COURT OF VINES AND VIPERS

Secrets of the Faerie Crown, Book 3

EMBERLY ASH

Copyright 2024 Emberly Ash, Cara Maxwell Romance

All rights reserved. No part of this book may be reproduced, or stored in a retrieval system, or transmitted in any form or by any means, electronic, mechanical, photocopying, recording, or otherwise, without express written permission of the publisher.

For permissions contact: caramaxwellromance@gmail.com

This is a work of fiction. Names, characters, places, and incidents either are the product of the author's imagination or are used fictitiously. Any resemblance to actual persons, living or dead, events, or locales is entirely coincidental.

ISBN: 978-1-964408-02-6 (ebook)

978-1-964408-03-3 (paperback)

Cover Art: Selkkie Designs

Beta Analysis: Made Me Blush Books

Map Design: A. Andrews

❦ Created with Vellum

For all of us who have ever doubted...
You are enough.
You always were.
You don't have to earn it. You don't have to ask for it. And you don't apologize for it—ever.

CONTENT WARNINGS

Secrets of the Faerie Crown is a fantasy romance series with elements of dark romance. While it is not a true dark romance, the themes are heavy and may be triggering for some readers.

Content warnings include: blood play, child abuse, references to rape, murder, death of a loved one, explicit sexual content, and graphic depictions of death, violence, and torture.

❦ I ❦
GUINEVERE

Sleep was a waste of time.

A weakness.

Sleep stole the hours that needed to be dedicated elsewhere.

Meeting, training, torturing.

Sleep brought dreams. Dreams turned to nightmares.

Nightmares were the only place Gwen saw her friends anymore.

Still, she avoided them. The white-haired queen, young and broken, who'd entrusted her with a kingdom. The Brutal Prince, commander turned friend turned king. When their faces came to her nightmares, they spoke words of disappointment. The queen's beautiful features filled with rage, the knife in her hand swiping for Gwen's throat.

She always woke before the queen could land her death blow.

That was the real nightmare.

Gwen had no doubt that the queen would come for her. That she would demand vengeance for her failures. Merlin gone. Parys dead.

Parys.

Perhaps her first true friend.

She had not deserved him in life. In death, at least, she would honor him. In the ways she knew, as well as those she was still learning.

She shifted in the tall wingback chair, arching her spine to stretch. That was fatigue curling around her bones, tightening her muscles. When she did sleep, it was always in her dark lioness form. She was lethal, in any form—and knew it. But knowing and believing were far from the same thing.

Fatigue she could tolerate.

Weakness, she could not.

She rolled her shoulders and refocused her eyes on the book in her lap.

The Travelers.

Parys had carried this book with him from the library, through the tunnels as they chased down Merlin, Igraine, and their Shadows.

It was important. It had to be. Otherwise, he would have left it behind.

Or he'd simply forgotten that he carried it at all.

Gwen shoved that thought away.

She would read the entire damn book, forward and backward again, if that was what it took to find some nodule of meaning. Something to mark Parys's contribution. His importance.

His absence.

The Travelers.

Few among us have the power to travel through space, to sense the grains of creation and bend them to our will.

What utter drivel. Nonsense.

She'd traveled the entire length of the continent. The humans had come from Eldermist. If humans could travel, anyone could.

Why had Parys bothered with this book at all? It had nothing to do with the rifts, as far as she could tell, or Veyka's void power. No mention of Avalon in the chapter headings.

She needed to go to the library.

She had ordered it sealed after Parys' death, but she had not gone to inspect it herself. Not yet.

First, she had to see the goldstone palace fully secured.

She had walked the entire perimeter, finding two more unprotected exits. It was a miracle Baylaur had stood unbreached for seven thousand years, with all its secret passageways and weak wards.

Not weak, she corrected herself. Foolish.

The wards were keyed to power. Specifically, royal power. Only the royal family could alter them. As the terrestrial heir, Arran had been able to manipulate them upon arrival. And Igraine had been able to open and close them to accommodate the Shadows as she willed.

A snarl built in Gwen's chest, a low rumble that grew and grew until she pushed to her feet. The book crashed to the goldstone tiles. She grabbed the back of the chair, desperately anchoring herself.

She'd almost shifted, without thought or intention.

Without control.

That had not happened in more than a hundred years.

Her lioness surged again, another snarl that sent her braids flying, her chin whipping to the side. She had no choice. She couldn't contain it. She threw her head back and screamed.

Half fae, half beast. Pain and torment and rage.

The entire room quivered around her.

She knew that if she looked down at her hand, she'd see claws digging into the upholstery.

That forced the lioness back.

She couldn't destroy the chairs. The twin wingbacks where she'd shared so many meals with Parys. Suddenly, they were more than chairs. They were infinitely precious.

She dragged in a breath. Then another. Breath by ragged breath, she fought back until she was in control. Until there was no weakness left.

Her eyes tracked around the room, the fatigue banished now as well.

Book. Table. Round Table.

The candlelight glinted off of the golden scrollwork of the Round Table. Mocking the engraving that had vanished when Parys did.

Gwen hated that table.

She ought to destroy it and the prophetic curse that Merlin had saddled them with. If Parys' name was not etched upon it then it should not exist at all—

Footsteps.

Her eyes went to the doors with keen feline awareness.

It was too early for dinner, a meal she wouldn't eat anyways. But the footsteps... not heavy, laden with trays of food.

Rushed. Running.

Gwen drew her sword.

No knock, no pleasantries.

A palace guard, sweat lining his face, fire sputtering at his fingertips. His pale, cream-colored uniformed was barely visible beneath the noxious black bile.

"The darkness," he choked out. "In the barracks."

The guard barracks. Tightly packed. Males and females lodging together.

All fae.

The darkness had come to Baylaur.

2

VEYKA

The perfectly round pebbles crunched under my boots with each step, grating over my already frayed nerves.

Already?

That implied that they'd been intact at some point in recent memory.

Well, that wasn't fucking true.

Frayed, damaged, broken. Words too mild to describe the state of my mind and heart.

I was shattered.

Entire pieces of myself were missing.

An entire half of my soul.

More, maybe.

Arran was more than half of me. Loving him, being his mate—it *was* me. My power. My heart. My sanity.

The latter was teetering dangerously close to oblivion.

I planted my feet on the beach, ignoring the melodic lapping of waves at the toes of my boots, and turned to face the ominous rolling mists.

"Morgyn! Get your skinny ass out here!"

Nothing happened.

I gave her exactly one minute, counting out each heartbeat.

The mists did not budge.

I closed my eyes, summoning the ember of power inside of me, ready to step through the void—

"I have not given consent for you to visit the Sacred Isle."

The human realm materialized around me. My magic groaned, protesting the leash as I pulled it back sharply. But it had only a fraction of my attention.

Everything else was focused on the wraith-like female hovering in the mists a few yards away. I hated the familiar arch of her neck. And the way she tilted her head to the side when she was contemplating. I hated that I'd seen both of those actions in the mirror more times than I could count. How was it possible that she could exist? How was it fair that I'd lost my brother only to discover a sister both foreign and eerily familiar?

I did not pray to the Ancestors or make an errant appeal for guidance.

The Ancestors had failed me in every imaginable way. They had been dead for seven thousand years, and I was done resurrecting them with foolish pleas.

They hadn't protected Arran.

Couldn't protect him, not from me.

I had failed to protect my mate once. Never again. And that meant I was done wasting time and hope by invoking useless beings.

"If you would let me see my mate, I would not attempt to visit your sacred little island uninvited." One heel dug into the gravel. Deeper, showing my anger.

Good. Let her understand what simmered in my veins.

Morgyn's full lips pressed together, thinning out until they almost disappeared. "The King lives."

"So you say."

"Your ability to access your power ought to be reassurance enough."

The rage boiled up inside of me, burning in my throat, demanding release.

I ignored it. My heart curled around the golden thread inside of me—taut, thin, but there. The tiniest whisper of Arran, inside of me, still.

I allowed myself half a heartbeat to savor that comforting reminder that my mate did indeed still live. Then I flashed an arrogant, vicious grin.

"What else do you know about my power, Morgyn?"

I'd tried to play her game. Before Gorlois attacked and upended my world. She'd been content to let me walk away with no knowledge of who she truly was.

Morgyn le Fae, the illegitimate daughter of the Dowager High Queen of Annwyn—my mother—and Gorlois, the male who had tortured me for twenty years. All for the Ethereal Prophecy. Because my mother and Gorlois believed that I was meant to fulfill that ancient prophecy and command the voids of darkness. For that prophecy, I'd been raped in desperate attempts to seed magic within me. For the power it would bring, Igraine and Gorlois had slaughtered Arthur and placed me upon the throne of Annwyn.

Arthur may have lied to me about Excalibur and the magical scabbards, the Sacred Trinity, but he had loved and protected me. Then, he'd been brutally murdered. Meanwhile, the Lady of the Lake, my half-sister, had watched as Gorlois attacked and took my mate hostage. As I made that fatal mistake.

She'd allowed it all to happen.

As useless as the Ancestors.

I stepped forward, letting the water wash over my leather boots. I didn't bother to reach for the blade at my hip or the curved rapiers strapped across my back. I'd strangle her with my bare hands.

Morgyn did not flinch. The Lady of the Lake only tilted her head to the side as she considered me.

"I do not wish you ill, young queen," she said.

"Veyka. My name is Veyka. I am your sister. Gorlois had our

brother, Arthur, murdered. We should be allies, yet you keep secrets. The Void Prophecy, my mate—"

"The acolytes and priestesses are my brothers and sisters."

Arran's beast would have been proud of the snarl that ripped from my throat.

I was absolute shit at this. Strategy was Arran's strength, not mine. I knew I needed reason and calm. But I couldn't sort it out from the rage. Such fire burned inside of me, I half expected flames to shoot from my hands. I was angry for myself and the loss of my childhood, a cursed existence. My very birth had doomed my beloved brother. Gorlois and Igraine had damned us all. And Morgyn claimed none of it. She could just walk away.

"Then you are as selfish as our mother," I spat.

Her gaze did not flicker. No telltale tick in her cheek. The only movement was the strands of her golden-brown hair where they were lifted off her shoulders by the morning breeze.

"I have duties to attend to. I expect I shall see you tomorrow morning," she said with that eerie, unshakeable calm.

"Take me to my mate."

"Goodbye, Your Majesty."

"I demand that you take me to him!"

But I was screaming at nothing.

Morgyn disappeared into the mists as suddenly as she'd appeared. Exactly as she had done every morning for nearly two weeks.

I was alone.

Again.

I stomped back across the clearing, through the dancing tendrils of the weeping willows. I drew the dagger from my waist and slashed —again and again and again. Until the graceful vines were a tangled mess at my feet.

An apt metaphor for my state of mind.

I slid the dagger back into my jeweled scabbard, my other hand sliding downward by habit. But only one found purchase.

The other scabbard was still fastened to Arrans' belt. Or maybe not. Maybe the priestesses had removed it.

I didn't fucking know, because Morgyn had told me next to nothing.

Is he alive? *Yes.*

Is he healing? Awake? Asking for me? *I will give you more information once there is something to tell, young queen.*

It had been a mistake—all of it. Coming to Avalon, engaging with Gorlois, begging Morgyn to help Arran.

She'd kept him alive, because no one could die on Avalon. But that didn't necessarily mean that he was healing. And I was not stupid enough to believe it meant that he was safe.

No one—not the Ancestors, nor the Lady of the Lake or a thousand humans-turned succubus—would keep me from my mate.

3

VEYKA

"I thought we agreed that Isolde is not allowed to cook," I said, dropping down to the stump they'd designated as mine. A makeshift throne, Lyrena had joked.

At least Lyrena was alive to make the joke. After Percival had stabbed her, with the fae magic in her blood stifled by the proximity to Avalon, her ability to crack jokes was nothing short of a miracle.

Even when they weren't funny.

"Unless you plan on joining the rotation, she gets her turn," Cyara said from the other side of the roaring fire. I could not tell whose flames they were—Cyara or Lyrena. But given that Cyara had kept the fire going for over a week on her own while Lyrena healed, I suspected the latter.

My harpy of a handmaiden had my spare pair of leggings spread across her lap, stitching the seam that had split along the inner left thigh. Given the way her teeth dug into her lower lip as she stabbed the leather with her needle, I decided not to press her. I turned to Lyrena instead.

Just as I had every single time I looked at her over the past two weeks, I cataloged each detail of her body, checking for strain or weakness.

But Lyrena didn't wobble or falter as she executed a series of training maneuvers with her sword. I'd refused to spar with her so far, but it looked like that argument was about to die a sure death. She swung the sword with smooth grace, perfect control. All while keeping that fire burning steadily.

She was healed, no question.

Which brought its own host of troubles.

I focused on the most pressing one—Isolde crouching on the other side of the fire, stirring a pot that dangled from a carefully placed tripod of sticks above the flame. I managed not to flinch as the earthy aroma accosted my nostrils.

"Have you just begun?" I asked hopefully.

One claw-tipped finger twitched in my direction. "It's nearly ready."

I failed to suppress my shiver and started digging into the pack resting at my feet. There were only a handful of travel cakes left, and they were past stale, but if they meant I could eat less of Isolde's stew, I'd take them gladly.

I let myself get lost in the mundane. The normalcy of cooking, mending clothes, washing dishes—there were hundreds of little tasks that needed doing to maintain ourselves and our campsite. I'd hated them before. But now, they let me pretend that things were normal. That my entire world had not been ripped apart. Not to mention the state of my soul.

Lyrena sheathed her sword and dropped down onto the ground beside me, sitting on a folded travel blanket to avoid the damp of the dewy grass. We'd retreated just far enough for the magic of the cursed clearing to wear off, to where Isolde's healing magic worked again, and Lyrena's innate fae mending ability began. And here we'd stayed for two long weeks. Each day wretched without news of Arran.

"Why won't the Lady of the Lake let you see him?" Lyrena mused, folding her hands.

Calm. They were all so infernally calm. As if it was not the High King of Annwyn we were discussing. A tremor shook down my arm to my hand.

"The Lady of the Lake does not *let* me do anything," I said sharply, staring into the fire. It did not need wood to burn, not with fire-wielders in abundance. But the act of splitting the wood, the perspiration and distraction, would hold the pain at bay.

As I looked around us for probable trees to fell, I caught Lyrena sliding her gaze to Cyara, who did not glance up from her mending to receive it.

"Morgyn can try to issue edicts, but I am the High Queen of Annwyn. I will do what I deem best for my kingdom." My kingdom. Another weight upon my shoulders. Another responsibility pressing down on my chest and threatening to crush me.

"Including sneaking into Avalon?" This time, Cyara did glance up. She pinned me with her commanding turquoise eyes, her white wings fluttering behind her.

I uncrossed my legs, straightening on that stupid fucking stump. "I need to assess Arran's wellbeing for myself. We cannot do anything else, make any other moves, if he is not safe."

Not we. *I.*

I was making a show of it, but the thought of statecraft, of ruling and making decisions without him, made my stomach turn. Ironic, considering how irritated I'd been only a few months ago, after our Joining, when I'd had to defer every impulse to his agreement.

But decisions did have to be made.

Taliya, still closeted below in the safety of the caves with the rest of the faeries, had said the succubus would come to Annwyn. I might personally detest her, but I had no reason to doubt her truth. The Faeries of the Fen remembered their history better than the fae.

Another thing that needed to be done—research. Parys' laughing grin flashed across my mind. He'd enjoy the new list of topics I had for him to research in the library of the goldstone palace. Likely, he'd use it as an excuse to never leave those winding stacks.

Succubus, nightwalker, the Great War, the Faeries of the Fen, who the Ethereal Prophecy did apply to, since we now knew it was not me...

"Eilean Gayl is not far."

Cyara's clear, confident voice stabbed into my thoughts with all the force of one of my daggers.

A dozen thoughts coalesced at once. Eilean Gayl. Arran. The rifts. Annwyn. More.

I blinked, my mind unable to sort through the torrent even as my mouth formed words. "Eilean Gayl is in Annwyn."

I didn't say the rest. We'd have to go through a rift. We'd have to leave Arran.

I shouldn't need to.

"What is Eilean Gayl?" Isolde asked around the claw she'd lifted to her mouth to taste her concoction.

"It is Arran's ancestral home," I said, wishing that raging flame of the campfire could do something to warm the ice spreading inside of me. The cold that had been growing ever since I'd plunged Excalibur into my mate's chest. "I am not leaving Arran."

Cyara did not waver as she stared right at me, the leggings in her lap seemingly forgotten. "You could open a rift to Annwyn."

And maybe I was more messed up than even I understood. Because instead of shutting the entire conversation down, I actually responded.

"I've never done that." I blinked again. My universal sign for overwhelm. "I've only been able to move between nearby places in *this* realm."

There were no feigned expressions of disinterest or sideways glances now. Lyrena and Isolde were watching us, eyes sparkling, the latter stirring the pot absently with one clawed finger.

"But you did it before, after the Joining," Lyrena said, leaning forward noticeably.

A beat of silence.

They probably thought I needed it to think.

Wrong.

I was trying to tame the terror clawing its way up from the pits of my stomach, through my chest and up my throat like bile. I remembered it, as stark and clear as if it had happened yesterday. The feeling of being ripping apart. Of falling headfirst, without a shred of control. The terrible cold that dug its claws into me.

I *had* done it at the Joining. And I never, ever wanted to do it again.

Moving along one realm was one thing. The idea of trying to travel between realms... and without Arran. Arran had been the one to push me, to show me how to reach into my magic and start to control it. To take this new step on my own... I did not want to contemplate what that might mean.

"We are not leaving Arran." A thousand years and a thousand more. That was the promise I had made. I would die on these blasted shores before I would leave him.

"How does the magic work?" Isolde asked quietly.

She did not express an opinion. Merely asked a soft, gentle question. It was telling—she considered herself my subject, but also an outsider. Less than Lyrena and Cyara, my Knights of the Round Table. I tucked that nuance away for later.

I sucked in a breath. "I wish I knew."

Stares from my friends.

Exhaled.

"I can enter the void between realms," I explained, as if that sentence actually did much clarifying. "Arran is my tether. Without him calling me back, without the bond to center me, I could become lost. I do not know if I can do it with him..."

Gone.

I could not say it.

My chest was going to cave in on itself. The shredded golden thread would not be enough to hold me together—

"You can feel the bond in your chest."

My teeth gnashed, a snarl rolling up through me as my focus

shifted outward once more, annoyance and relief at being pulled back to reality.

"Do you know everything?" I bit out.

"I know you," Cyara countered. "If you could not feel Arran, you wouldn't be sitting here calmly waiting—"

"You call this calm?" Lyrena interjected, her grin stretching across her face, her golden tooth catching the rays of the rising sun.

"—you would be slaughtering your way across Avalon." Everyone stared at her—myself included. But Cyara was unwavering. "You can use your power."

She was right, of course.

I'd been about to use it on the lakeshore, to spite Morgyn and her edicts.

I turned back to face Isolde, now scooping the concoction she called a meal into bowls. "Moving between places in the same realm is simple. I can step into the void, then step back out. I'm hardly even there. Jumping between realms is something else."

Isolde nodded, passing the bowls around the campfire.

She paused when she reached me, one claw-tipped white finger tapping against the side of the wooden bowl she held. "But you can do it. Create a rift."

I swallowed. "Yes."

I did not want to.

But in my bones, in the center of my soul where that shining ember of power slumbered, I could feel that answer with certainty. Even if nothing else in my life was certain anymore.

Isolde slid the bowl into my hands, retreating back towards the fire. Instead of sitting, she crouched down, balancing her own bowl in the cradle of her curved claws. Close enough to the fire, she ought to have burned. But her translucent white skin glowed softly instead.

She did not reach for a spoon or lift the bowl to her mouth to eat.

I swallowed back my own saliva, too tense for a bite, knowing more was coming. Already tense because I knew what came next.

"And you could take someone else with you, from one realm to another?" Isolde asked.

Another swallow. "In theory." My eyes darted to Cyara, eating her bowl of mushy green stew and ignoring me; letting me sort through the feelings and fears on my own. The first time I'd brought someone through the void with me, when I hadn't been ready, hadn't meant to... I looked down at my arm, half expecting to see the bloody stump of her hand there. I sucked in a breath. "But it is not safe. You could end up maimed, or worse."

It was impossible to tell for sure with her already white skin, but I imagined that Isolde paled.

We ate in blessed silence for a few minutes. Maybe I would get lucky, and they would let the conversation drop. I needed time with my thoughts, anyway. To figure out my next move. Ancestors, how I missed Arran's warmth and strength at my side.

You don't appeal to the Ancestors anymore, the voice in my head reminded me.

Right.

I broke a stale travel cake in half, dipped it in the green stew, and tried not to wrinkle my nose as I forced down bite after bite.

Of course, I was not actually lucky. Not in the way I'd hoped, at least.

Isolde was fascinated. Eager to press, she leaned forward on her toes, dangerously near to the fire. "So, if you moved through the void, from the human realm to Annwyn, you would emerge on the same spot?"

I nodded. "Like one of the rifts."

"But that is not what happened at the Joining," Cyara said between bites.

I was going to strangle her. Even if it meant facing the harpy hiding beneath her skin. "No. It is not."

I turned to Isolde, the only one who hadn't heard the story. "I crashed through rifts, realms, uncontrollably. Painfully." I shot a look at Cyara, to remind her. As if she needed it, after all she'd been through. "I saw the Split Sea, and a castle I did not recognize, and Avalon."

Isolde nodded along, her white eyes sparkling as she considered. "But those are not in the same location, through the layers you describe."

I shoved the last bit of travel cake into my mouth, the stale grain sticking in my throat. "No."

"So you could enter the void here... and step out on the other side in Baylaur? On the other side of the continent, in an entirely different realm?" Her voice was full of wonder. What would it have been like to learn about my void power in safety? To explore it as a gift, a beautiful wonder, instead of a means to an end? A weapon for battle?

It did not matter, I told myself. Making my body into a weapon had been my choice from the beginning. The only way of protecting myself.

There was no use in second guessing that reality.

"Yes," I said to Isolde. She was right—in theory. But I hadn't done it.

"And other realms? What about other realms? The monolith above the faerie caves showed many layers." Isolde's mouth hung open with excitement.

Of course, she'd have examined the monolith. It was directly above the entrance to the refuge of the Faeries of the Fen. Perhaps they'd erected it at some sort of marker, thousands of years ago.

I looked accusingly at Cyara and Lyrena. Had they been discussing this with Isolde? Had clever Cyara set up this whole conversation, to push me to make decisions, to move forward?

There would be no moving forward. Not without Arran. And if my Knights were foolish enough to believe otherwise, then as their queen I owed them a lesson in reality.

"I haven't done it," I said sharply.

Isolde licked her lips. "But you could."

"If I truly command the void..." I closed my eyes, pushing down the flare of power and light inside of me. The void called to me, eager for me to come and play. As if my power knew what we discussed and yearned for me to try. I shoved it down, willing that ember to rest. "I do not know what I could do."

That was the starkest truth.

I wondered if I would ever stop hating this vulnerability. Sharing these suppositions aloud. Not about the wellbeing of Annwyn or some plot, but about *myself*.

A shiver slid up my spine, through my shoulders, and down my arms like lightning to my fingertips. I tried to shake it out; pulled the cloak that I wore around my shoulders. It was always so damn cold in the human realm. Yule was only a few weeks off, and then it would turn even more frigid.

I hated the cold.

But if I had to sit here in the snow drifts until my mate was healed, I would.

I stared into the fire, unable to meet any of their eyes. I heard the familiar sound of steel being drawn from its sheath, then the repetitive swipes of Lyrena polishing her sword. Goldstone Guard, Knight of the Round Table. That was the warrior who finally broke the silence. "We would have allies in Eilean Gayl."

I let my eyes get lost in the dancing orange and yellow flame.

Lyrena's blade sang as she applied pressure to a particular spot. "You could be back here in a second."

The cold inside of me was not the same indifference I'd felt after Arthur's death. Then, my focus had been singular, selfish. Revenge at the cost of all else. Now, too many emotions flowed through me to process. Too many responsibilities and too many friends to worry about. So much, that my mind and body began to institute an icy freeze to stop them from overwhelming me completely. "Maybe. Or maybe I'd end up back in Baylaur, or at the Crossing."

"What are our other options?" Lyrena said, her voice still carefully diplomatic.

I did not answer her. So Cyara did. "Return to the faerie caves.

Return to Baylaur. Or go to Eilean Gayl." She paused, drawing in a delicate breath before adding, "And on to Wolf Bay."

I ripped the dagger from my belt, hurling it through the air. Well over their heads. It embedded in a tree on the other side of the clearing, all the way to the hilt.

"We are staying here." My voice was cold enough to freeze water.

The flames of the campfire flickered.

But Cyara did not back down. "You are the High Queen of Annwyn."

I slid off the stump, landing easily on my feet. Towering over the fire, over my friends, all still seated.

"Arran is the High King. And my mate. I will not leave him."

Lyrena and Cyara exchanged a look that I didn't even pretend to ignore.

I stepped into the void, blissful and silent, free of their expectations, and went to retrieve my weapon.

4
VEYKA

I spent the afternoon sweating. But that ice inside of me did not thaw, no matter how many times I moved in and out of the void, pushing my power to its limits. Perhaps ice was better than fire. It kept the horror of the feelings at bay.

Through the void I went. Along the edge of the lake, ten feet, fifteen feet, another ten. My feet landed on grass and dirt and sand, but my eyes always went right to the center of that lake, to the mist-shrouded isle. I arrived in that cursed clearing where no one could heal. I did not let myself think about what would have happened if Avalon had stolen all of our magic, not just our healing ability. Even after two weeks, my sharp fae senses could detect the blood that had disappeared into the grass.

The scent of Arran's blood on the shore nearly undid me.

This was not the blood I'd licked from his lips, tasted on my tongue. I did not shiver with delicious need. The blood that had disappeared into the sand and pebbles was fetid, old. It spoke of death.

I fell to my knees.

He's alive. He's alive. He's alive.

I repeated it like a prayer. I let my focus go inward, checking that the bond was intact.

He's alive.

The cold lake air filled my nostrils. Brine and waterweeds and... blood. But not Arran's blood.

Slowly, I staggered to my feet. Willed my muscles to move, my nose to inhale deeply again. It was nearly impossible to sort out after all of these weeks... but there. I found it. Thin, mellow, a mere footnote in the cacophony of scents. Human blood.

I took one step into the clearing. Sniffed again. A few more. Then I was jogging. But that was too slow. I stepped through the void again, appearing at the edge of the clearing, pausing only long enough to inhale deeply, mark the scent, and disappear once more.

◆

Humans moved slowly, but they'd had weeks. I had the power of the void.

They were not even trying to hide themselves, arrogant fools. The scent of human blood ebbed away as the miles stretched. I found no decaying bodies. Their wounds must have healed.

I paused beside a massive tree, its branches wickedly curved. A beautiful, ancient sentinel standing guard over the creatures of the forested mountain foothills. And a human man had pissed on it.

The green sludge in my stomach threatened to make another appearance at the intensity of the scent. The whole lot of them had used this area as a latrine. Not just humans... I realized as I pressed the back of my hand to my mouth. Fae as well. That is probably why the humans were still alive at all.

I resisted the urge to jump away through the void, following the scent through the trees, knowing I was getting closer and afraid of moving too far.

But walking was slow. Walking over the frosty debris on the forest floor was even slower. No one had ever taught me to track. I was relying on all the fae abilities in my veins. It would be enough. That, and the cold rage inside of me, would be enough to find them.

I carefully maneuvered over a stream, extending my legs as far as they would reach. It took all of the muscles in my core to keep my balance and not go pitching forward into the icy water. The humans and their fae companions had not been so careful. They'd trudged through the stream, leaving deep tracks in the thick mud. I hardly needed to, but by now it was habit. I lifted my face and inhaled deeply—just as the wind shifted.

And my heart stopped.

One hand went to my ear, checking the amorite studs that lined it. Not that I was in any danger of possession, being female. They were a comfort nonetheless. But it was the blade I drew from my waist that would save me. In the filtered light of the pine forest, turned silver by cold and frost, I could just see the swirls of amorite blended into the metal blade itself.

The only thing that could slay a human taken by the darkness—the succubus—was an amorite blade. Fire could hold them back, but they'd rise again eventually. We'd learned that in the jungle clearing before Isolde had rescued us from the horde of death.

I moved in silence. I had no idea if they could smell or how they sought their prey. They'd managed to clamber through the thick vines and trees of the jungle, so they must have some sentience. But did they hunt? Were they searching for the same thing as I was?

Every instinct in my body screamed in unison—*run*.

I had spent twenty years learning to survive, honing my body into a weapon to ensure that no matter who or what attacked me, I would be able to face them. Now, I had my power as well. I could step though the void and escape them.

But the time to run had past.

I forced my legs to move forward, the muscles of my powerful thighs to keep me going in a steady, silent rhythm. Closer. Closer. Until the scent of that black bile filled my nose and the cold began to permeate my bones.

I was close. It had to be just behind the next tree, so close I started scanning. The trees above my head, the branches—I imagined I'd find a black demon of death, squatting above my head. But there was nothing. No unwieldly clambering through the frosty forest. Just cold and that awful, awful scent of death and decay.

My gaze traveled down, below my direct line of sight—

Every muscle froze. My fingers did not tremble, my heart did not beat. But I was too late. It had seen me or heard me or scented me.

At the base of another massive pine tree, the dark-shrouded form rose. Pushing itself up from the ground, a jagged bone poking out of one of the elbows, it turned those unseeing black eyes to me. The mangled jaw fell open in what might have once been a smile. But noxious black bile poured from its mouth as it hauled itself up. Tried to—and failed.

My eyes began to sort out what I was seeing. The legs were not just mangled—they were gone entirely. Only the upper torso of the fae male remained.

Fae.

But that did not slow it.

It began clawing its way across the ground, an unearthly strength lining those desiccated muscles that should have been unable to move. Whatever senses remained honed in upon me. That gaping black maw would tear me wide open, feasting on my flesh until there was nothing left to heal, nothing for my companions to find.

I did not have to think. A few yards of frozen pine needles separated me from the monster. I made use of every inch, digging in my heels and launching myself forward. I came down on top of it, the lines of the wolf carved into the pommel of my dagger digging into my palm. My wolf was with me as I slammed the knife into the creature's neck, the tip lodging in the dirt below.

The succubus stopped moving immediately, but I did not. I pressed all my weight into my knee, pinned in its back, and sawed my dagger side to side. I did not flinch at the crunch of bone or the crackle of frozen pine needles as the succubus' head rolled off of the remnants of its body.

I dragged in a breath, nearly gagging at the reek.

There was no trace of fae scent left on him. There wasn't much left of him at all. The pointed fae ears were the only way I knew.

It wasn't a fae I'd killed. It was a succubus. Not him—her. All the succubus were female.

It was time to start calling them what they were. No more nightwalkers, no more talk of possessions or being taken by the darkness. I'd killed a succubus. I suspected I would kill many more before this was all over.

I recognized the remnants of clothing beneath the black poison. One of the fae warriors who'd fought at Gorlois' command. All of them had worn amorite pendants in the clearing. It was supposed to protect from this...

Even as new fear and alarm lit in my gut, I kicked over the remains, toeing around with my boot. There was no amorite pendant, no earring, anywhere to be seen. Maybe the amorite pendants had not been about the succubus at all. Gorlois had certainly known about the effects of the cursed clearing, the way it prevented healing and preyed on the mind. Maybe that was all he had known. And when the warriors retreated, when this one stupidly removed the amorite...

The shiver that snaked down my spine had nothing to do with the ice encasing my heart or the descending cold of late afternoon.

Taliya had spoken true. The succubus could overtake the mind of a fae.

If they had come to the human realm, they would come to Annwyn. I might be afraid to jump between realms, but the succubus was not. They had come for the human messenger sent from Eldermist, held in the bowels of the goldstone palace all those months ago. Now they would come for my kingdom as well.

Above my head, a lone brown leaf from one of the few deciduous trees in the forest shook loose. I watched it fall, drifting side to side, but ever down, until it came to rest on the bed of evergreen needles.

The true horror of what I faced, what Annwyn faced, came down upon me as surely as the downward path of that leaf.

We would not be battling succubus in human bodies, terrible but distinct, distant, without fae strength and magic. It would not be strangers from a different realm who faced us on the battlefield. It would be our sons, our fathers and grandfathers, uncles and cousins. The males we'd once called friends and family who would attack us while we slept. While our children played.

Children—Evander, the horrible Goldstone Guard I'd dispatched all those months ago to see to the children's disappearances near the Split Sea... what chance was there that those were not related to the succubus as well? But if Parys and Guinevere knew, if they'd heard from Evander, made progress... I had no way to know. Because I was in another realm. On the other side of the continent. With a mate hovering near death who I wasn't even able to fucking see.

I shivered again.

It was a reminder—ice. Cold and hard. That was the only way for me to survive being crushed by the weight of it all. I could not buckle. Not now—not when I was on my own.

I dragged in another breath and instantly regretted it. Still, my stomach had the audacity to rumble, reminding me that I'd been out all day with nothing but stale travel cakes and mushy green stew as sustenance.

I would kill a dozen succubus if it got me a chocolate croissant.

Carefully modulating my breath, I surveyed the trees around me, the barren ground, the pockets of gray sky visible overhead.

The sun was well past its zenith, and my steps though the void had taken me miles from the lakeside camp.

I did not have time to wait and see if the succubus would rise again if I did not burn it. I missed the absence of Lyrena and Cyara's flames as I gathered tinder and kindling, and then left what remained of the succubus to burn.

5

VEYKA

Cyara was cooking. I opted not to spoil everyone's appetite by describing what I'd found in the woods. It did not change anything, not really. The facts all remained the same as they had an hour ago, a day ago, a fortnight ago.

But I could not sit and stare at the fire for another evening. I couldn't even bring myself to do the mundane chores that had been my salvation these past weeks. I needed something more.

I drew the twin curved rapiers from across my back as I walked past Lyrena, sharpening the dagger she'd gifted to Isolde. I'd yet to see the white faerie wield it, though I doubted those claws were merely for show.

"Spar. Now," I said without pause.

I could feel the weight of glances being exchanged behind me, but I did not acknowledge them. I heard Lyrena stand, hand off the knife, then the soft hiss of her sword sliding from its sheath.

"Magic?" she asked casually, her feet moving with quiet grace to the opposite side of the small area she'd been using to train.

"Blood and blades."

The oval of stomped down grass was only six or seven yards long. A few yards wide. That close, the fighting would be all quick, sharp movements. No room for sweeping approaches. We'd be close enough to scent each other's sweat. Good. That was exactly what I needed.

I did not even wait for her to fully turn back before launching myself forward.

Lyrena met me easily, anticipating my approach, a lazy smile climbing her face as she parried the twin blades. She forced them down with her bigger, wider sword, swinging for my stomach.

I danced out of her way, using the momentum to cut upward with one rapier while I brought the other in from the side.

"Tsk, tsk," Lyrena clicked with her tongue. She deflected the blade at her ribs with her sword, then caught my other hand unprotected—chopping her hand down hard on my wrist. The rapier fell from my hand, landing noiselessly on the grass. Before I could reach down, Lyrena had kicked it away. "You aren't going easy on me, are you?"

Good. Lyrena understood what I needed.

I didn't have to reach for my magic. This power—the ability to kill and maim with blades and my body—this I'd mastered long before that glowing ember of magic awoke inside of me. I did not need to rapiers to defeat her. I probably could have managed without a blade at all.

I gave myself fully to the exertion. Let the sweat sliding down between my breasts give me that extra bit of lubrication to move faster. I used the narrow field to work Lyrena to the side, stunting her movements with the longer, wider blade. I could see the frustration in her eyes—she wanted to beat me, to prove to herself that she was fully healed.

But I was not ready to lose. I knocked the sword from her hand.

Lyrena made no move to retrieve it. She pinned me with her bright eyes, narrowed slightly over her perfectly straight, patrician nose. "What happened?"

I grinned wickedly. But the ice inside of me did not thaw. Not even the tiniest crack as I smirked. "I want to see if you've fully recovered."

Lyrena's eyes darted to the sword a yard away on the ground. I followed her gaze. I stretched that smile wider across my face as I tossed aside my rapier, leaving us with only our bare hands.

A slight tick marred her otherwise perfect cheek. "Planning something, Veyka?"

I winked. "Trying to decide the best way to hand your ass to you." Then I moved.

She thought I was going to leap, to use my height and my powerful thighs to tackle her to the ground. But she misjudged. I dove at her legs instead, the knees she'd made the mistake of locking. She went down hard and fast.

She drove her fist up into my gut, swinging her other hand for my windpipe. But I was on top of her and I weighed more. I used every pound to my advantage. Knees on either shoulder, one hand on either side of her head, I could have snapped her neck in a second.

I held the position for one long breath; long enough for both of us to recognize the truth. Then I rolled off of her and offered her a hand up.

She took it, her lovely face caught halfway between a grin and grimace.

We collected our weapons and dropped onto our respective seats at the campfire. I chugged the entire contents of my canteen, as well as the lukewarm tea in the special cup that Osheen had fashioned for me when we first arrived in the human realm. It now seemed a lifetime ago.

I pulled out the flask of aural I'd been keeping at the bottom of my pack for months.

No one spoke.

I took a deep draw, savoring the burn of the amber spirit down my throat. I let my eyes close, let my world center on the sensations in my body. The heat spreading into my stomach from the aural, the tingling in my muscles from the exertion... discrete, tangible things that I could focus on without repercussion or implication.

Even with my eyes closed, I felt the shift in the camp. There was the slight crunching of the frozen grass as Lyrena adjusted her seat. Isolde's claws clicked together like they did when she was nervous. Which meant the heavy feeling of eyes upon me was coming from one copper-haired female.

"Lyrena is fully recovered," Cyara said. It may have been staged as an observation, but there wasn't an ounce of neutrality in it.

I didn't open my eyes. "Seems like it."

She cleared her throat. Such a delicate sound, for a female with more balls than most of the males in Annwyn. "We ought to discuss the implications."

The weight of two eyes became six.

I opened my own. Surveyed the three females arrayed around me, each powerful in their own way, each motivated by their own perceptions.

One glance, and I knew I was late to the party. "It seems like you've already been discussing them."

None of them bothered to deny it. Only Isolde averted her eyes, the white orbs dropping to her lap where she appeared to be knitting something on her long claws. The faerie never ceased to amaze me with her accomplishments.

But Lyrena held my gaze, her smile turned grim. Set. Ready for a battle.

I half expected to see the harpy when I turned to face Cyara. But she was as calm as ever. Her gray tunic and pants were freshly laundered, neatly pinned into place with the leather harness she'd fashioned to wear atop them, similar to the one I sported. Mine held weapons. Hers had several smaller pockets for needles and cooking knives and who knew what else.

A flick of her wrist, and a carefully wrapped leather roll appeared from the pocket of her cloak.

"I've plotted it out on the maps," Cyara said as she tugged loose the twine that held the leather roll in place. Leather to protect the delicate paper of the maps that were revealed. I recognized the sprawling continent, even at a distance. But Cyara was not looking at the maps. She was looking directly at me as she said, "Eilean Gayl is not far."

Not far? I laughed aloud—a cold, mirthless sound that matched the state of my heart. "Eilean Gayl is in Annwyn."

But she was not cowed. She'd never been intimidated by me. I'd often thought that was why Arthur had chosen her as my chief handmaiden. What had once seemed an asset made the aural turn to poison in my stomach as she continued, "Indeed. But it lays north of the Spine, on the banks of a great lake. Almost exactly where we are now."

"In another realm." I could feel my temper rising. My voice was steady, but it would not stay there. The ice inside of me was cracking.

"And you are a queen who can move between realms as easily as the rest of us walk from one room to another," Cyara countered. She never raised her voice, never needed to. But I was escalating for the both of us.

I slid to my feet. "And what will the rest of you do, Cyara? I doubt either of you," I jerked my head toward Lyrena, what remained of my Goldstone guards, "Would be content to wait here."

Cyara's wings twitched, her throat bobbing. "Take us with you."

She did not have to reach for her wrist for me to know what was going through her mind. The first time I'd used my void power to take someone with me, just from one side of the room to the other, I'd severed her hand from her body. Ripped her into pieces.

"Do you have a death wish?" I breathed.

She tensed, the crumple of those maps she'd protected filling both of our pointed ears. She inhaled slowly and then spoke on the exhale. "I wish to serve Annwyn."

"And I am the High Queen of Annwyn. Which means you serve me," I ground out, advancing one step.

Cyara did not flinch. She held my eyes with her turquoise ones, her wings tucking in tight to her body. "I only want what is best for my kingdom."

"That sounds a hell of a lot like the justification that Gawayn used when he slaughtered Cyara and Charis."

I hated myself the moment the words left my mouth. But I could not take them back. Worse, I was not sure I wanted to. They'd hit their mark, Cyara dropping the maps on the ground, her wings drooping.

The fire to my left leapt, flames reaching toward the sky, spiraling up above my head. Her flames, then. They crackled for several long seconds before settling. She picked up the maps, rolling them carefully and tucking them away.

I needed to walk away before I said or did something worse. It was my fault that my mate was near death, and I was just as surely going to destroy my closest friendship. But I could not move. Could not give in. Could not see past the collision of feelings and attempts to ice over them inside of my body.

Cyara straightened, her wings pristine as they arched over her head. "We cannot stay here forever. Are you at least considering what we will do if—"

I exploded.

"Of course, I have been thinking about it! You are so fond of reminding me that I am High Queen of Annwyn. As if I could ever forget it. As if every beat of my heart, I do not know what that means. Annwyn is meant to be ruled by us—two of us. Arran and me, a balance of elementals and terrestrials. I was never meant to do it alone!"

I'm not fit to do it alone.

I did not want to know if my friends heard the words I was too afraid to speak.

I turned my back on all of them, taking another gulp of aural before throwing it down in the dirt beside my pack.

"It does not matter how close we are to Eilean Gayl," I said to no one... everyone. To myself. "I am not leaving Arran."

I disappeared into the falling darkness, my body craving release. But I was no longer hungry for food.

6
VEYKA

They were easy to find, in the end.

The scent of their fear left a trail from where I'd killed the succubus straight to their camp. Even after a day spent jumping through the void again and again, it only took me three jumps to cover the many miles between our camp and theirs.

When I'd first gone through the void, during those arduous training sessions with Arran, the fatigue would grow. Each jump a bit slower than the last. But now, the beating of my heart was from excitement, not exertion.

My power was growing.

Even as I looked down on them from high in the branches of a pine tree, where I'd made my final appearance from the void, I could feel the hungry hum of my power. *More*, it seemed to say. *Further. Again.*

I tightened the leash, just as Arran had taught me. *Soon*, I whispered to it lovingly. I only needed a minute to plot my course.

Three humans and seven fae.

All that remained of the force Gorlois had attacked us with on the shores of Avalon.

It would have taken me ages to find them without my void

power. But now? Less than a day. The other scent I'd caught on the pine-scented wind as I moved in and out of the void... I was still deciding what to do with that. But it did not affect what was about to happen.

The humans passed around a flask of some watered-down, human made spirit. The fae warriors did not deign to drink it. I could not recall if they were elementals or terrestrials. If they were terrestrials, they'd been stupid to select this campsite. The branches of the pine trees did not begin until nearly twenty feet up; too far for any but the most powerful of their flora-gifted to make use of. The dead pine needles on the forest floor would not answer their commands. That much, I'd learned from months of traveling with Arran and Osheen.

If they were shifters... my magic flared inside of me. *It does not matter.*

No, it did not. Either way, they were dead.

❦

Once, I might have been outmatched. But I commanded the depths of the voids of darkness. Each time I stepped into the void and reappeared, another soldier died.

I thought I'd killed all the humans. But my memory of that battle in the clearing... I started to shudder, but shoved the impulse back. No weakness, not now. No fear. Only ice.

I'd been mistaken before when I characterized the rage as fire. The ice was there to sharpen the rage into something useful— something deadly.

With each swipe of my knife, each spurt of blood that dripped down my hands, I rebuilt the wall of ice inside my chest. I could not afford to fall apart. I could not afford to be rash. Every decision had to be calculated. Every one of these deaths had meaning.

For Annwyn.
For myself.
For Arran.

7
VEYKA

I stopped at the lakeside long enough to wash the blood from my weapons and my hands. It would not fool the razor-sharp senses of my companions. But I was in no mood to answer questions about the blood. This at least gave them an excuse to pretend.

When I finally re-appeared at the camp, Lyrena and Cyara were already bedded down for the night. Isolde was on watch. She let me eat the roasted pigeon they'd left for me in silence. But instead of crawling into my empty tent, I tossed the bones into the fire and caught her eye. Tipped my head to the side, toward the line of willows the demarked the boundary of the cursed clearing before Avalon.

Isolde did not even glance at the other tent.

She waited only until we were beneath the swaying tendrils of the willows to whisper, "Where are we going?"

I shrugged. "You wanted to know about my power."

Her bright white eyes lit with excitement. I was too mentally exhausted to question the wisdom of that. I nudged her forward through the trees, into the cursed clearing.

"Is it dangerous?"

"Probably," I said honestly.

She paused only a moment as we cleared the cursed clearing and disappeared into another set of trees.

"Excellent."

I snorted softly, speeding up my steps. Even with her much shorter stature and legs, she kept up. It still would have been faster to take her with me through the void. But I wanted to save my focus.

When I glanced back, her eyes were shining. I swallowed hard. "You spent too long in those faerie caves."

"My entire life."

Caged—she'd been caged just like me. A newfound surge of warmth built in my chest. We stepped out onto the beach, far from our companions, far from where the boat had crossed from Avalon. But still on the edge of the lake.

I extended my hand. "Are you ready?"

"Always, Your Majesty."

The warmth in my chest twisted painfully. For all that I might feel connected by our similarities, Isolde saw me unequivocally as her queen. Which made her mine to protect.

Mine to use.

The warmth inside me turned back to ice. But I reached into my ember of power anyway.

I'd imagined that the mist merely encircled Avalon. That once I set foot upon the sacred isle, the thick fog would melt away. But I was wrong.

I felt the magic—the power—before I'd even fully materialized back into my body. If that cursed clearing where I'd faced Gorlois was the absence of magic, its suppression, Avalon was power unleashed.

Would it have felt like this, before? Before the Joining and my void power? Or would I have been blissfully unaware of the power crackling along my skin, the magic that tickled the inside of my nose as I drew in a breath?

Joints cracked at my side. Isolde, rolling her neck, rotating her tiny shoulders. She felt it, too.

Feeling was all we could do. We couldn't see shit through the mist.

Isolde, even standing directly at my side, would have disappeared entirely if I hadn't still been holding her hand. With her white skin, white hair, white eyes, she almost seemed to be made of mist.

But her hand tightened on mine, her tiny white braids settling back onto her shoulders as she looked up at me expectantly. Awaiting orders.

I could not see more than a few steps in front of us. We stood in thick grass, the dew discoloring the toes of my leather boots. The sun had not fully risen—not that I could see it through the fog. But time was immaterial when I stepped through the void. One second we were beneath the weeping willows, the next second we were shrouded in Avalon's mists.

I couldn't hear the lapping of the lakeshore. Which meant Avalon was larger than I'd supposed, and we were further inland than I'd intended.

Not good. But I'd analyze the implications of that later.

Now—*Arran*.

I reached for the bond, wrapping myself around the golden thread of connection. Slender, taut, and *pulling*. Pulling me toward him. The mating bond was very much alive within me, and stronger now than it had been in weeks.

Was Arran healing? Could he feel it too? Would he emerge from those mists, whole and hard and perfect?

No. If he was up and able, he'd already be at my side.

As I stepped forward into the fog, Isolde at my side, I desperately tried to temper my expectations. To remind myself to be realistic, that Arran had been so gravely injured...

But hope lingered inside of me.

Foolish hope that maybe, just maybe, this part of my ordeal was nearly over.

***

We followed the pull of the bond, step by agonizingly slow step. Even as the demand in my chest intensified, I forced my feet to move with deliberate slowness.

After several minutes of walking, I could not see more than a few steps ahead. The mist was relentless. I'd never seen a priestess wield a blade, but they must have sentries of some sort guarding their sacred fortress.

Was it a fortress?

So far, all we'd seen was thick green grass that was almost eerie in its perfection. No patches of mud, no weeds or wild flowers. Not even a sloped incline to indicate we were moving toward the center of the island.

But the magic buzzing all around us... where was it coming from, if not living beings?

My hand fell to the scabbard at my belt. The sacred trinity. Objects of magical power created here in Avalon. I should not presume to know how magic worked here. Not with ancient prophecies and demons from other realms at play.

I nearly choked on the thought.

But not merely that. Something else was rising up in my chest. *The bond.*

I'd been so determinedly ignoring the demand, only acknowledging it enough to let it lead me. Now it overtook me, demanding satisfaction.

I couldn't breathe.

Isolde's hand fell away. So did the mists.

Or maybe I just ceased to see them. To see anything, notice anything. My entire existence narrowed.

Right there. Right there in front of me was my mate.

8
VEYKA

Arran.

My heart twisted inside my chest. Pain, longing. My eyes raked over him, checking every curve of muscle and long plane of his body.

His boots were clean of the mud and blood of battle. His leather trousers were immaculate as well, stretched across his hips. But his armor was gone... the vest that buttoned across his chest, the battle axe, the scabbard... nothing but the linen shirt he wore beneath.

A pale gray, fashioned in the terrestrial style, with buttons that started in the center of his chest and angled upward to where they ended at the shoulder. Open now, revealing a triangle of perfectly golden skin and the upper branches of the tree tattooed across his chest—his Talisman. The physical marker of the power within him, to bend even nature to his will.

He did not move. Not even to draw breath.

But it was his eyes that struck me the most.

His eyes were closed.

That strong, muscular body was prone. Laid out on a slab of granite. Utterly still.

I stumbled forward, my chest exploding with emotion. My eyes burned. I could barely see. The granite jarred my knees as I fell, but that pain was nothing.

Arran. Arran, please.

Arran, wake up! I cried down the bond. Screamed. Reaching for any shred of him on the other side of that precious golden thread.

But there was nothing.

Arran can't be gone. I would have felt it. No one can die in Avalon. How can he... No... no, no, no, no...

Gentle claws landed on my shoulder.

I felt the brush of Isolde's leg as she climbed up onto the base of the granite slab beside me. She lifted her other hand toward Arran, then paused, looking down at me.

"May I?" she asked softly, her voice barely audible through the keening of my soul.

Words were beyond me. But the plea in my eyes must have been enough.

Isolde's white eyes shone. Sympathy, reverence, kindness – she showed more emotional depth with one glance than I'd ever managed with words and actions combined.

Then she turned that focus to Arran.

She laid her hand on his arm with a gentleness that belied the long, sharp claws at the ends of her fingers.

I felt her power before I saw it. A warm wave, washing over my skin, radiating from the white faerie. The glow beneath her palms was brighter than when she'd healed Lyrena. As if she was drawing from the latent magic of Avalon, humming all around us.

Later, I'd wonder if that was why my void power had carried us further onto the sacred isle than I'd intended. Some strange amplification...

But now, my thoughts, my eyes and heart—they were all for Arran.

Isolde's hands drifted over his arm to his chest. The unbuttoned flap of his shirt fluttered open—

I doubled over, my stomach emptying itself violently onto the grass, bile splattering the edge of the granite slab.

I was wrong. Wrong about everything. He couldn't live—not in Avalon, not anywhere. Not with that gaping wound his chest. His heart—

Another wave of bile rose in my throat.

Arran's beating heart was visible, right there, through the wound *I'd* inflicted.

This was all my fault. I'd killed my mate, the male I'd finally allowed myself to love. I'd doomed myself. I'd doomed Annwyn.

Arran's beating heart.

Beating.

His heart was beating.

"The king lives."

Morgyn.

I reached for the edge of the granite slab, digging my nails in hard enough they cracked as I hauled myself up. She stood on the other side of Arran, a few feet back on that perfectly emerald grass. As always, her pale lavender gown fell as flawlessly as her sheet of brown hair. One neat braid, the width of a finger, fell from each temple. And she stared at me with those blue eyes, with the same unshakeable calm.

I wanted to gouge those eyes out.

"The Lady of the Lake speaks the truth," Isolde said before I could launch myself through the air and start ripping her apart.

"I have no reason to lie," Morgyn said, watching the faerie.

I put a hand on Isolde's shoulder. "You would do anything to preserve your precious neutrality," I spat at the priestess. At my sister.

The word was loathsome. A mockery of what Arthur and I had been to one another.

He lied, too.

My heart was breaking inside my chest.

"You were supposed to heal him. Help him!"

"Your Majesty...." Isolde tried to interject.

"His chest is cleaved open! He is dying! You left him alone in this infernal mist to die!"

"My queen..."

"What is wrong with you? Are you every bit as heartless as our mother? Do you blame me, is that it, for being their precious chosen one?"

"Veyka."

Isolde's quicksilver voice finally penetrated. But I was beyond words anyway.

I was going to kill Morgyn. And then every priestess in this cursed place. Even if I spent the next hundred years hunting them all down through the mist.

Morgyn held my gaze. Her lips did not curve or press down into a line. But her eyes... they swirled with feeling. I couldn't have named which ones. But I recognized the storm swirling inside of her.

My hand slid to my knife.

But Morgyn simply lifted her hand, spinning her palm in a graceful wave.

The mist disappeared.

And hiding beneath that velvety white blanket...

Dozens of priestesses. Males and females, dressing in indistinguishable flowing robes. Reminiscent of the ethereal styles of the elemental court, but with thicker, heavier fabrics against the cool air. That remained, even with the mist gone.

All shades of purple, from palest lavender to rich aubergine. All the forms moved with graceful purpose. Walking between buildings carved from the same granite as the slab where I braced my palms. Some carried platters and bowls toward stone altars. Another led a group of children—young acolytes—into a copse of aspens. A small white crystal dangled around each neck. Communication crystals.

But not a single word was spoken. Maybe that was another bit of magic, like the fog.

Beside me, Isolde exhaled slowly.

They'd been here all along, hidden by the mist while we

bumbled about. They'd let us walk right in. After denying me access for weeks, Morgyn had let me walk to my mate unhampered.

What sort of cruel, twisted game was she playing?

Anger curdled in my stomach. But when I glared back at her, the Lady of the Lake's eyes were unreadable once again.

"What have you done to my mate?" My voice was steady. I knew she would recognize that calm for what it truly was—lethal.

But it was not Morgyn who answered.

"He is in an enchanted sleep," Isolde said.

I bit down hard on my lower lip to keep it from trembling. "Why?"

"To heal," Morgyn answered. She did not even smirk. Cold, unfeeling creature.

"He is healing, Majesty," Isolde said quickly, before I could start screaming at Morgyn again. "Look," the faerie implored.

I did not want to look. I did not know how I would survive it. Not without Arran at my side to catch me. Not when Arran was the one lying there...

"The edges of the wound have smoothed, the damage giving way to healthy tissue," Isolde explained.

I forced my eyes down.

It was better than it had been in the clearing... I shivered. Shivered, shook, trembled.

Arran had once promised to cleave open his own chest to find that golden thread between us, to use it to find me if I was ever lost to the void. In the end, I'd done it for him. And nearly lost him in the process.

I pressed my eyes closed, focusing all of my energy on the bond in my own chest. I could not see it. But I could feel it there.

A shaking exhale. "How long?"

I expected Isolde. Got Morgyn instead. "We cannot predict. It is mighty magic, as will be the price."

All magic had a price. Cyara's aching wrists after she used her flames to build my fire. Lyrena's catatonic sleep after quieting the flames that consumed the human village. I'd take a missing limb or a natural disaster or whatever terrible cost the Ancestors demanded. Anything, so long as he lived.

I turned to Isolde, those magical white hands now folded behind her back. No glow in sight. "Can you help him? Heal him faster?"

I watched her eyes fill with tears, knew the answer before she spoke it. The shake of her head was so small, her tiny white braids hardly moved.

"My magic is different here," she said. Whether her sadness was for me or Arran, I felt the weight of it settling in my chest.

"What if I moved him? Brought him to our camp using my power."

Isolde's braids did move this time. "I am afraid he would not survive the journey."

So was I.

I did not know what the void would do to him in this state. Rip him apart, but then find there was not enough of him left to put back together? When I'd moved with Lyrena during the succubus attack in the forest, she'd been injured, but not so gravely.

I sank down to my knees, the vomit I'd spewed up earlier magically enveloped by the unnatural green grass. I kneeled on the edge of the granite, the sharp corners digging into my knees, and let my head fall forward against the cool stone.

"He is safe here," Morgyn said.

I did not believe that for a second.

9
VEYKA

I kneeled there for hours.

Isolde and Morgyn exchanged more words. I only half heard them. My mind lent just enough focus to determine they were non-threatening. But not a fraction more. They came and went. None of the other priestesses approached. If they had, I would have stabbed first and asked questions later.

Or maybe I would not have even bothered with a knife.

Maybe I would have ripped their throats out with my teeth for daring to approach my mate.

The sun beat down on the back of my neck, no mists left to provide cover as it tracked across the sky. I did nothing to cover it. Felt my pale skin burning, and healing, and burning again. I savored the pain. Pain was the least that I deserved after what I'd done to my mate.

My fault.

That gaping hole in his chest?

My fault.

The once strong golden thread of our mating bond, now reduced to a tenuous frayed remnant?

My fault.

Arran's closed eyes.

I had been so focused on my vengeance, on killing Gorlois, that I did not even consider the possibility. Arran wore the scabbard. He was safe.

Safe from everyone but me.

The ice inside of me spread, turning brittle. One well-placed blow, and I would shatter.

You cannot shatter.

I wanted it to be Arran's voice offering that reassurance. But it was my own sad internal monologue whispering to me.

You have a kingdom to protect.

And the Faeries of the Fen. A kingdom in Annwyn, an entire race trapped in the human realm. At least they were safe—for now. Taliya believed that their hidden cave refuge would hide them, that with the amulets of amorite around their necks, the faeries would be safe from the succubus.

But the succubus already knew where they were. What else could explain the mass of them in the forest right above the entrance to the faerie caves? Eventually, the succubus would come. They may not take over the faerie's minds and bodies, but they would rip them apart. There were no warriors among the fierce but peaceful faerie colony. Osheen and Arran had verified that.

Arran.

The granite where I rested my head had turned warm from the contact with my skin. Strange, that my skin still radiated warmth when my insides were cold and frozen.

Folly. It had been such folly to allow myself to care about the world beyond myself. Had I left before the Joining, like I'd always planned, none of this would have happened. My void power would never have awoken. The succubus would not have found the entry they needed into Annwyn and the human realm. My friends and my kingdom would be safe. So would Arran. The guilt rose up in my chest, threatening to melt the ice, to burn me from the inside out. *My fault.*

No. No, no, no, no, no.

I shoved it back down. Guilt wasn't useful, not now. It would not save my kingdom, or my friends, or my mate. Guilt was a private luxury. I could cry alone in my tent, in the cold, empty bedroll. The ice protecting my heart had to remain in place. Without it, I would never get up from this grass. I would stay here at Arran's side forever.

Which is when I realized I'd already made my decision.

Voices floated through the mist. Morgyn and Isolde, approaching. The latter was chattering endlessly. The Lady of the Lake hardly spoke at all. But I could feel her presence. If magic flowed through the very air of the sacred isle, it centered on her.

She'd been a disappointment to Igraine and Gorlois. Abandoned —how had she come to live here? Not just a priestess, but *the* priestess. The Lady of the Lake.

Morgyn had spent two weeks evading my questions and denying me access to Avalon and my mate. Yet when Isolde and I appeared, she was neither surprised nor angry.

Why?

Though, she could have been both of those things and I wouldn't have known it. Not with her perfectly neutral face. On her perfectly neutral island. Which meant that attempting to convince her to aid us in the fight against the succubus was a total and complete waste of my time. Even if it would keep me here at my mate's side for longer.

But still... she was allowing me access now. Why?

Because she realized I wasn't going to leave if she did not.

Everyone seemed intent on me moving on. On leaving Arran.

Fuck all of them. Fuck all of it. Arran was my mate. Leaving him was a betrayal. I'd promised to wait a thousand years. I'd wait that and a thousand more. Eternity. That's what I'd promised to Arran— to myself.

And we'd pledged those years together to Annwyn.

Fuck, fuck, fuck, fuck.

My heart was going to break. Ice or no. It wasn't going to be enough to hold it together. To hold me together.

You can do this, Princess.

A tear slipped down my cheek.

I knew it wasn't real. That it wasn't really Arran, that he couldn't speak to me through the tattered bond, in that enchanted sleep. It was my deluded mind, my broken heart, conjuring his voice in my head to give me strength. But I clung to it nonetheless. If I'd still believed in praying to the Ancestors, I would have beseeched them for strength and courage. Prayed for that voice in my head to be followed by a growl, a growl to fill me up.

But the ice remained, uncracked. Unthawed.

Morgyn and Isolde were close enough to hear their words clearly. Isolde's, at least. My perfectly neutral sister didn't speak at all, keeping her own counsel as always. But I had a plan for that too, I realized.

I blocked them out as I stood, refused to let their voices intrude on this moment. It belonged to me and Arran.

He might have been sleeping. He *was* sleeping, I reminded myself. But he did not turn into my hand as I stroked my fingers along the side of his face. After a fortnight, he should have had the beginnings of a beard. But the stubble along his chin and throat was unchanged from that awful day. He was as frozen as me.

I leaned down, pressing my forehead to his. His skin was cool, none of the eternal warmth I'd come to cherish. It was all so wrong. But I did not pull away. I inhaled deep, filling the chasms inside of me with his scent of earth and spice. And though it nearly broke my heart to do it, knowing he wouldn't pull me close or respond to my touch, I pressed my lips to his.

I let one more tear fall.

And as I rose, the wall of ice inside of me thickened.

10

VEYKA

It was farther than I'd ever jumped before in a singular use of my power. But I did not even pause long enough to wonder if I'd make it. Maybe part of me didn't care if I did... a secret hope that I'd be caught in the void, that I'd find some remnant of Arran there.

But I landed on the ground with my own two feet. Alone.

To find Lyrena and Cyara completely unruffled. The latter spared me a glance only long enough to confirm that it was indeed me who had appeared at the edge of the campsite.

Lyrena was dressing a hare, blood and discarded entrails at her feet. She paused in her gruesome task to say one word, "Avalon?"

I jerked my chin in confirmation.

The golden skin of her throat bobbed in response. "What now?"

"Isolde will stay to watch over Arran." I'd explain the rest to them later. I needed to move now, or I would start second-guessing my decision and wouldn't be able to move at all. "If we are to battle the succubus, we will need allies."

Cyara lifted her eyes to meet mine, their turquoise depths looking into me in that keen way that was slightly unnerving, and yet comforting. She saw what I couldn't yet say... was ready for what I did.

"We are going to Eilean Gayl."

Lyrena's inhale was sharp, her gaze cutting from me to Cyara. My handmaiden held my gaze as she reached behind her and lifted her pack from the ground. Her tent was rolled and affixed to it. In the corners of my vision, I realized all the tents were down, the debris and laundry we'd scattered over the last weeks tidied. Everything was already packed.

It was time to go.

11
VEYKA

"This is not the way to Eilean Gayl."

The crumple of maps should have been my first clue.

I'd seen her sketching them out on the paper gifted to her by the Faeries of the Fen before departing their cave city. Cyara was a librarian's daughter, through and through. And so damn clever. No wonder she and Parys had become allies.

I put aside the thought of my smiling friend, acknowledged the wave of thankfulness that he was safe in Baylaur.

"We need to make a slight detour," I said as we circled the lake. The same route I'd taken nights before, jump by jump, now walking. Even with the speed of our fae legs, it felt impossibly slow.

Cyara let out a controlled exhale behind me. "Back to the faerie caves to retrieve Osheen and Maisri?"

I couldn't fail to note the change in pitch, the hope in those words that she tried and failed to disguise. Faithful. Above all, Cyara was faithful. Even when I did not want to hear what she had to say, she always spoke with truth and love.

What had I ever done to deserve her?

Any of them, really.

At my right, two steps ahead of me, positioned so that the

lakeshore was on one side and she was on the other, Lyrena's entire body was primed for movement. Alert, scanning, assessing every blade of grass or whipping willow vine.

"Not yet," I said. Not until I was certain of what we were walking into, of our safety. Arran laid unconscious in Avalon because I hadn't taken my time; because I'd rushed headlong into danger.

I should have checked the clearing. Should have formed a perimeter, explored the area around Avalon, before standing exposed on that lakeshore and asking Morgyn stupid questions she only half answered.

My fault.

I would not lose another person I loved because of my temper, my brashness. My selfishness.

He is not lost.

I shivered, the ice that filled my chest reminding me not to think. Not about Arran. Not if I had any chance of holding myself together.

I shook myself again, this time to regain control. "Lyrena, how's your tracking?"

"Not as good as a wolf."

She didn't mean it. It was a joke. Always a joke.

Shit, shit, shit.

I ground my teeth together hard enough I was sure they would crack. I reached for my dagger in the scabbard at my waist. Began searching out targets. Something, I needed to hurl it at something—

Thunk.

I barely registered the feeling of the wolf-pommel in my hand before it was gone, flying through the air, landing fifty yards away. Lodged directly in the knot of a tree stump.

I blinked. I'd never thrown that far. Never hit a target that far.

I watched in open-mouthed silence as Lyrena cut to the side. She exchanged a look with Cyara, who stepped up to my side, white wings flaring. Taking on guard duty.

Lyrena walked with unflinching precision. Wrenched the knife free. Walked back to me. Sank to her knees. When she lifted her eyes, the apology was there. I wanted to tell her I did not need one. That having her at my side was enough. That I appreciated her loyalty and laughter and joy.

But I said none of that. The ice inside of me wouldn't allow it. Ice was strong. But it could be melted.

I sheathed the dagger. Dropped my chin a fraction of an inch.

Lyrena rose, stepping up in front of me as Cyara fell back to guard my rear. Asinine, considering that of the three of us I was the superior warrior. But I was also their queen. I knew that both of these females would give their lives to slow down an attacker, to give me time to jump away through the void.

Another shiver of ice through my veins.

"My skills are adequate. My Goldstones training included tracking would-be attackers," Lyrena said before turning to resume our path along the edge of the lake. "What are we tracking?"

"Hunting," I corrected. "We are going to hunt down the one who betrayed us. And this time I won't be stupid enough to fall for his tricks."

12
CYARA

She had hoped she would never have to see his face again. Percival St. Pierre was the sort of clever that made Cyara's stomach turn. Not like Parys, quick and genuine and ultimately, kind. Not even her own brand of intelligence, borne of careful observation and educated leaps of intuition.

Percival was conniving. He paid attention not so he might learn, but so he could subvert. She had noticed it early in their journey through the human realm, but had ultimately decided to keep her own counsel on the matter. Veyka did not need to know every thought in her head. Veyka did not *want* to know. And that was perfectly well. The more time she had to mull things over, the surer she would be when she finally spoke.

But Percival had been a mistake.

Cyara had recognized his true nature, but had deemed it secondary to the value he provided in guiding them to Avalon. That mistake had nearly cost the life of a fellow Knight of the Round Table and the High King of Annwyn.

Cyara considered herself a merciful female.

But she would not try to stop Veyka when she sank her blade into the half-witch's chest.

"The tracks from the clearing are old, but there hasn't been rain. I should be able to make something of them," Lyrena was saying, hands on her hips. "But we are going the wrong direction."

Veyka merely stepped around the golden female, as if she had not noticed the guarding formation that Cyara and Lyrena had agreed to. Cyara rolled her eyes, shot a glance to Lyrena, and resumed her spot guarding the queen's back. Lyrena had to jog to catch up, but was in place in a moment as well.

Lyrena was still figuring Veyka out, even after all of these months. Who could blame her? She had been lost in her own grief after Arthur's death, though she was careful to keep her bright, gold-studded smile in place for all the elemental courtiers to see. But Cyara had seen the cracks in her goldstone armor; the way her smiles did not quite reach her eyes, the brash overcompensating. As Veyka had emerged from her grief, so had Lyrena. Only then had they truly begun to see one another.

Cyara, however, had been watching her queen keenly for nearly two years. Ever since Arthur had appointed her and her sisters as handmaidens.

The memory of Charis and Carly stung. It whispered to the monster inside of her. But she could not think when the harpy was in control.

She was not a true shifter, like Gwen or Arran. Their beasts were never wholly gone, even when in their fae forms. And when they shifted, they retained their ability to think and reason.

Not Cyara.

When the harpy took over, she shed all remnants of who she was. The harpy's only objective was to shred and kill.

She would let Veyka do the killing today. The queen was determined, her body coiled with unspent, lethal energy. Cyara noted everything as she walked two steps behind her.

The thick cloak was thrown back over Veyka's shoulders despite the frigid air and cutting wind off of the lake. It would give her easier access to the daggers fastened to her belt—one in the jeweled scabbard, the other in an ordinary one that Lyrena had fashioned for her during their weeks spent in stasis.

Excalibur was nowhere in sight.

The curved rapiers strapped across her back would be harder to access with the long layers of the cloak. Which meant that Veyka did not plan on accessing them at all.

Percival's death would be at the end of her daggers. And Cyara doubted that the queen would throw them.

No, Veyka would want to feel the traitor's lifeblood on her hands as it drained out of him.

Cyara considered herself a merciful female. So, perhaps there was not as clear of a demarcation between the fae and harpy. Because she knew she would savor Percival's death almost as much as the queen.

13
ARRAN

Light flashed, filling my vision, blinding me. Such light, I'd never seen such light. No, that wasn't light searing through me.

It was pain.

Pain that filled every crevice of my body. My toes in my boots, the lines of the Talisman inked across my chest, my head. Oh, Ancestors, fucking Ancestors. My head ached.

My heart beat and it sent pain shooting through my veins. I tried to drag in a breath, but the small act of opening my lips was impossible. Every twitch of muscle brought pain sharper than anything I'd experienced in my immortal life.

I had endured torture before, but it had never felt like this. It went beyond physical. As if the core inside of me, my very soul, was being shredded. My insides were tearing themselves apart, searching for something.

Something was missing.

I tried to take stock. Tried to hone in with the warrior's focus that had saved me from terrible, life-ending situations again and again. But I couldn't order my mind, not with this pain.

I could not fight it.

Not without... whatever it was that was missing...
I could not fight.
And the pain swallowed me whole.

14
VEYKA

We were a mile past the last sign of tracks before Lyrena caught the scent on the wind. The same one I'd stumbled across while hunting for Gorlois' soldiers. Percival was clever, indeed, dragging his feet through the thick mud, only to change direction and head west instead. Had it been anyone else, I might have applauded the attention to detail in a moment of crisis. He and his sister had run while the battle at the lakeside still raged.

But he was arrogant as well as clever. And after more than a fortnight of relative safety, he'd let his guard down and hadn't bothered to be clever anymore. Which was how we walked right into his camp.

It was so simple it did not even require a plan. Lyrena, Cyara, and I exchanged glances, pulled our weapons, and encircled the meager camp.

I left Percival's long-lost sister, Diana, to my companions. She wasn't a warrior. Cyara could likely have subdued her on her own. But Percival was mine.

He managed to get a dagger out and up. The same blasted dagger I'd pressed into his hand in thanks for saving my life when we battled the succubus. The one he had slid into Lyrena's back the instant it benefited him.

Diana was whimpering in the background. Not much fight in her.

Percival's dark eyes darted around the campsite, trying to take stock, to weigh his options. He had none. His deep ochre skin paled at the realization. I smiled.

"You really thought it would be that easy, did you?" I crooned, pausing a few yards away. Propping a hand on my hip, chuckling mirthlessly. "No matter who triumphed in that battle, you were always going to be hunted down like the vermin you are."

Percival's chin notched upward. "Lord Gorlois promised—"

"Gorlois is dead. If you were stupid enough to trust him, then you deserve the consequences." I took a casual step in his direction, then another.

I made a show of examining my knife, the twin to the one he held. Percival gripped his hard enough that the red-brown of his knuckles nearly glowed. Mine—casual, loose. Deadly.

There was a slight crunch behind me. Diana hadn't stop whimpering from the moment we had entered the clearing, so I doubted the intentional, quiet sound came from her. Lyrena or Cyara, then. Trying to remind me of something?

I summoned a slow, malicious smile as I turned to look at Percival's sister. Her lilac robes, a variation of what the other priestesses on Avalon wore, were filthy. The hem was caught on the log she'd been sitting on when Lyrena dragged her backward. It would not be the first rip in the ragged garment. Her brown cloak—which I recognized from Percival's shoulders in the weeks before we arrived at Avalon—was in only slightly better condition.

But none of it was as impactful as the tears rolling down her cheeks or the way her soft chin trembled against Lyrena's small knife. My golden knight had not even bothered to draw her mighty sword.

I rolled my eyes, rolled my shoulders, and looked back to Percival. "She doesn't seem worth the effort."

His eyes burned with anger. He wanted to stab that knife into my gut, to twist it again and again. The feeling was entirely mutual.

But I could not allow myself to be governed by rage. Not anymore.

So, each move was carefully calculated.

Springing toward Percival. Knocking my knife out of his hand and catching it with my empty one. Burying my knee between his legs and then smashing it into his face as he doubled over. It took hardly any effort to push him down to his knees; especially with a knife pressed to his throat.

Diana cried out behind us. I ignored it, pressing my blade tighter against Percival's jugular as his head snapped up, trying to see past me to his sister.

"If you behave, we have no reason to hurt her," I said reasonably. Really, I was being very reasonable. I had not executed them on sight, which was my due for the part he'd played in Gorlois' plot. For what it had meant for Arran.

"Do whatever you want to me. But leave her alone," he ground out.

Yes, Percival would do anything for his sister. Even betraying those who had helped him.

"Lucky for you, I have decided to be merciful," I said, not bothering to loosen my stance or the tension of my blade at his throat.

"Merciful?" Cyara echoed behind me. I swung my gaze around, just to let myself savor the disbelief on her face. It was so rare that I managed to surprise my crafty friend.

Anger contorted her lovely face, filling her turquoise eyes. For a moment, I thought we might meet the harpy once again. Messy, but it would scare Diana and Percival shitless. However, she managed to master herself. Her eyes flared, wings twitched, but no talons appeared.

"This isn't mercy," Percival spat, earning back my attention.

I rolled my eyes. "Would you rather I killed you?"

His entire face screwed up, trying to hold his mouth closed. Pain arched his body—magic. Different than the terrestrial or elemental or even the void power inside of me. This was ancient, part of his very essence. As old as our world itself.

"No." He scowled at the word, passing involuntarily from his lips.

I laughed aloud. Not at his will to live. But at how beautifully it worked. A witch at your mercy must answer three questions. Percival wanted to live. That was certainly something I could use against him.

He realized it as well, glaring at me with an impressive amount of bravado. "You would have done it already," he added of his own free will.

I shrugged. "Fine. I will kill her, then."

Lyrena was ready. She pulled her sword in one long, graceful motion, without disturbing the knife she pressed to Diana's throat.

True terror flashed in Percival's eyes. Tears bubbled out of Diana's.

I knew it was cruel. I had spent twenty years being tortured by the same monster who had held Diana hostage.

But my heart was encased in ice. I had a kingdom to protect.

I pinned my attention back to Percival. His eyes remained on his sister. Good—he ought to remember the stakes.

"How do the communication crystals work?" I asked.

His dark eyes flared—not the question he'd expected. I had plenty of others. But I'd enjoy torturing them out of him later.

For once, though, his response was not pained. He was compelled to give it, but he did not fight the command in his blood.

"They work on intention. You must know who you wish to speak to, and they must be open to receiving your messages. Otherwise, you are just talking to a rock."

I compared that against what I'd seen so far, checking the veracity of it. The priestesses in Avalon wore them. That made sense, since to become an acolyte or priestess involved taking vows. Surely that would cover the intention necessary to make the crystals function.

It also fit with Percival stealing the crystal during the festival at the Crossing. He knew Diana had one, and hoped she would be willing to receive his message even while in Gorlois' clutches. Or Percival had used it to communicate with Gorlois himself.

My stomach tightened, my muscles as well. I fought to keep my breath steady, my heartbeat even. Even as a half-witch, Percival could not perceive those changes. But I hid them nonetheless. Let no one see my struggle, my weakness. Even my friends.

I was the High Queen of Annwyn. I could handle it.

For all that Percival had given the answer about the communication crystals freely, there was plenty he'd left out. He'd answered the bare minimum; given no details about how the mechanics of sending and receiving messages actually worked. Another question, for another time, then.

I tucked the knife that was not pressed to Percival's throat into the crevice between my breasts. With my now free hand, I casually slid my palm along the side of Percival's face. Down, until I cupped his chin firmly. My other knife still pressed to his throat. One jerk of my hand, my fae strength combined with the muscles I'd built from years of training, and I would snap his neck.

As a human, there would be no healing.

I leaned in, whispering the question into his ear like a lover. "Will you betray us again?"

Percival swallowed, his throat bobbing against my hand, the stubble of his unshaved chin rough against my callouses. But he did not appear to resist the answer he gave— "No."

I released him. Sheathed my knife. Lifted my eyebrows at Lyrena, who had not shifted a fraction from where she held Diana.

"He is telling the truth now. But he could change his mind in the future," Lyrena argued.

"Then we'll make a habit of tying him to a tree and torturing him for answers," I said. I checked him for weapons as we spoke, but found none other than the knife I'd already taken back.

Lyrena was right, of course.

He spoke the truth of his intentions now, but those intentions could change. Cyara was watching me, her protest silent. I could not see the struggle on her face; she was too skilled of an elemental to allow that. But I knew the twitch of her wings. She was considering all the angles. Understood my decision, but did not like it.

"Arran will remain in Avalon indefinitely. Isolde is with him." The words hurt, threatened to shatter me. But I pushed past them. Cold, ice, unbreakable. "The priestess who made the Void and Ethereal Prophecies may be dead now, but she dwelt on the blasted island for seven thousand years before that. At some point, these two did as well." I jerked my head between the pair.

"Until I am confident I've leeched every bit of useful information from their brains, they live." I smiled at Percival, in case he'd entertained any doubts about what happened next. "They are coming with us."

15
CYARA

She understood her Queen's motivations, she truly did. But that did not quell the rancor swirling in her stomach or the harpy lurking beneath her skin from trying to tear her way out. There were about a thousand more questions they needed Percival and Diana to answer.

How did one actually use the communication crystals to send a message? How had Gorlois used Diana to open rifts and travel through the void when neither of them possessed the void power? What were the Lady of the Lake's true motivations?

But wringing answers from Percival was torturous.

Veyka had sent Percival to the front of the group, where she could keep watch on him herself. She had not even bothered to bind his hands with rope. Cyara recognized the tactic—ensuring his good behavior through threats rather than tethers.

The motivation walked between Cyara and Lyrena. Lyrena held the leash—ten feet of rope that trailed from her belt back to Diana's bound hands. Cyara scanned from the rear, eyes examining every angle and step. She knew Lyrena would have preferred this position. But she would not leave Veyka's side.

Missing Osheen and Maisri had been one thing. Leaving them

in the faerie caves had reorganized their structure of guarding and chores. But Arran's absence was something else entirely. It changed the way Veyka walked, breathed, spoke.

She did not smile.

Sure, she had flashed a wicked, intimidating grin here and there. She pretended to laugh at Lyrena's jokes. But something had shuttered inside of the Queen.

To have found her mate, accepted the bond… only to lose him so quickly. Cyara shivered.

She knew, perhaps better than anyone, what it had cost Veyka to accept Arran as her mate. So much had been taken from her. Loss after loss after loss punctuated with torture and betrayal. To commit to Arran, to love him, meant to risk the pain of his loss. The pain she was experiencing right now.

If half of the things Cyara's father had told her about mates were true… it was a miracle that Veyka was standing. Let alone leading them—or trying to.

Cyara shook her head, her wings heavier than usual, twitching more as well. Worry was a physical weight. She would watch Veyka, care for her, and push her as best she could.

Caring meant helping—lessening the burdens that the Queen carried. Cyara could do that, starting with the woman stumbling through the forest in front of her.

She increased her speed, one flap of her wings, until she stood nearly at Diana's side.

"Are you cold?" Cyara asked, infusing her voice with the careful gentleness she had used when speaking to Maisri the first few times.

Diana lurched, her matted dark hair swaying as one thick sheet when she shook her head. "No."

The rich red-brown of her skin made it difficult to detect any flush, but a thin veneer of sweat coated her face even in the frigid morning air. Cyara had noticed it earlier, but attributed it to nerves rather than exertion.

Her stature was similar to Veyka's, though the acolyte lacked all of the latter's easy predatory grace. As Cyara watched, Diana stumbled over a log, barely preventing herself from splaying face down in the pine needles.

She lacked the Queen's endurance as well. However Gorlois had been using her, it had not required physical stamina. From what she had seen, Cyara doubted Diana had been treated well. Which suggested mental exhaustion instead—and would account for the tears that had been running down Diana's face off and on since they had taken her and her brother prisoner the day before.

Forceful tactics would likely break the scared young woman.

Cyara had always been better with the subtle sort of manipulations, anyway.

Keeping her movements slow, her steps heavier than usual so that Diana would sense her approach, Cyara moved a few paces ahead. Until she was positioned in front of Diana, out of her reach, but not quite to Lyrena.

She grasped the rope between them and tugged lightly. Lyrena whipped around, hand already reaching for her sword. But the expression on Cyara's face stilled her. Lyrena slid a glance up ahead to Veyka, then back again. She hummed in disapproval, but untied the rope without breaking step and handed it back to Cyara.

Lyrena watched, her bright eyes sharp, until the rope was firmly affixed to the leather harness that Cyara wore. Only then did she turn back to monitoring Veyka.

Diana blinked a few times, dark eyes—the twin to Percival's—widening with terror. A whimper escaped her lips.

Percival whipped around at the sound, only to find Veyka pressing the tip of her dagger into the small of his back.

Veyka rolled her eyes at Percival's glare, then followed the direction of his gaze with a lazy glance of her own. Sweeping them over Lyrena, and Diana now tied to Cyara. Veyka dug the knife in a little harder. Percival cursed under his breath and stomped off, feet crunching over the frosty wintry debris beneath their feet.

Veyka followed him without a backward glance.

But Cyara knew the decision was deliberate. Veyka had noted

the change in who held Diana's leash. She knew her handmaiden well enough to intuit that there was a reason for the switch. Cyara would either report or be questioned later. Or maybe Veyka would keep her mouth shut and wait to see what happened.

Unlikely, though.

She put Veyka's considerations to the side, for the moment. She would deal with the queen's tempers and expectations later.

Her focus narrowed to the woman now walking near her side, a yard or so away. Cyara had not put that space there; Diana had. Wary, even of her, the handmaiden. What had Percival told her? Did she know about the harpy?

Cyara swallowed as silently as she could, then remembered the woman's human ears could not detect such things in any case. Even as a half-witch, Diana could not hear the thumping of her heart or scent the worry that flowed off of Lyrena, who kept looking over her shoulder.

Cyara caught Lyrena's gaze the next time. Rolled her eyes. Nodded forward.

Lyrena stuck out her tongue and turned her full attention back toward the front, to Veyka. The queen's safety must be prioritized over everything; especially with Arran now laying in an enchanted sleep in Avalon.

Veyka was the only one who could save Annwyn.

If she was willing to try.

If she could overcome her grief and guilt.

When she was ready, Cyara would be as well.

She waited more than an hour, until they had settled into a quiet rhythm of movement, before she began humming. Just a gentle, soft sound. The tune was one from her youth, from the times when she had played with two younger sisters, all white winged and full of mischief.

She did not dare reach out and touch the captive woman

directly for fear of startling her. But she slowly increased the volume of her humming, letting Diana adjust to the resonance of her voice.

When she stopped, and the woman's head turned slightly, almost against her will, Cyara knew the time was right.

"I am going to ask you some questions," Cyara said, keeping her voice carefully even. Nonthreatening.

Diana sucked in a breath, her heartbeat speeding up. Her muscles went tense, easy to see even under her flowing pale purple robes.

"I am not going to hurt you," Cyara said. "But you are at my mercy." She tugged on the rope, just enough to apply pressure to Diana's hands.

Veyka took the harsh approach—pinning Percival down and putting a knife to his throat. Arran had done the same before her, without even realizing it, by tying Percival to a tree before questioning him. But that would not work with Diana. She was one wrong step away from shattering, and then she would be useless to them.

And shattered.

Cyara inhaled slowly, speaking on her exhale. "How long did you dwell on Avalon?"

She watched the woman's throat, visible just above the modest cut of her purple robes, bob up and down. But she answered without flinching, without any outward sign of pain.

"My brother and I pledged ourselves as acolytes after our parents' deaths twelve years ago," Diana said.

Her tones were naturally high-pitched, but they did not rise as she spoke. Another indication that she was not fighting the command of the witch-blood in her veins to answer the questions.

Cyara had used her time mindlessly humming to consider her questions. She certainly could not afford to spend it dwelling on her own grief, on the sisters she had shared that melody with, the sisters she had lost.

Her voice remained steady as she asked her next question. "Did you leave Avalon willingly?"

Diana pressed her eyes shut. Stumbled. Hauled herself back up.

Her voice had risen by an octave when she spoke again. "No. I was taken."

Cyara let the words hang in the cold air between them. With each huff, they could see their breath. The words were as real as those clouds of air—real but intangible.

The words that came next were the ones that truly mattered.

Veyka's head twitched to the side. Listening to every word. Lyrena was subtler. Both waiting. If Percival listened as well, he gave no indication.

"How did you come to be Gorlois' captive?"

Diana's lower lip started to tremble. Then her hand, her arm. Her shoulders and then her entire body were moving. Tears tracking down her cheeks. Shaking. The name had set her off—set her shattering.

Cyara stilled the urge to press her own eyes closed or to press her fingers to the bridge of her nose in disappointment. She did not know how much gentler she could be. She opened her mouth to retract the question, to ask something different.

But it was too late. The command of the witch curse in her veins had Diana's mouth opening, even as tears streamed down her face.

"He lured me with the communication crystal and then he took me from Avalon." Each word was pained, the syllables stretched until they were jagged and sharp. Diana's face crumbled and she buried it in her hands.

Percival's footsteps crunched through the underbrush as he stormed to his sister's side. He tucked her in against him and glared at Cyara, telling her without words that he was unafraid of the harpy he knew she could become.

Cyara looked away from the tender moment, unable to bear the gentle shushing of Percival's voice. It was too close, too reminiscent of the sibling bond now lost to her. She sucked in a breath, letting Lyrena step closer and keep watch on the two.

Only to find the High Queen of Annwyn staring at her speculatively, tossing her dagger idly between her palms.

One eyebrow lifted toward the crown of shimmering snow-white hair.

Cyara ducked her head, avoiding Veyka's eyes, afraid of what she would find there. Admonition, for pushing an already fragile captive toward the breaking point. Or worse—approval, for getting information they sorely needed. She was not sure which would make her feel worse.

16
VEYKA

In the northeastern foothills of the Spine. Arran's words, spoken months and months ago when we'd first wondered so naively about rifts. I let the meaning of the words fade to nothing, let myself bathe in the memory of the syllables scraping over his tongue, the rough stubble on his throat moving as he spoke.

Would things have been different if I had listened to Parys all those months ago? Would I still be standing in a brutally cold pine forest, alone?

Fire crackled behind me, then the hushed voices of Lyrena and Cyara arguing over who would take the first watch of the night. Lonely, but not alone, my fragile heart amended.

We were moving painfully slowly with our human prisoners in tow. Diana, in particular, was a mess. Cyara was the gentlest soul among us, and even she had not been able to coax much out of her before the woman collapsed in on herself.

I had been broken like that before. Before Arran came and stitched my soul back together. Before I had friends.

Even now, it was a minute by minute battle to keep myself from falling to my knees and sobbing at the ache in my chest. Only the layer of ice I'd encased my heart in, that I'd built in my chest, kept me upright. If I could not feel the other parts of myself fully, if I was dangerously close to that numbness I'd felt after Arthur's death... I could not dwell on that. I had to protect Annwyn. I had to stop the succubus. I could not fall apart.

Cyara could work on Diana. I still had Percival to torture. Once he outlived his usefulness, I'd remove his head from his body. The terrestrial realm was known for its brutality. They'd probably think nothing of me spiking his head to the battlements of Eilean Gayl or Wolf Bay.

But first we had to get there.

After several days of travel, we were close.

I did not need Cyara's maps, however well-crafted they were by the librarian's daughter. The rift called to me. It was a soft hum in my bones, a trill in the back of my mind that never quite stopped.

It hadn't been like this before, back when we went through the rift at Eldermist. But I had not accepted my power then, either.

Now, I knew that if I closed my eyes, stepped through the void, I would appear at the rift itself. I'd have done it to save us from this tedious journey. Except I had never taken more than one other along with me through the void. The glowing ember of power inside of me was strong, but would it be strong enough to carry two or three companions at once?

I had never even taken myself from one realm to another, let alone done so with another. Had never taken another step like that, deeper into my power, without Arran at my side.

Even if I took my companions through one at a time, there was nothing to stop Percival from using the moment of vulnerability to slide a dagger between my ribs. I was not stupid enough to believe his compliance would last one second beyond his first opportunity to escape.

This was the best way, the safe way. Over land to the rift near the Spine. It would deposit us in the exact same geographical location, but in Annwyn. Then we could travel on to Eilean Gay.

I would not endanger my friends. The arrogant use of my power had already lost me my mate. My partner. The strategic one, the steady one. The warm body that wrapped around mine at night and soothed away the fears that the others could sympathize with, but only Arran could truly understand.

I stood on the edge of the camp, staring out into the darkness. I listened to the sounds of Diana and Percival being settled in for the night, even more tightly bound, separated. The rustle of a tent flap, the even quieter rustle of wings. Cyara was going to sleep. Lyrena was on first watch.

I lingered still. Until Percival stopped grumbling about the cold the open tent flaps let in—open so that Lyrena could watch both him and the camp—and his breathing evened out. The rhythmic sound of Lyrena sharpening her blade on a whetstone merged with the animal sounds of the forest around us.

When the moon was fully overhead, just visible, and all human and fae sounds had ebbed away to nothing, I shot a look back over my shoulder to Lyrena.

Her bright eyes were already waiting.

I tipped my head toward the darkness of the forest.

She shook her chin sharply to the side. *No.*

One casual step. *I am going.*

Her lips thinned into a line. *No.*

I glanced up at the moon, then back at the tents. *I will be back in time to take the next watch.*

Lyrena stood up, hands on her hips, gripping her sword. As if she might charge me, try to subdue me and tie me down to keep me from slipping away. But mere ropes could not hold me now.

She looked meaningfully at Percival, a dark form in the tent a few yards away. She could not leave him and follow me. She took a step toward Cyara's tent.

I shook my head sharply. But it was everything else about me that held her in place. The way I squared my shoulders, the imperious tilt of my face. The command from a queen to her sentinel. *Stay.*

My golden knight dropped back down to her seat and glared at me.

I winked, and then disappeared into the night.

17
VEYKA

I did not use my void power this time.

I wanted to feel the earth beneath my feet. As I wove my way between the roots of the mighty pine trees, I tried to feel the power that lay there in wait. Arran could pull the power up in a second, use the roots and branches to do his will. I knew it was a desperate, sad attempt at a connection to him. But I tried nonetheless.

It did not come.

The trees were just trees, the roots solid and unmoving.

When I settled myself against one, my thighs cradled by the thick roots on either side, I did not let myself imagine it was my mate holding me. That was much too dangerous to my precious wall of ice.

My hair was just long enough to braid now, though tendrils of it still snuck free. Most days I left it loose around my shoulders, enjoying the lightness of it. But tonight I took the time to braid it back, though even the motion of flipping it over my shoulder had a few wisps of white coming loose at my temples.

I ignored them, turning my focus inward.

I closed my eyes.

Inside of me was darkness. Not emptiness. Not quite what it had been after Arthur's death. The parts of me that I'd rebuilt were still there, but they were shrouded in moonless night. I could feel them, but I could not see them. And around all of it was that wall of ice, protecting the things that were most precious to me. If I let that ice melt, I'd have to feel. If I let myself feel, I would be paralyzed.

But beneath that wall of ice, deeper inside of me still, was the ember of my power. A shining light that slumbered now. Once, stroking it awake had terrified me. Now, I could step through the void and out the other side with half a thought. I released the leash I held on my power only a tiny fraction.

Moving between realms would require something else. Something more.

I would have to reach deeper into that ember of power, fully awaken it.

Without Arran.

If I left the human realm and ended up somewhere else, who would know? I was sitting alone in a forest, for Ancestors' sake.

No, damn the Ancestors to hell.

You could have done this with your friends, my inner voice admonished.

But then they would see me utterly failing.

I hadn't failed yet. I hadn't even tried.

I closed my eyes again—had not even meant to open them. Shit. I needed to focus.

I eased the ember of power awake, stroking it lovingly. I had come to love my power—my cursed power that had brought the succubus into this realm and cost my mate—

Shit. Shit. Shit.

Focus.

Into the void, the darkness of nothing pulling me apart, stretching my limbs and spine until I scattered into fragments. Bit by bit, I put myself back together, willed myself to linger in the void a bit longer, not to move laterally, but... what? Up, down? Where were the other realms? Somewhere. Go somewhere.

I tried to imagine a low snarl, tried to summon Arran's beast, begged it to come. But there was no answer at the end of the golden thread of our mating bond. My body slammed back together, reassembling so fast and hard—

Shit.

I opened my eyes.

Absolute fucking shit.

I was sitting in the same damn clearing, against the same damn tree, in the same blasted realm.

Fuck this.

We were close to the rift. By tomorrow, we'd be there. Through the rift, into Annwyn, and on to Eilean Gayl.

I shoved the power still humming in my veins back down and pulled the communication crystal from my pocket instead. Intention, Percival had said. I knew who I wished to speak to, but it remained to be seen if she would be open to receiving my summons.

"Morgyn."

Silence.

"I am addressing the Lady of the Lake," I ground out, focusing all of my energy and attention and intention of the pale crystal in my palm. "Tell me about my mate. Tell me he is healing or that he is awake or anything."

Absolute fucking silence.

I shoved the crystal back into my pocket. I hadn't really expected her to answer, had I? I would go back and check on him, then. It had been my intent all along, really. The communication crystal was a stupid idea. Morgyn could say whatever she wanted, and I would have no way of verifying it.

Get to Eliean Gayl, get my friends to safety, and then I would go back and check on Arran. That is what Arran would prioritize—the good of the kingdom. I could not be selfish, not anymore.

I needed to focus on being High Queen of Annwyn, ruling without my king. I did not have time for this trial and failure.

I gripped the tree roots, ready to shove myself up—

And fell right back on my ass in shock.

Not ten feet in front of me, silent and serene as always, was the fucking Lady of the Lake.

"What are you doing here?" My mind scrambled, trying to fit this new reality into my understanding of the world, even as my body did not shift an inch. Not a tremor, not a twitch. I held myself with obstinate stillness.

Maybe Morgyn and I had more in common than I realized.

I hated that thought.

I cut her off before she could open that perfect mouth and speak. "You lied about having the void power. It was you all along. You lying bitch." It was the only explanation for her being there.

She didn't interrupt me. Her pale blue eyes didn't even flare at the insults I leveled. It made me want to throw out a dozen more. But I held my stillness, staring her down, trying to place what this meant.

Fuck, fuck, fuck. I was going to kill her. I did not move, but I inventoried my weapons. Checked my power. I could step through the void and be behind her in less than a second, dagger pressed to her throat.

"Are you done?" she finally asked, voice barely above a whisper. She did not want to wake my companions; did not realize they were far enough away they would not hear the sound of her head hitting the ground when I removed it from her body.

There was no one to talk me out of killing her for her deceit.

I was already calculating how long it would take me to get to Arran, how many long jumps through the void.

When I did not hurl any more epithets in her direction, Morgyn continued in that breathy voice. "You are the one and only wielder of the void power," she said. "I am neither a queen nor blessed with a mate to tether me. The voids of darkness remain solely at your command, Majesty."

"Then how are you here?" Even as I asked, I noticed the inconsistencies through my haze of icy rage.

Neither her gown nor her hair moved in the breeze. She'd always seemed to hover above the ground, the mist providing as sure a footing as anything else. But as I blinked, I realized there truly was an inch between the hem of her lavender robes and the stony ground.

"You ask the wrong question."

I rolled my eyes, hoping that the irreverence would annoy her even if I never saw any outward sign of it. My heart was slowing down, reality sinking back into me. The need to fight and kill still simmered just beneath the surface of my skin.

But if Morgyn sensed it, she did not react.

She merely inclined her head—the movement slower than it should have been, stuttering. "Avalon has kept its secrets for tens of thousands of years. I will not share them now."

I unfolded to my feet, carefully silent but seething. I swiped a rock from the ground, deciding to test the theory that had taken root in my mind. As I straightened, I chucked the rock right at her head.

Where it sailed through Morgyn's crown of brown hair without even touching her. She did not truly stand there at all—this form a mere shade of her corporeal self.

"Fun trick," I spat. My fingers twitched for my blades, but I forced them to still, crossing my arms over my chest instead. "I tried to use the communication crystal because I wanted to know about Arran. If you have no news of him, then I do not wish to speak with you."

Morgyn blinked. A long-suffering tell. I was annoying her. Good.

"You ask the wrong question," she said again.

"I did not ask any questions at all," I countered. "Tell me news of my mate, or go away."

Morgyn opened her mouth to respond, but I cut her off. I did not give a fuck if she was the Lady of the Lake. I owed her no allegiance. She'd kept Arran alive, but only in the most nominal way. If she was any use at all, he'd be at my side now.

I was so tired of being alone.

"I don't want to do this bullshit again. I played your game on the lakeside, and it ended with Gorlois attacking and my mate nearly dead." So tired of everything.

I turned my back on her, starting in the direction of the camp. I suddenly wished I had not walked so far, alone through the darkness. Every step now seemed impossible, the distance interminable.

"Ask the right question," Morgyn said to my back. I stilled, if only to rest my weary soul for a second. But I did not turn back to her as I spoke.

"Why was I unable to contact you using the communication crystal?" I ground out.

"Because I did not wish to receive your message."

I spun, dagger in my hand, even though it could do nothing against her in this form. "We may technically be sisters, but I will kill you. Lady of the Lake or not, whether you are a hundred years or three hundred years old, you are still fae. And I am very good at killing."

Morgyn didn't flinch. "Ask—"

"Why did you refuse my message?" I demanded, close enough to her I should have been able to smell her, hear her heartbeat. But there was nothing. Only the hollowness of my own soul.

"I fear that the communication crystal will become a crutch. A distraction, keeping you from where you need to be and what you must do."

"That does not sound very neutral."

"I allowed Gorlois to attack. I am helping you by giving this counsel." Was that remorse in her eyes, or a flickering of this strange apparition she'd conjured?

"Those are not remotely equal."

"Arran is safe in Avalon and will continue to heal. But you must not interfere."

I heard the subtext. No more using the communication crystal.

No uninvited trips through the void to her sacred island. Or she may very well dump my injured mate on the shores of that cursed clearing.

"You must use your power," she continued calmly, as if she had not just threatened my mate's life, and by extension, Annwyn itself.

"My power—the one that summoned the succubus. Yes, great things have come from this power."

"Your mate wanted you to hone it, not hide from it."

Ice. Ice around my heart. Ice in my chest. Ice to protect the golden thread of my mating bond, so fragile and taut now. "My mate is in an enchanted sleep, fighting for his life."

"You do not deny the truth of what I say." Morgyn did not even bother to sound smug as she said it.

For a second, I was envious of her. What must it be like to be immune to the pain of the world? Even when I'd lost myself in the sullen numbness of grief for Arthur, I'd felt the clawing need for revenge. But Morgyn, she got to be above it all. She had not been tortured for twenty years. She'd been discarded, yes. But that had saved her.

Anger rose in me, icy walls thickening and sharpening. I hated her. I hated everything she meant.

"We may share the same heartless harpy of a mother." I paused. Harpy now felt an inaccurate term for the Dowager. "But you do not know me or my mate."

She did not argue. "Train your power, Majesty. You will need it in the coming battle."

I turned on her, ready to stab my knife into that mirage form even as I knew it would be unsatisfying, would do nothing. The blade was in my hand, the muscles of my arm already tensing in readiness. "And how am I supposed to do that without my mate—"

She was gone.

Of course, she was.

I stabbed the dagger back into the jeweled scabbard at my waist, my fists tight with fury. That wasn't enough. I grabbed it out again and threw as hard as I could, lodging it to the hilt in the tree directly behind where Morgyn had appeared.

Even with my strength, both inherited and honed, it took me several tries to dislodge the blade. I finally managed to get it out, shoved it back into the scabbard, and stomped off.

"Thanks for nothing, sis," I said to the emptiness over my shoulder. "As usual."

18
VEYKA

"There is no way."

"Perhaps we could shift the rock."

"You would have to find a way up there first."

I listened to my friends debate. Even Percival weighed in, the bastard. But it was like listening through water. I may as well have been back in that massive golden tub in the washroom of my apartments in the goldstone palace. Or behind a wall of ice.

It was impossible. Even if I brought them along, one at a time, I couldn't be sure they'd land securely. I could jump with them out of the void and find ourselves a foot away from the ledge, freefalling through the air.

If it were just me, I could have risked it.

I still might have ended up in freefall, but I had enough belief in my own sense of self-preservation—and my power—to suspect I'd throw myself back into the void to avoid crashing into a pulp at the bottom of the ravine.

"Could you fly up there? Start shifting the rocks enough that there is a ledge? Then Veyka could bring me up and the two of us could move the rest."

"I do not think I am strong enough on my own. The harpy

could, maybe. But I have no control in that form. Without a battle to fight or someone to defend, I might just fly off in search of something to kill."

Lyrena's lips twitched, despite the weight of the situation before us.

Literal weight. A landslide. Huge boulders that had collapsed down over the ravine, blocking our way up the side of the mountain to the rift that I instinctively knew waited on the other side.

"Veyka can move from one place to another. She could take us across, to the rift on the other side, one person at a time."

"You. Then Percival..."

"I am not leaving you alone with the two of them."

"He will run off if he goes first."

"I will not."

Cyara lifted on hand to her temple, massaging gently. "This is like one of the horrible logic puzzles my father used to give us as children."

There was no safe way to do it. This had all been a waste of time. I should never have left Arran's side. I had decided to be the queen he always challenged me to be, to try and do what was best for Annwyn, and now there was a literal roadblock in my way.

Who knew what awaited on the other side, in Annwyn. The realms were geographic mirrors of one another. Did that mean if a rockslide happened in the human realm, it also happened in Annwyn?

I would have to take them all over the landslide to the rift. Everyone through the rift. Then take them one by one back over it, because if Cyara's maps were correct Eilean Gayl lay behind us. It would take forever, deplete my power. Leave us vulnerable. Who knew what the cost would be for such an expenditure of power. If I collapsed into a days-long nap, like Lyrena had after containing that fire in the human village, we'd take even longer to reach Eilean Gayl.

Time. All of it was a waste of time. Time I did not have. The succubus could be in Eilean Gayl already, or in Baylaur, eating my kingdom alive.

Shit. Fuck. I was spiraling. The ice was melting. I was going to fall apart.

"Just... wait!" I screamed. "Wait!"

It was the only command I gave before throwing myself into the void.

I had to get away from them. I could not think, even with my mind trying to filter out their suppositions.

I stepped out of the void at the edge of the forest, where it dipped down into a bare brown mound before continuing on in sylvan hills. Beyond my vision, I knew those hills gave way to the softer knolls and lakes and islands where Avalon lay. Behind me, the towering mountains were capped with snow. I wasn't certain how far I'd gone, but I could not hear voices.

Not any that spoke out loud.

Train your power, Majesty.

I wanted to claw Morgyn out of my brain. How dare she make demands of me... coddled priestess, safe in Avalon while I had suffered for decades. She said I would need my power for battle, not for this. It was too soon to battle...

I have filled her as best I can. We must give the seeds of magic time to take root.

My stomach rolled over, ready to dump its contents among the pine needles. Gorlois and my mother had tortured me for years trying to awaken the void power within me. Did that taint my magic? Make it into something ugly, when I'd just begun to love it? How dare they still be able to creep into my thoughts, to torture me even now. All because of that stupid prophecy.

A faerie queen shall rise to command the depths of the voids of darkness.

The prophecy that Parys had known about from the beginning. Clever, Parys. Parys, my sweet friend. If I mastered this, if I truly could move between realms, I could go to him. I could tell him about the pain in my heart, and he would eat with me and hug me tight and it wouldn't be enough to stop the pain but it would be something.

I will tear apart this world, realm after realm, until I find you.

Oh, Arran.

My love, my husband, my mate.

How could I possibly do this without him at my side? To train me, to believe in me, to pull me back from the edge of darkness?

"You were supposed to be with me," I whispered, across mountains and realms and eternity. "We were supposed to do this together."

A single tear slid down my cheek.

Slid over the cracks in my shield of ice, sealing them once more.

I took a deep breath, wrapping the shreds of my soul around the mating bond inside of me. The weight of that tether was enough to hold me when I moved through the void. But this was a bigger jump. One I'd never made intentionally before.

Quietly, softly, I stoked the ember of power inside of me to life. That shining white ember of power, the same color as my hair, the same shade as the fur of Arran's beast... I released the hold that I kept on it, as Arran had taught me to do. Then I released it further —a bit further than I ever had before.

I stepped into the void, let it tear me and rearrange me and massage my soul with that painfully sweet stretching sensation I'd become used to over the past few months. Just as quickly, as if I were going to appear at Cyara or Lyrena's side, I reassembled. Except this time, when I stepped out of the void, I was not in the human realm.

The mountains were not just capped in snow, they were covered in it. The pine trees were there, but taller, sparser, as if the energy they took to soar hundreds of feet above my head made it impossible for them to grow any denser.

I turned slowly on the spot.

Without the dense pine trees to block my vision, I could see the hills spreading out before me. Deep emerald, craggy, sharp rocks that jutted upward, bare of the trees I'd left behind. In the distance, far enough away that I should not have been able to see it, the sparse winter sun reflected back at me off a lake.

But it was not the scenery that told me what I'd done. It was the magic that thrummed through me. The ember of power inside of me was dancing, singing. And those emerald hills, those snowy mountains, the majestic trees... they all sang back in answer.

I had made the jump to Annwyn.

19
ARRAN

Da-dum.
 Da-dum.
 Da-dum.

The pain never stopped. It changed, alternating from blinding white that seared through my veins to an intense throb in my skull that was surely building toward implosion. But all of that was secondary to the pain in my chest. It felt like my heart itself had been ripped from my body.

That couldn't be. That was the sound of my heartbeat, wasn't it?
Da-dum. Da-dum. Da-dum.

Every twinge, every ache led back to that—the gaping hole in my chest.

Every dream...
How long had I been sleeping?

Dreams became nightmares. I saw the emerald hills of my homeland, scented the thick pine forests of the Spine—only to have it all dissolve away into nothing. The green faded to brown, the mighty trees withered and died.

Open your eyes. A voice—a command that felt like the space between breaths as it washed over my soul and filled in the cracks.

But I couldn't.

Fuck, it hurt to try. Every muscle protested—

Fuuuucckkkk.

I couldn't fight it. I was being torn away, ripped into fucking shreds—

Until I wasn't.

Until I landed in the middle of a barren valley, orange-red dirt spreading all around me. A ring of towering mountains surrounded the empty plain, the same color as the dust beneath my feet.

But it was only a momentary reprieve. Shock and confusion had taken precedence, but with my feet firmly planted, the pain came roaring back. I fell to my knees, clutching my head. Death would be better than this…

Maybe this was death.

The hell I deserved, for all the pain and destruction I had rained down over the past three hundred years.

But if this was hell, I wasn't alone.

I saw his boots half a breath before I heard his voice—

"I did not expect so much screaming."

20
CYARA

When she appeared again, it took one look for Cyara to know.

There was no joy in her face, not as there had been when she mastered that first level of her power. Then, she had jumped around the clearing in the jungle laughing; disappearing, reappearing, tapping Lyrena's shoulder, only to appear behind Arran and kiss his cheek.

Now, there was only cool determination in the lines of her round face, strength of will in the icy blue shards of her eyes. She had made this descent deeper into her magic alone, without Arran, and it had cost her something. A part of her soul.

But she did not share that with them. Did not speak of the cost or explain what it had meant to her. How she had done it. She crossed her arms over her chest, a protective gesture that was not even intentional but was telling all the same. She had added another layer over the shirt she usually wore, the flowing black fabric that revealed her midriff even in the cold. There was no hint of the metal brassiere that held the shirt in place while showcasing her physical assets. All of it was hidden beneath the thick wool of a deep green tunic.

Arran's.

Cyara's heart ached for her friend. But now was not the time to comment upon it, not when Veyka moved with purpose. Especially not in front of an audience.

So, Cyara kept her face carefully neutral when the queen spoke.

"I will take you one at a time through the void to Annwyn." She turned to Cyara, eyes slightly glazed. As if she was in her body, but her mind was not fully present as she issued her command. "Plan it."

Cyara.

Percival.

Lyrena.

Diana.

Veyka did not question the order or the reasoning that Cyara and Lyrena had worked out. She double-checked Percival for hidden weapons before taking his still-bound hands. Cyara doubted he would try anything stupid while she carried him through the void. It would mean risking losing himself in that terrible in between, or worse, leaving his sister unprotected.

But Cyara did not share this reasoning with the queen. She did not say any more than was necessary as she steeled herself to go first.

It felt exactly like going through the rift at Eldermist. They jumped through the void, the rift that Veyka created for them, and landed with their feet on the snowy ground of Annwyn. Cyara fell to her knees, boots crunching in the snow.

Veyka hauled her back up, raked her gaze over her, and disappeared again.

Cyara used every second to compose herself. She dusted the clinging snow from her gray leggings. Conjured a bit of fire around her fingers to warm them. Her wrists would ache later, but she would take the relief now.

She blinked, and Veyka reappeared with Percival.

The queen did not bother with words for him either. She snarled in his face, teeth gnashing. She lacked the sharpened canines of the terrestrial fae, but the message was clear enough—she would rip his throat out regardless if he made a move against Cyara.

But it was uneventful.

Percival turned his back and glared at the mountains. Cyara divided her attention between him and the spot where Veyka had disappeared. She kept fire dancing at her fingertips, in case she needed to subdue Percival.

Lyrena arrived. Then a quivering Diana.

The latter fell to her knees, then her elbows, and vomited all over the pristine white snow. Only Percival bothered to help her. Lyrena monitored them both.

But Cyara watched her queen. Her friend.

Veyka did not pause to wait for any of them. She started walking down the mountain, toward the emerald green hills that awaited them. Cyara knew without looking at her map where the queen was going.

She watched for any sign of weakness or exhaustion. But there was none. Veyka stomped through the thin layer of snow in the foothills without a hitch, her shoulders perfectly squared.

It could be nothing but a huge expenditure of power, to move between the realms like that. Cyara had felt the void pulling her apart. She wanted to lay down. To at least sit and sip water for a while before continuing on. And Veyka had done it again and again, using her power to not just jump herself between the human realm and Annwyn, but four others as well.

Veyka was strong and honed. But the cost... there had to be a cost.

All magic had a cost.

A slither of unease slid down Cyara's spine

If Veyka had not paid it yet... What would the consequences be when she did?

21
VEYKA

I am the Queen of the Elemental Fae. I am the High Queen of Annwyn. I am the prophesized queen of the Void Prophecy. I command the depths of the voids of darkness.

Why am I so fucking nervous to meet my mother-in-law?

Because Arran loved her, and I loved Arran, and he was not at my side.

Easy enough answer. The resolution was not so simple.

"We should take an extra day to tidy ourselves, to make plan," Cyara reasoned.

Our clothes were dirty. My hair certainly needed a good untangling. We'd been using buckets of glacial runoff to bathe, warmed by Lyrena or Cyara, but none of us had seen anything resembling a tub since the faerie caves.

I drove us hard through the mountains and hills until Diana had nearly collapsed.

"We should watch the gates, see who comes and goes, make sure we walk in with the advantage," Lyrena added to Cyara's arguments.

I shook my head.

"No."

They both opened their mouths to argue.

"I am either the High Queen of Annwyn, or I am not. They will greet us and treat us with the due respect, or I will start stabbing."

"In Arran's home?" Cyara asked quietly.

"If it is as he's described it, there should be no need for violence."

"And if it is not?"

"Annwyn does not have time for disloyalty. I do not have time to play political games. The succubus is coming—may already be here."

If we'd been seated at the Round Table, they surely would have kept arguing. But without the table to anchor us, without Arran at my side to negate or bolster my authority, the fact remained. I was either the High Queen of Annwyn, or I was not.

My Knights chose to obey me.

That was the first hurdle conquered.

I pushed myself up the hill, the final barrier between us and Eilean Gayl. Cyara had scouted ahead, her white wings blending into the overcast sky.

Overhead, a hawk screeched, swooping above us in a graceful curve.

"What are the odds that is not a fauna-gifted terrestrial?" Lyrena said, her usually melodious voice grim.

Cyara's eyes followed the hawk as it dipped down, disappearing over the top of the hill. "They will know we're coming. They will be ready."

"Good. So will we," I said over my shoulder. One more step, and I pulled myself up, cresting the hill.

The sight stole the breath from my body.

A familiar castle floated in the middle of a lake. Except this time, I could see that it was not floating. It occupied the entirety of a small island, the outer battlements reaching right out to the water's edge. The only approach was a narrow bridge, stretching from the base of the hill where I stood to the gates of the keep. Gates that were opening in welcome.

The memories flashed through my mind—the still, unbroken

surface of the Split Sea, the misty shores of Avalon, and the castle. This castle.

And just as I had when I landed on the lakeside more than two months ago, in those intense moments of falling through the void after Arran and I's joining... one word rose in my senses, my chest, until it fell from my lips.

"*Home.*"

22
VEYKA

We all watched in awe as the hawk soared down, circled the castle once, and landed with a graceful shift just as the iron doors of the keep swung open.

As we picked our way down the steep hill, the delegation filled out behind her. I counted as I walked, half an eye on my companions as they fell into place behind me. Lyrena at my left, Percival at hers. Cyara at my right, one hand guiding Diana forward. Both Diana and Percival were still bound.

Ten, fifteen, eighteen… the party that started across the bridge was nineteen terrestrials strong. I had two fire-wielders and two human prisoners. If this turned into a fight, my bravado would not be enough to save us.

I am the High Queen of Annwyn.

I am powerful.

More convincing than either of those statements was the feeling of rightness as I stepped onto the stone bridge. *Come*, the bricks seemed to say. *Relax*, the moss whispered. *Home.*

Arran loved this place. I loved him more than life itself. Did that somehow account for the force pulling me forward, causing me to throw caution to the wind?

I checked the amorite studs in my ears, questioning whether this was the same disorienting magic we'd experienced in the cursed clearing on the edge of Avalon. But everything was in place. Cyara walked at my side rather than raging as a harpy overhead. Lyrena's hand was oh-so-casually on her sword while idle flames danced at her fingertips. Totally in control.

I swallowed hard and led them to face the female leading the group. The fauna-gifted terrestrial could be none other than the mistress of Eilean Gayl—Arran's mother.

She was the most beautiful female I had ever seen. Given that my mate was the most brutally beautiful male in Annwyn, it should not have surprised me. Yet nothing about her fit with the image I'd constructed in my mind.

Even with the diffused light of overcast skies, the world seemed to brighten around her. The gold headband that stretched across her forehead contrasted sharply with her dark hair, braided back and coiled up at the back of her head so that not a single strand swayed as she approached.

Her gown was just as perfect, the heavy burgundy falling in flawless, unwrinkled panels despite the fact that she'd been in her hawk form minutes before. Every step was assured, and she lifted her dark eyes to meet mine long before she reached me.

From Arran's descriptions of her kidnapping, the brutality that had followed and the quiet life she'd sought away from the terrestrial court at Wolf Bay, I'd expected someone demure and retiring. Neither of those words sprung to mind as I used the brief seconds to study the female approaching me across the narrow stone bridge.

I had been tortured for years. And I doubted *demure* or *retiring* had passed a single set of lips—fae, human, or faerie—in reference to me.

A foolish mistake, to assume anything at all.

I had to be better at this. Arran wasn't here to be the strategic one.

My fault.

I am made of ice. I am impenetrable. I am immovable.

I repeated the chant. Thrice more, hoping it would give me the strength to face the formidable female approaching me. The mother of the male I loved—the mother of the male I'd nearly slaughtered.

Ice. Ice. Ice.

I was so busy willing shards of ice into my veins, around my heart, that I almost did not notice the terrestrial male who walked at her side. It was the blooming roses that alerted me. Bright, shining white roses on thick emerald vines, crawling along the stone ledges on either side of the bridge in perfect time with the approaching steps of the delegation.

Where her face was elegant and composed, his smile was easy and wide. His golden-brown hair, long enough to be boyish, caught the same light as the metallic band on his wife's forehead. He seemed like an accessory himself.

We stopped. So did they. Mere steps separating us. My heartbeat sped up, pounding against that wall of ice, trying to get out. Trying to get home.

We were dirty, tired, worn out from months of traveling and weeks of frustration. Our ranks were depleted, and we looked little better than the prisoners we brought with us.

But none of that mattered as the Lady of Eilean Gayl sank to her knees, followed by every single one of the eighteen terrestrials who had followed her out to greet us.

I exhaled.

I counted my heartbeats. *One, two, three, four, five...* The silence stretched out. A wing brushed against my shoulder, the gentlest of reminders.

They were waiting for me.

I choked back the hysterical laugh that bubbled up in my throat. *Be the queen you were meant to be.*

Oh, Arran.

"Rise, Lady Elayne and Lord Pant." I knew their names now. Arran had whispered their history to me while he held me in our bedroll, sketching out the broad lines of life in Eilean Gayl and his childhood. He'd been happy here—the happiest he'd ever been... until he met me?

Until I threw Excalibur and nearly killed him.

"We are honored and pleased to welcome you to Eilean Gayl, Your Majesty," Elayne said, rising gracefully without reaching for a hand for assistance. At nearly seven hundred years old, she ought to be showing the first signs of aging. But there was no gray in her dark hair, no wrinkles around her eyes. She appeared only a few years older than me. Except for the eyes—those dark, fathomless eyes spoke of centuries.

I affected an easy half-smile that was not easy at all. An imperious lift of my chin. Hand on my jeweled scabbard—the only sign of opulence on me. How ironic, that my first diplomatic foray into the terrestrial kingdom and I was robed in grime rather than jewels.

"As you can see, we have come to you after a long journey." It was the only acknowledgment I would give to the sorry state of our appearance. I was a queen. And despite the careful attention I'd always paid to my appearance, I did not need clothing to show it.

"Then you must be famished," Pant said, his grin wide and genuine. At least, in my initial estimation. I did not know him well enough to truly judge.

But terrestrials were not known for their ability dissemble.

I inclined my head, though my eyes stayed on the female at his side. "Indeed."

"Arran is not with you." Elayne did not disguise the surprise in her voice.

My throat closed. Panic, hot and fierce, that would melt my icy exterior in a second.

"The High King was detained," Lyrena said, her bright smile nowhere in evidence. Even without polish, she shone with the light and confidence of pure gold. She was every inch the courtier her parents had hoped she would be, the Goldstone Guard she'd trained to become, one hand on her mighty sword. My Golden Knight.

"It seems unlikely that he would allow his mate from his side, so soon after your Joining," Elayne said sharply, eyes cutting to me rather than Lyrena.

They'd heard about us being mates, even here in Eilean Gayl, almost as far as one could travel on the continent of Annwyn. Then they had also heard about my power, that explosion of light and my disappearance. They knew we had left Baylaur, might even have been waiting for us to arrive here, at Arran's ancestral home.

But they had not expected us to arrive without Arran.

The Battle of Avalon was still unknown.

I could use this to my advantage. I shoved the panic down. Anchored myself to the friends standing on either side—one gold, one white, both eternally steady and unflinching.

"Duty has always been paramount to Arran. I look forward to telling you of our travels," I lied. If Elayne and Pant realized the falsehood on my tongue, neither of them showed any hint of it. "My Knights and I will need adjoining chambers, if you have them. We will keep our prisoners in our custody."

"Knights?" Pant asked, nonplussed by the mention of prisoners. This was the terrestrial kingdom, I reminded myself. Pant's vines had paused their advance down the bridge, though one now moved to his hand.

"Knights of the Round Table," Cyara answered this time. A declaration that she would not be ignored. I felt a surge of pride in my chest—and gratitude. I may be made of ice, but I was not entirely unfeeling. Not when it came to the two females who stood unflinchingly at my sides.

Hushed whispers swept through the small crowd behind Arran's parents. Not courtiers, exactly. This wasn't the official terrestrial court. It was a family home—though still a castle. My education on the terrestrial kingdom had been superficial at best. Arthur had been the one trained on their customs, the structure of their noble houses.

They did have noble houses, I knew. Arran had been born into one of them, as had Gwen. But in the end, those historical lineages meant little to the terrestrial fae. All that mattered in this kingdom was strength and power.

At least now I had both.

All eyes deferred to Elayne, even her husband's. Which told me enough. She was the power here.

But Pant played his part well. He stepped forward, one white bloom in each hand, and offered them to the Knights at my sides. "Welcome to Eilean Gayl, Knights of the Round Table."

Moving on impulse and instinct, only the barest strategy sketching itself out in my head, I stepped forward and offered my hands to Elayne. A gesture of goodwill, of welcome. Of family. What I hoped we might be... what I'd never had before.

"You shall have everything you request, Your Majesty," Elayne said, taking my hands. "Eilean Gayl and all of its resources are at your disposal."

She stilled, lifting my hands slightly higher between us. The pad of her thumb stroked once and then again. The ring. Her ring—given to me by Arran. Slipped on my finger in the quiet, stolen hours before we went to the Tower of Myda. That night in Baylaur seemed thirty years ago, rather than a mere three months.

I sucked in a breath, ignoring the thaw that threatened in my chest. I could not give it to her. No matter what diplomacy demanded. It was the only part of Arran I still had, the only connection, this narrow band of gold.

But Elayne said nothing. Only squeezed my hands a little tighter and then released them. As she turned to address the surrounded groups, elemental and terrestrial, I reached inside myself. Found the golden thread of the mating bond and clung to it.

"Tonight, we shall feast in honor of our royal guest. Let it be known across our territory—the High Queen of Annwyn has come to Eilean Gayl."

The group assembled behind Elayne recognized it for the command it was. A blink, and half the terrestrials had shifted into their animal forms. Birds took to the sky. A fox and several hounds bounded past us. What might have been a seal disappeared over the side of the bridge into the water before I could get a good look.

How the flora-gifted terrestrials would send their messages, spread the word of our arrival, I did not know. But Elayne had made this move without asking for my approval.

As I followed her into the castle, more vines slithered out along the stones. Some moving so fast, curling like they meant to close around my ankle, to trip me up.

Maybe my instincts about Eilean Gayl were wrong.

23

ARRAN

I had been tortured before. I was little more than a child when I was stolen away, tortured until my beast exploded out of me.

The pain did not ebb, but my thoughts cleared.

Thoughts or dreams?

I could not open my eyes, no matter how often the command echoed in my mind—my soul.

This pain... it was a soul wound. Deeper than anything I'd ever felt... ever allowed myself to feel...

I landed softer this time. Did not land at all, really. Just appeared on that dusty orange plain, trapped by the ring of mountains. But this time was different. The pain was gone.

Most of it, anyway.

I pressed a hand to my chest, where the dull ache remained. The place where I should have felt—

"Perhaps now we might actually have a conversation."

My hands went for my weapons, only to find none. Reached for my power, but there were no plants in this wasteland to command. But my beast, I could feel him inside of me, the snarl building.

"Where have you taken me? Who are you? What do you want?" The demands flew from my lips, more growls than words.

The male who stood before me raised one dark brown eyebrow, scanning me up and down, then dropped it. Thoroughly unimpressed. "At least you have stopped screaming."

He waved his hand and two simple wooden chairs appeared. He lowered himself to his with casual grace, every movement refined, guided by muscle memory. He propped one foot across a knee, folded his arms over his chest. "Sit."

Not likely.

"Where am I?" I did not have weapons, but I had the strength of my body. More than enough to kill.

The male rolled his shoulders. He did not flick his hand this time.

The pain roared back, spearing through every muscle and tendon, fogging my brain. I knew I was screaming, but I could not stop it. Whatever willpower I might have had ceased to exist in this nightmare realm. I hit my knees, clawing at my head, anything to stop the pain—

Gone. Just as quickly as it had come.

It took every ounce of will to keep myself on my knees, rather than collapsing to the dusty ground with relief.

"I have taken away the pain so that we may have a coherent conversation."

A different sort of torture then. Not continual pain, but the stop and start of it. I began to adjust my expectations, my approach for managing the pain—

"Stop planning your attack and sit in the blasted chair." The voice was harsh even behind the refinement. A noble. Powerful. Pointed ears, fae like me. Terrestrial or elemental?

"What in the Ancestors-damned hell—"

"I have not damned anything. I saved it. Now sit down so I can tell you how to do your part." It was not an entreaty or suggestion. That voice was pure command. A voice that expected to be obeyed. I recognized it as the sibling to my own—the one I used to command legions in battle.

Ancestors... this male was an Ancestor.

I summoned all the strength and control that three centuries had given me. I did not question what portions of myself I could access in this nightmare. I commanded the strength to rise, and it came. If it was because this male had taken away the pain... didn't matter. What did was using it to my advantage.

One foot on the ground. Pushing myself up. Two feet. Lowering myself into the chair. Playing by his rules, for now. For long enough to pick him apart and decide how to flay my enemy.

For anyone who would give and take pain like that could not be anything else.

There were no identifying markers on him. Well-made leather clothing, the style neither elemental nor terrestrial. Close fitting, like it was meant to be worn beneath armor. A warrior sat across from me. That fit with his lethal grace and air of command. There was only one Ancestor known as a warrior. *The* warrior.

"Accolon."

He lifted his chin and gazed across the dusty orange yards between us. I'd seen portraits in Wolf Bay, could see the resemblance now. The aquiline nose, the imperious tilt of his green eyes as they judged me. A warrior. A shifter like me. A king.

"Very good," he said into my sullen silence. "Where are your questions now, Brutal Prince?"

My hand itched for my battle axe. "You were not going to answer them."

"You are correct about that," Accolon agreed. "Sit there like a good dog and listen to what I have to say, and I will consider answering your asinine questions."

I forced my hands to loosen. Forced my face to neutrality. Brutal cold.

Accolon marked the motions with a flick of his eyes—first to my hands, then to my face. A small smile curled the corners of his mouth, but there was no warmth in it.

"You have gotten so much better at masking your emotions," he said. "When you were a child, every tiny feeling exploded outward."

I refused to let my fingers curl, even as the growl of my beast built within me. "What do you mean, when I was a child?"

Accolon ignored the question. "It's a skill I never quite mastered, no matter how long I spent with my mate and her court."

His mate—Nimue. The Queen of the Elemental Fae. Accolon had ruled the terrestrials. Their union had ended the Great War, brought peace between the two ever-warring fae kingdoms, and set in place the procedures for the Offering and the Joining of the elemental and terrestrial heirs for seven thousand years to come.

"We went to the priestesses seeking help in ending the war. We were cursed with the prophecy instead."

He'd spoken true. There were so many emotions in those sentences I struggled to parse them. Disdain, anger, hate. Maybe sadness in his eyes as he flicked them away, gazing at the sharp red-orange mountains that rose in the distance. So different from his terrestrial home—our home. A land of green and trees and lakes. Of life—while this place was devoid of it entirely.

Accolon spoke again, his voice low and fathomless. Devoid of emotion. Careful. Reciting each word with tenacious, agonizing accuracy.

"Then comes a queen in the age of uncertainty, when shadows cast doubt upon the realm. Born under a double moon and marked by a radiant star, a faerie queen shall rise to command the depths of the voids of darkness. Twice blessed, the realm of shift and mist, when comes the awaited queen who shall possess ethereal might. With a touch, she will feel the heartbeat of her subjects and she will unlock the secrets they guard within.

Together they must stand, to defeat what once thought dead. Together they must give, if any shall live to the end."

The Void and Ethereal Prophecies.

But those last two lines... "You have botched the ending."

Accolon's eyes swung back to me. Yes, that was sadness lining them. "History has forgotten those last two lines, but I have not. It cost my mate everything, to write them down." His dark eyes clouded with a feeling I recognized instinctively—anger. "And of course, you all forgot."

Understanding flickered through me. "You took away my pain, brought me here, to tell me the prophecy in its entirety. So that I would remember."

Accolon inclined his head, lifted his hand.

I knew what that meant—this reprieve was at an end; the pain would come rushing back.

"You said you would answer my questions."

His hand stilled. "Ask."

Who are you? What do you want? He'd answered those without me having to ask again. "Where are we?"

His shoulders shook in a harsh, acerbic laugh. "You do not recognize the Effren Valley?"

There it was again—understanding. I looked at the dusty red plain and the sharp mountains, dotted with narrow trees, fronds at the top the only sort of leaves. Bits began to fit into place.

This was where the last battle of the Great War had taken place.

I was not a student of history, but I was a battle commander.

Accolon surveyed the valley around us, his eyes colder now. Similar to how I imagined my own looked. "This is how I knew it. Before Baylaur was a mighty city, when the goldstone palace was carved into the mountain itself and did not yet rise above it."

I opened my mouth to ask him more, the questions bubbling up in my chest. New questions, infinitely more important in light of what he'd told me—and the gathering dread in my stomach about what those forgotten words of the prophecy might mean.

But Accolon was standing. I was too, compelled by some phantom urge. The chairs disappeared. "I would have given you more time to heal, but alas." The dust kicked up around us, swirling faster and thicker until it swallowed the mighty mountains entirely.

"Your rest has ended, Brutal Prince," Accolon sighed. And it was not sadness in his gaze any longer. It was pity. "She needs you now."

Then he was gone, and there was nothing but darkness. Nothing but me and my pain and that ache in my chest, that demand that superseded all else. The hollowness that called out, that could only be filled by one being, in this realm or any other.

I opened my eyes.

❧ 24 ❦
VEYKA

"They are going to fall over at the sight of you," Cyara said, her turquoise eyes glinting with blatant satisfaction as she stepped back to observe her handiwork.

I tilted my head to the side so the jewels falling from my ears caught the firelight of the braziers anchored on either side of the mirror. "When I packed the essentials for a journey to Avalon, I did not think I would need jewelry and gems."

Cyara rewarded me with a small smile. "Then it is fortunate you thought that you needed me," she said. "And I knew that you would need jewels."

I shook my head, still managing my disbelief at the sheer quantity of finery that Cyara had produced from the recesses of her travel pack. Strands of black diamond and amethyst to be woven into my now nonexistent plait. Earrings so heavy with sapphires they brushed my shoulders. Golden bangles studded with amorite. I would be digging those out and distributing them to the males in Eilean Gayl. The only protection I could give, other than my warning, against the coming darkness of the succubus.

I focused my attention back on the towering mirror leaning

against the gray stone wall. Tonight, I would be fighting a different sort of battle.

While Lyrena had searched our quarters—two adjoining suites with a shared washroom and sitting room between them—for secret entrances or peepholes, Cyara had heated a bath and polished the golden brassiere I'd worn off and on since our departure from Baylaur. She'd scrubbed away all the grime, getting it to shine just as brightly as it had in the throne room of the elemental court.

But the true wizardry was her rendering of the gown.

A servant had delivered the news that I'd expected from my brief glimpse of the occupants of Eilean Gayl. Not a single one of the terrestrial females of standing here possessed a gown that would fit me. They were all willowy or thin to the last. And while Cyara might be able to stash jewels in her travel pack, she could not produce a gown.

I'd almost said fuck it all and gone down in my soiled traveling clothes. I was the High Queen of Annwyn. They'd all strip naked if I told them to.

But clever Cyara had managed something so much better.

She'd used her petite knife to cut open the seams of the flowing black shirt I'd worn while we traveled, held in place with my golden brassiere. But instead of sewing it into another garment, she'd looped it behind my neck, then brought it straight down on either side, in front of my breasts. The golden brassiere fitted atop it, holding the panels in place and leaving my back bare. Even the dusky rose of my nipples was visible through the translucent black fabric, if one looked close enough.

For the skirt, she'd lobotomized a forest green gown, delivered to us as the largest they had. What did it matter if the skirt was too small? My body was too perfect to hide. The skirt she'd contrived was a mockery of the thick ones I'd seen on the welcoming delegation, with slits cut nearly to my waist, my powerful legs on display with each sway and step.

It was nothing short of marvelous.

I stopped admiring myself in the mirror long enough to notice that Cyara had sat down, still wearing nothing but a loose nightgown.

"You still have to change."

Cyara's wings shot inward, the tips nearly colliding with one another. "I beg your pardon?"

"Lyrena must stay to guard those two." I jerked my head to Percival and Diana, their rope bindings exchanged for thick metal ones. Maybe I ought to have felt bad for shackling them to the wall like animals. But I was not going to give Percival another opportunity to stab one of mine in the back.

I swung my gaze back to Cyara, pinning her with the same force she liked to use on me. "I am the brawn." I patted the daggers at my waist. "You are the brains. I want you to watch, listen, and analyze. What you do best." I smiled, and it was only half faked.

I felt more like myself than I had in weeks. Without the thick boots and leather and weight of travel, with my skin on display and jewels in my ears... with my power buzzing through me, waiting for my call.

All of it was a distraction from the empty, ever-present ache in my chest. I wanted to collapse into the luxurious, silk-lined bed and cry for a week. I wanted to poke into each and every one of the rooms in Eilean Gayl, to search for something that might speak of Arran. Something that might connect me to my mate.

But what I wanted did not matter.

The safety of Annwyn did.

I would fall apart later.

That ice would shatter. I could feel it already, deep within my soul.

But I would make use of every minute between now and then. If I still prayed, I would have asked the Ancestors for it to be enough... that when my mate woke, he would find a world of light, rather than darkness. That I would be enough to save it.

25
CYARA

Cyara knew what Veyka wanted this place to be. Salvation, refuge. But that was not what she had seen as she trailed her queen through the narrow halls and winding staircases of Eilean Gayl, up to their chambers. They had been placed at the very top of the tower. One look out the windows was enough to confirm—no easy way in or out. Either for their protection, or to trap them.

Dressed in another female's gown, a dove gray silk in the restrictive terrestrial style, Cyara followed Veyka into the corridor. Guards were positioned at the end of the hall on either side, but not directly at their doors. She was sure Lyrena had already noticed, but she tucked the observation away for later, just in case.

Veyka took one look at the guard, the narrow hallway and even narrower staircase—she had to turn sideways to fit her wide hips up the stairwell—and turned back to Cyara with that wicked smile in place. "How about we go a different way?"

Cyara rolled her eyes, but accepted Veyka's proffered hand. The queen winked at the soldier over Cyara's shoulder, and then they were gone.

26
VEYKA

The terrestrials' gasps and screams of surprise were as good as any dessert or crusty bread. Nearly as good as an orgasm.

They fell back from where Cyara and I appeared in the center of the great hall, giving us a wide berth. The males' eyes nearly popped out of their sockets as they got a good look at my outfit. Many of the females, as well. More than one set of eyes began to glow with desire, the curse of our passionate race.

Good. If they were busy lusting after me, they'd be distracted from plotting.

Even Elayne and Pant had fallen back, the latter's hand on the sword at his waist. Arran's mother was a second from shifting. I'd spent enough time with Arran and Gwen to recognize the signs—the clenched fists, the feral gleam in the eyes, the curve of the body that was not fae at all. Pure beast.

A low growl rumbled in my mind.

I nearly fell over.

Impossible.

None of them noticed; too busy gaping.

It was an aching memory that threatened to derail my resolve. I shoved it down. Later, I promised myself. An hour, maybe two. Then I could sleep and dream of him.

Elayne regained herself first, gliding around the long table situated at the head of the hall. "Your Majesty, we did not expect you so—"

"So soon? So suddenly? So lovely, considering the state I arrived in?" I cut in, flashing a long leg as I walked to meet her.

"So comfortable as to appear among us without a formal announcement," Elayne said smoothly, taking my hands and squeezing. A mother-in-law greeting her son's wife, rather than a subject meeting her queen. An interesting way to play it. "But you do indeed live up to the rumors."

"You shall have to tell me which ones." I winked for everyone to see.

Irreverence—I could play that. It was a cousin to apathy, which I'd worn so well for so many months after Arthur's death. No amount of jesting or wicked laughs could melt the ice in my heart. Only one thing—one male—could achieve that.

The great hall had been transformed in the time we'd been upstairs. The tables that had occupied the space were now lined up against the walls, creating at wide rectangle in the middle. They were draped with thick embroidered tablecloths, sumptuous golden place settings, endless bottles of wine down the middle of each in lieu of a centerpiece.

Nothing to compare to the opulence of Baylaur, but it was wealth all the same. The terrestrial fae lining the walls, standing behind each chair, reeked of it. Standing as they stared at me. Every pair of eyes, trained and waiting.

They would not sit until I did, I guessed.

I skimmed my gaze over all of them, trying to detect who was fauna or flora gifted among them. I failed, but flashed a small, knowing smile anyway before I gave my attention back to Elayne.

"I was under the impression that you did not stand on ceremony in the terrestrial kingdom," I said.

"You are correct, of course." She waved her hand, and a small army of servants appeared. "Begin."

There was a flurry of action and sound, as it all did, fully, begin.

Trays heaped with food appeared balanced on servants' shoulders. Different from the fare in the elemental kingdom, but no less appealing. Thick cuts of meat, seared crisp on the outside, crusted with nuts, bathed in a thick wine sauce that had me licking my lips. There were vegetables I did not recognize, roasted whole and stuffed with herbs and grains.

I willed my stomach to silence. It did not obey. A tick in Elayne's cheek was the only sign she'd heard it.

Like mother like son.

Arran's cheek did just that when he was trying to keep something in.

My heart threatened to break. I reached for a bottle of wine. Cyara must have sensed something was wrong. She swooped in, filling my glass before I could reveal my shaking hand.

I took one long gulp. Another. It wasn't nearly sharp enough—not like the aural that had drowned my pain after Arthur's death.

Arran is not dead.

Arran is healing in Avalon.

Arran is safe with Isolde.

I drained the goblet. Lifted it in mock salute to the crowd, many still watching me, and then held it out for Cyara to refill. She did, but the warning in her aquamarine eyes was clear.

I slowed to a sip, rather than a gulp. Then a trickle on my tongue. When I lowered the glass back to the tablecloth, my hand was steady.

Ice, my ass. I was a sheet of ice above a frigid sea, one good knock away from shattering.

But I did not let myself look at Elayne to judge her reaction, to try to read what she'd seen in my face. Instead, I stared at the spectacle unfolding in the center of the hall.

It was not just the meal that she'd signaled—but the entertainment as well.

A huge cage had appeared, borne in by four males with muscles popping against their wool tunics. A beast of nightmares waited inside.

If the dank scent coming off of it hadn't been enough, the massive claws made it clear that whatever it was, it came from the depths of the lake outside of Eilean Gayl's walls. My first thought was of the scorpions that lurked in the mountains surrounding the Effren Valley. Those were intimidating enough—tails as long as my arm, with a stinger that would render an immortal unconscious long enough for the venom to kill. But this creature of the deep was bigger than Arran, even though it stood no more than three feet tall. A thick shell covered the incredible width of its body, its claws the size of my entire torso. The pointed spikes that covered the thick umber shell promised to impale anyone who got too close in any futile attempt to pierce the armor.

But that was precisely what was about to happen, I realized. Even as the lake beast thrashed against the metal bounds of the cage, the crowd's attention shifted to a slender female on the other side of the empty rectangle. An arena. For the battle about to begin.

A parade of servants delivered platter after platter of food, but no one noticed. Not as that impossibly small female shifted, a giant serpent appearing in her stead.

The door of the cage lifted. The serpent did not waste a second before swiping, fangs the size of my daggers flashing.

My mate had described the communal meals, the brawls that often broke out, but Arran had not warned me about this. I recognized it for what it was—a test. Fifty terrestrials, servants, lords, guards, watched to see how I would react in the face of this brutality.

And maybe if I had not been tortured for twenty years, or had not lived through the massacre of Baylaur and the Battle of Avalon, maybe my stomach would have turned at the sight of the shifter and the beast ripping each other to shreds.

Instead, I sat down and helped myself to a bowl of candied nuts.

I popped one into my mouth, the thick toffee sticking in my teeth as the serpent wrapped herself around the creature's claws—and lost the end of her tail for her trouble.

Blood spewed.

I drank my wine.

Whether my lack of reaction disappointed or impressed them, the terrestrials started claiming seats for themselves. I watched idly, dragging a finger around the rim of my wineglass, trying to detect if there was an order or hierarchy to the positions they took.

They seemed most interested in drinking and watching the spectacle.

"Is this exhibition on my behalf, or is this your usual nightly entertainment?" I asked my hosts. Elayne had taken the seat directly to my left, Cyara on my right. Pant was on the other side of his wife. They were all watching me, rather than the brawl happening before us.

I would make sure I gave a performance worth watching.

"The fuath has been terrorizing the village on the other side of the lake for some time. It happened to be captured this morning," Elayne said smoothly.

Not an answer to my question.

I helped myself to the food sitting untouched before us. We had been travelling for months; I was not about to let a little blood dissuade me from a real meal. "And the fauna-gifted female?"

"The one who caught the beast," Elayne explained, serving herself as well. "From a low-born family in the village. She hopes to win a place here at Eilean Gayl by defeating it."

That fit with my understanding of the terrestrial kingdom. To be born into a family of power was a start, but if you did not exhibit strength of your own, you would never rise. Never gain true standing. Strength mattered here above all else.

The serpent leapt from a coil, aiming for the tiny strip of exposed flesh where the fuath's claws met its body. She missed. She was slowing.

"My gold is on the fuath," Pant interjected, leaning around his wife.

They were a startling pair. Elegant, composed Elayne and brash, quick-talking Pant. Not at all what I had expected from Arran's parents. *Not what I'd hoped.* No, it was too soon to make that judgment.

Elayne delicately cut a slice of meat, chewing it fully before speaking again. "What sort of entertainment is favored in Baylaur?"

My finger paused its tracing. "I like to watch the acolytes dance."

Cyara snorted into her wineglass.

Elayne cut her a look, then opened her mouth to say more. But I spared her the explanation. "Is your priestess here as infuriating as the one in my own court?"

It was all mine, I remembered. Eilean Gayl, Wolf Bay, Baylaur. My court. I could take this ancient castle, Arran's birthright, as a private holiday residence and kick every occupant into the frigid lake outside.

And I would pay the consequences.

Torn allegiances. Uprising. Coup attempts. I'd dealt with enough of that shit already.

But the power thrumming in my veins, the blades at my hips, they begged me to do it. To make myself a queen of blood, not just in name.

"They are mostly docile, since the Great War," Elayne said. "They steep themselves in prophecies and lore, and only come out to bother us at festival time."

Prophecies and lore. I'd had enough of that nonsense as well. But if the priestess here was a student of history, if she studied the prophecies of old... maybe she would know something about the succubus, even if it was called by a different name. Maybe she would have theories about the missing Ethereal queen. If Parys was right, and the Ethereal and Void Prophecies were really one, then that was the only missing piece.

Pant propped one elbow on the table, ripping into a leg of lamb with his teeth. "Are you so devout yourself, Majesty? Arran was only ever interested in the festivals that involved fucking." He punctuated his statement with a broad wink.

Elayne did not tense at his brazen implication. She did not even roll her eyes—as if she was used to it by now. A theory began to form in my mind as I sipped my wine and lifted an imperious eyebrow at the Lord of Eilean Gayl.

"Hardly," I said. "My interests are well aligned with my mate's."

Elayne did stiffen then, at that word. Mate. A fairytale, a myth. An inexplicable, unforeseen link between her beloved son and me.

Let them remember—he may be their son, their heir. Even their king. But he was my mate. And if they did not understand what that meant, I did. If Arran returned—*when* he returned—they would learn as well.

Pant could make his crass jokes to try and unbalance me. Elayne would let him, slipping in her perfectly timed, polite questions. A cleverly orchestrated partnership. But nothing compared to the twisted threads of the elemental court where I'd been raised. Nearly murdered.

Elayne refilled my wine herself. "We were shocked to hear of your mating," she said. "And pleased."

Was she trying to get me inebriated so my mask would slip? It would take more than three glasses of wine.

I took a deep drink and smiled, letting just a hint of wickedness show. "Weren't we all."

Ask about my power.

It was the next logical question. She'd even implied it. *Shocked to hear about your mating*—and the mysterious explosion of power that had poured from me. I'd appeared from nothingness into the middle of the hall. Every terrestrial in this castle was wondering about my power and what it meant.

But Elayne held her silence.

"Arran always was a protective bastard," Pant chortled, rubbing his finger and thumb over the close-cropped beard the covered his chin. Such an irreverent way of referring to the protective instincts that governed Arran's every action. That had almost torn us apart. Did they truly not know him? Or were they betting that I didn't?

"We doubted he'd ever marry," the lord continued. "Let alone take a mate, only to let her go running across the kingdom without him."

Well-played.

So masterful, it was almost worthy of an elemental. They'd been building to this since the beginning of the conversation. Every word chosen to get to this question—where was Arran?

Like hell was I going to tell them the truth. I needed to rally the terrestrial kingdom to push back the succubus. Trying to explain that I'd nearly killed their King was more than a mistake. It was gambling with my own life as well.

Even if these were Arran's parents.

Even if this castle felt like home. A place I belonged, when all I'd had were gilded cages.

Being myself here was dangerous. Especially without Arran to guard my back.

"The King and I were forced to separate temporarily," I said smoothly. A bit of creamed potatoes. "We are united in mind and purpose." A bite of sweet glazed carrot.

A crash drew our eyes back to the fight in front of us. The terrestrial had wrapped her powerful body around one of the fuath's claws and was attempting to squeeze it off with the ever-constricting pressure of her coils. It wasn't going to work.

I kept my eyes on the spectacle as I spoke, underlaying the boredom with command. "I wish to inspect the amorite mines. I am given to believe they are nearby?"

Elayne blinked. At her side, Pant sank back in his chair, huffing out a chuckle that was half sigh.

"Nearness is relative, I suppose," Elayne said, brow creasing. "They lay to the west, where the Split Sea yields to the Northern Way." She wanted to ask why I was interested in them. I had not decided yet what I would tell her. When—because the eventuality of the succubus was inevitable.

Eyes still fixed, I withdrew the dagger from the jeweled scabbard on my hip. "How many days' journey?"

Pant shifted in his seat. To make the sword that hung at his side easier to grasp, I'd imagine. It was treason to pull it on his queen, but Arran had told me of the love between his mother and father. I knew firsthand how that particular emotion did not play by the rules.

Meanwhile, Elayne lifted both of her hands to the tabletop and placed them palm-up. Showing she was unarmed. A gesture of submission. "It would depend whether you travel alone or with your human guests."

"Prisoners," I corrected. "Would you like to hear how I acquired them?"

An elegantly inclined head.

I stroked my thumb over the pommel, tracing the familiar grooves of the wolf carved there. Another piece of the puzzle that I had not yet unraveled—Arthur had gifted me daggers carved with white wolves... only for me to mate a terrestrial male whose beast form matched my prized blades.

No time for mulling over Arthur.

Or Arran.

Everyone I love suffers.

Find the ice. Bathe in it. Let it seep into your soul.

"One of them slid a knife into my golden knight's back," I said, my voice cold. "The other used her feeble magic to lure me into the clutches of my lifelong enemy."

No one moved. Not even a shuffle of Cyara's wings.

"And yet you keep them alive," Elayne said softly.

The battle had reached its zenith. Both serpent and fuath were bloodied. The former had gotten in a few jabs into the tender flesh that was mostly protected by the fuath's shell, but not enough to inflict fatal damage. The serpent was in worse shape—missing her tapered tail, green and black scales awash with blood that did not seem to clot. Some strange magic of the fuath, no doubt.

But there was still plenty of fight left in the serpent's dark eyes.

Wrath, and a desire to win that went beyond the sentience in the monster she faced.

I already knew how it would end.

I pricked my finger with the tip of the dagger. Lifted it to my mouth. Painted my lips with my own blood. "The King taught me many things about punishing one's enemies."

They scented it. Elongated canines emerged, so much more prominent in the terrestrials, revealed as their lips pulled back and their noses lifted to trace the scent on the air. Primal power. That was what they could scent in my blood.

The tick in Elayne's cheek moved furiously. Enough, she pretended to tuck back an invisible hair to cover the tell.

I doubted the scent of my power was what unnerved her. No, it was Arran—his blood had twined with mine at the Joining. Even now, it ran through my veins. Sat on my lips, red and vibrant and with a power all its own.

"Yule is only a few days away. After, we will send you with an escort to the mines," Elayne said. To her credit, the strain was barely noticeable.

"After we've recovered from the celebrations," Pant chuckled, clapping his wife on the shoulder, attempting to lighten the moment.

I drained my third glass of wine.

"I look forward to it." Punishment, Yule, the mines. Let them sort out what I meant.

I leaned back in my chair and watched with mild interest as the fuath ate what remained of the terrestrial serpent.

27

VEYKA

"The Ancestors know, I'm a good sport. But I am sick of ending up on my ass," Lyrena griped. She took my proffered hand, pulling herself up from the muddy ground of the island's small courtyard.

It was either there or walk out to the mainland and spar on the lakeshore. Here, at least, I could keep my eyes on the terrestrials. And they could all get a sense of me, their new queen. They could learn exactly how sharp my blades were.

Lyrena sheathed her sword and hobbled over to the water trough. No elemental magic needed to cool it. When we'd come down earlier this morning, it had taken a blast of her fire to melt down enough for drinking.

"You won the last bout," I said, lifting my arms overhead and returning the two curved rapiers to their sheathes across my back.

The look she shot me was hotter than the fire that had singed my hair. Fair recompense for when I'd accidentally chopped off several inches of hers in the jungle above the faerie caves.

"You let me win." Disdain dripped from every syllable. Even my affable golden knight didn't like to lose.

"I would never," I protested.

I pressed a hand to my chest, my pale skin heated and flushed. I was back in my traveling leathers. By tomorrow, Cyara would have an assortment of gowns for me to wear. She was up in the tower chambers now, glaring at Percival, pitying Diana, and sewing rapidly.

Lyrena rolled her neck in time with her eyes. "Try stabbing Cyara and see if you can get the harpy to come out. I am done for today."

We'd dueled with magic, knives, and swords. My entire body was coated in sweat. But it was either this, or politicking, or wallowing in my own misery. At least for now. Until Yule, when the priestess and her acolyte would appear for whatever obnoxious ceremony. Until after Yule, when I would get to those amorite mines and start distributing the best weapon my kingdom had against the succubus.

The succubus I still had not told Elayne and Pant about. Because I still was not sure where I stood with them.

Fuck all of it. I hated being queen. I hated it ten times more without Arran at my side.

Maybe I would go back to my room and lock myself in. Summon that ember of power, step into the void. Return to Avalon —see Arran. Even for a few moments, just to see him...

And risk his life, again.

Fuck, fuck, fuck.

The sweat and exertion were supposed to take the edge off, not melt the icy interior.

"I'll spar with you, Majesty."

Lyrena's head snapped to attention, her hand already on the blade she'd sheathed moments before. The courtyard was a strange trapezoidal shape, following the shore of the island, the lake itself waiting just on the other side of the mossy stone walls. Along one side there were alcoves. Doors that led up to the towers, down to the kitchens. Who knew where else. The voice had come from one of those alcoves, where a male loitered in the shadows, leaning against the door.

I rolled my shoulders, not bothering to draw a weapon yet. "You won't be the first terrestrial I've beaten."

The male stepped fully into the gray early-evening light. I got the sense he was grinning, though it was hard to tell beneath the bushy brown beard. For a moment, my heart stopped. The resemblance to Arran...

The thick locks were the same, the tight bun at the back of his head... but this male's features were lighter. Brown hair, not black. Green eyes. Shorter, too, though not by much.

He looked at me with equal alacrity, his unnaturally green gaze sweeping over my face and body. A lip quirked at the dirty boots. The other side joined it when he arrived at my normally white hair, which I knew was closer to gray now, caked with dirt and sweat until it hung limp around my shoulders.

The male lowered a hand to the weapon hanging from his belt. A mace. A fucking mace. "Arran certainly chose well."

"Arran did not choose at all." *False.* He'd chosen me. We'd chosen each other. Despite the Offering and the Joining and all the other bullshit.

But this male who dared to look me over like I was something to eat, a mated female, a queen—he did not get to know any of that.

He smiled through the gross, bushy beard. "The male I knew never acted against his instincts. Even for Annwyn. Even for duty."

My throat closed.

I will tear apart this world, realm after realm, until I find you.

"Who are you?" I said. If the male did not recognize the lethal softness of my voice, more the pity him.

The mace was in his hand now, the cast iron tips that covered its round head swallowing the gray light around us. "My name is Barkke." He tossed the mace into the air, caught it in one sweeping movement, gaze still holding mine. Challenge issued. "I am a friend of Arran's."

Accepted.

I drew my dagger—just one. That's all I would need.

Lyrena hissed.

I blocked it out. Shuttered every impulse, every shred of guilt, every queenly instinct, as I launched myself into battle.

He tried to sidestep my dive, but I put all of my weight and speed behind it. I knocked one knee out from under him. By the time he shoved himself back up, I was on the other side of the courtyard, back to the wall.

I didn't give him time to rest. I scuttled along the wall, not caring how ridiculous I looked. My movements were fluid, strong, but unpredictable. If he'd been watching me spar with Lyrena for the last two hours, then that was the only way to best him.

"Come and play, Majesty," he crooned, fingering the leather-wrapped handle of that mace.

I sprung before the last word finished falling from his lips. But he got the mace up, catching my arm against the thick wooden handle. I pressed up, using my feet as leverage, my powerful legs bracing.

"I did not see you at my feast last night," I said into the inches between us. The bastard was not even winded. He hadn't been sparring all afternoon.

Barkke had the audacity to smile. "Your feast?"

I pushed in, up, then spun away just as quickly before he could nick me with one of the iron spikes. "A feast to welcome me. My feast." I considered pulling my other dagger to use as a distraction. Decided against it.

Barkke charged, no chance to catch my breath. Using it against me. But this was nothing. The cold air burning blue flames down my throat? I welcomed them. A lifetime of torture had its benefits. Pain focused me.

I threw him off easily.

"So?" I smirked.

He took the pause I offered, his gaze reassessing. "I was seeing to a matter in the Spine."

"How mysterious." I shrugged. He could try to figure me out; good luck to him.

"When I heard you'd come to Eilean Gayl, I hoped you would have brought pretty Guinevere along." *Hell.* I'd judged this Barkke as one of those males who liked the sound of his own voice a bit too much. But it seemed he was a male with a death wish as well.

"I assume you have never met her. Because if you'd called her *pretty Guinevere* to her face, she would have skewered you with her sword. Or just shifted into her dark lioness and eaten you for her evening snack."

Amusement or ire, he used it to drive me back. Knock me down. Flat on my back, the terrestrial approaching with mace in hand. I felt the burst of flame from Lyrena's fingers. A warning for now.

"Fire wielders," Barkke paused, "Am I meant to be intimidated?"

"They are as effective at burning flesh as they are wood," I said in the same breath as I launched myself up to stand from flat on my back. A move I'd learned from *pretty Guinevere*.

Our weapons clashed, then our bodies.

"Where's Excalibur?"

I gnashed my teeth. "I only bring it out for special opponents."

"You wound me."

"You had better speed up, or I actually will."

He threw back his head and laughed—leaving his throat exposed. Fool.

I lunged. He brought his arm up to block, exactly as I'd known he would. I sliced down his arm, long and brutal, right through the wool of his tunic and into the skin and muscle beneath.

He stumbled back, blood seeping down his arm, a few drops falling in the mud.

I sheathed my weapon.

"You were warned," Lyrena said with a mocking grin.

Barkke did not bother to bind his wound. He stared at me across the courtyard, the half-smile on his face shifting that infernal beard. I wiped my hands on my leather leggings, ready for a bath and supper. I opened my mouth to say something snide—

But the words died on my lips.

Even across the courtyard, it was unmistakable. Maybe it was the unusual green color or the falling dark that made them so bright. It was impossible to miss. His eyes were glowing.

28
VEYKA

Shit fucking Ancestors-damned hell.

I'd been looked at like that all my life. I couldn't go anywhere in the goldstone palace without glowing eyes haunting my every step. When I came of age, when I escaped the water gardens, I'd deliberately dressed myself in provocative clothing. A taunt to all those who judged my body as less than ideal, twisting the knife by reminding them that their husbands and wives lusted after me anyway. I'd employed the same tactic in the great hall, in front of all those terrestrials.

This should not have been different.

But to see that ring of desire shining in eyes whose angle was so similar to Arran's... the tendrils of hair that had fallen forward from Barkke's bun around his face, just like Arran's dark hair did... to be sweating and sparing and trading verbal snipes... it was too much.

It was just lust. Desire. It should not fucking matter.

But it didn't have to make sense to be real.

The ice inside of me shattered.

I spun on my heel, desperate to get away before I shattered into a million tiny shards. I shoved past Lyrena, not knowing where I was going. Not caring.

Away.

My fault.

I stumbled on the stone stairs, scraping my knees through the leggings.

Arran.

My clothes kept catching on the walls. The corridors were so narrow. I wasn't narrow. I didn't belong here.

Home. Not my home. Not for me.

I had to get out. Get away. I was going to suffocate under the weight of it all. Expectation. Salvation. Separation.

Arran. I need you.

I threw myself into the void and did not care where I came out.

29
VEYKA

I was in freefall.

The void pulled at my tired muscles, my shattered soul, ripping them apart until I was nothing but stardust in the space between realms. I ceased to be a queen or a friend or a warrior.

I was the space between stars, the darkness that sucks everything into it, swallowing all light. In the void, there was no hope or fear. I did not even exist, not in a way that anyone could recognize. I was myself in my most distilled form.

Unfathomable.

Untouchable.

Free from pain.

But not from that tug in my chest.

Except I did not have a chest, so I could ignore it. I could bask in the nothingness. No feelings... what had I ever felt that had sent me here? It did not seem to matter. Not in this infinite inhale.

I could go anywhere, be anything. Everything and no one. Free of... what? What was I free of? I could not remember.

There it was again, that tug.

It was important, but I could not quite recall why. But I knew it was trying to pull me back together, to reassemble the parts that were free and flowing and gloriously unfettered.

I tried to shake it off, to will the particles I'd become away from that restricting force—

It solidified.

I could see the golden thread wrapping around... my wrist? There, I had a wrist. Then my arm, my chest. I looked down and saw where that golden thread speared for my heart. Right there was the blasted organ, beating stronger and brighter as the golden thread wrapped around it again and again and again...

I wrenched control of my magic back just in time to avoid being splattered on the cold stone tiles of my bedchamber.

Even so, I landed hard on my hands and knees, sweat pouring off of me. I gulped down air, but did not open my eyes. I was too busy inside, shoving the ember of my power down inside of me. It hadn't been an ember that took me into the void this time. It had been an inferno. A flash of power stronger than anything I had ever felt.

Not a new magic, uncontrolled, like after the Joining.

Oh, no.

This was different, and I did not need to explain it to anyone or have it explained to me to understand.

This was magic *in control*—of me.

In my desperate desire to get away from my feelings, I'd lost track of who I was and what I was—not just a queen, but a wife. Arran's mate.

I'd almost lost myself to the void.

30
VEYKA

Breathe in, breathe out.
Breathe in, breath out.

Two more times and then I ran out of patience.

I shoved myself to my feet, forcing the tired muscles in my legs to compensate for my sweat slick palms and keep me from falling on my face on the flagstones.

Even without falling into lakes and beaches, my clothing was soaked through. I was so cold—I needed to get this clothing off. Needed a hot bath. Where were Cyara and Lyrena? I couldn't have been gone long.

I turned toward the door that connected the bedroom to the shared sitting and bathing rooms—

"Welcome back, Your Majesty."

I did not reach for my weapons. I did not dare reach for my power. She was not threatening me. She was sitting in a high-backed wooden chair against the wall. It had to be uncomfortable, but she still sat up ramrod straight. Not that I'd tried it myself. I had taken one look at the narrow seat with its high armrests and knew my ass was not going to fit.

But the Lady of Eilean Gayl looked perfectly comfortable,

hands curved around the ends of the armrests, her silk skirts as smooth as always.

"Where are my Knights?"

"Here," Lyrena said from behind me. At the window. Planning some sort of escape route? "Cyara is with Percival and Diana," she added.

I took a step back, keeping both females in my sights.

"How long?" I asked Lyrena.

"Only a few minutes," she answered. "I came up here to tell Cyara what happened. Lady Elayne arrived just ahead of me, demanding an audience with you."

"Requesting," Elayne corrected, her voice calm but firm.

Lyrena ignored her. I could have kissed her perfect golden face. "I will not leave until commanded."

I clenched my teeth to keep from chewing my bottom lip. I was in no shape for this conversation. I'd nearly disappeared into nothingness forever, for Ancestors-sake.

Fuck the Ancestors.

Right.

But maybe it was a reminder, too. Without Arran, with me still learning to control my power... we were the only ones who knew the full truth of the succubus. Isolde, Lyrena, and Cyara did as well, but they were not rulers. They were not terrestrials. No one here would listen to them. And Morgyn probably knew more than either Arran or I, but she wasn't doing anything in her precious, neutral Avalon.

I'd been debating how to tell Elayne and Pant, how to ask for their help. Trying to judge if I would weaken my position by asking rather than demanding. I was so bad at strategy. I needed my Brutal Prince.

Instead, I had his mother.

That was something, I supposed.

"Go. Rest, eat, and then relieve Cyara of guard duty," I ordered Lyrena. "She's been stuck with Percival all day. I would not be surprised if she'd stabbed him in the eyeball with one of her sewing needles."

Lyrena laughed aloud at that, her golden tooth flashing as she passed me. By the time she reached Elayne, the smile had hardened into something different. A smile still, but one of challenge and promise. A surge of warmth filled my chest.

I did not bother trying to encase it in ice. That stupid strategy had failed spectacularly.

I should have squared my shoulders, shoved my ass into a chair, and met Elayne like the queen I supposedly was. But I was just too fucking tired to manage it. Instead, I unfastened the belt with my scabbards, slinging them onto the trunk at the foot of the bed while I scrubbed my hand over my face.

"I thought you would be better at hiding your feelings. You are an elemental," Elayne said from her throne.

I'd seen my own mother sit on the throne for twenty-five years. I'd stopped being impressed by it decades ago.

I sighed heavily, working on the harness that held my rapiers across my back next. "What do you know of elementals?"

The wood creaked as she shifted in the chair. "Before Arthur's birth was prophesied, there was every reason to believe Arran might one day become the terrestrial heir. I educated myself accordingly."

"How industrious of you."

Elayne chuckled softly. Not quietly enough for me to miss.

Weapons gone, I turned to face her, planting one hand on each hip. Exhaustion surely lined every feature and muscle, but I let her see it. I was so tired of playing games. The terrestrial court was supposed to be about strength. Well, here I was—strong, facing my problems, minutes after I'd lost my sanity and nearly myself.

Arran's mother was not smiling any longer. She appraised me openly. Probably the most honest expression I'd seen on her face since arriving. Maybe that was the true difference between the elemental and terrestrial courts. Here, they tried and failed to hide their feelings. At least in Baylaur, we knew how to lie.

A small sigh and then pity in her eyes.

My throat threatened to close with emotion. I ordered it to remain open.

"You have enemies here, Your Majesty," Elayne said.

Truth. I could read it in her face easily. But it wasn't her warning that struck me.

"I thought you would call me Veyka." I hated the vulnerability, the honesty. I was not good at it. Nor at strategy. Hell, what was I good at?

My hands fisted against my hips.

Elayne's eyes softened, but she held her silence, waiting for me.

I swallowed past the emotion in my throat. "Arran said Eilean Gayl would be a safe harbor."

This time, she laughed aloud. "Arran said no such thing." She pushed herself up from the chair with an ease that belied her advancing age.

I held her gaze, unflinching. "He implied it."

Truth for truth. Arran had spoken of Eilean Gayl with such love and affection. I had assumed this would be a safe harbor for me and my companions. We'd been welcomed, yes. But formally. As a queen visiting a distant noble, not a daughter-in-law visiting her husband's family. No warmth.

Why? What had changed here? Or worse... what had I done wrong?

Elayne waved her hand as if stating the obvious. "Arran has not been to Eilean Gayl in decades."

I was too well trained to let my jaw drop open in surprise. But the tell must have been there just the same, because Elayne frowned and said, "He did not tell you that."

I shook my head—not in agreement, but in disbelief. "He was happy here."

Another sigh from Elayne. "He was a child here," she allowed. And I was reassessing everything. Had I misunderstood Arran's recollections of this place? Had he lied to me? No, Arran did not lie. It was endemically contrary to his nature. He was who he was, and he did not apologize for it. It was one of the many things I loved about him. But why... why paint me a picture of a place, a reality, that no longer existed?

Elayne watched me closely. And even though I had relaxed my guard, I knew that I kept most of the emotions off of my face by habit. Despite what she said, I was good at hiding my feelings. My survival in the elemental court had demanded it.

"Arran has not been happy for a very long time," she said quietly. Sadly.

"That is not true." It cost me to say it. But it was the truth. We were happy.

Even with the threat of the succubus hanging over us, the mystery of my powers and all of Arthur's lies and what that might mean for Annwyn... I'd never felt happiness like I did when I was in Arran's arms. Or when I was kicking his ass in the sparring ring. Or trading pointed barbs that turned sharper and hotter until we were clawing at each other in desperation to get closer, to join our bodies along with our souls.

I opened my eyes, realizing for the first time that I had closed them. Maybe I'd been standing there for minutes, rather than seconds, letting myself get lost in the memories. Only weeks separated me from the faerie pools where we'd finally consummated our mating bond, and yet it felt like years. Decades. Maybe another lifetime entirely.

Elayne watched me with such sadness in her dark eyes. Eyes that were familiar. Arran's eyes.

"Why did you come to Eilean Gayl?" she asked. I watched her throat bob as she swallowed. Now was the time, then.

I sucked in a breath and shoved my sadness, my heartbreak, all of it to the side. "How many amorite blades do you have?"

Elayne's dark brows joined together, arms coming across her body as she stared at me like I'd grown a second head. "Amorite blades?"

I unsheathed one of my daggers, then one of the rapiers, holding the blades across my palms non-threateningly. I held them out into the light, so that the swirling gray and silver of the blades was easier to see. "Like these."

Elayne examined them closely—touching neither. She leaned down, cocked her head to the side to get a different angle of light coming off of the braziers pegged into the stone walls, but she did not reach for the blades. Interesting, given Arran's comfort with them. But that was an observation to be analyzed at another time.

"We have finely made weapons, to be sure. But nothing like this..." she said, shaking her head. "Why?"

I sheathed the blades once more, exhaling slowly. Giving her my back, just for a moment, to gather myself. "The amorite blades are the only weapon that can kill a succubus."

Her voice did not shake, but her body was stiff when I turned back to her. "What is a succubus?"

I told her all of it.

The darkness that we had first seen in Baylaur—the human messenger from Eldermist and then the witch in the Tower of Myda. I left out the details of Arthur's murder, the betrayals of Gawayn and Roksana, their attempted coup. I was not ready to bare those parts of myself to her yet. She was Arran's mother, and she'd shown more openness in this conversation than the two days since our arrival. But I was not ready to give her those parts of myself.

I spoke briefly of the Faeries of the Fen, giving minimal details about their locations and their caves. Whether they considered themselves my subjects or not, I knew they were mine and I would protect them as such. I would not risk exposing them to the terrestrials. But I did reveal what Taliya had told us about the first time the succubus had come to Annwyn.

And finally I told her about the Void Prophecy and my place in it. That it was my void powers that had allowed the succubus entry into our realm once again.

My fault.

I did not speak of Gorlois or Percival's betrayal. Or what had come after.

"If you cut off their legs, they will crawl. If you burn them with fire, they will pause. But the only way to kill them is to cut off their heads or stab them with an Amorite blade," I finished.

Around my recounting of the Void Prophecy, Elayne had sunk back into that hard, high-backed wooden chair. The silence stretched out between us as I watched her trying to comb through everything I'd told her. The world I'd turned upside down with little warning.

I forced myself to remain standing. If I sat down, I'd lay down. If I laid down, I'd close my eyes and lose myself in trying to forget this entire mess.

Elayne lifted one hand, pinning two fingers to her temple while her elbow rested on the arm of the chair. The weight of the truths and considerations I'd dropped too much to bear. A huffed exhale. "The Great War... it was not about elementals and terrestrials at all."

I jerked my chin to the side. "Or at least, not wholly."

Her next thought— "The amorite mines."

I nodded, more steadily this time. The erasure of our history was unsteady ground. Weapons and solid actions, I could handle. "We need weapons. And as many amorite necklaces, earrings, and trinkets as we can manage."

She was nodding along now, that arm dropped. Good—she was moving into acceptance.

"You are the queen from the Void Prophecy."

My chest constricted but I ignored it. "You must have expected it. You were waiting here, expecting me to reappear."

That earned me a half smile. Hell, even the shape of her mouth was like Arran's. Would our own children bear this uncanny resemblance? A dozen emotions roared to life within me at the musing I'd stupidly allowed to sneak out. I shoved all of them back down.

"I knew your magic was special," Elayne said. Maybe she'd supposed it some type of wind magic, like Arran had once suggested. Terrestrials did not come to the elemental kingdom. It was entirely possible Elayne, Pant, and the rest of their retainers had written off my strange power as an elemental oddity. That was easier than accepting vague historical prophecies as fact. "But the succubus appeared before you came into your power. How can they be linked?"

Exactly what I needed to get out of Diana and Percival. I rubbed the palm of my hand over my brow and down my cheek. Question Diana. Get the amorite. Warn the terrestrials. Figure out the nonsense with the sacred trinity and Arthur's secrets. Get back to Baylaur. Arran. Fucking hell. Tired? It was a wonder I got out of bed each morning.

For a long time, you didn't.

"Perhaps the Offering acted as some sort of trigger. From what I can glean, human minds are easier to take over than fae. But in the end, they will come for all our males. Turn them against us, rip us apart, until we are dead defending our children, and then they are carrion as well."

Morose. But it was the truth.

My heart ached for Maisri. She was safer in the faerie caves then she was here in Eilean Gayl. The succubus had not come here yet, not that Elayne had heard of. But that was a blessing that would not last.

"Perhaps," Elayne allowed, tapping her temple with those two fingers. She shifted in her seat, the struggle on her face evident.

Because she'd revealed all of her tells to me? Or because she'd decided on honesty?

Sadness, calculation... and worry. "Arran was with you at Avalon."

Don't ask.

I nodded.

"You came to warn us, but he did not. Is he seeing to some other task, something you cannot tell me?" Her voice was hopeful. The golden thread in my chest squeezed tighter, trying to protect my heart.

I shook my head.

Please, leave it at that.

But she loved him. I saw it in her eyes, recognized the emotion I'd seen reflected back in Arran's long before I'd been able to give him those words.

"Where is my son?"

I sank down onto the bed.

"Sleeping," I said, my voice a hollow, dead thing. And still, I could not deny the truth to this female who loved my mate. "The King sleeps in Avalon. And it is all my fault."

31
VEYKA

"Veyka."

A soft voice. Imploring but gentle. Not across the room, but beside me on the bed. A warm hand encircled mine, the fingers daintier but the will they manifested so strong.

"Tell me, Veyka."

I wanted to collapse. I wanted to scream and cry. But that hollowness was taking over again. I tried to shove it back, tried to let myself feel. Feel Arran, feel the love he'd given me, the love I'd finally let myself feel in return.

"He was holding Arran. He was going to kill him. And Arran was going to let him."

Go, Veyka.

"Arran was ready to die, so that I could live."

I love you, Veyka.

"He did not realize…" I couldn't breathe. My voice was hoarse, gasping. "I don't want to live without him. I can't—"

My voice broke.

Please.

I broke.

The hollow emptiness was no match for this—my love for

Arran, my heartbreak at his loss. I felt everything. Every inch of my body screamed at the loss, the acute pain of a part of myself ripped out and missing.

The hand tightened around mine.

I clenched it tighter. Bones cracked. But I could not stop myself. "How? How could he not know? That without him there is nothing? I am nothing?"

Save yourself.

I couldn't see through my eyes. I was wet. Not with sweat now, but hot salty tears that covered my face, fell on my chest, slid down between my breasts. I was melting. Dying.

"I used my power. I threw the sword. I killed G—" I choked on the name, unable to let it past my lips. "But I was thrown off balance. The sword went into Arran's chest..."

Elayne gasped. I held tighter, lifted our joined hands until they were between us. Trying to make her understand.

"We were wearing the scabbards. Each of us. Our blood cannot be spilled while we are wearing the scabbards. He was supposed to be safe."

Hair flying. Longer hair. Hair Arran had tangled his fingers in. Arran, oh Arran. My mate, my love. My mistake.

"But not from me. I can draw my own blood, even with the scabbard. And the mating bond... we are not safe from one another. He wasn't safe from me."

"I begged the Lady of the Lake to take him to Avalon, where no one can die."

I released her hand.

All that remained of me was the bond. The fragile, tenuous golden thread now stretched across realms was the only thing about me that mattered anymore. But I did not deserve it. I did not deserve him. I knew it, and now Elayne did as well.

"And then I left him. I came here to warn you, to try to save Annwyn. I left my mate." And I hated myself for it every second of every breath of my miserable, cursed existence.

It should have been me.

I should have taken the blow. Arran was the one who should have ruled. The strategic one, the commander, the most powerful fae in millennia. The greatest power Annwyn had ever seen. Lying prone and injured in the human realm because he had made the mistake of falling in love with me.

Elayne grabbed by my hand. This time she held it much tighter, so I could not twist away.

"It is not your fault," she said. I recognized where Arran had gotten the steel that so often lined his words.

My lips were trembling. No, that was my chin. "I nearly killed my mate. The High King. Your son." My entire body was shaking with the force of silent sobs.

I did not see Elayne shaking her head in the periphery of my vision until she lifted her free hand to my face and turned it, so I had no choice but to look directly at her. I did not have the will to fight. I was not even sure how I was still upright.

Her dark gaze bore into mine. "I absolve you."

"You can't," I whispered.

She held my chin tight between her fingers. All the command of the Lady of Eilean Gayl, the female who had survived rape and torture and somehow found love, raised a male like Arran, was in her gaze and in her words. "I love my son. And I have no trouble at all seeing why he fell in love with you. He would be proud of you now for trying to do what is best for Annwyn."

I tried to shake my head. She would not let me. I tried words instead. "I promised him a thousand years. I promised him I would wait."

"For Arran, there is no higher calling than duty."

"Except love." I dreamed about the first time I'd realized it, standing on the cliff edge on the other side of The Crossing. When I closed my eyes, that was the moment that came back to me most often—not when he'd told me, but when I'd felt the absolute certainty of his love through the mating bond.

"Why must they be in opposition?" Elayne released my chin but waited, perhaps to see what I'd do. But I sat still. Frozen. Broken.

"You can love Arran and your kingdom, Veyka. There is enough of you to love both."

I actually laughed. A terrible, unhinged sound that mocked the word. "My mate, my friends, my subjects... the more I love, the more I stand to lose."

"I see."

She did not try to argue. I was thankful for that.

"You are soaked through. I will call for your handmaiden. How convenient that fire of hers must be at bath time. Then you are to bed." She spoke with such calm conviction. Do this, then this, next this. Simple steps to move through the next minutes and hours, when nothing about my life was simple anymore.

"People do not usually give me commands," I said vaguely.

A hand landed on my shoulder, squeezing. "Mothers are exempt from such strictures."

I knew my chin was wobbling again, my whole body trembling as I looked up at her. Maybe it hadn't stopped. I probably would not have noticed.

Mother.

I hardly recognized the word.

Understanding flashed in her dark eyes. I did not have the energy left to protest, to explain, to deflect... not as she eased me back onto the bed and walked to the adjoining door to summon Cyara.

"Rest, Veyka. You are safe for tonight. Tomorrow, we shall plan."

32

VEYKA

The heat built in my body slowly. So deliciously slowly. Hands that were not my own stroked, reverently tracing every inch. They cupped my full breasts, teasing the nipples with fluttering touches until my breasts were heavy and aching. But then they moved away, tracing the midline of my body, pausing to circle my belly button and the soft rise of flesh above my navel.

Then the calloused fingertips disappeared, replaced by impossibly soft lips. Stubble scraped across the tender plane of my belly, just a little too rough, pushing me a little too close to the edge. Much more and I would lose control.

Control... an illusion. I was not in control of this. Had never been, since that first moment. This was destiny. This was a joining preordained by Ancestors and gods and whatever forces governed the endless realms of existence—human, fae, faerie... all bowed before our union.

Those soft lips kissed down my body, hands pinning my legs down and apart. A long lick of that sensitive seam where my body met my legs. Down, down, down towards my center. Until that was being licked, too. A long, luxurious lick up my slit, then back down again. This time, his tongue slid between my folds, tasting the desire that was already flowing hot and fragrant.

I could smell my desire as he tasted me, hear his groan in my ears as he savored and nibbled at my flesh. It was so impossibly decadent, no hurry at all to those long strokes. We had all the time in the world for these touches. Unending minutes and hours and days to discover one another, to worship at the altar of our love.

I arched my hips. More. Fingers slid inside of me. Two thick, strong fingers at the command of a male so powerful, I trembled. Trembled with need, but also with awe. This male loved me. He had chosen me above all others, not because of duty or a bond but because he loved me. This male was mine.

Those two fingers worked inside of me, curling until they found that spot that I was never able to reach on my own. Only he had the power to draw this sort of pleasure from me. Only he had ever discovered the depths of pleasure that my body could know, and coaxed them from me with loving demand.

He stroked again and again over that spot. I heard my own sobs, begging him to go faster. But there was no answer, not in words. Only the silent, constant demand of his fingers. Then his mouth, back on my stomach, sucking me hard enough I knew I would bear the marks.

I was going to die of this pleasure. Fall into the void and lose myself, willingly, so that I might stay in this spiral of perfection forever. This was not sex, it was so much more. It was my body honoring what my soul knew, what my heart felt with every beat of that golden thread that tethered us.

Please, please, please, I chanted. Aloud or in my mind, through the bond, to the beast—it did not matter. I needed him to go faster, to push me over that edge.

But he refused with every punishing stroke of his fingers inside of me. Until I could not argue anymore. I could not think. I usually came in a gush, an explosion of liquid pleasure that coated our skin and the bed around us. But this was so much more intense. My climax came in waves, undulating with each scrape of his fingertips inside my pussy. It dragged out over minutes, a wave of pleasure that dripped down around his wrist; another a few seconds later, drenching my thighs. So much, so sweet, that his mouth left my stomach, desperate to capture every drop of me.

I was no longer in my body. I obviously could not be alive. No one survived coming like that. I had no fluids left in my body, I was reduced to a heartbeat and a gasp.

But a hand touched my waist, applied slight pressure. An invitation.
One I would never, ever refuse.
I rolled over—

I jolted awake. My fingers curled into the silk bedsheets, trying to find purchase, searching for something that was not there. Someone.

"Arran?" I whispered into the darkness, my voice pitifully small and broken.

No answer.

No rasp of breath or huff of beastly warmth.

It had been a dream.

I closed my eyes again. And even though I didn't believe in the Ancestors' ability to help me, even though I'd cursed them to hell and beyond, the prayer still flitted across my consciousness. Unspoken, but no less real.

Let me dream of him again. Please, oh please, oh Ancestors. Let me see him in my dreams.

Because I knew that when I woke again, I would be alone. Living in my nightmares.

33
CYARA

"Is this how you celebrate Yule in Annwyn?" Percival spat, blood and spittle mingling as they slid down his chin, slowed by the weeks' worth of black stubble.

"You ought to know by now that I consider any day without blood spilt to be an utter waste," Veyka said, wiping the blood from her knuckles on a handcloth. At least she had spared the gown that Cyara had spent hours finishing for her. "Now that we've established that you're at my mercy—"

"The chains weren't fucking en—"

"—it's question time." Veyka crossed her arms under her breasts.

She wore no weapons, though Cyara knew she would not leave the suite of rooms in the tower without her daggers and the scabbard. But for now she was unarmed. That was a decision. Much like hitting Percival and blatantly ignoring Diana.

Veyka had a plan. Not that she would share it until she was good and ready.

At least when Arran was with them, he could intercept her rash schemes.

But that was the least of the reasons to miss the Brutal Prince.

Cyara averted her eyes and went back to folding towels.

"Why was Diana taken instead of you?" Veyka asked.

There was a pause. Cyara counted the seconds. Either Percival did not want to answer at all and was fighting his own nature or he was trying to formulate a response that was truthful but avoided what he did not wish to reveal.

"She had shown potential in the gift of foresight and prophecies," Percival finally said.

Veyka snorted. "One can easily assume that you showed no potential for anything at all."

Silence from Percival.

That was telling, as well. They had assumed that he left Avalon and the priesthood to search for Diana, eventually being blackmailed by Gorlois and tricking them into following him to Avalon. But perhaps Percival had not left the sacred isle of his own accord after all. Maybe he had failed to prove useful, and they had ousted him.

Cyara slowed the pace of her folding, drawing out the task so that no one would notice her. Veyka listened to the words. Cyara read the spaces in between.

"What do prophecies have to do with opening rifts?" Veyka asked.

"I don't know." Percival answered immediately.

Veyka cursed under her breath.

Somehow, Gorlois had used Diana to move himself through rifts, between realms, as if he had the void power. Some facsimile of it, based on the villain's words at the Battle of Avalon. Diana was a half-witch. Surely that had something to do with it. But their female prisoner currently huddled in the corner, watching her brother's questioning from behind trembling fingers.

Veyka tapped the foot of her slipper on the ground, the sound muffled by the thick carpets strewn over the otherwise frigid stone floors. Cyara missed the inherent warmth of the goldstones of Baylaur. She missed her flowing, clean white gowns and familiar food for every meal. Her parents... she had no way of getting word about how they were. Even if they sent a message from Eilean Gayl now, with a flying fauna-gifted terrestrial, it would take more than a month to hear back. No one would try to cross the Split Sea, which meant the winged shifter would have to cross the Spine, sail over the Shadow Wood, across the Spit, beyond the Barren Dunes and back up to Baylaur. By the time a return message came, they likely would not be in Eilean Gayl to receive it.

Still, she knew that Veyka had written missives. Closeted away with the Lady of Eilean Gayl the day before, the two females had sent letters off in every direction. Cyara did not need to guess at the contents. They were warnings. Watch the males. Gather your amorite. Prepare for the darkness to come.

If they would take those warnings with any degree of seriousness remained to be seen.

"How did you use the communication crystals to communicate with your sister?"

Cyara heard the rapid uptick of Percival's heart in his chest. That meant Veyka and Lyrena did as well. It was well done, to switch topics so abruptly. Veyka would not need the witch magic compelling Percival's answers to read his reaction. She had a lifetime at the elemental court to teach her how to do that.

Percival answered quickly this time as well. Probably hoping that the sound of his voice would cover the staccato rhythm of his heart.

"I said the incantation, and then I said my message," he said.

Before, he told them that the communication crystals worked on intention. The person on the receiving end had to be open to hearing from the speaker. Now, there was an incantation required as well.

He was leading them in circles.

But to what purpose? Escape? To protect Diana? Did he think that if he led Veyka on, she would keep questioning him and forget that his sister was half-witch as well?

A shiver of awareness snaked up Cyara's spine, into her wings so that they twitched. Just slightly. But she saw Veyka mark the motion. So, she was totally unsurprised when Veyka grabbed Percival's arm and hauled him to his feet.

"Make him presentable," she said, shoving him at Lyrena. "He's going to celebrate Yule with us down in the hall."

His red ochre skin paled. "What... what about Diana?"

Cyara set aside her laundry and let the harpy inside of her show through, just in her eyes. "She and I shall spend some quality time together."

34

VEYKA

I sent Lyrena and Percival down ahead of me, through the winding stairwells and narrow corridors. I needed a moment of silence.

For the last two days, there had been none. First that horrible sparring with Barkke, then my unplanned debacle in the void, and then plotting with Elayne. She was a brilliant female. She admitted she could not touch a weapon, not after the brutality she'd suffered before Arran's birth. But she was formidable with a pen and as a fauna-gifted terrestrial whose animal form was a hawk, she knew precisely which airborne terrestrials to call on to deliver our letters.

Writing to Parys and Gwen had been the hardest. Not because I needed to convince them; I knew my Knights would believe me and heed my warnings without question. But writing to them, when all I wanted was to talk to them... to hear Parys' laugh, to spar with Gwen... it hurt more than I'd expected.

But I'd also sent letters to Skywatch and Outpost, the elemental and terrestrial garrisons on either side of the Spit. Another went on to Cayltay, the capital of the terrestrial kingdom on the shores of Wolf Bay. For the latter two missives, Elayne had included her own notes as well.

She wrote them, but they were signed by Pant.

I remembered what Arran had said, huddled in our tent all those months ago. His mother was not well regarded in the terrestrial kingdom, despite her son becoming the Brutal Prince. I'd suspected at the time that disdain had been what motivated him to the bloody title. Getting to know Elayne only confirmed my guess.

I reached the first spiral staircase and lifted my eyebrows at the guard.

Once he picked his jaw up off the floor, he moved out of the way.

Self-satisfaction warmed me as I angled my body to fit down the narrow stairwell. Which was damn good, because the castle was drafty and a lot of my skin was on display.

The general style in Eilean Gayl was either a high-cut gown that covered everything but the throat, from the long, pointed sleeves all the way down to the voluminous skirts, or a white underdress with sleeves covered by a front-lacing overgown. There were laces and belts and embroidery for accents, and the bodices were close fitting to show off the females' figures. The attire matched the cold weather outside. But it was just sad to look at.

After seeing the desire burning in Barkke's eyes, I'd almost asked Cyara to dress me in one of those sad, boring gowns.

But she'd worked hard on the others, creations more suited to my own preferences, and in the end I'd allowed her to dress me without making a fuss.

I had to angle my body down the staircase, or my hips would brush against the stone walls. I would not risk undoing Cyara's hard work.

I dragged one hand along the central column as I navigated each stair.

I would have missed it entirely if my hand had not passed over the indentation.

An engraving. One that had not been there the first time we were led up this staircase.

My fingers traced the outlines. Two upright triangles—fire. Two inverted triangles with a line through the lower point—earth. Humans. And one circle.

Cyara, Lyrena, Percival, Diana. And me.

Smeared with a dark substance. I did not need to lift my fingers to my nose to know they were tinged with blood.

A message left by someone in Eilean Gayl. Enemies, Elayne had said. Both within this castle and beyond.

The peace in Annwyn had always been precarious. It was why the Ancestors demanded the Offering and the Joining, to bind our two kingdoms together. Elementals and terrestrials may both be fae, but that was where the similarities ended. I'd never thought about it much, before Arran—how essential the balance was.

Arran was control, I was feeling. He spoke his truth without reticence; I dissembled to get what I wanted. A terrestrial heir and an elemental heir. King and Queen. Co-rulers.

Except that I was alone, now. And whether the terrestrial who'd carved the threat into the stone hated all elementals, me specifically, or the fact that our Ancestors had joined these two kingdoms together, did not really matter.

I lowered my hand to my side and let my own preternatural balance guide me down the remaining stairs.

Let them come. I'd enjoy cutting them down one by one.

I managed to make it down the narrow spiral staircase without tripping or ripping my gown. Next was an empty dining room, mostly unused based on Elayne and Pant's quick description when they'd shown us up to our rooms that first day.

Bookcases bracketed two chairs set beneath an arched stained-glass window. This castle was more than seven thousand years old. It predated the Great War and the unification of the terrestrial and elemental kingdoms, though it had been largely destroyed in that conflict and rebuilt in the centuries that followed. Had those seats once been occupied by a King and Queen of the Terrestrial Kingdom, enthroned here at Eilean Gayl? Maybe the territory north of the Spine had been a separate kingdom entirely. A flora-gifted fae could easily have kept the ornately carved thrones in good condition, shoring up any damage over the centuries.

But it was not the thrones that snared my attention. It was the stained glass.

A slender female figure stood at the center. Having met the Lady of Eilean Gayl, there was no mistaking her even in this simplified form. The artist had rendered her with unmistakable care, from the angle of her eyes to the graceful sweep of her skirts.

In each hand, she held a smaller one. Two boys, one dark like her, the other the image of his father.

My brother is long dead.

He'd never offered an explanation. Fae children were not susceptible to the same range of illnesses that often took human children young. For his brother to die, the circumstances must have been extraordinary...

But Arran was three hundred years old. His brother could have died in adulthood, long as it was.

"The boys broke this window squabbling," Elayne said, her sigh long-suffering. "Their father forced them to stand for a portrait, which was then used for the artist to create the stained glass, as penance."

"It is lovely," I said truthfully.

The sadness in her small smile was plain. "It is a beautiful lie. They never got along, even as young children."

They'd been young together. Usually fae siblings were separated by decades. What had become of Arran's brother? But that was not the question I asked.

"What was Arran like as a child?"

That sad smile softened slightly as Elayne slid her gaze to me, approval in her dark eyes.

"Much like he is as an adult," she said. "Solemn. Cognizant of the gift and curse of the magic in his blood. Once he learned to control his power, he never let it slip."

But he had for me.

The first time I'd seen him in his beast form, in the tavern in

Baylaur when the agent of the Shadows tried to kill me, he'd lost control. Had his beast known that I was his mate, even then?

For all that I trusted Elayne, I kept my face neutral. Those moments belonged to me and Arran. A low growl rumbled at the edge of my consciousness.

I spun, half expecting, not believing—

But we were alone and I was being ridiculous.

I followed Elayne down to the great hall and ignored the slight pulsing in the back of my mind.

35

CYARA

Cyara waited until the trio was well gone before she unlocked Diana's shackles.

Percival had been trussed up like a chicken in a blue embroidered tunic and brown trousers that were ill fitting—she had to roll the pants to accommodate his human stature—but they were, blessedly, clean.

Lyrena refused to wear anything other than her Goldstones uniform. But she had sent it to Eilean Gayl's laundry to have it cleaned and pressed. With a strand of rubies borrowed from Veyka braided into her blonde hair, she looked every bit the noble courtier she was. Anyone who had watched her spar with Veyka the last few days knew that it was a thin veneer over the warrior beneath.

Veyka, though, was the real accomplishment. Her glorious white hair, near glowing now that they had access to a bathtub, was still too short for the customary elemental plait. So instead, Cyara had braided it starting at one pointed ear, then up over the crown of her head and back down. When she tied off the end, the tail had just brushed Veyka's collarbone.

For all the Cyara missed the pleasant monotony of brushing out

Veyka's long hair and teasing it into intricate designs, she could admit that the shorter length suited her friend well. It drew attention to her beautiful face and stayed out of her way better when she sparred.

Cyara finished brushing out and plaiting her own waist-length copper hair just as the supper tray arrived. As a servant set down the tray, Cyara walked over to the wall and unceremoniously unlocked Diana's shackles.

The woman did not move.

She did not even blink with Cyara so close to her.

This was going to take longer than Cyara had thought.

"You are welcome to come and eat," Cyara said, settling herself back at the table. She did not wait for Diana before dipping her spoon into a thick potato soup swirled with cream.

Diana did not move.

Cyara kept eating.

"You may as well enjoy an hour with free range of movement. Veyka would skewer me if she knew I had unshackled you, and Lyrena would be there to finish off whatever was left." She methodically cut off a chunk of dark brown bread and dipped it daintily into the soup.

Movement.

Slow, so very slow. But Diana was pushing to her feet, clinging to the unevenly stacked stones of the wall to pull herself up.

Cyara pretended she had not noticed the movement. She finished her bowl and cut herself a section of glazed meat, and Diana was still stagnant.

"The food will get cold if you stand there much longer." Cyara tilted her head to the side. "I have never been much good at using my fire for cooking. You will not like the mess I make of things trying to reheat them."

"Why are you doing this?" Diana squeaked.

So many ways to answer that question. Cyara decided on the most literal, for the moment. "Because I think you are caught up in a situation that is not your fault. I cannot release you, would not even consider it. But I can give you a decent meal while the rest of them are away."

And if you talk to me more easily...

Diana took one step, stumbled, clawed her way back to the wall, and started whimpering.

Cyara refilled her wine and prayed to the Ancestors that the Yuletide revelry kept her companions downstairs for the next several hours. She would need every minute.

36
VEYKA

Elayne had arranged for dancing.

Lyrena burst out laughing when the music started and the parade of performers appeared. Apparently, Cyara had shared that particular quip with her.

I did not plan on stabbing anyone at the Yuletide feast. But we were only on the first dinner course.

The stone walls that I'd once judged as austere hung with rich emerald tapestries, all manner of terrestrial shifter depicted in woven gold. They were lovely, but it was clear that the festival of Yule belonged to the flora-gifted terrestrials.

Massive evergreen trees stood in each corner, each of their tops ending a scant inch below the arched stone roof—too perfect to be anything but magic. They were ornamented by glowing red winterberries magically grown to the size of my fist. I could have plucked one off a tree and eaten in like an apple.

I tested the flesh with my thumb, pressing until my fingernail pierced the ruby red skin. 1 glanced around—by some miracle, no one was watching me. They were all busy watching the dancers, or eating and drinking. I caught the muffled sounds of other pleasures as well.

My stomach tightened.

I sucked the berry juice off of my thumb and pretended not to notice.

I savored the tartness on my tongue. Drank in the elegant movements of the dancers. A handful of the terrestrials who resided at Eilean Gayl were joining in, selecting the handsomest and most beautiful of the performers to partner with.

The priestess and her acolyte arrived without ceremony—exactly as Elayne had said. No ridiculous prophecies or overwrought water magic in sight. Maybe I would take a terrestrial priestess back to Baylaur with me and kick Merlin out on her smug, power-grabbing ass.

This is not the terrestrial court, I reminded myself.

Eilean Gayl was its own microcosm of the terrestrial kingdom. What awaited in Cayltay, the capital situated on the edge of Wolf Bay... I took a deep drink of my wine, wishing it was aural. Elayne skirted around the topic of the capital. But it was not a conversation we could avoid forever. Not even for long. Once I'd dealt with the amorite mines, that was my next stop. I needed to warn the terrestrials of the threat of the succubus, convince them to take precautions... without Arran at my side.

For a second, I could almost feel the scrape of the engraved wall against my fingertips. Scent the blood. A threat, a reminder.

I might not be enough.

I had to be enough. For Arran and for Annwyn.

I drained my wineglass.

37
CYARA

"Slowly. You will make yourself ill," Cyara warned. She was nibbling at a small square of bitter chocolate that was meant to be dessert.

Probably a good thing, she reflected, as Diana shoved another oversize hunk of bread into her mouth. Watching the woman eat was the opposite of appetizing.

Diana ignored her, fully given over to the frenzy of food. She licked gravy off her fingers, took her next bite before she had even finished chewing the previous one. Cyara had once seen a skoupuma devouring a child who had wandered too far on the outskirts of Baylaur. This was revoltingly similar.

When the woman paused long enough to gulp down some wine, Cyara tossed one of the towels she had folded earlier across the table. "We have been feeding you."

Diana blinked several times, her eyes going hazy and then refocusing on Cyara. As if she had forgotten that she had an audience, when it had taken every bit of the last two hours for Cyara to entice her to the table.

She lifted the towel to her lips, licking them thoroughly before wiping away anything she had missed. Her fingers were filthy—she had not bothered with a fork or knife. But she sucked each of them clean rather than use the towel.

"You have never been held prisoner," Diana finally said, smacking her lips.

Cyara shook her head slowly, her braid swishing softly against the simple pale-blue dressing gown she wore.

Across the table, Diana started in on a second round. "Serving yourself. Choosing what to eat because you want it, not because you do not know when food will be offered again... it means something."

The thought had never even entered Cyara's mind. Some might have considered her constrained by a life of service, but she was well-born. She had never wanted for necessities, never had simple choices taken away from her. She dressed how she wanted, ate as she wanted, and had her pick of esteemed positions within the goldstone palace.

She was not foolish enough to think herself immune to the influence of those privileges. But her usefulness to Veyka and the Round Table had been predicated on her ability to observe, to see what others missed and string those observations together into coherent supposition.

Yet when she invited Diana to the table, she had thought only of the impact of removing the shackles. Not of the food and act of eating itself.

Cyara's pride wobbled in time with the twitch of her wings. Maybe she was not as observant as she thought.

Diana's eyes tracked the movement. They tracked everything, darting rapidly around the room in constant search of threats. When she found none, they came back to Cyara. "You are a harpy."

"Yes."

"It's unusual, yes? To be both a shifter and a fire wielder?"

Somehow, she had ended up answering questions, rather than asking them. But she responded, for the goodwill it might win her. "I am not a true shifter. Not like the terrestrials here. The harpy is something different."

Diana seemed to accept that, digging back into her food. A thin line of brown gravy trickled down her chin, gleaming against her deep red-brown skin.

Cyara took a slow, silent breath in. Now or never.

She kept her voice carefully even, no aggression or threat to be found in the perfectly enunciated syllables. "The doors are locked. I am armed, and you are not. If you try to escape, the harpy will bring you back. She will not be kind or gentle about it."

Diana's chewing slowed.

"You are going to ask me questions," she said around a mouthful of food. Her eyes had blown wide, the dark brown turning glassy.

Cyara shook her head. "Do not fall apart."

"I can't help—"

"Do not fall apart," she commanded softly. *Or a worse fate awaits you.*

Diana closed her mouth and chewed slowly, her eyes still round. But no tears fell, and when she swallowed she did not look away from the force of Cyara's turquoise gaze.

Now or never.

"Percival said you have a gift for prophecies. How were you useful to Gorlois?" Veyka could not say that monster's name, but Cyara could. Diana flinched, pressing back into her chair. But she did not melt into a pile of tears. Nor did she reach for more food.

She did not fight the answer the way that her brother did. "He used me to make the rifts."

Cyara did not give her a pause to think or fall apart. "How?"

Diana was slower to answer this time, but Cyara got the sense that she was trying to decide the best way to explain, rather than avoiding the question. The corner of her wide mouth twitched, a sigh so soft that Cyara almost did not mark it.

"What are prophecies if not the mind traveling to another time and space?" Diana finally said.

Only years of training in the elemental court kept the surprise from Cyara's face. The power of prophecy... some distant vestige of Veyka's void power? Akin to the similarities between water and ice powers among the elementals, perhaps. But the implications of that... Cyara kept her hands loose as they rested on the table, not allowing them to clench into fists.

"He used ancient spells, stolen from the witches generations ago, before they were terminated. Combined with my witch blood and my power for the sight, he was able to travel through the void. Short distances, fixed points. Not like your Queen."

Two questions asked, two answers received. Answers that implied so much... but that in actuality, might not change anything at all. Cyara had to ask one that would.

"Do you bear any ill-will to my Queen?"

Diana met her gaze, eyes still full of unshed tears. In the low candlelight, the brown of her irises was softer, flecked with gold. Such a contrast to her sharp, abrasive brother Percival.

"No," Diana whispered. "All I want is to live in peace."

Cyara would have believed her even if she had not compelled the answer. So she gave a true answer of her own in response. "There will be no peace until we banish the succubus for good."

Diana's lower lip wobbled slightly. "And how will you banish it?"

If Veyka had a plan, she had not yet shared it with Cyara. Beyond writing letters to warn the far reaches of the kingdom, obtaining the amorite and distributing it... she had mentioned journeying to Cayltay. Did that mean she would try to rally the terrestrial armies?

But who would be fighting... the fae against the humans? The lower and less powerful classes who did not get the amorite before it ran out? Who would be left as prey to the succubus... and who would make that decision?

Cyara swallowed the chocolate and wine past the lump in her throat. "Did Gorlois ever mention a way to close the rifts, to control the void so the succubus could not get through?"

Diana looked away, toward where the two sets of shackles waited, set into the stone wall. "That is your fourth question."

"You do not have to answer," Cyara said gently, and meant it.

The human woman's eyes lingered on the shackles. Perhaps

remembering a different set, another captor. Bile swirled in Cyara's gut. She was not certain that when the time came, she would be able to close the iron manacles around this young woman's wrists again.

"Gorlois was not concerned with the succubus. His only concern was power. He wanted to open rifts big enough to let entire armies through. To conquer the fae realm, the human realm, and perhaps others we have not yet discovered. The realms are the same, layered on top of each other. He knew the terrain of the human and fae realm. He felt that with the rifts, he would be unstoppable." Diana's voice was as devoid of emotion as Cyara had ever heard it. A kernel of unease skittered up down her spine.

"Is such a thing possible?" Cyara whispered.

Diana turned back to face her, her teeth digging hard into her full lower lips. She released it to say, "Your queen commands the depths of the voids of darkness. What she might do is limited only by her own willingness to try."

"How do you know?"

Cyara watched as Diana's eyes threatened to glaze over again. But she managed to keep her eyes clear, her posture steady as she answered. "I was Gorlois' prisoner for nearly three years. There was no one alive, in this realm or any others, who knew more about the Void Prophecy."

The implication her words held—was it an offer or a threat?

Cyara's hopes and instincts told her the former. But she was not ready to give into them, not quite yet. In either case, what came next was entirely genuine.

"The others will not be back here for hours, yet. While you are unshackled, you might as well enjoy a proper bath."

❧ 38 ☙
VEYKA

I slowly worked my way around the great hall of Eilean Gayl, course by course and drink by drink. There was no formality to it, but there was a cadence. Servants would appear with heavily laden platters. The terrestrials would murmur and growl their appreciation before digging in, serving themselves from whatever platter was nearest at that given moment. Eventually, interest would shift back to dancing or fucking or fighting. Only to be renewed again thirty or forty minutes later, when the next course appeared.

Every bite was delicious, every sip of wine thick and luscious. But none of it could touch the aching void inside of me.

No one approached me, which struck me as odd, when they were clearly watching every step and mouthful. So different from Baylaur, where the courtiers would have been fighting one another for a chance to reach my side and ply me with honeyed words.

The terrestrials watched me instead, assessing my strengths and weaknesses. I was determined to show them none of the latter. At least I did not have to speak with anyone.

Which left me too much time to watch them, in return.

There was just as much fucking as the elemental court, though here they did not even bother going into the recesses of the alcoves or corridors. I watched as a female mounted a male right there beside a tray of golden, crisp sausage roles. The servant had to reach around them to clear the last course's dishes.

Plenty of weapons as well, though a wider array that what I was used to seeing. The elementals I knew preferred daggers or thin, elegant rapiers. A handful wielded mighty swords such as Excalibur. Lyrena was one of them. But the terrestrials had all sorts of wicked weapons hanging from their belts, leaning against the stone walls, or just dropped onto the tables next to the platters of food. Spears taller than I was, thicker than my arm, kept company with pick axes and what I thought was called a flail, with a lethal Morningstar hanging from its chain. All of which was secondary to the claws, talons, and teeth that would emerge when the fauna-gifted among them shifted.

I settled myself at a table near the massive wooden doors as the next course appeared—entire game birds the size of my head roasted whole and dripping what smelled like plum sauce. My eyes followed the line of servants marching back into the kitchens, past the head table where Elayne and Pant...

My hand froze an inch from my mouth, the tender meat forgotten.

Elayne was not in her seat. She stood at the door where the servants were disappearing with empty platters, monitoring and exchanging words too lost to the din for me to hear. But Pant remained in his ornately carved wooden chair, the pair at its side empty, and his lap full of female. A petite, beautiful female with pale gold hair cascading loose down her back and breasts that rivalled my own.

For a second, I thought the wine had addled my brain. Or had someone slipped something into it? There were poison experts among the flora-gifted terrestrials. Arran had described how certain talented males and females could coax the poison from a plant, make it more potent or enhance certain features.

"Have you been introduced to Lady Sylestria?" Barkke's gravelly voice said from the periphery of my consciousness.

I had not seen him since our bout in the training courtyard. Whether he realized how deeply he'd disturbed me with that glowing gaze of his, I did not particularly want to know. I was barely holding myself together as it was, that wall of ice I'd tried to build around my heart nothing more than a puddle.

I inclined my head to acknowledge his presence, but gave nothing else. He'd already noted the direction of my gaze and my blank face. That had been enough for him to guess the direction of my thoughts.

But Barkke was unbothered by the lack of warmth in my welcome.

He leaned back easily, his huge body swallowing up the chair. Even went so far as to kick out the chair on the other side of the table and prop his feet up on it. Utterly at ease. He swept his gaze over me—a little too appreciatively—and then refocused on the scene unfolding at the other end of the hall.

"She's been his mistress for the last forty years or so," Barkke said, swigging back his ale. No aural to be seen here, even if I'd wanted it.

"Arran spoke of the love and tenderness between Lady Elayne and Lord Pant," I said, lifting the wine to my lips to spare myself expanding on that thought.

Barkke operated under no such subtleties. A terrestrial through and through. "Since when are love and sex preclusive?"

I blinked. There was no way I would ever let another female sit in Arran's lap. If I so much as saw one with desire glowing in her eyes, I'd stab her and be done with it. But... Arran and I had never spoken of it. He'd intimated that sexuality was different in the terrestrial kingdom, even freer and wilder than in Baylaur. But he couldn't have meant this...

"Not much for sharing, are you, Majesty?" Barkke said, grinning broadly. Even adding a wink. I wanted to stab him.

I swirled my wine and contemplated dashing it into his smug face. "Certainly not one to discuss my sex life with a terrestrial brute."

He leaned back further, tucking his hands behind his head. Boldly exposing his throat even as he blatantly played with fire. "Yet you married one."

"Arran is not a brute," I said. No room for argument in my voice. Which, of course, the rude and irritating terrestrial took as a challenge.

"I have known the Brutal Prince a lot longer than you, Majesty. That is precisely what he is. But if it works for you..." He trailed off, waggling his bushy brown eyebrows.

I crossed my legs, knowing the action would expose the long length of my muscular legs. He wanted me, that was blatant. Too damn bad. Let him look, let him be jealous. Let him worship me. So that when my mate did return, I would have the pleasure of watching him flay this ass of a male alive. "What does and does not work for me is, and never will be, any of your concern."

"Maybe." He winked again.

I pulled my dagger.

He threw back his head and roared, beard bouncing ignominiously. By the time I thrust my hand forward, he was well out of reach.

***

Uneasiness was building steadily inside of me. I tried to drown it with another glass of wine, but it seemed even a whole bottle would not be enough.

Lyrena gave me space, dividing her attention between smiling at the dancing, watching me, and glaring at Percival. Whatever Cyara was up to with Diana, I hoped it proved useful. If being separated from his sister was torture for Percival, even better.

Barkke, mercifully, did not return. I spotted him an hour later on the other side of the hall, a slender terrestrial winding vines around his massive biceps.

Jealousy rose in my throat, hot and sharp. No, not jealousy. Barkke may lust after me, but the feelings in my stomach had nothing to do with him. The self-pity, the longing... those belonged to Arran. All of me belonged to Arran.

But still, it burned.

A low growl rolled through me, past my lips. My fingers tightened around the stem of my wine glass. Whether it came from my longing or the shred of Arran's soul that was wrapped around mine... the power of it threatened to slice me in half. Melt me. Until I was a useless puddle of longing and loss that all the dancers had to step around—

The wine glass shattered.

The stem snapped, the foot shattering into tiny pieces on the stone floor. The shards of the glass bowl dug into my palm, my fingers, deep enough that blood dripped down my wrist onto the floor.

That was what caught the attention of the terrestrials around me. Not the sound of the glass shattering, but the scent.

Nostrils flared. Eyes began to glow. The power in my veins filled the hall, until every single terrestrial was staring at me.

My power tugged at its restraints. A tingling started at the tips of my fingers. Once, that sensation had sent terror roaring through me. Now, the void was a comfort, an escape, beckoning...

A sharp movement across the hall caught my gaze—demanded it.

Barkke.

He'd dumped the lusty female somewhere, now stood against the stone wall. Towering over everyone, his mace resting on his shoulder. That was the movement I'd seen—him pulling it from his belt and swinging upward in one swift, brutally efficient motion.

Challenge.

My hands moved for my daggers. I'd slip into the void and slit his throat before—

His startlingly green eyes flashed, but not with desire this time.

A warning, not a challenge. A reminder not to give in to the power. To be the queen I was playing so hard at being—irreverent, powerful, superior.

I curled my bloodied fingers into a fist. Then quickly, just as suddenly as I'd shattered the wine glass, I flung my fingers wide, my blood flying in droplets around me. I smirked at the terrestrials, the ones with my blood now dappling their clothing and skin.

"Go ahead, have a taste of true power," I purred.

The music began again at a signal from Elayne. Conversations began anew. When my eyes again found Barkke, his mace was back in its place on his belt. He lifted his hands and silently applauded.

I held that smirk in place on my face, even as every drop of wine I'd consumed threatened to reappear.

I couldn't remain at the feast much longer. Elayne had mentioned gifts. They would be presented to her and Pant, as Lord and Lady of Eilean Gayl. She'd warned me that some of the more powerful terrestrials in the area might present some to me as well. Power acknowledging power. The true currency of the terrestrial kingdom.

But she'd have to accept them on my behalf. The pressure in my chest was nearly unbearable. Perhaps something I'd eaten—

The entire hall went dark, every flame doused. Blades sang as they emerged from their sheaths. Screams. Snarls and flapping wings and even a hiss as terrestrials all around shifted. The gush and scent of blood.

It was just like when Arthur was murdered. The sudden darkness, the confusion, the blood. *So much blood...*

My daggers were already in my hands, but I didn't raise them. I couldn't.

I wasn't in control of my body or the snarl, the rolling growl that built until I was howling.

The massive doors of the hall flew open, icy winter cold sweeping in off of the lake.

Another howl. Menace, command, threat—and not mine.

Lyrena's fire flickered, a single plume of it cast straight up toward the arched stone ceiling, illuminating the great hall of Eilean Gayl.

And the massive white wolf framed in the doorway.

A half dozen terrestrials were dead.

Some stood proudly over their kills, daring those nearby to challenge them, give them another opportunity to prove their strength. Others were content to let the dead lie unclaimed. I did not care what scores had been settled in those moments of all-encompassing dark.

My heart was beating so hard I thought it might explode out of my chest. The golden thread, so frayed and stretched these weeks... now strong. And pulling hard.

I stumbled forward. One step, two. My body struggled to catch up with my heart. I felt the sob pushing up through me, as unstoppable as the snarl and howl had been.

"Arran." A whisper—raw and full of aching need that not even my elemental blood could disguise.

A blink and he shifted.

My mate stood before me, seven feet tall, dark hair pulled loose from the knot at the back of his head, deep bronze skin glowing. Whole. Black eyes blazing with fury that I wanted to taste.

His brows knit together, the cruel slant of his mouth thinning before opening again.

His eyes pinned me to the spot as one dark brow lifted. "Who are you?"

39
VEYKA

It was a nightmare. It had to be.

Any second I would wake to find myself alone in that stone bedroom, the four walls closing in on me like a prison. The place I'd thought was a refuge, that had called out to me with the promise of family and home, was slowly making me lose my mind. Tomorrow, I'd leave for the coast and the amorite mines. Whatever excuses I had to make to Elayne, I'd find them. I just could not stay here. The echoes of Arran were too strong. Now I was having visions of him while waking.

"Who are you?" he asked again, singling me out from the crowd of terrestrials.

Wake up.

I blinked my eyes rapidly, trying to clear the fog that had conjured this vision. Nothing happened, nothing changed. The wine must have been drugged. My hand flailed behind me, reaching for—

"Your Majesty," Lyrena murmured, appearing at my shoulder. I recognized the warmth of her flames, still dancing at her fingertips.

Arran's dark brows rose higher still on his golden forehead.

"Elementals," he growled.

Damn it, Veyka. Wake up.

Wake up. Wake up. Wake up. Wake up.

"Arran," Elayne's voice sounded in my ear a second before she swept by me, putting herself between me and Arran.

There was only one reason she would do that.

I had come to know the Lady of Eilean Gayl over the last few days. I believed I had seen her true heart, and I'd shown her mine in the ways that I could. I knew that there was only one reason she would stand between me and my mate, knowing the depth of my loss, the guilt and longing that plagued my every breath.

This was real.

I was not dreaming.

My mate had risen from his enchanted sleep, healed and whole and powerful once more. And he did not know who the fuck I was.

※

There was such stillness, we could have been a painting.

Arran and I, staring at each other, while every single being around us held their breath.

He might not know who I was, but he'd marked me nonetheless. I was not wearing a crown, no magic danced around me. But he still singled me out. Some part of him knew, even if his mind did not.

A low, rumbling growl filled me. Arran's beast brushed up against my consciousness, sliding into me with familiar ease, caressing the parts of my soul that not even I was brave enough to touch. But Arran's face did not shift. The male was not aware of the what the beast did. Or, at least, did not recognize the meaning of his beast's reaction to me.

I could not move. I could not think. The golden thread of our mating bond was strong around my heart, compelling me to go to my mate and seal our reunion with a physical touch. I'd always been able to sense his nearness or distance through the bond. But over the last few weeks, it had been so frayed I'd detected nothing beyond its existence. Now, the force was strong enough that it took all of my own strength to keep myself from falling into his arms.

Arms that would not close around me. Would shove me away. Might even draw the battle axe from his belt.

His belt—the jeweled scabbard.

It was there.

Relief washed through me. He was safe, at least.

Arran seemed to realize at the same moment, his thumb stroking over the lip of the scabbard while his eyes fixated on the one at my waist, the twin to his own. The matched pair. As we were meant to be.

Oh, Ancestors. Oh no.

I sucked in a breath. Another. Too fast. I was going to start hyperventilating. I could not do that here, could not fall apart in front of all of these terrestrials. I had to be the Queen. They knew who I was, even if he did not. *Oh, Arran. Ancestors fucking hell...*

Elayne grabbed my arm.

But she spoke to Arran.

"We will speak privately. There is much to apprise you of, son." She did not call him Majesty. Did not reference his title. Because if he did not remember me... did he remember that he was the High King of Annwyn?

Fuck. Fuck. Fuck.

The Offering, the Tower of Myda, the Void Prophecy... even the succubus? How was I supposed to face all of it alone? Without Arran... with Arran, but alone still? This was worse than death, this was—

No.

Not worse than death.

Pant and Arran were walking now, exchanging words I could not hear over the roar in my own ears and the sounds of the Yuletide celebrations resuming. If no one was going to die, the terrestrials weren't overly interested. I'd never been more thankful for their base brutality.

The Lord of Eilean Gayl steered his son out of the great hall, down a corridor I had not yet explored. Elayne kept her grip on my arm. Later, I'd be grateful for her steady guidance. Then, I could not process any of it.

I saw the flash of white in the corner of my vision. Tiny, hovering near the door, bright white eyes dashing to and fro. My mouth opened and closed like a fish, trying to acknowledge Isolde. She'd brought him here, to me. Watched over him and gotten him here safe and whole. I owed her everything, but I could not form words. Lyrena spoke, but it was muffled, like hearing underwater. I was vaguely aware of a flash of white. Movement, as Isolde fell in line with my Knight.

Elayne and Pant guided us to a comfortably appointed room at the end of the corridor. Thick carpets, lush hangings, heavily stuffed furniture. There was a book left here, a sewing basket there. Private quarters of some kind.

Much smaller than the great hall and left unheated. No one had planned for it to be in use tonight. Lyrena lit the braziers in the walls with a flick of her wrist. A fire raged to life in the hearth. She lingered at my side, Percival nowhere to be seen. I could not bring myself to care if he was alive, escaped, or dead on the floor with the terrestrials.

Arran's eyes flared at Lyrena's fire, marking us for what we were —elementals.

Deceptive, self-serving elementals. That was what he'd thought of us when he arrived in Baylaur. What was worse... it had been true.

"I do not need to be managed," Arran said sharply, loud enough that Pant blanched.

Elayne, standing between us once again, was steady as always. "You certainly do not," she agreed. "Out. Everyone, out."

Pant followed her without question. Lyrena did not move from my side, Isolde behind us at the door. What reaction she would garner from the residents of Eilean Gayl, what Arran had made of her upon waking... I'd sort through that later. Deal with it *later*.

"Go," I said softly to my golden knight, knowing she would never leave my side otherwise. Percival be damned. She opened her mouth to protest, staring daggers at Arran. He looked her up and down and then dismissed her with the ease of someone who knows their own strength. The Brutal Prince.

"He will not hurt me," I said, knowing that he heard the words as well. Nothing I could do about that—nor that I wanted to. Anything, to trigger his memory. *Anything, Ancestors, please. I will do anything.*

I'd said I would never beseech the Ancestors again. Wrong. All it took was true desperation.

Lyrena was not convinced. She gave me a pointed look before retreating to the door. "Use your power." *If you need to get away.*

Arran and I had hated each other once. But never... he would never hurt me. He couldn't. That bond in his chest would shred his heart before he could bring me harm.

At least, intentional harm.

I'd done plenty of damage without meaning to.

Is this my fault?

My eyes stung. No, no, no. I could not allow myself to cry. Not now. Not yet.

The door fit snugly into the archway behind us, and then Arran and I were alone.

For several long seconds, I just stared at him, cataloging every feature. His boots were dirty from traveling; so were his woolen vest and leather trousers. His shirt was fastened all the way to his throat, hiding the expansive tattoo of his Talisman splayed across his chest. But there was the stubble on his chin that he never quite managed to keep at bay. The sharp cut of his cheekbones, precisely the same. He fingered the head of his axe as he returned my stare, as I'd seen him do a hundred times when appraising an enemy.

Is that what I am now?

No. I refuse.

I planted one hand on my hip, drawing attention to the curves of my body that he'd lusted for from the moment we'd met in the clearing outside the goldstone palace, before either of us realized who the other was.

"You do not know who I am." It took every bit of courage and strength within me to speak the words without my voice cracking.

A small but not silent part of me hoped the façade would fall away then. That the entire thing had been an act, carried out in service of some larger plot that he would reveal to me once alone.

But the flash of his eyes—cold and dark—killed my last shred of hope.

Nearly killed me as well.

"You think that I should." He lifted one dark eyebrow. "Care to tell me why?"

My fingers drifted to my weapon as well. The hilt of the dagger, so prophetically carved into the shape of a wolf. If I drew it, it would be to carve out my own heart. That would be less painful than this.

"I'd rather you tell me," I managed, a slight movement of my hip, forward. A bravado I did not feel.

He lifted one arm to rest casually against the mantle of the fireplace. It was one of his tactics. To lean back on something—a wall, a fireplace, a pillar—to make it seem like he was only casually interested. To distract his opponent from the pure brutality of every muscle. "Presumptuous thing, aren't you?"

Call me Princess. Stride across this room and drag me against you, rake those canines down my throat, and punish me for my presumptiveness.

But none of that happened.

I shrugged my shoulders. "Being a queen comes with a few privileges." Irreverence—so easy to slip back on the mask I'd been wearing since my arrival at Eilean Gayl.

But I did not want to wear a mask, not around Arran. Before the male who had seen all of me, the darkest, ugliest parts of me, and told me I was beautiful and worthy and strong. Before Arran, all I wanted was to be loved.

"Queen of what?"

His broad hand stroked the wood of the mantle. Like he had stroked my body.

My teeth stabbed into my lower lip. Tiny droplets of blood beaded up. I saw the scent hit him—watched his nostrils flare—before I could swipe them away with my tongue.

The composure he'd managed, the scowling battle commander that intimidated and killed, fell away before the scent of my blood. I could see the shift in his stance, subtle but there. The wolf inside of him battling for control. A low growl rolled through me.

"What *are* you?" my mate growled.

Yours.

But I couldn't say it.

"They call me the Queen of Secrets," I said instead. No irreverence, no pretending. I let my voice be gravelly and raw. Let him see that if he was broken, his memory gone, I was as well. What he'd do with that knowledge...

"What is your name?"

It was almost a stammer. He had not wanted to ask, but something inside of him demanded it. The beast, the bond... some echo of the love we'd shared.

How do you forget that you love someone? Not just a female, but your mate? How could he forget the single most important thing in my life? His life, as well.

I'd asked Morgyn to save him.

But this... would I have sent him to Avalon, knowing that this would happen?

Yes.

I would do anything to save my mate's life. Anything. Even at this cost.

Cost.

All magic has a cost.

I thought my heart had been broken before. The pain of

Arthur's death. The threat of Arran's. But this was worse. *I had done this.*

My eyes traced his body again, checking the outline of every muscle. He was whole, but not. My mate stood before me, healed. But he did not know he was my mate. *What if he did not want to be?*

I reached his face. None of the devastation tearing apart my soul showed there. Only mild curiosity. Arran did not know what he'd lost, so he could not be hurt by it. I wanted to hurl something at him, to rage at the fact that I was suffering while he was not. Even as another part of me was thankful, so thankful, that my mate was spared this pain.

My eyes burned, sharper. I was running out of time. The façade I'd managed was crumbling.

"My name is Veyka," I said softly.

Arran's chin dipped slightly, but no recognition lit his black eyes.

"Veyka." He tried it out— the syllables that should have been familiar but were painfully foreign on his tongue.

Fuck, fuck, fuck.

This was so much worse.

"Arran." A prayer. A plea. To the Ancestors, who I'd vowed never to ask for anything again. To the gods the humans worshipped. To anyone, in any realm, who would listen to the desperate begging of a female in love.

His eyes widened slightly, like he noted the desperation and intensity of that plea. But he did not move.

"Oh, Arran," I sobbed into the void as I disappeared.

I didn't aim or plan. I moved on instinct, but even those failed me. I crashed into the stupid ornate chair where Elayne had sat days before. I cried out, a reaction to the pain I could not hold back. But physical pain was nothing.

Cyara would come soon. I vaguely heard her footsteps through the shared sitting room. But I could not wait for her or explain. Just drawing a breath was more painful that it had ever been. Even after the water gardens. Even after Arthur.

I threw myself into the plush bed, burrowing into the pile of pillows and thick quilts. I stuffed my face down into the soft mattress, until I could hardly breathe. Only then did I let myself cry and scream. I sobbed into the mattress and did not bother to pray that it would muffle the sounds of my agony.

40
ARRAN

"High King of Annwyn?" I shook my head, refusing to believe it.

I hadn't decided who I was going to strangle first. That white-skinned faerie who had followed me all the way here, but would not tell me anything beyond her name and a few vague details about the Faeries of the Fen being more than a bedtime story. Or maybe the glowing, moon-haired elemental who looked at me like she fucking owned me.

My beast was clawing to get out. It had guided my journey here, through the lake lands to the rift in the foothills of the mountains. The rockslide was nothing to my bounding paws. How the faerie got through, I did not pause to see. Once I emerged on the other side, I could practically smell the misty waters of Eilean Gayl.

"Indeed," my mother nodded sharply. It had been too long since I'd seen her. Decades since I'd been to my ancestral home. She looked exactly the same—dark hair, graceful bearing. But she was being utterly ridiculous.

I crossed my arms over my body. "No."

"Yes," she said simply.

As if any of this was fucking simple. My father sat in the chair beside the fire, his fingers tapping an irritating rhythm on the book in his lap, which he had no intention of opening. He just needed something to hold. He'd always been so damn fidgety.

Whereas my mother stared at me with unwavering stillness.

"How?" One word. A command. Never had I needed to use such a tone with the female who'd given birth to me. But the veneer of control that slipping into the battle commander's form gave me was the only thing keeping my head from spinning right off my neck and onto the floor.

My mother glanced at the other chair before the fire.

I remained standing, arms over my chest, every muscle at attention. Every muscle aching from the unrelenting sprint to reach Eilean Gayl.

She pursed her lips and took the seat herself. "King Arthur was murdered, and his twin sister Veyka Pendragon ascended to the elemental throne. You were appointed the terrestrial heir and sent to Baylaur—"

"What about Gwen?" I cut in.

Guinevere was the terrestrial heir. She had fought in the pits, killing every other contender in order to achieve the title. I'd witnessed it myself.

"She went with you," my mother continued, her voice sharper. Reprimanding me for interrupting. Ancestors. Why did it feel like I was twelve years old again? "It is my understanding that she became a guard of sorts, and that she remains in Baylaur at this time."

I actually laughed at that. "No. Gwen would never debase herself into being a mere guard. She was supposed to be the High Queen of fucking Annwyn."

This was all a joke. It had to be. I must have taken some sort of head wound in battle... though I could not recall which battle... and this was the result.

"Guinevere has always done her duty. As have you, my son," my mother said. Pride rang in her voice. Pride... because I was the High King of Annwyn?

Ancestors... Could it be true?

Another detail of what my mother had said clicked into place in my mind. "Veyka Pendragon... the female who looked at me like..."

My mother did not finish that sentence for me.

Like I belonged to her.

And my beast... recognized her. *Wanted* her. A female I had never met.

"The High Queen of Annwyn," I said slowly. "My wife."

"Your mate."

The beast inside of me surged. I yanked back on the restraints I always kept around it, keeping that side of me tethered. Even as pressure contracted in my chest, around my heart. What the fuck was that?

Another possibility occurred to me. Not a joke, but a plot. I'd been targeted my entire life. I had been stolen away from this very castle when I was a mere child, locked in a dungeon, and tortured for the prophesied power in my veins. This was another attempt, and I would kill all of those involved, like I had every time before. I loosened the hold on my beast...

"I don't know who has convinced you to do this, or to what purpose, but I will slaughter them for you, Mother. Tell me what is really going on—"

"It does seem more the sort of jape I would orchestrate," my father interjected. Rarely, so rarely, did he step in. He'd always been the beta to my mother's alpha. Which gave his words more gravitas as he said, "Your mother speaks the truth."

This was madness. I was the commander of the terrestrial armies. I had earned the title of Brutal Prince by killing my way across battlefields for the last three hundred years. I was a weapon of terror and death, not a king. Certainly not *the* King. Nor a husband. Least of all the mate of a female who had simply vanished in the middle of a conversation.

"And she can just disappear? What cursed elemental magic is that?" I'd drawn my axe at the quick flash of movement, ready to fling it against whatever magic she—Veyka—had rallied against me. But she was just *gone*. As if she'd never been there at all.

My mother stiffened. "That is for your mate to explain."

"Mates do not exist," I growled back.

"They have not existed for seven thousand years," she said. "But they do now."

I bit back the snarl that rose in my chest, the need to gnash my teeth. I needed to shift, to run, to claw something apart. The fell creatures of the lake would be a good place to start. Blood. Blood would clear my mind.

Blood—her blood. I'd scented it and known she was different. My beast had wanted to lick it off of her lips, and then lick the rest of her as well. But a mate... no.

My mother rose, smoothing the folds of her silk skirts by habit, as I'd seen her do thousands of times. "Look inside of yourself, Arran. The bond between mates... it is the stuff of legend. You must feel it."

The pressure in my chest. The unexplained urges of the beast inside of me.

"Why did you wake from an enchanted sleep and come here? Why not Cayltay? Why not go to the war camps? You were drawn here, because *she* is here."

Even now, that feeling in my chest was painfully intense. It had driven me to Eilean Gayl, bound by bound, softening fractionally with every mile. But I thought it satisfied, it had eased—

In her presence.

Veyka.

If she was my mate then why did her name mean nothing to me?

My father rose to stand beside my mother, the two of them a steady wall, one strengthening the other. As it had always been. I had never seen their alliance falter.

They walked in tandem to the door, my father stepping ahead to open it for his wife, my mother letting him.

But she paused to look back at me, assessing. Reproving. "You look terrible. Go up to your room. Bathe. Sleep."

She did not wait to see if her order would be obeyed. The door shut behind them, and I was alone. Me and my beast.

Scolded like a child.

The Brutal Prince. High fucking King of Annwyn.

I slammed my fists into the wall hard enough that the room shook around me. But the stones of Eilean Gayl did not care about my anger or frustration. They held steady.

My head fell forward to join my fists.

Sleep.

My mother was right in that at least. I'd made plenty of battle plans, led armies to victory on less sleep and more exhaustion than my body was dealing with now. But this was more than I'd ever faced before. I was a hairsbreadth away from losing control to my beast. And if I did, there was no telling what havoc he would wreak.

41
VEYKA

I begged the Ancestors for sleep, my vows to never ask them for help again swallowed by the misery that filled every corner of my body and soul. To lose a husband, a mate... what did that mean? I thought I had understood. Living these last weeks without Arran, knowing I was the cause of his pain and near death, I had died myself. A little bit each day. Until I was nothing more than a shell around what had once been, for such a short time, a full and beating heart.

Dead.

Arran was not dead.

Arran is alive. He is alive. My mate is alive...

I started, suddenly awake. Rolled over, reaching for—

Nothing. No one. Alone. I was meant to be alone. *I deserve to be alone...*

Shivers wracked my body, dragging me from nightmares of swirling darkness and screams.

Cold... I'd been cold ever since we left Baylaur and crossed into the human realm. Was I never meant for warmth? Was warmth a privilege I did not deserve? *Like love...*

I was alone again in the forest, hunting down Gorlois' soldiers. There was the succubus, clawing its way across the frost-gilded forest floor. Bits of dried leaf and pine needles clung to the tarry black bile that coated its hands, its jaw, its face—Arran's face. I couldn't pull my amorite blades. I could not run. I fell to my knees, ready to let it take me. Let him take me. It was no more than I deserved. That fetid darkness, cutting through the crisp air to fill my nostrils... but it was not. It was spice and earth and warmth and Arran...

I didn't open my eyes. I was a fucking coward. Arran had known it from the moment he arrived in Baylaur. He'd called me useless, a waste of my crown. He was right. I was nothing without him, and now...

My eyes popped open against my will, an ingrained need to survive, to escape the darkness that found me even from behind what should have been the safety of my own eyelids.

A white wolf sat at my bedside, preternaturally still.

I blinked, trying to make it go away.

I was still sleeping. Still dreaming. I shut down that part inside of me that cared about my own survival and closed my eyes, even though I knew there would be no escape from this agony.

There was no longer a difference between sleeping and waking. It was all a nightmare.

42

VEYKA

Cyara had not managed to produce cosmetics from her secret stash. Not that it would have mattered. I doubted anything, human or fae, magical or otherwise, would have covered the dark circles under my eyes. I'd have looked better if someone had punched me. At least those bruises would heal.

"You should eat," Cyara said as she knotted the tail of my narrow plait. She'd braided from my right temple, over the top of my head, and down the left side, leaving the back of my hair loose to skim my shoulder blades. A strand of garnets glittered in the braid. A far cry from the ornate plaits she'd fashioned in Baylaur, but effective. Elegant. Regal.

A reminder to every terrestrial I encountered of who I was.

Perhaps a reminder to my mate as well.

My stomach clenched painfully. No, I would not be eating.

Cyara stepped away, sipping her tea as she went. Maybe I would be spared—

"Why haven't you gone to him?"

"He does not even remember my name," I said through clenched teeth.

"Maybe something has changed."

"Do you think if Arran remembered me, that he would be patiently waiting? That he would be anywhere but here?"

I watched Cyara's jaw clench beneath her otherwise smooth cheek. She was the consummate elemental. But she was also my friend.

"I think his chances of remembering you are better if you are in his company," Cyara said carefully. So careful, because she knew what she was proposing.

To spend time with Arran, to feel the pull of our bond, the growl of his wolf... but not to see the love in his eyes... it would be torture.

Cyara set down her tea, the rattle of the cup in its saucer unmistakable. Her hands were trembling. So were mine.

"This is not your fault, Veyka," she said, her voice steady even if her hands were not.

Of course. Cyara, only my keen and observant Cyara, could have plucked the thought so deftly from my mind.

"I begged the Lady of the Lake for his life."

"You did what you had to. I was there on that shore. I saw you, ready to take your own life rather than lose him," Cyara countered.

"But I did lose him."

I inhaled slowly—through the tender membranes of my nostrils, past my throat, sore from sobbing, into my lungs, somehow still functioning alongside my broken heart.

A hand curled around my shoulder. Strong. Steady. Constant.

I lifted my eyes to meet Cyara's in the mirror's reflection. Her chin may still have wobbled slightly, but the depths of her turquoise eyes were eternal. My friend, through all the battles to come.

"Then you should find your way back to him." She squeezed my shoulder tighter. "And I shall be at your side, no matter how long the journey."

"As will I."

I hadn't even heard Lyrena enter. It was a testament to just how lost I was.

My golden knight just grinned, resplendent as ever in her goldstone armor, and reached for my other shoulder.

My heart swelled in my chest. And it was still broken and I was broken and the world was royally fucked up. But at least in that moment, I was not alone.

But our peace was brief.

A knock sounded at the door. Not the one connecting my chamber to Lyrena, Cyara, Percival, and Diana. The one that led to the rest of Eilean Gayl. To reality.

Lyrena winked, squeezed my shoulder, and went to answer it. Cyara handed me the shadowvein tea, though I doubted I would need it anytime soon. Arran's beast may want to fuck me, but the male had looked at me with such contempt.

"He wants to see you," Lyrena's voice cut into my self pity parade.

I blinked.

He. Arran.

My eyes slid past Lyrena to the liveried guard standing in the arched doorway.

He didn't even bother to come himself.

Lyrena turned back to the guard expectantly. He eyed her, then me, clearly hoping he'd be allowed to escape now that he'd given my Goldstone Guard his message.

We all stared at him.

The other two were surely waiting for me to speak.

The guard's hand twitched. Then his jaw.

"His Majesty the High King requests that her Majesty join him in the study," he repeated. No one moved. "Promptly," he added, unable to hide his cringe.

His Majesty the High King requests that her Majesty join him in the study.

I could feel the pull in my chest, that incessant demand. I'd learned to trust it, to use it to determine how far away Arran was at any given moment. He was in this castle, maybe even in this same tower. No more than a floor or two away.

His Majesty the High King requests that her Majesty join him in the study.

We may as well have been on different continents. In different realms.

Cyara moved first. She reached for the heavy fur mantle she'd acquired in an ongoing attempt to keep me warm in this frozen hell.

I reached for my blades instead.

"Tell Arran that if he wishes to speak to me, he can come find me himself. No one summons the High Queen of Annwyn." I watched the color drain from the male's face as I strapped on my leather harnesses, then my belt with the scabbard and dagger.

Maybe it was cruel.

But if I stood in front of Arran just then, I did not know how I would keep myself from coming apart. And that could not happen. Not now, with the safety of Annwyn hanging by a thread.

I had already lost my mate.

I would not lose my kingdom as well.

43

ARRAN

"She said *what?*"

"If he wishes to speak with me—"

"I heard you the first time," I growled, slamming my fist down on the broad wooden desk. The oak groaned beneath the force but did not give. Less could be said for the messenger quaking before me.

He'd been sheet-white when he re-entered the chamber, one of my father's unused studies. The place I'd chosen to meet my wife again, on my own terms.

Wife, mate, queen. *Fuck.* It was too much. My head was already pounding.

I'd chosen to focus on the latter—queen. High King and Queen of Annwyn. Surely there were matters of state to attend to. Hence, the desk. I could not imagine Uther Pendragon, the former High King, ever sitting at a desk.

I could not have imagined any of it.

Which was the best justification I'd yet found that this might all be real.

"No one summons the High Queen of Annwyn," I repeated under my breath. I could just imagine the words leaving her full, lush lips. Lips that begged to be bitten. Lips that were far too clear in my mind for someone I had only met once.

Who was my mate.

Fuck.

The most grating part was that she was right.

As High King and Queen, we were co-rulers. Equals. It was how the balance between our two kingdoms was kept, generation after generation, for seven thousand years. I hadn't been an attentive student of history, but I knew that much.

That was bullshit.

I'd lost my Ancestors-damned memory. The least she could do was meet with me and explain... something. Everything.

"Fuck!" I slammed my other fist down.

The guard in front of me shivered. Little use he would be in a fight. I'd speak to my mother about having him reassigned. I would not have trusted him to guard my breakfast, let alone my home.

My fists clenched tighter.

Eilean Gayl had not been my home for many years. The Brutal Prince's only home was a war camp, a battlefield, with my battle axe in my hand.

The ever-present ache in my chest intensified. *Home.* I pressed my fist into my chest, rubbing in vain. I'd learned on my bounding trek to Eilean Gayl that nothing would soften it.

Someone would.

The beast inside of me yanked at his restraints.

It took more energy than it should have to shove my beast back down. When I looked back out of my fae eyes, I found the guard framed in the doorway, back pressed flush against the wood, as if he hoped he could melt through the ancient cracks.

"Where is she now?"

I could taste his fear. So could my beast.

"Her Majesty was going to the training yard, I believe," he mumbled. More coherent than I'd expected.

I walked to the window. It faced the wrong direction for me to be able to see her. But even through the leaded glass, my fae ears could hear the clash of metal.

I fingered the head of my axe, then the jeweled scabbard that had been on my belt since I'd awoken on the misty isle.

The queen wanted a fight?

I'd bring one to her.

The ache in my chest eased with every step. I wanted to resent that pull she had on me, but my beast would not allow it. As soon as the feeling rose in my chest, my beast devoured it. I tightened the restraints I held, ever present, to keep him in place.

I was so preoccupied trying to master myself that I did not realize where I was, how quickly I was walking. I was in the courtyard before I meant to be, quicker than should have been possible. Had I run through the hallways of Eilean Gayl without realizing it?

Then I saw her, and everything else ceased to matter.

The thread around my heart was so bright, so hot inside of me that it burned. My fingers tingled, my muscles tightened. I was burning from the inside out. Burning for her. Veyka.

No one had told me what to expect from my queen. But as I watched her move around the courtyard, I reassessed every presumption I'd made in the last twelve hours.

Last night, she'd worn a revealing gown that highlighted a luscious body meant for one thing. But in the gray light of morning, she'd put it to a different purpose entirely.

She was still breathtakingly beautiful, her moon-white hair swirling behind her as she swung and parried with such speed, unnatural even for a fae. Jewels studded her ears, from the soft lobe to the pointed tip, and there were gemstones braided into her hair as well. A queen, yes. But something else, something more.

A warrior battled before me, deadly curved blades held with loving ease as they swiped at her opponent. She'd traded the revealing gown for leather leggings and a cropped tunic that revealed a swath of pale skin around her midsection. The longer I looked, the more I recognized. The leather armor she wore was an approximation of my own, modified to fit her luscious curves.

Not just luscious, but deadly. I knew precisely where I'd fit her in my legion. But she fought without magic... what was her power? The abrupt disappearance from the great hall—why did she not manifest that same power in battle?

The answer came to me as I watched the duel barreling toward climax.

She did not need to.

That was how skilled she was.

She did not flinch when her opponent brought his blade down at a sharp, sudden angle. But I did.

My axe was in my hand before I formed the thought. Instinct guided my movements, experience paired with fury that sprang from a well inside of me deeper than any I'd accessed before.

The growl ripped from my throat, reverberating through the training courtyard. A fucking mistake, a warning to my enemies.

Her cry of ire battled mine, ricocheting off of the ancient, moss-covered stones. Her blade swiped across her opponent's side, the rich sent of blood flooding my senses. He staggered backward, out of range of my axe. I was so focused on him that I missed her attack entirely. She struck my chin with enough force to send my head reeling back. I struggled to right myself—*Fuck!* Pain sliced through my kneecaps.

I staggered, axe useless in my hand. I shoved it upward anyway, the instinct to protect my head and throat ingrained by three hundred years of battlefield slaughter. But no more blows came.

I kept my feet, but only just.

She'd tried to swipe my knees out from under me. The growl built in my chest, the beast inside of me insistent. Fine—I'd shift. I'd give in and—what? What would I do?

Fuck. Hardened battle commander? I was a fool.

This warrior queen had not only defended herself from attack, but she'd fought me off as well. She'd thought I was attacking her, not trying to save her.

What in the Ancestors' living hell did that say about our supposed marriage?

Our cries and growls had faded to nothing, leaving behind only ragged breathing. Mine was as tortured as hers, my chest moving in time with the rise and fall of her own as I dragged my gaze up her body to her face.

Her eyes—how had I not noticed them instantly? They raged with blue fire. She was an elemental, she ought to have been able to dissemble. But either the emotions were too much or she wasn't bothering to hide them as they blazed in her eyes. Anger and frustration, but that was not all. A bright circle glowed around the center of the black pupils. The one thing she could not hide, even had she been trying. The glow of desire.

She felt it too.

The pull of her gaze was magnetic. My heart beat faster, the tangle in my chest solidifying into something almost tangible. If I looked down, I might see the thread that stretched from my chest to hers, connecting us inexplicably.

Except it had been explained to me. She was my mate. This feeling in my chest, this compulsion, was the mating bond making itself known. My fingers ached, urging me to reach out and touch her. That was ludicrous. She'd just shoved me backward, almost knocked me on my ass in front of half of Eilean Gayl.

Terrestrials lined the battlements. Her own companion, an elemental dressed in ornamental goldstone, watched us with arms crossed over her chest. The white faerie who'd dogged my steps since Avalon hovered at the golden one's side.

But I noted all these details without really internalizing them. They were part of the landscape, the periphery of relevance. I was aware in the way I might be on a battlefield of the fighting happening around me. Just enough attention to ward off threats, but not enough to distract from the challenge directly in front of me.

My mate.

To my right, someone scuffled and sighed. Her defeated opponent, sent sprawling across the flagstones on the far side of the training ring.

The male grumbled. "What the Ancestors—Arran."

Ripping my gaze away from her was almost painful. But I knew that voice. I recognized the figure clambering to his feet. "Barkke."

My longtime friend, sometimes rival, brushed the dirt off of his ass where she'd thrown him into the dirt. He winced as he stood, which is when I remembered the scent of blood. She'd slashed at his side. A minor wound, knitting back together even as Barkke approached, eyes wary. But his words belied the caution in his gaze.

"I would tell you that you looked well, but terrestrials don't lie," Barkke said, clapping me on the shoulder. Very few would have dared. Certainly not a member of the terrestrial armies. But Barkke had known me since childhood, and obviously felt himself entitled to certain intimacies. Which is why he dared to add, "You look like utter shit."

Slowly, so slowly, I turned my head to look at where his broad hand rested on my shoulder.

"Says the male who was just on his ass," I bit back. I lowered my axe, returning it to the notch on my belt. My control had snapped so quickly, I did not even recall drawing it. Instincts were one thing. Loss of control was another. Who had I become, that the mere threat of injury—an injury she could surely have healed from—had rendered the control I'd fought hundreds of years to master utterly useless? What was it about this female that unhinged every carefully moored tether of control?

"Not for long. Never for long." Barkke chuckled, retracting his hand and running it through his overlong hair. A few shades lighter than mine, it was just as long. He'd let his beard grow out, thicker than ever. But other than that, he looked the same as he always had. And he elicited the same feelings in me. Mostly annoyance, but buried deep within me, there was a grain of affection.

Not that I planned on showing it to him. I scowled. He just smiled broader. Ass.

"Come to claim your prize?" he said, nodding to the center of the ring.

She was not feigning any sort of indifference. She watched our exchange closely, the blazing blue fire in her eyes only slightly dimmed.

"I am not a prize to be won," she snapped. As she spoke, she reached her arms overhead, sliding the twin rapiers into their sheaths across her back with practiced ease. "Nor did either of you do any winning."

I felt the tick in my jaw, clenching my teeth together to still it. "He had you. I only intervened—"

"I know why you intervened," she said sharply. "I had him, and I had you."

Her eyes were still glowing. I knew that if there'd been a mirror to hand, I'd have seen black fire in mine as well.

"Spar with me."

Barkke had melted back, leaving Veyka and I staring each other down in the center of the training courtyard with two dozen terrestrials looking on. There was nothing to be gained by sparring. We valued strength above all else. If the High King and Queen dueled, one of us would beat the other, and that would leave the other diminished in the eyes of their subjects. But I didn't take it back.

Something inside of me wanted to tangle with her. Not just sexually, though my cock was tight at the mere thought. But I wanted to test myself against her, to see if my body would move in complement to hers. I suspected that it might.

Her chin cut a sharp, straight horizontal line through the brisk air. "No."

I stepped closer—compelled, again. My beast, the mating bond, the lust that was burning in my cock, it did not matter which of them was in charge. They were all in agreement as I lifted one eyebrow. "Afraid?"

Veyka threw back her head and laughed, planting her hands on her generous hips. "I don't want to embarrass you."

"You could try," I growled.

"I would succeed." Her voice slid over me like a lover's touch. The sultry whisper, for me alone, slid past every defense I had. Her eyes flared—she knew. She fucking knew how easily she was able to get inside of me, to appeal to my beast and my baser instincts.

"Prove it."

Her tumultuous eyes flashed once more, then shuttered. There was the cool, calculated façade I'd expected from the Queen of the Elemental Fae. She lifted her chin a fraction of an inch, determination set in every line of her pale, angular face. "Not here."

"Not here," I repeated, under my breath.

Because she got to choose. She understood the stakes, better than I ever hoped to. The last few months of my life were completely blank. Yule had just passed. But my last memory was of a war camp on the eastern edge of Wolf Bay. Months and months ago. Now, King Arthur was dead, I was mated and High King, and there was more. I could feel it in my mother's gaze, in Veyka's careful aloofness. There was more at stake here than I could puzzle out, and I knew nothing.

I was so fucking angry.

I drew my battle axe. "Here. Now."

I did not care if it was a mistake. I did not care if it was politically infantile. I wanted to make her suffer the way I was suffering. I wanted to make everyone suffer. I tensed my muscles, ready to spring forward—

She disappeared.

Gone.

My axe did not even have a chance to fall before I felt her, my senses filling with primrose and plum a second before she reappeared at my side.

She grabbed my arm. The beast inside of me howled his approval at the contact, the blood in my veins rushing at such speed I could hear it in my ears. My entire being narrowed to that point of contact, everything else melting away. Not quite pain, but something close to agony. Memories swirled through my vision. A barren valley, a half-remembered male face. Pain. Such unbearable pain...

I forced my eyes open, unwilling to lose myself to the pain again.

But there was nothing to see but the swirling black void.

44
VEYKA

My mind mirrored the whirling eddies of the void. Arran showing up in the training courtyard, looking every inch the male he'd been before that horrible day in the cursed clearing. Watching Barkke and I sparring. I could feel the weight of his gaze, the pressure of the bond between us so demanding I'd nearly staggered under the force of it.

But the mate I'd known would not have intervened. He knew me well enough, trusted my skills enough to let me defend myself. My Arran would have known that Barkke, for all that he was a well-trained and brutal terrestrial warrior, was no match for me.

The urge to spar with him when he demanded it had almost overwhelmed me. Were we ever more whole, more attuned to one another than when we battled hand to hand, blade to blade? Yes— when we fought side by side.

Because the only thing I missed more than the warrior who had challenged me in the sparring ring of the goldstone palace was the male who had taught me to trust myself and my magic.

And I almost gave in. I knew that fucking him would be devastating. But feeling the weight of his battle axe, pushing it away, battling against someone who was actually my match... I craved it. I craved him. And still, it would have been a mistake. For so many reasons, not the least of which was it made me vulnerable, and I could not allow that in front of the terrestrials. Not if I wanted them to heed my warnings about the succubus, to truly accept me as their queen.

Then the anger in his gaze, the fury that set his eyes burning not with desire but with wrath... I had to get him away before he shifted. I had not seen Arran in the moments after my disappearance from our Joining, but I understood the loss of control and the consequences of it. Ripping apart our enemies was one thing, punishing those who betrayed us; those I would always support. But the Brutal Prince was known for his control; we could not afford for him to lose it, no matter what damage I'd done to his soul by shoving a sword through his heart.

I moved quickly. Even with my mind in tumult, my heart threatening to shatter inside of me, I was in control of that ember of magic inside of me. I stepped through the void, bringing Arran with me, and knew that it would work. That even though my power was tied to him, and our relationship was in fragments, I still commanded the void.

Arran, however, had no idea what to expect.

He hit his knees hard as we landed on a mountain top, one of the many we'd woven our way between on our journey to Eilean Gayl. Still firmly within Annwyn, but far enough away that even a flying terrestrial shifter would struggle to reach us in the time it took to have this conversation.

"What was that?" Arran demanded.

No blades of grass elongated to reach around my boots and hold me in place. I supposed that was as good a sign as any. He was angry, but he did not view me as the enemy. At least, not as one who needed to be restrained. Not yet.

I licked my lips, taking a step back to give him space to gain his feet and still keep plenty of cold mountain air between us. "The void power."

His laugh was sharp, humorless. "That is a legend."

"If you have trouble swallowing that, just wait until you hear what else I have to tell you." He did not laugh at that. I crossed my arms over my chest. For once, not to highlight my breasts and taunt him, but to protect myself from the inevitable pain. "Not a legend. A prophecy. One that you and I fulfilled on the day of our Joining."

He stood, and suddenly the several feet of space I'd put between us was not nearly enough. I could see the fight in every inch of his powerful body. He'd dressed in the terrestrial style, drawing from an armoire or bedroom that had probably been his for hundreds of years. Despite the cold, punishing wind ripping across the mountaintop, he did not shiver. No hint of gooseflesh rose along his exposed throat. I imagined I could see the uppermost branches of his Talisman. I wanted to trace every line with my fingertips, to feel his heart beating beneath. Maybe that would ease this shattered, broken thing inside of me.

But Arran did not move toward me, and I would not force myself upon him. His jaw ticked and the familiarity of it nearly brought me to my knees.

I'd never known anyone so well, not even Arthur. There had not been enough time. But Arran... I recognized the clench of his muscles and the tightening of his jaw. I knew him intimately, and I'd let him know me. That loss felt as painful as the memories.

When he opened his brutal slash of a mouth and spoke, his voice was hard but calm. "Tell me."

A command from the Brutal Prince. Not my husband or mate.

Half a day he'd been at Eilean Gayl, and he already knew something was wrong. Why else would we be here and not in Baylaur? Why else would he be missing his memories?

Slowly, I exhaled. I forced my arms to relax and hang at my sides. Arran's expression was hard, that unforgiving mask he wore to keep all other emotions at bay so that he could make clear decisions and intimidate those around him. I was not intimidated by him, but by the scope of explaining the last year of my life. Everything had changed. I had changed.

I turned away from him, looking out across the tall green mountains. The higher peaks around us were dusted with snow, but this one was all grass and craggy rocks. It was still brutally cold. I did not bother trying to encase my heart in ice as I summoned up the words to explain. There was no protecting my heart from Arran. There never had been.

"Seven thousand years ago, the Ancestors fought the Great War," I began.

"I know the history—"

"No. I don't think you do," I said sharply. I leveled him a look that promised violence if he interrupted me again. He stared right back. When I did not back down, he crossed his arms and lifted one black eyebrow. I would not get any more agreement than that.

"The Great War was not about the Terrestrial and Elemental Kingdoms. Or at least, it was not entirely about that. The exact details are vague, but..." I chewed over my next words. What to explain, how much, to a male who did not know me and had no reason to trust me. The truth; or as close to it as I could manage. I owed Arran that much. "Our Ancestors were not fighting each other. They were fighting something else, something worse. A great darkness."

I waited for any sign of recognition. A flicker of his black eyes, a shift in his stance, anything to indicate that he sensed the gravity of what I was explaining, that he recognized the importance of this on some subconscious level, even if he could not fully place it.

Nothing. He truly does not remember.

"The succubus."

He did not react.

"It takes over the minds of men while they sleep. It sinks into their consciousness, rendering their body into a monster. They feel no pain. They will stop at nothing to feed, to tear apart those around them." The only sign that Arran was internalizing any of it was that infernal tick in his jaw. I wanted to scream. "Entire villages destroyed as husbands and fathers wake in the night, taken by the succubus, and feast on the flesh of their wives and children. Hundreds of them moving in packs, waves of darkness that overcome even the most skilled fae warriors, because they simply *do not stop*."

I could see the horror of it, playing across my mind with the clarity that could only be conjured by memory. The human village burning. The mass of succubus encircling us in the clearing above the faerie caves. The half-body of the fae male crawling across the forest floor.

For a second, I envied Arran the loss of those terrible memories. They still haunted me, waking and dreaming.

Arran uncrossed his arms, one hand fingering the head of his axe. "How do you kill them?"

I saw the calculation in his eyes, then. This was why he was such a successful battle commander. He did not allow himself to be overwhelmed by these horrors, which allowed him to make a plan. Ancestors, I'd missed him. I'd missed having a true partner.

I curled one hand around the hilt of a dagger to keep from reaching for him. "Flames will hold them back temporarily. Beheading seems to work. The surest way is with amorite blades. Once one has been taken by the succubus, there is no redemption. There is only death."

His face betrayed him, black gaze narrowing in disbelief I was certain he did not mean to show me. "Amorite is a gemstone, not a weapon."

I held his gaze. "Until now."

Without breaking eye contact, I drew one of the curved blades from my back. Arran did not flinch, but he tracked the movement. His eyes changed, so slightly that months ago, I would have missed it. But now I recognized the beast within him, straining for control.

Did his wolf see me as a threat? I would have thought that even if Arran could not remember me, that his beast would recognize me for who—and what—I was. But maybe even that had been taken from me.

I lifted my other hand, laying the blade across my palms so that he could examine it. "Gifted to me by my brother. The rapiers, my knives, and Excalibur."

A step closer. He leaned in. I tilted my hand so that the blades caught the watered-down winter sunlight overhead, clearly illuminating the swirls of silver. It was beautiful, the sparkling amorite contrasting with the steel to create a pattern like curling smoke, unfurling along the delicately curved blade.

Arran examined it closely, but did not reach for it. Nor for me. When he stepped back, I slid the blade back into its sheath.

"Five blades. Against an enemy that comes in the darkness."

I nodded. "The amorite is effective against them even in its gemstone form. Wearing it will prevent possession, though they can still tear you apart just fine."

Arran's fingertips lifted to trace the stud in his ear. I'd given him one of my own earrings after we found out the truth in the faerie caves. "You said men. This is a human plague."

If only.

"It began in the human realm. Perhaps because they are weaker and more feeble-minded, they were easier to possess. But I've seen them take a fae male as well, in the forests outside of Avalon. Annwyn is not safe."

The words were hardly out of my mouth when the Brutal Prince spoke, his voice clear and strong. "We must protect Annwyn."

There he was—the male I'd fallen in love with. The one who had taught me not only that I was worthy of love, but that my kingdom was as well. The king Annwyn needed.

I searched his face, trying to find some sign that the male who had loved me lived inside of Arran still. The thick arch of his brows was just as it had always been. The muted sunlight deepened the shadow of stubble along his strong, square jaw. His dark hair would feel exactly the same curling around my fingertips, impossibly silky for a male who'd rightfully earned the title of Brutal Prince.

I felt my façade, the placid elemental mask I kept in place, beginning to slip.

I wanted to reach for him, to throw myself into his arms and let him comfort me. It had taken me so long to allow him in, to admit that I loved him, only for him to be ripped away. First physically, and now... I did not even know how to describe the agony of having my mate standing right in front of me, but feeling him lost.

My fault.

Every terrible thing that had happened came down to me. Arthur was murdered to put me on the throne. We were lured to Avalon so Gorlois could capture me. The succubus had returned to Annwyn because I had begun to open the rifts.

Maybe it was stupid and selfish. But I could not bring myself to tell him the part I'd played in it all. That my void power was the reason the succubus had come to Annwyn again after seven thousand years.

He would figure it out. He would have more questions. Arran Earthborn had not become the commander of the terrestrial armies by being stupid.

But he already looked at me with such conflict in his ominous black eyes, I could not give him one more reason to doubt me. The Arran who loved me would never have blamed me, would have helped me work through my guilt. But this Arran? I didn't know, and I was too scared to find out.

I hooked my thumbs around the daggers on my belt. Arran marked the movement. His eyes had not left me since I'd brought us here. But if there was desire burning in his eyes, I could not see it. Not behind all the other emotions. Maybe that was why I did not see the next question coming.

"What about us?"

All the air was sucked from my lungs. My fingers began to tingle. The void called to me, promising sweet escape. If I let myself go now, maybe I could travel to another realm entirely. A place without this love and attachment that had led to such pain.

A low growl rolled through me, rooting me to the spot. Issuing a command.

Arran's eyes remained unchanged, expectant.

"What do you want to know?" I said, hating the choked whisper.

"Our marriage was arranged, demanded by the Ancestors to keep peace between our kingdoms."

"That is not question." But I still knew the answer he wanted.

Another faint growl, this one from his lips. "But we are more than husband and wife, king and queen."

I waited. A second, then five, ten. A full minute. Arran stared at me, waiting.

Fine.

I planted one hand on each hip, readying for a different sort of battle. One that would not involve blades, but would hurt so much more. "We are mates."

He shook his head slowly. My hands curled into fists.

"It is more than a legend." I felt my frustration rising. It was not fair to be angry at him. He was trying to piece it all together. But I could not stop it. I was held together by my own stubbornness and the echo of a love lost. It wasn't enough.

"You were the one who recognized it for what it was, this bond between us," I said, my voice rising with each word. "And now, you don't even believe me."

I felt the growl of his beast rolling through me. It was so fucking perfect. I'd missed him so much. And even though I was coming apart into a thousand tiny pieces, still desire for him unspooled inside of me. The way that growl soothed all the broken edges of my soul, saw the darkness within me and did not retreat...

Arran's brows knit together. "I do believe you. My beast—"

"Thinks I am fucking delicious. I know what that growl means."

Arran's eyes blew wide, his mouth curling into something like a snarl. I wanted to regret my brash words, but it felt so damn *right*.

"You can hear my beast."

I can talk to him too.

"Get out of my head."

Fuck. Me.

It wasn't going to be a blade or a succubus that killed me. It was the male I loved—systematically chipping away pieces of my heart.

The heart he had healed.

Maybe some of us just weren't meant to be happy.

Maybe it had been foolish to think I even deserved it.

I turned away, stalking to the edge of the mountain where a sheer drop fell away, a thousand feet or more. If I was lucky, maybe a strong wind would come along and knock me off of it.

I waited for Arran to join me. Knew that he would. I even knew what his line of thinking was going to be, because we'd been here before. In Baylaur, he'd spent hours lecturing me on duty and trying to ignore the desire raging between us. I had changed since then, but Arran had been thrown backward—to the male who would do anything for the sake of his kingdom, rather than his mate.

"We need a plan of action. If the succubus is coming for Annwyn, we must be ready," he said from behind me. From the pressure in my chest, I knew he'd left a solid two yards between us.

"What do you think I've been doing here?" I said, refusing to look back at him. "We need amorite. It is the easiest form of protection. Every piercing, every necklace, is one less terrestrial we need to worry about ripping us to shreds while we sleep."

"There isn't enough. Not for every male in Annwyn. We must prepare for a fight. Summon the armies. We should be using the amorite to forge weapons." His voice was full of command.

"How typically terrestrial of you, to choose the violent approach."

"Do not pretend that you are above violence."

I closed my eyes. Forced myself to feel the weight of the blades strapped across my back, the daggers hanging at my waist.

"I crave it," I said truthfully. "But it was you who taught me the importance of strategy."

"Then listen. Learn."

The superiority in his voice had me spinning on my heel. "You may be three hundred years old. But until a few days ago, you were in an enchanted sleep. Nuance is not a terrestrial strength, even when you're not incapacitated."

It almost felt normal. Like we might have been sitting at the Round Table, sparring until we came to an agreement. But Parys was not here to offer a clever quip. Cyara had not been listening carefully, waiting to share her insight. I even missed Gwen's brutal but efficient way of cutting through the bullshit.

Arran's black eyes were unreadable. The commander's mask, firmly back in place. I knew that expression well. He might believe me, but he did not trust me. He also did not understand all the intricacies at play, not yet. If he did not trust me, then I had to make the best decisions I could without him. I still had Lyrena and Cyara.

I extended a hand, even knowing that touching him would be torture. "Let's go back."

He did not reach for me. "Why was I in an enchanted sleep?"

I blinked. No. *No, no, no, no, no.*

"You are the only one who can tell me."

My throat was closing, but somehow I managed to get words out. "Lyrena and Cyara were there as well. And Isolde."

His eyes flickered with recognition, then shuttered again. "The faerie refused to tell me anything useful."

"Isolde is a loyal friend."

"Tell me the truth, Veyka."

My name on his lips was my undoing. I could not hold back the dam, the flood of words, my confession breaking in an uncontrolled wave.

"We went to Avalon to learn about the Void Prophecy. We were lured into a trap and attacked by an enemy from my past." I did not go into detail about Gorlois or who he'd been in the twisted story of my past. I could not give him those parts of me again, not now, not like this. "I killed him. And in the process, I nearly killed you."

"Y... you..." I had never seen Arran stumble over his words. Not once. Not ever.

"Me," I whispered, watching his face crumble. Watching any chance I might have had of winning back his love disappearing as I spoke. "I was the one who stabbed you in the chest with Excalibur. I am the reason you nearly died."

45
VEYKA

Arran shifted into his beast form and sprinted off without another word to me. Maybe I should have gone after him, but the message he sent was clear. He did not want me.

I sank into the void, letting it wrap around me and offer the comfort that my mate no longer could. I landed in my bedroom far too soon. A moment. That was all it took to move through the void. What would it feel like to linger there? There were other planes of existence, other realms beyond the human, succubus, and Annwyn. What if I went to one of those? Would the pain of my shattered heart still exist?

But my feet landed on the thick scarlet and gold carpet that failed to warm the stone chamber. I missed the warmth of the gold-stone walls of Baylaur. Once, they'd been my cage. Now, I wanted to curl up against them like a cat.

The bed called to me. It, at least, was warm. Each night, Cyara heated bricks with her fire, layering the stones beneath the foot of the mattress. The thick velvet draperies and heavy quilts sealed in the heat. When I caught Cyara rubbing at her wrists, I'd ordered her to stop, insisting I would be warm enough. But the next night, the bricks were in place as usual.

When my feet moved, it was not toward the comforting softness of the bed. That was the escape I'd taken once. I missed it. My world had been simpler when my only concern was revenge.

The door to the chamber opened, Lyrena sweeping in with a laugh on her lips.

My world had been emptier then, too.

"Welcome back," my golden knight said flippantly, flashing a smile that showed her gold-capped tooth. "Did you and Arran have that duel?" Her razor-sharp grin was edged with double-sided innuendo.

My heart gripped, but I forced myself to smile through it.

The corners of Lyrena's mouth softened in response. It must have come out as a grimace.

"Where is Cyara?" I asked.

Lyrena nodded over my shoulder, to the door that connected my room to the shared sitting room.

I met her nod with a sharper one of my own. "We don't have a round table, but we'll make do with what we have. You get the food."

※

The spread was impressive given the short notice. Lyrena must have charmed the terrestrials working in the kitchens. Not a surprise, really. It was impossible not to be charmed by that easy laugh and golden smile. It was part of what made her so formidable as a guard. She looked like she'd rather laugh than fight. And maybe that was even the truth. But she was deadly with the massive sword that hung at her waist, and anyone who underestimated her did not deserve my pity.

Right now, she was using her gilded golden teeth to rip into a yeast bun that looked like it was more air than dough. I held out the crock of honeyed butter to her before reaching for a roll of my own.

Cyara fluttered around us, pouring wine and fixing plates for

Diana and Percival. I did not comment on the kindness as I dolloped a crushed tomato spread onto my roll, topping it with a thick slice of ham and an even thicker cut of cheese before taking a bite. I did not even try to restrain the audible groan of appreciation that spilled from my lips.

Lyrena shot the layered bun in my hand an appraising look, then reached for the tomato spread herself.

Cyara paused before each dish, glancing sideways. She was being very subtle, but I was much too attuned to food to miss the action. On the other end of that glance, Diana's chin rose and fell, or twitched side to side, equally subtly. The potatoes mashed with cream and so much garlic it brought tears to my eyes? No. The slices of sweet red apple and soft, blue-veined cheese? Yes.

When those two plates were filled and delivered to the prisoners, only then did Cyara return to the small rectangular table and serve herself. I dabbed at my mouth with a napkin, took a long drink of my wine, and then crossed my arms. "Something you care to share, Cyara?"

She did not look up from buttering a roll of her own. "You called this meeting of the... Round Table, Majesty."

I rolled my eyes.

"I have sent word to Baylaur and Wolf Bay, warning them of the threat of the succubus. Gwen will take the proper precautions, I have no doubt. As for those in Cayltay..."

Lyrena paused mid-bite. "You are the High Queen. They should listen to you without question."

I laughed at that, wishing it were true. "If the directive came from Arran, maybe they would. But Cayltay is a long way from Baylaur. My own court barely knew my face until a few months ago. I may technically rule the terrestrial kingdom, but without enforcement—"

"—they can do whatever they want," Cyara finished. I almost missed the days when she kept her quiet observations to herself. "It is why there is usually a royal progress shortly after the Joining," she added.

"I don't have time for a progress, and I doubt Arran would willingly accompany me on one anyway." I let that hang in the air for a few beats. Lyrena suddenly found her cutlery very interesting.

Cyara's turquoise eyes held mine.

"Have you been speaking with Lady Elayne?" I asked, fingers tightening around my now empty wine glass.

"No. But it does not surprise me that she's mentioned it." I lifted my eyebrows for the rest of the explanation. Cyara pursed her lips, as if it should be obvious. "She's been at the center of Annwyn's politics for most of her life, against her will. She'd be wise to anticipate events such as the progress and their implications."

First as the foretold mother of a child of unforeseen power, then as the mother of the Brutal Prince who eventually became king. Cyara's point was clear—Elayne was a formidable ally. I had accepted her comfort and her advice, but I hadn't thought to use her on the offensive. Arran would hate the idea—and probably me—for even proposing it.

I'd think more about that later.

"One thing at a time. We must give enough time for our missives to be delivered to Baylaur, and for Gwen to send a response." The idea of sitting around and waiting made my legs twitch beneath the table. But Annwyn was a vast kingdom. Even with airborne terrestrials bearing my missives, it would take weeks to hear back. Though there was another way.

"You could go to Baylaur faster," Cyara said, stealing the thoughts from my head. If I had not known better, I might have thought she was part of the Ethereal Prophecy with the way she always seemed to know what I was thinking.

I opened my mouth to respond, to excuse, but—

"She would be unguarded," Lyrena cut in sharply. There was no food in her hand now, and her bright eyes were fixed on Cyara with a look of absolute reproach.

My handmaiden's white wings shifted softly. "Go with her."

I did not know what that would mean for my power. How many jumps through the void would it take, and how would carrying

Lyrena with me affect my power? What would the cost be? I had not yet seen an impact from my magic, nothing like the near comatose sleep that had taken Lyrena after she'd staunched the flames of the burning human village. But such a huge expenditure of power, surely there would be something.

Would I wake to find my memories gone, like Arran?

I remembered to set down the wineglass before it shattered in my hand.

Once, I would have welcomed the loss of every gruesome memory. It would have seemed a brilliant reprieve. But now, losing my memories meant losing *them*. My friends. Even if Cyara and Lyrena were currently yowling at each other like skoupuma kittens.

"And leave the King behind? I am also his Goldstone guard." Lyrena's usual grin was nowhere in evidence on her face. Was I imagining it, or was the tip of her golden tooth slightly pointed?

Cyara shrugged with contrived irreverence. "You haven't been doing much guarding down in the kitchens."

Lyrena had a reputation for carousing in the kitchens and guard barracks in Baylaur as well. But I did not realize she'd made friends here at Eilean Gayl… Unsurprising. She was the easiest person to love.

I shook my head, bringing my hand down flat on the table with more force than I'd intended—startling them into silence. "What is happening here? Are you two arguing? With each other?"

"Yes," they said in unison.

"Why—what in the Ancestor's frigid hell is happening?" I rubbed my temples. "Usually you are too busy arguing with me to squabble with one another."

Lyrena grinned, and it was more than a little predatory. I felt a rush of heat, suspected that if I looked down I'd find flames curling around her fingertips.

Which reminded me of another. "Where is Isolde in all of this?"

"Avoiding terrestrials who want to touch her skin and examine her claws," Lyrena smirked. "She is keeping an eye on Arran," she added, golden brows lifting in time with her lips in a smug smile aimed directly at Cyara.

Cyara would not do anything as indelicate as roll her eyes, so I did it for her.

Which gave her the opportunity to ask, "What about Arran?"

Across the room, the sound of cutlery scraping against plates ceased. Everyone was listening now, even our prisoners. I sucked in my cheeks, teeth catching on the soft flesh inside my lower lip. When the tangy taste of my own blood met my tongue, I spoke. "We move on without Arran."

Cyara's wings flared above her shoulders. "He is the High King of Annwyn."

"He's the next thing to an invalid." It was cruel, but it was the truth. "We can't trust him."

Lyrena reached for me next. Actually reached for me, her hand closing over my arm. "Veyka—"

"He does not trust me."

Arran could not be told what to do. As much as I wanted to throw myself into his arms and beg him to love me, to trust me and believe me and *remember me*, it would mean nothing. Not to the Brutal Prince. The male who had emerged from Avalon was not the mate I'd left behind.

"Arran has to figure out where he stands in all of this. We cannot do it for him. I've explained the threat of the succubus." I caught Cyara's eyes cutting to Diana and Percival. She was too good at hiding her thoughts and feelings for the motion to have been anything but intentionally meant for me. I ignored it. "Until Arran remembers... or he decides... this discussion stays between us."

"We await word from Gwen. But in the meantime, we need to get to the amorite mines. Until we know how much there is, we cannot decide what purpose to put it to." I heard Arran's voice in my mind. He wanted to make weapons. I wanted to protect as many individuals as possible. The argument was immaterial until we had quantities.

I could almost understand it, the deep place of calculation

where Arran went when assessing a battle. That was exactly what this was—a race against time. Before the succubus came in numbers we would have no hope of beating back. Pretending it was nothing more than numbers, than movements in a dance, might make it easier to bear. But if the shattered wall of ice around my heart had taught me anything, it was that now that I'd released the cage on my heart and its capacity to love and care, there was no closing that door ever again.

46
CYARA

"What are you doing?"

Cyara managed not to flinch at the clear shock and reprimand in Veyka's sharp voice. She had been expecting it and had prepared herself accordingly. Not even a flutter of wings to betray her nerves.

The queen did not usually make her nervous. But she understood the enormity of what she was about to ask. There was every chance that Veyka was going to react horribly. To be anything other than nervous would be foolish.

Willing her wings not to twitch, she finished unlatching Percival and Diana's restraints and stepped aside to let them approach the table. "They are taking the trays down to the kitchens, where they will assist with the dishes."

Veyka did not move from her seat, did not even reach for the daggers always at her waist. But the look in her blue eyes was clear —it promised pain, dismemberment, and murder if either of the half-witch humans made a move out of line.

"They are prisoners, not servants," Veyka said.

Cyara waited in silence, hands folded in front of herself while the pair gathered up the remnants of the meal. She had been laying the groundwork for this conversation all afternoon. She had spoken with Lyrena about it.

Cyara had no problem contradicting her queen. But she rarely did so without careful thought and preparation.

When Percival and Diana stepped away from the table and started toward the door, Veyka shot to her feet. Cyara was ready for this as well.

"Lyrena will accompany them," she said smoothly. And before the argument in the queen's stormy blue eyes could make its way to her lips, she added, "Your Majesty—Veyka—if we might speak privately?"

The anger melted away from Veyka's eyes instantly. She held her posture, rigid and aggressive, until the door to the outer corridor closed behind Lyrena and the two prisoners. Then she melted as well, her muscles softening, concern clouding her eyes.

"What is it? What's wrong? Are you ill? I told you to stop with the damn bricks." She advanced as she spoke, a mixture of admonition and concern that only Veyka Pendragon could have managed so authentically.

Warmth kindled in Cyara's chest. But she only allowed a small smile to grace her lips.

"It is not the bricks, Veyka," she said. This time when her wings twitched, she did not try and hold it back. Veyka's sharp eyes tracked the motion, the frown lines around her mouth deepening. Cyara hated to manipulate her like this, but she had to win this argument. "You are going to dislike the idea I am about to propose, but I hope you will do me the courtesy of hearing my reasoning to its conclusion."

Veyka took a step backward, unsteady on her feet. The back of her calves hit the footstool that stood by the sofa. She sank down into it, her tall, commanding stature deflating.

"You doubt that I would?" She tried hard to disguise the pain that edged her voice, but Cyara knew her better than anyone, save her mate.

That was not a blow Cyara had intended to level. *Ancestors.* She wanted Veyka to listen, not to hurt her. She should have known better. The queen was making a good show of it, but her entire world had been ripped apart for the second time in as many years.

But Cyara swallowed back the need to comfort her friend. This was for the good of Veyka, Arran, and all of Annwyn.

"I believe it is time to loosen our hold on Percival and Diana," Cyara said.

Veyka's hand darted to her waist, curling around the hilt of her dagger. Cyara knew she would not draw it. It was an instinctual reaction, a way for Veyka to remind herself that she was in control. "Percival is the one who led us to Gorlois. He stuck a knife in Lyrena's back—*my* knife."

Cyara nodded. Her hands were still folded in front of her, maintaining the careful picture of composure and calm. "He did so to protect his sister. Surely you can understand that."

Veyka was as good as any elemental at hiding her emotions. It was her default when those emotions ranged high, threatening to surge out of control. But she did not pull that mask into place now.

Another surge of warmth crested in Cyara's chest. Admiration rose as well. To have suffered as Veyka had, to have lost her mate, but not to retreat back to that place of dark apathy…

"Go on," Veyka said. Cyara could not let herself get caught up in her own emotions, either.

"Diana is safe with us. Safer than she would be outside of our protection, on her own in the human realm, even with Percival at her side. No human can protect her the way a fae can." She had thought about it at length and even discussed it with Diana. Diana wanted safety. Percival wanted to protect Diana. Those were motivations they could use to their advantage.

"Not all fae will protect her. The only reason none of the terrestrials have slaughtered her is because she is my prisoner," Veyka countered. There was an edge of brutality in her voice, as if she wished one of the terrestrials would just take care of the problem for her. But Cyara charged on anyway.

"Which is why I do not believe they should be allowed to freely roam Eilean Gayl," she explained. She took a careful, low breath that did not betray her next words. "I think we should give them over into the care of the priestess here."

Veyka's bright blue eyes blew wide with surprise. Followed quickly by a low growl that Cyara vaguely noted would have made Arran proud, before rushing on with her proposal.

"Lady Elayne has told us that the priestess here is loyal to her, that she and her acolyte do not grasp for more power than their due. They are also the keepers of the ancient texts, in lieu of a formal library."

Veyka's mouth went from surprise, to snarl, and then to pursed as she realized what Cyara was implying. "There could very well be a library in Cayltay."

"There is," Cyara agreed. She had confirmed as much by speaking to the friendlier terrestrials at Eilean Gayl. "But we are not leaving for Wolf Bay yet. We do not know the disposition of the priestesses there. But here, we might use Diana and Percival to our own purposes. They grew up in Avalon. They are more likely than any of us elementals to be trusted by the terrestrial priestesses, taken into their confidence, and given access to the ancient tomes."

Veyka exhaled slowly through her nose. "You think the priestess may have information about the succubus."

"I think that they may not realize what information they hold." That was the truth. Cyara doubted that they would find the word succubus anywhere in the lore of the terrestrials. If Lady Elayne was half the female Cyara expected she was, she had already asked the priestess about it. But that did not mean there was no record of their foe. Only that it had not been named as such.

But all of those musings were immaterial if the queen refused.

Veyka stared at her for several minutes. The time stretched out between them, but Cyara did not breach it. She had asked Veyka to listen, and she had. Now she must give her the time to sort through it all in her head. Cyara knew that for all that Veyka proclaimed them equals, and discussed her thoughts openly with the Knights of the Round Table, the only person with her full confidence had been

Arran. With him ripped away, she could not fathom what eddies swirled and tugged at Veyka's mind.

Finally, she signed and pushed to her feet. "You have spoken to Diana?"

Cyara nodded. "Yes."

"And you believe that Percival will comply as well?" Veyka asked, eyes drifting to the place on the wall where the traitor had been anchored since their arrival. The expression in her eyes was clear—she still thought him a traitor.

"I do," Cyara answered steadily. No twitch of her white wings.

Veyka's chin stabbed the air sharply as she turned away, decision made.

"Fine," she said over her shoulder. "You will stay and monitor them while Lyrena and I go to the amorite mines. Isolde will stay with you as well. The Faeries of the Fen did not forget the succubus, even when the rest of the fae did. She may be helpful to you."

She walked to the door that connected the sitting room to her own chamber. Not a retreat, but a dismissal. The decision was made, she would not question it. At least, not to anyone but herself. But she paused in the doorway, turning back and spearing Cyara with a look so intense, she found herself unable to move.

"You did not expect me to agree," Veyka said.

Cyara's swallow was audible. "I was not certain."

"That must have been difficult for you." Veyka smirked. But then her gaze softened. "I love you, Cyara. You have my trust to see this through."

Veyka turned for the door. But before she could open it, the other clanged open noisily. To both of their surprise, it was Percival who stood panting in the arched doorway. The queen had a dagger in her hand before he even got the sentence out. "Isolde is missing."

47
VEYKA

"Where is she?" I demanded as my feet pounded down the last few steps to the stone landing.

A stupid question. Percival had already said she was missing. But I was not thinking. Not about the words coming out of my mouth, at least.

I had brought her here.

If it were not for me, Isolde would still be safe in the faerie caves. She'd followed me to Avalon out of an ancient loyalty that I did not deserve.

My fault.

Lyrena was already striding my direction, the door to Isolde's room hanging half-open behind her. "I knocked on her door on the way down to the kitchens to see if she needed to eat."

Our suite of rooms was full. Elayne had given Isolde the next best thing, a room on the floor directly below ours.

"She could be somewhere else in the castle, exploring." Cyara said from behind me. Her voice was calm, but I heard the telltale rustling of her wings. We both knew that Lyrena would not raise the alarm if that were a possibility.

Lyrena pressed herself to the wall as I hurtled past, flinging the door open the rest of the way. My eyes took in the scene in a second. Cyara arrived at my shoulder, and I knew hers did the same.

There was the tray of food that Percival must have set down before running for us. The surge of gratitude I felt for the human was eclipsed by the rest of the scene. A chair flat on its back, one leg broken off entirely. Curtains in shreds—what had done that? Isolde's claws?

I inhaled deeply, instinctively searching for some clue. No coppery tang of blood met my nostrils, but something else did. Something earthy. Terrestrial.

"Cyara, stay here in case she comes back."

I did not have to order Lyrena to my side. She was already there, a half step behind my left shoulder.

"There were terrestrials in there," I said, hitting the stairs again. I tried to follow the scent, but even with my sharp senses it was too difficult. This was a terrestrial castle, everything blended together. "Where would they take her?"

"The towers are all occupied by the family," Lyrena answered. She'd explored the castle extensively as soon as we arrived—part of her goldstone training, to assess all potential threats. "Dungeons monitored by Elayne and Pant's guards. I doubt they would have taken her there."

"Why would they have taken her at all?" My voice was deceptively calm. I could feel the void pulling at my senses, my fingertips tingling. But I did not know where to go to find her. Right now, it was smarter to stay where I was, to walk these halls and courtyards looking for any clues to where my friend had been taken.

Isolde wasn't defenseless, precisely. Her tiny fingers were tipped with sharp claws, and we'd all seen the white flame she could summon. But she was not a warrior. She was a Faerie of the Fen— an Ancestors-damned legend. One I'd sworn myself to protect, if only within the silence of my own mind.

"Because the terrestrial bastards think they can take whatever they want," Lyrena growled behind me. The viciousness of it almost made me stumble.

She'd never shown any sign of distrust towards the terrestrials here or in Baylaur, beyond what was reasonable for strangers. If she held some personal prejudices, I'd never seen them. But the ire in her voice mirrored the rage in my soul—one of our own had been taken.

We hit the training courtyard. The cold air and wind whipping against my face did nothing to calm the blaze within me.

"Where?" I demanded again.

Lyrena's hand was tight around the hilt of her sword, knuckles bright white against her golden skin. Precious seconds passed as she considered, and I knew she counted every one of them. "There are old passageways in the walls around the outer ward. Most of the entrances are sealed. But it is more likely than taking her to someone's private chambers."

Because there would be no one to hear her cries for help.

I traded the rapier I'd grabbed for a dagger instead. It would be better for fighting in close quarters. "You start in the northwest corner. I will go to the southeast."

Lyrena did not wait for more. She was already running. But I knew she heard me when I said, "Show them no mercy."

I forced myself to stay on this plane. The void was faster, but I might miss something. Every step between me and the entrance Lyrena had pointed out felt like it lasted a lifetime. But I focused on the details—tried to catch a scent of burning embers on the wind or the crunch of brutality.

Nothing.

This was my fault.

I should have arranged for Isolde to stay with us, even if it had meant close quarters. We'd shared worse while camping and traveling. But like a stupid fool, I had believed we were safe here. Even after I'd found the threat carved into the staircase that led to our suite.

The entry to the passageways was partially walled off by a half-caved in stone wall that otherwise could have been mistaken for an accident. But there were tool marks, the scrapes faint but visible, where someone had used a metal blade to pry apart stones and enlarge the opening.

I'd reward Lyrena for her cleverness later.

I shimmied through the opening, slower that I wanted at the price of silence. Whoever had taken Isolde, they would not hear me coming.

It was dark, the only light seeping in from the opening I'd climbed through. Once I turned the corner that marked the southeast tower, even that would fade to nothing. But I knew the darkness like I knew my own soul.

I cleared the corner, no sounds from ahead or behind. I kept going, knowing that Lyrena would eventually sweep behind me.

Each step was a moment lost, and there were too many steps. The passageway curved with the edge of the island. The next turn was more of a slope, but there was still a tower. A larger opening that would mean more space for—

No. I did not let myself consider what torment they'd wreak on Isolde.

My ears captured their voices a half-breath before the faint flickering of light reached my eyes.

Males and females, hushed but excited.

I stepped around a pile of debris.

One, two, three separate voices.

I slowed my pace, inching around the curve with by back pressed into the stone wall. The shadows would not hide me for long, especially in these close confines. But they were distracted. There was a thud—were they jumping?

My breathing so shallow it was imperceptible, I was finally able to see why.

They were indeed in the base of the tower, a slight male with dark hair, a larger one who was turned away, and a female I'd definitely seen during the feasts in the great hall but could not place otherwise.

Isolde was above them—out of reach. Thank the Ancestors.

The ache in my heart eased slightly.

Somehow, she'd managed to get free and climb up where they could not reach her, using her size and those sharp claws to her advantage. Those claws were embedded in the wooden supports for the floor above. But the terrestrials were dragging over stones. No airborne shifters among them, then. Or none whose wingspans would fit in the tight space.

I tugged the other dagger from the scabbard at my waist, muscles poised to move. Then another terrestrial stepped into the light.

"Quite a little morsel you've found yourselves," Barkke said laconically. My heart beat out the question—friend or foe? His mace was in his belt, but he made no move to reach for it.

The smaller of the two males turned, baring his teeth at the much larger male. "She's ours. Find your own elemental to taste."

Barkke was, understandably, unimpressed. He was twice the other male's size. "Did your mother never tell you bedtime tales about the Faeries of the Fen? She's no elemental."

"She has fire," the bigger one said. He was the one climbing atop the stones, trying to reach Isolde. Who, for her part, was not quivering at bit. No, she was spitting like a cat up there in the rafters, brandishing her claws.

"There will be repercussions for this," Barkke said, flicking his emerald gaze up to Isolde. But it did not quite sound like a warning. More like advice—like he was telling his fellow terrestrials to do what they must, but be prepared for the consequences.

Barkke would be harder to kill. And I might even regret it, because he was a friend of Arran's. But I could not suffer a powerful warrior like him to live.

The big male jumped, nearly reaching Isolde's foot. She tugged it up, white eyes darting around for a way out. I saw her realize what I already had—she'd gotten away, but only temporarily. Eventually, they would reach her, and she was backed into a corner.

"I have heard the tales," the female terrestrial said, her voice dripping with poison. "Her kind are little more than animals."

Above them, Isolde hissed.

I had known, but I'd let myself forget. As I'd become close to Arran, accepted Gwen as my Goldstone, became friends with Osheen and adored Maisri, I'd forgotten the truth. The terrestrials hated us. We hated them.

And without Arran standing at my side, unified and strong and in command, they saw me as no more than an elemental interloper. And Isolde, by extension, as prey.

A stupid, stupid mistake.

But not as big as theirs.

My fingers twitched around my dagger, eager to be coated with their blood. But before I could move, Barkke did. The crunch of the spiked flanges of his mace against the male's skull reverberated against the walls. Another swing, and the male's head was on the ground.

I did not give the traitors a second to retaliate.

If Barkke was surprised by my sudden appearance, he did not show it. He did not even pause his next swing as he said, "Welcome to the fray, Majesty."

My reply was the spurt of terrestrial blood as I slashed my dagger over the female's throat.

Lyrena was there a few heartbeats later, drawn by the commotion. But there were no terrestrials left to fell. She took quick stock of the situation, the bodies on the ground, and climbed upon the pile of rocks to help Isolde down.

"Hissing like an animal was a nice touch," Barkke complimented with vague amusement when the white faerie was on solid ground once more.

She hissed again through her pointed teeth. "They did not deserve my regard."

I choked back an unhinged laugh and crouched down so I could speak directly to her. "Are you all right?"

Her white skin was unmarred, her braids wild but intact. If she'd had any wounds, she'd already healed them herself.

"They wanted to draw out their fun. Hurting me too soon would have spoiled it." Isolde inclined her head, white eyes glistening in the torchlight. "Thank you for coming for me, Majesty."

I reached for her hand, undeterred by the sharp claws, and held it tight. The dark centers of her pupils expanded in surprise, but she did not pull away. I held her hand while I counted the pulsing beats of her heart, letting my frayed nerves realize that she truly was all right.

When I straightened, my heartbeat had slowed to calm again. But the rage within me was hot. I kicked aside the terrestrials to make room for us to walk out.

Maybe I should have shown mercy. Left them injured but alive. Killing them like this was going to elicit a reaction, and I doubted it would be positive. But the terrestrials owed me their allegiance—and I would punish any who withheld it.

Arran would have known—who to kill, who to leave alive, how to spin it as an act of strength rather than wrath. But I was doing this alone, now.

Lyrena led Isolde back toward the exit. I inclined my head to Barkke. He lifted his fist and placed it over his heart—a sign of respect between terrestrial warriors. Arran had described it to me. Even in these small moments, I could not separate myself from my mate.

I lifted my own fist to my heart.

It beat harder in my chest.

Isolde and Lyrena's footsteps fell away. I waited until they were fully gone to give my order. "Spike their heads to the battlements and dump their bodies in the lake. No funeral services. No blessings from the priestess."

Barkke did not question his queen. "It shall be done."

A few minutes later, I followed Isolde and Lyrena back into the tower rooms. Isolde was on the bed with Cyara. From the look on the latter's face, I knew Lyrena had already related the events of the last few minutes.

Lyrena straightened when I entered, and I addressed my first order to her. "I am done wasting time. We are leaving for the amorite mines today." I turned to Cyara, one arm still tight around Isolde's shoulders. "Keep her close."

My friend nodded, her turquoise eyes solemn. I waited another half second as she turned her attention back to Isolde, who was still muttering curses under her breath.

I would not wait around another moment while those I cared for were in danger. Not when I could feel the enemies, from this realm and others, circling us ever closer.

48
ARRAN

I stayed in my beast form for nearly an entire day.

No one tried to speak to a wolf that could rip their head off, severing bone and sinew with fangs the size of a child's forearm. No one spouted off about the sacred bond I now shared with a beautiful, brazen queen who could speak directly into my mind.

Even standing on that barren mountaintop, listening to her explain what might be the end of our world, my beast had been feral with need for her. He'd urged me to fill my hands with her breasts, to lay her back on the grass and rut with her like an animal, claiming her for all of the earth and sky to see.

But worse than that was the strength of the bond inside my chest. I felt the urge to gather her up into my arms, to kiss the tension from her face, to feel her melt and relax against me. That was even more foreign to me than the insatiable physical desire.

When I finally shifted back into my fae form, in the same bedroom I'd occupied in childhood, I stared at myself in the tall mirror. I examined the familiar lines of my Talisman, the rugged muscles that had been forged by battle, and by some strange magic, had not atrophied while I laid in Avalon in an enchanted sleep.

But for all that my body was unchanged, a stranger stared back at me through my black eyes.

I had nothing left of myself. No longer the Brutal Prince, but the High King. I'd never spent more than a month in the same female's bed, and yet supposedly I'd pledged myself for eternity to Veyka Pendragon.

I understood why I had done it. My entire life had been given in service to Annwyn. To prove that I was more than the monster inside of me, I had become an angel of death and destruction. I claimed every bit of the power in my veins, fauna and flora, and then I controlled it. The control was what had been most meaningful, not the power. That was the part that few understood. Power that was unclaimed, unchained, was meaningless. Dangerous, but not useful.

I had spent three hundred years making myself indispensable to the terrestrial kingdom. They needed me, depended upon me. Me—the son of the female they had debased so cruelly, then shunned.

I would never be beloved by the terrestrials or Annwyn at large. Their fear did not allow it. But every time I led legions onto the battlefield, pillaged a city on a distant continent and brought back riches to Wolf Bay, I carved myself deeper into the history of the terrestrial kingdom. Of Annwyn.

Duty, above all else.

Now, duty at the cost of myself.

I stalked away from the mirror, unable to bear the sight any longer. My dark hair was matted over my shoulders, but I did nothing to tame it. For the first time since I'd awoken, the beast inside of me was quiet.

So it was the mating bond in my chest that pulled me toward the window.

I was so exhausted that I did not fight it.

A party of five moved across the long, narrow bridge connecting Eilean Gayl to the mainland. Two terrestrials I did not recognize led the way. Behind them, the unmistakable form of my wife followed, her long strides eating up the ground. I watched as her gait slowed. She was taller than the two terrestrials in front of her and moved faster. Suddenly they sped up. I could not hear it, but I imagined her barking an order.

The golden elemental—Lyrena, I recalled—walked just off of Veyka's shoulder, guarding her back. And behind them, another figure I recognized. I could see his beard from my window. Barkke.

His swagger was only slightly impeded by the travel pack strapped to his back.

They were leaving.

The amorite mines.

Veyka had not even seen fit to send me word that she was leaving.

What reason did you give her? When she explained the threat against Annwyn, your first instinct was to argue.

That voice of reason in my mind sounded disturbingly like my mother.

But it was not the Lady of Eilean Gayl's rational thought that guided my footsteps away from the window. It was my beast. He had awoken.

49
VEYKA

For a few blessed weeks, I'd eaten delicious food prepared by competent cooks and had not washed a single dish. Now I was camping once again.

As if every breath that sawed in and out of my body was not already torture enough—longing for an Arran that did not exist, worrying for the friends we'd left behind in Eilean Gayl, the loom specter of the succubus.

The amorite mines were only a few days' travel away. Lyrena and I could have reached them in a matter of hours if I'd taken her with me through the void. Except we did not know where the fuck we were going. The terrestrial guides looked as dubious of me as I did of them. I doubted they'd have allowed me to take them through the void, even if I had offered.

All except for Barkke, who still looked at me with a little too much interest. But after what had happened with Isolde, I'd endure the awkwardness to have at least one more companion I could trust.

He was Arran's childhood companion and longtime friend. Yet, I knew that if Arran caught him with the glow in his eyes that flickered to life when he looked at me, my husband would rip him to shreds.

Or would he?

The bite of buttery pastry in my throat suddenly turned dry, the flakes scratching painfully as I swallowed them down. I finished the rest of the croissant—*not* chocolate—without noticing the taste. I did not reach for a second from the bag I'd pilfered from the kitchens at Eilean Gayl. They'd only keep for a day, and I did not intend to waste them on a foul mood where I would not fully appreciate their decadent taste.

"I could get used to having a magical fire," Barkke groaned in appreciation, stretching out. His length took up the entirety of one side, but by the way he tucked his hands behind his head and closed his eyes, he was unbothered by the possible inconvenience to our companions.

The two other terrestrials had mostly kept their distance—a flora-gifted female named Vera and a fauna-gifted male named Kay whose beast form was a boar with tusks that rivaled the skoupuma's horns for wickedness. Kay was on watch near the tree line; Vera ignored Barkke entirely, focused on coaxing flowers to grow on one of the many plants she'd casually picked as we walked.

Lyrena, however, sent a whip of fire to burn Barkke in the ass.

Barkke howled. Lyrena laughed so hard she nearly fell off of her log. The campfire flared and danced in time with her magic, flashing a bright red and then fading through a gradient of oranges and yellows before finally settling itself into a steady flame. It was beautiful.

I realized how little I'd ever seen beauty in magic. In Annwyn, power meant survival. Even among the elementals, who prized ancestry over everything, the strength of one's magic was seen as an indication of the strength of the bloodline overall. I had spent so long fearing my own lack of power, hiding it, that I had not been able to appreciate the beauty and nuance. Lyrena's flame was an extension of herself—merry and warm. Parys' warm wind could carry gossip but also provide comfort. I sighed at the memory of my friend. I missed Gwen and her razor-sharp barbs. I could hardly believe that I was longing for Baylaur.

Lyrena must have noted my sigh, because she sat up and nudged Barkke, this time with foot rather than flame. "I thought you were going to set up the tents?"

"In a minute," he groused.

"What if her Majesty wishes to retire now?"

That got his attention.

Barkke's green eyes popped open, spearing in my direction. I hoped it was just the firelight that made them appear to be glowing. "Are you tired, my queen?"

Unease curled in my chest, but I papered over it with bravado. "Tired of you."

To punctuate my words, I stood up and crossed to the other side of the fire, as physically far away from Barkke as I could manage. Vera looked less than welcoming as I settled onto the other end of the log she'd dragged up to the fire, but she did not outright deny me.

I was her queen. I didn't suppose she could.

Nor could she argue as I watched her with increasing interest.

I'd watched Maisri wield her daisy fae magic constantly during the months we traveled from Baylaur to Avalon. She could take a single shredded flower petal and grow it into a bloom the size of her head.

But what this flora-gifted female was doing was different. The modifications were minute, and different for each plant. For one, she'd gently twirled her finger until elongated stamen arched out of the center of the fully opened golden flower. For another, she stopped her ministrations just as the dark green bud appeared at the end of the stem.

Arran's father, Pant, had summoned thorny roses. I'd seen Arran manipulate trees, vines, grass, but never flowers. Was there an order to the types of flora powers, or were they like elemental magic, manifesting in ways specific to each individual?

"What are you doing?" I asked bluntly.

Vera glanced up at me for only a second before returning to her task—a leafy green plant that was wilting in her hand. But that second was enough for me to read the emotions in her dark brown eyes. She wanted to lie. But she was a terrestrial.

"I am ensuring each plant is at its optimal stage of life."

Not lying, but certainly avoiding.

"Optimal for what?"

"So that the unique properties of the plant will be at its most powerful."

Recognition dawned in my memory, a conversation with Arran about the affinities of different flora-gifted terrestrials. "Poisons."

Despite her hesitation, Vera's smile was absolutely wicked. "Some of them," she said. "Others are for speeding healing, beyond even our natural predispositions."

She held the plant she'd been slowly bringing along through its death and drying aloft for me to see, before curling her fingers around the clump of leaves. She crushed the dried-out leaves in her hand and held them out to me so I could see the gray-green shreds freckling her palm. "This is merely to make Kay's cooking more palatable."

"I am a more than adequate cook," a sharp voice said from the darkness at the edge of the camp. Something about the tenor of it, reprove and annoyance, piqued my instincts.

"Are you two related?" I asked, glancing over my shoulder.

It took me a moment to pick out his outline, even with my sharp eyesight. The darkness of the night had fully descended, even though it was not yet late. I pulled my fur-lined cloak tighter around my shoulders.

"He's my mother's elder brother," Vera confirmed.

"And his husband is *my* brother," Barkke said from the other side of the fire. His eyes, blessedly, were once again closed. "We're a happy little family."

A flick of her hand, and Vera held the little plant whose bud was not quite open. "I will slip some of this into your morning tea."

Barkke appeared thoroughly unbothered. "You would not kill me."

Vera's wicked grin returned. "No. But I'd have you shitting yourself for the next two days if it would keep you from running your mouth."

"You impudent little—"

"Quiet." I shot to my feet as Kay's voice sliced through the camp, recognizing the threat at the same moment he did. A low growl filled the air. My head whipped around, checking my companion's faces—I was not the only one who heard it.

"What is that?" Vera asked softly, eyes scanning the tree line. In the seconds it had taken me to turn and draw my daggers, she'd whipped the bow off of her back and knocked an arrow. A formidable fighter, then, in addition to her talent with poisons.

Lyrena moved soundlessly across the camp, drawn to my side by the invisible rope of loyalty. But her question was to our terrestrial guides. "What sort of beasts are there in these woods?"

"The kind that won't bother to rip our heads off of our bodies before they eat us," Barkke answered grimly. I did not need to look over my shoulder to know that he was no longer reclining.

The growling intensified, interrupted by a vicious snarl. It was getting closer.

"Everyone up," Kay ordered. Superfluous. Maybe it made him feel better.

It certainly did not help me. Dread unspooled in my stomach as the feral growl filled the air around us, pushing into all the corners of my consciousness.

"That is not necessary," I said.

"Veyka, behind me." Lyrena did not bother to wait for my compliance, stepping between me and the invisible threat. It would not remain hidden much longer.

"Absolutely not." I tried to shove her aside, but she held her ground.

"We can argue later, I—"

"Sit back down, Lyrena," I commanded. Her head whipped

back, eyes widening as she saw me sliding my daggers back into the scabbards at my waist. Another snarl rent the air. We had seconds now.

But she did not obey my command. She turned, sword high above her head and ready to strike as the white wolf leapt from the trees into the clearing.

50
ARRAN

I'd have found her anywhere.

It was a realization I did not want to make sense of as I bounded through the dense woods that separated Eilean Gayl from the Split Sea. I found their camp well before nightfall. But instead of going directly there, shifting and walking into camp, I found myself circling. Around and around, searching for any whiff of a threat. I ripped apart one of the mighty solabears as it slept in its cave for the winter. They never woke before the spring. It was no threat at all. But I could not stop myself.

Only when my beast was satisfied that no threat, beast or fae, lingered within striking distance, did I approach. I expected to find them on guard, blades drawn. They did not disappoint me.

Except Veyka.

She stood before the rest of them, arms crossed over her chest, weapons sheathed and annoyance etched in her beautiful face.

Annoyance.

No one else had ever dared.

She did not wait for me to shift before starting in. Her attack came not from those luscious lips, but directly into my mind.

I left you at Eilean Gayl for a reason.

The snarl that ripped from my maw was involuntary—and conflicted. Anger, that she could speak so easily into my mind. And was that... relief? It felt like a piece of me slotted into place. She spoke with such ease, confidence that she belonged this close to me, in my innermost sanctum.

Whether she could read the nuances of that snarl, I did not know.

I am not afraid of you or your beast.

Your mistake. I had not meant to speak back to her. But it came as easily as breathing.

Veyka's blue eyes glinted. Glowed. Her back was to the fire. That glow was entirely for me. *I have made plenty of mistakes in my life. But that is not one of them.*

She did not give me enough time to pick apart the implications of that before adding, *Why are you here?*

I am the High King of Annwyn.

She took a step forward, putting space between us and the rest of the group. They all remained frozen behind her. *Good for you. That does not answer my question.*

We did not agree on how the amorite would be used.

The glow in her eyes transformed into something sharper. It should not have been possible for simple blue eyes to show such a range of emotions. Swirling storm cloud, crystalline pool, icy blade.

Now they were daggers. *You did not trust me to do what is best for Annwyn.*

I do not know you well enough to trust you.

Veyka's arms dropped to her sides. Crossed over her body, she'd been protected. But now she was open, vulnerable. Even with the thick fur cloak over her shoulders, the skin along her throat pebbled. That was the only skin I could see. If she wore that tantalizing golden brassiere beneath the thick green knit tunic—my tunic. She was wearing my tunic.

Something surged through me, primal and hot. Another growl ripped from my throat, but different. Just as feral, equally dangerous, and all for her.

And yet, your beast is growling for me, Veyka purred through the bond.

There was no mistaking the glow in her eyes now as she stepped closer still. Close enough to touch, the low breath she exhaled lifting the scruff of white fur around my beast's head.

Are you hard for me, Arran? If I reached for you, what would I find amid all of that lovely, thick white fur? What if you shifted? Would that magnificent cock of yours be straining against your leathers, eager to bury itself in my cunt?

She was taunting me. It was a tactic. It had to be. She wanted to distract me, to gain the advantage in the new order that my arrival had created. Fuck if I didn't want to give in to her. Even covered up, with only the alabaster skin of her throat and face visible, she was fucking perfect. It would take more clothing that she had to hide those luscious curves. I could imagine what it would feel like to sink inside of her, to skate my canines along her throat while I inhaled my scent mingling with hers on the tunic.

The tunic she'd worn without knowing I was coming. She was taunting me now, that was certain, angling to get control. But that tunic... she had not worn it for me, but for herself. That did something to my heart that was worse than what her taunts did to my body.

What is the point of this? The strain in my voice was impossible to miss, even in the privacy of our own shared bond.

Veyka licked her lips. *I can feel your need through the bond. You want me.*

I wanted to suck her tongue into my mouth. Fuck. I had to get control of myself. *Wanting you is not the same as trusting you.*

I felt her bravado flicker. The next thought was softer. *We've built a foundation on less.*

What does that mean?

You used to hate me. And now?

The need to shift was becoming stronger with every beat of heat and meaning between us. Once I was in my fae form, I did not know what I would do. But I hardly trusted myself. And even though my wolf wanted to, and the bond in my chest practically demanded it, I could not quite bring myself to trust her.

That's what I thought.

I could *feel* her sadness. Not just sadness, but pain. Pain that I recognized. I could not remember. But I knew what torture felt like.

And maybe I was just as much a monster as the world thought, every inch the Brutal Prince. Because instead of offering the female who was my mate, wife, and queen comfort, I let out a thought that should have stayed buried. *I did not invite you to share my mind.*

Veyka stumbled backward a step. I might as well have struck her. For just a moment, I glimpsed the devastation on her face. But that was all she allowed me.

For all that I valued my control, it was Veyka who showed all the restraint as she shut off my access to her feelings, to her soul. *Your beast did.*

Don't worry, Arran. I won't bother you again.

She completed the exodus by turning and stalking away into the darkness, depriving me even of the sight of her. Her golden knight shot me a look that promised painful death before following her queen. When there was no sight of Veyka left, not even an outline in the dark, not even a hint of primrose and plum that only my beast could detect, only then did I shift.

The camp slowly resumed motion around me, but I stayed still, fixed at its edge.

I had what I wanted. Then why in the Ancestors-damned hell did I feel so bereft?

51

VEYKA

We'd traveled for months with little rest in our quest for Avalon. When I was in Baylaur, and later in Eilean Gayl, I spent hours each day in the training ring. But the three days journey between the lake-locked castle and the amorite mines on the edge of the Split Sea felt like they lasted for *years*.

Being so close to Arran, yet having this yawning void between us... it left me drained at the end of each day. Honestly, I was drained by midday. Lyrena had taken to supplying endless hot tea in the special cup that Osheen had fashioned for me all those months ago, magically keeping the tea warm even as the snow thickened beneath our feet. I suspected she'd appealed to Vera for the brew. It wasn't poison, so I didn't ask.

Lyrena shared my tent, but she always took the first watch of the night. Which meant I was alone. The exhaustion should have helped me sleep, yet each night I had still been awake when Lyrena crawled into the tent hours later.

One more night, and we would arrive on the coast. That, according to Vera and Kay. I'd asked Barkke about the terrestrial lord who held the amorite mines, but he'd been useless, as usual. Only commented that the male had killed the previous guardians about a year ago, snuffing out a lineage that had stretched back thousands of years. I was preemptively exhausted by the negotiating that awaited me.

One more night of staring up at a tent, shivering in the cold. A thousand more nights until my mate was here to warm me. Maybe. If I was lucky. If he ever remembered. Or decided to love me again, despite his missing memories.

Fuck.

I rolled over to my side, trying to find some sort of comfort. Even the padding of my curves was not enough to make the hard ground comfortable.

A painful lump poked into my back. When I'd shared a tent with Arran, I'd barely noticed the rocks beneath our bedroll. I was much too distracted by the warm, hard male pressed against me.

I was depressingly used to sleeping with lumps in my back after all the traveling. But this one was particularly sharp and stabby. I dug around, shifting up onto an elbow and arching my back, trying to shove it out of the way. My fingers brushed against it, just out of reach, only to find it was smooth. My fingers closed around the column of faceted quartz, realizing before I saw it what I held.

The communication crystal.

Cyara had suggested I bring it with us so that I might stay apprised of their work with the priestess at Eilean Gayl. Another carefully laid piece of her plan to convince me that Percival and Diana could, if not be fully trusted, then at least used. She'd been terrifyingly clever in how she presented that proposition. If we survived the succubus, Cyara would become one of the most cunning and effective courtiers Baylaur had ever seen. She'd even convinced Percival to fully explain how the crystals functioned, step by step, as a show of good faith.

I pulled myself up to sit, holding the crystal in my palm. The light from the fire Lyrena kept burning all night in the center of the camp was scant, but I supposed I did not need light to hear.

I murmured the incantation. The crystal flared bright white in my hand, then softened to a luminous glow. I inhaled sharply, awe filling my chest. Then the crystal flared with light again, and Cyara's voice spoke into the tent.

"Veyka?" Her voice was as clear as if she sat by my side. I could hear every nuance—the slight annoyance as she tried to get the crystal to work, the lining of hope that it would.

"Ancestors," I breathed. "I did not expect it to work."

There was a long enough stretch of silence that I wondered if the connection had faded away. But the crystal maintained its soft glow, brightening as Cyara spoke again. "It is very strange."

"And damned useful." No wonder Gorlois had used them. And the Lady of the Lake. Why hadn't my long-lost sister given me one, instead of appearing as a wraith in the woods? Probably because she did not actually count me as a sister.

I realized there was silence stretching between us when Cyara spoke again, voice cracking subtly. It was so strange, talking to a crystal. "I feel that I ought to warn you—"

I cut her off. "Arran is already here."

More silence. I expected to hear a soft sigh, but maybe the crystal only communicated words.

"I suspected when he left Eilean Gayl. He did not even tell Lady Elayne where he was bound," Cyara said.

I found myself laying back on the bedroll, tucking one hand under my head as I settled on my side and resting the other on the ground in front of me, crystal balanced on my palm. "He may hate the bond between us, but its demand is impossible to resist. The only time it is satisfied is if we are near." And even then, it was still a constant ache—begging for physical consummation.

Cyara's response came through immediately. "He does not hate it. Or you."

I pressed my eyes closed. "I do not know what he thinks. He does not want me in his head."

Another long pause. It was so easy to get lost in your own thoughts and forget you were actually speaking to someone when you could not see them. But when her words came, I knew it was because she'd been struggling to find the right ones. "I am sorry, Veyka."

There was really nothing else to say.

"Thank you."

I stroked my thumb along the smooth facet of the crystal, wishing my friend was with me. "Have Percival and Diana discovered anything?"

The response was a long time coming. "There are mentions of a darkness. But all the references we've found so far are vague. They are not the primary sources."

"Always the librarian's daughter."

A soft laugh. So, the crystal did communicate more than just words. "The oldest histories are carved in stone."

I wished I could see the expression on her face, let her read mine. One of the best things about Cyara was her ability to know my thoughts before even I did. It was also one of her most irritating traits. "Carvings like Arran and I found in the water gardens, and on the standing stone in the jungle," I mused aloud.

"Yes. But there are none here in Eilean Gayl. This castle was destroyed in the Great War and rebuilt afterward, like many of the northern strongholds. The only surviving older constructions are in the south," she explained.

I realized the thrust of her thoughts immediately.

"Near Wolf Bay." Another place we needed to go, another hurdle between me and Baylaur and being back with Parys and Gwen. I missed them even more acutely now, with the state of things between Arran and I so fraught. I sighed heavily and hoped that Cyara heard it. "Keep looking. We should arrive at the coast tomorrow."

She made a sound on the other end, a sort of hum but without a tune. An attempt to soothe and offer comfort, even from miles and miles away. How had I gotten so lucky, to have such loyal and loving friends? In those months after Arthur's death, I had done nothing but lash out and hurt. But Cyara, and before her, Charis and Carly, had offered their friendship and support unconditionally.

I supposed that now, I would prove that I deserved it. By saving all of us from the succubus. That had to be my priority, even at the cost of mending things with Arran. I may not have the time to do both.

"Veyka...," Cyara finally said, her voice low and soothing. "I know it hurts. But you let him in once. You can do it again."

"Maybe." That was the most I could manage.

Several heartbeats later, the crystal went dark. Whether that meant that I was no longer receptive to the conversation or that Cyara was, I was not certain.

52
ARRAN

I was a heartbeat away from losing control.

The beast inside of me tugged at the restraints I kept on him constantly. Never, since the early days after my beast had emerged, had I struggled to keep him leashed. The power of my will had always been stronger. But not where Veyka Pendragon was concerned.

Every step, I had to force my foot forward or it would have angled in her direction. The breaths I inhaled begged to exhale her name. Food tasted like ash in my mouth, because the only flavor I wanted on my tongue was her.

I was nearly ready to give in, to fuck her just to get her out of my mind. I was at war with myself, unsure if that would even be enough. The pull between us was more than physical. The swagger with which she walked, the confidence and command in her words, all of it drew me to her. My logical mind screamed at me to go slowly, to approach this female with caution. But every instinct wanted to know her better. I did not know how much longer I could fight it.

And then we arrived.

The scent of brine and sea salt flooded my senses moments before we crested the hill.

There it was.

A long downward slope, slick with snow, just like every other mile we'd trudged since leaving Eilean Gayl. This close to the water, the layer was thinner. We ought to have been able to see footprints left behind by guards, residents, animals. But there was nothing. An undisturbed blanket of white that stretched from the toes of my boots down to the unmoving edge of the Split Sea. And in the center, a castle so black it sucked in the light of the untouched snow surrounding it.

It was a blight upon the landscape.

While Eilean Gayl rose up from the lake as if by magic, a strong, unfaltering sentinel in the brutal northern reaches of the terrestrial kingdom, there was no sense of protection emanating from the black stones of the castle. No moss clung to the grooves between stones. I knew without having to reach out my flora power that no living thing touched that castle. If there was grass on the plain before us, beneath all that snow, it died away long before the cursed black stones met the earth.

I recognized Veyka's presence at my side before she spoke. Or rather, my wolf did.

"That looks very welcoming," she said, planting a hand on each hip. Wide hips. Hips made to be gripped and—

"What is this place?" Lyrena asked, cutting off my thought. Thank the Ancestors for that small mercy. I needed to be thinking strategically about how to obtain the amorite in the mines, not about how to bring my wife to climax.

"The new lord has named it Castle Chariot," Kay said from my other side. He and Vera had taken up positions on the outer fringes of our group, precisely as I'd commanded. I had never led either of them into battle, but they were loyal to my mother and, therefore, loyal to me. Barkke lingered in the woods, a lifeline if things went badly.

"The same lord who killed the previous occupants?" Lyrena

asked, recalling the brief story Kay had told us around the campfire two nights before.

The boar shifter nodded. "A line of powerful aerial shifters held the fortress and the mines for thousands of years."

Held.

But no longer.

I vaguely recalled meeting the male who had held this castle sometime in my youth. He had come to Eilean Gayl to express his goodwill to my mother and father in the months after the full strength of my power had manifested. Every lord of any importance north of the Spine had come crawling to Eilean Gayl in those early days, eager to get a look at me. And to prove to their peers that they were brave enough to stand in the same room with the flora and fauna gifted child so powerful, he'd left a trail of bloodshed across the continent before his eleventh birthday.

"I don't care who he's killed if he gives us the amorite," Veyka said, her sharp blue eyes scanning the tableau before us. I wondered if she noted all the same things I did—the impenetrable walls without even arrow slits, the strange position at the bottom of the valley rather than the apex of the hill where we stood, assuring that any approaching enemy would always have the high ground. With the Split Sea at its back, the fortress should have been nearly indefensible.

Everything about this place screamed its wrongness.

"He could very well try to kill us," I said, loud enough that all of our travel companions could hear. I wanted everyone on alert. No matter what we were walking into, we would not be facing an ally.

Veyka smiled, a wicked, feral thing that made my cock harden instantly. "He could try."

I cleared my throat, shoved down my beast, and took the first step down the hill. "Kay, Vera, guard our backs." When I stepped forward, I expected the rest to follow.

Of course, Veyka remained on the hill, hands still planted on her waist, pushing back her fur cloak and highlighting the lines of her figure. Ancestors. Did she do that on purpose just to distract me?

Her wicked smile deepened.

Yes, she did.

"No brilliant battle plan?" she challenged.

I ground my teeth. "This is not battle." Not yet.

The smile dropped off of her face. "That is where you are wrong." She was not looking at Castle Chariot as she said, "Every day, every breath, is a battle."

<hr />

There was no one to greet us. The castle was just as deserted from ten yards away as it had been from a hundred. I scanned the battlements, the towers, the gatehouse—nothing. I kneeled, pushing my hand through the snow to feel the ground below. A mealy of mixture of dirt and sand. No plants. I could summon them, even at this distance, but they would be less powerful, slower.

Fine. My beast could handle anything that came from those dark walls.

I stood again, frowning.

"Were you expecting a welcome party?" Veyka said, her sultry voice turned mocking.

Veyka's voice had not echoed in my mind since she'd given her word. But I wondered if she could sense my thoughts just the same.

She's elemental. She can see the thoughts I do not guard right on my face.

I turned the same dark glare on her that had cowed thousands of warriors on the battlefield. "We are the High King and Queen of Annwyn."

Veyka snorted. "And in the months since I've been queen, an assassin has snuck in through my window, the captain of my Goldstone Guards has turned traitor and tried to murder me, and a half-human witch lured us to Avalon only for us to be attacked by an enemy I thought long dead." She rolled her eyes, like she was exhausted, explaining this to a child. "Being king is not exactly what you might have dreamed."

I'd never dreamed of being king. The only thing I'd wanted was to do my duty and be left the hell alone. But that thought melted to nothing as I realized the full enormity of what she'd said.

Targeted by an assassin. Betrayed by the captain of her guard. Attacked in Avalon.

I remembered none of it.

"There were fires burning in the round towers," Lyrena said, reminding me that despite the force of her presence, Veyka and I were not alone.

"How can you tell?" Vera asked from Lyrena's other side, frowning.

"I can sense them." As Lyrena spoke, the broadsword she held casually in her hand began to glow slightly. No, not glow. *Burn.* But her golden face showed no hint of untethered emotion as she continued. "They must have doused them when they saw our approach, that's why there is no smoke. But the embers are still burning."

"But how did they see our approach at all?" mused Kay. "There has not been a speck of movement on the battlements since we crested the hill."

But they had seen us—someone had. There was no reason for this mysterious lord to take over the castle and then abandon it, when doing so would mean also leaving behind the prosperous amorite mines.

"Check the perimeter," I ordered. Kay and Vera moved immediately. Lyrena, unsurprisingly, did not. She was steadfast at Veyka's side. *Good,* my beast growled in approval.

Veyka waited until the other two terrestrials were out of earshot before she spoke. "This is a waste of time."

This time, I was the one fighting the impulse to roll my eyes. Veyka may engage in childish antics; I did not. "We need the amorite," I said. A simple fact *she* had insisted upon.

Another flash of that wicked grin to belie the seriousness of her words. "We ought to just kill the mysterious lord and be done with it. Take what we need. We do not have time for games."

"Another ambitious terrestrial would rise up in his place, and there is no guarantee they would continue to supply the amorite. We need the mines operating and delivering amorite for as long as they can. We are better of convincing the current lord to acquiesce now." Though her strategy sounded infinitely more gratifying.

What I did not say was that if we did as she suggested, we'd have to spare loyal soldiers to work the mines. And we might need those soldiers in battle.

"As long as they can?" Veyka said, voice quieter.

"Amorite is rare. These are the only mines on the entire continent," I said. If the situation was truly as bad as Veyka had described, the succubus as formidable, then these mines could very well mean the salvation of Annwyn.

"I know that." There was more steel in her voice this time, though it remained soft.

"Mines do not last forever. Eventually the veins will run dry." I'd been contemplating it since our conversation on the mountain top. The amorite was a finite resource. We could make weapons to destroy the succubus as they came or protect individuals from possession. Some combination of the two. Either way, if the succubus came in larger numbers, it would not be enough.

"I know that, too," Veyka said softly. Her face was unmoved, but her voice showed all the emotion her countenance did not.

She understood.

Several more interminable minutes passed. Vera and Kay had not returned, but enough time had not yet passed for me to be concerned. Veyka muttered something I did not catch. Lyrena chuckled softly, then—

"I am going in."

"Absolutely not," Lyrena said.

"No," I growled, the force of my beast behind the sound.

Veyka smiled sympathetically, glancing between me and Lyrena. "Neither of you is my keeper."

Before either of us could argue, she was gone.

53
VEYKA

I was torn between wanting to throw myself into Arran's arms and beg him to remember me, or stab him with one of my daggers. Unfortunately, neither action would achieve anything productive.

Productive.

Was it only months ago that I had slept my days away, drowned the hours in aural and food and orgasms? At least when I had been lost in melancholy and revenge, I did not have to deal with so many Ancestors-damned feelings.

I half-expected the black stones to launch some sort of trap, dropping me through the battlements into a torture chamber or for restraints to spring up. Not that either could have held me. But my feet landed on the even stones of the gatehouse without incident.

My daggers were already in hand, well-suited to the close combat an attack between the rising stone walls would demand. But none came. The battlements were exactly as they'd appeared from below—deserted.

Slowly, I rotated on the spot. No one jumped out from the recesses of a hidden refuge. No doors opened to reveal a fighting force. There were not even any plants to be summoned by a flora-gifted terrestrial. Maybe nothing could grow this close to the Split Sea.

I'd sensed Arran's unease. Mine concurred.

There was something very wrong with this place.

The next question—a feature of Castle Chariot itself, its location, or its new owner?

Even from a considerable distance above his head, I felt Arran's growl of disapproval. I paused in my exploration to throw Arran and Lyrena an irreverent wave from the top of the round tower.

The growl deepened.

I licked my lips and swallowed down the needy, lustful part of me that wanted to answer. I was only partially successful. But it was enough for me to control my step through the void into the inner bailey of the black castle.

54

ARRAN

I was going to kill her.

Turn her over my lap and spank her for her insolence. Then kiss her. *Then* kill her.

Fuck.

I scrubbed my hand over my face, through my hair. Dark strands fell forward out of the knot at the back of my head. Veyka was picking me apart piece by piece, even when she was not standing in front of me.

I'd started counting the seconds from the moment she disappeared. I started to rally my power. If she did not return, I would scale those impenetrable black walls and drag her back to safety.

"You'll get used to it again."

I blinked, several seconds passing. I'd lost count. *Fuck.* I managed a response.

"I was used to it before?" That seemed impossible.

Lyrena sword was no longer gleaming with flame, but it was still an impressive weapon. She brandished it easily, despite its massive size. Gold gilded the hilt, gold that matched the tooth that glinted in her mouth as she smirked at me and said, "I think you secretly liked it."

"What? The irreverence, the impetuousness, or the fuck-you attitude?"

Lyrena grinned fully. "All of it."

Ancestors fucking hell.

I was about to ask Lyrena how she did not tie Veyka to her bed in her sleep when the High Queen of Annwyn appeared before us, hands on her hips and mouth pouted out, looking like she'd never left us.

My beast growled.

Veyka's eyes flickered.

She fixed them on Lyrena as she spoke. "I did not go inside. But there is no one on the battlements or in the inner bailey, either. They haven't been deserted long, though. The fires are just as you said."

Before I could flay her, verbally or otherwise, Vera and Kay reappeared, approaching from either side of the castle.

"Nothing" and "No one" they confirmed.

A plan began to take shape in my mind. We would not bother to take the castle. It was not the prize—the mines were.

I felt the weight of Veyka's eyes on me, trying to read my expression. Just like I knew that she would find nothing. I'd been a battle commander for three hundred years before whatever twists of fate had landed me here, a high king without the memory of ever becoming one. There was no way she would find the answers she sought on my face. I was not that stupid.

But her gaze did not linger, moving beyond me. Over my shoulder.

Widening.

I turned on instinct, battle axe in my hand, growl ripping from my throat.

Veyka whipped past me, dagger flying.

She missed. Her dagger landed blade-down, buried in the snow.

No.

My beast sensed it even before the faint his filled my ears. *Hisssssssssss.*

Veyka stalked forward, leaving heavy brown footprints in the snow as she approached her target.

A snake so pale, it nearly disappeared into the snow around it. Only the hilt of Veyka's dagger and its milky blue eyes provided contrast against the solid white ground. And the horrible forked tongue, bright red and darting out again and again as it writhed against the blade that impaled it.

Veyka pressed her booted heel into the vertebrae just behind its skull.

"Shift," she crooned.

Lyrena and I flanked her, moving in silent parallel, weapons drawn. Was Veyka fast enough with her void power if the shifter lunged for her—

She was the fastest female—elemental or terrestrial—that I'd ever seen. The male's shift had not even solidified before she had her hand around his throat, her fingers tight. One hand, that was all she would need to snap his neck. It would not kill him, but it would render him unconscious long enough for her to divest him of his head.

The male glared at her, unkempt dark hair plastered to his sweaty forehead. Now that he was returned to his fae form, blood started to drip from the wound in his thigh, where Veyka's dagger was still impaled.

"I'll have that back, now," Veyka said, voice dripping with sweetness.

She held out the hand that did not hold his throat.

He looked like he wanted to spit in it.

Lyrena casually brandished her sword.

This was a dance they'd executed before.

He was close enough to stab her with the dagger, but doing so promised a swift death at the end of Lyrena's mighty broadsword.

Veyka watched with unhidden satisfaction as he pulled the dagger from his leg, blood spurting. He swayed on his feet, and her smile deepened. Only when he'd placed the hilt of the dagger into her palm did she release his throat and step away. Lyrena immediately stepped into the space she'd left.

Veyka reached down to scoop up a handful of snow, using it to clean the blade, careful not to touch a single drop with her own fingers. As if the male's blood was repellant. Beneath her.

She was much, much better at this game than she'd let on. Admiration kindled like a small flame in my chest. Veyka had a plan—one she had not judged me worthy of sharing. The warrior within me admired the caution. But the male, the one who longed to be close to her at a level deeper than consciousness, growled with disappointment.

Veyka slid the dagger into the jeweled scabbard at her waist—the one that matched my own. A Joining gift, I guessed. I had not asked and she had not offered an explanation. There were too many questions between us, and too many of them threatened to scrape over raw wounds.

Veyka opened her mouth, no doubt to parry some sassy comment that would equally inflame and enrage me.

But a voice boomed across the plain. From behind us. From the battlements.

They were no longer empty.

"Welcome to Castle Chariot, Your Majesties."

55

VEYKA

Every single one of them wore amorite. The slimy snake shifter I'd wounded wore a torque around his neck. The whisper-thin female that stood on the other side of the throne was practically dripping with gems—they fell in ornate configurations from her ears, a three-tiered necklace at her throat, multiple sparkling rings. The lord's circlet was studded with them, as was the prominent signet ring on his left hand.

But it was not just the ruling trio. The guards stationed around the perimeter of the throne room each wore matching metal torques, two large chunks of amorite on each end with a gap of maybe an inch of bare skin at the base of the throat.

A reference to the mines commanded by the residents of Castle Chariot, or something more?

Arran was at my side, rigid as we approached the throne at the end of the great hall. The layout of the castle was similar to Eilean Gayl, though built on a barren plain instead of an island in the middle of a lake. But the black walls around us were foreboding. They swallowed all the light. Not a single tapestry or banner hung to soften the effect. Arrayed around us were our companions, though I counted no less than twenty guards, ten on each side. Plus the trio waiting on the throne.

It could not be described as anything else. And on it sat the lord that had appeared briefly on the battlements above the gatehouse, his booming voice projecting unnaturally across the field. I'd have thought he had a wind-wielder in his employ, except that most elementals thought their terrestrial counterparts little better than beasts. An elemental would never willingly serve a terrestrial. And terrestrials loathed elementals just as much. I could still taste the fear I'd felt in the moments after Isolde's disappearance. A potent reminder as we faced this new foe.

"Welcome, Venerated Royal Majesties," the male said, his voice only slightly modulated now that we were indoors. "I am Lord Palomides, keeper of Castle Chariot and Guardian of the Mines."

Not the amorite mines. Just *mines*. It could mean nothing.

But I doubted that.

Everything about this male was calculated.

I looked him over slowly. So slow, there was no way to miss the insolence.

No, insolence was the wrong word. That implied a power dynamic that did not exist.

Palomides of the Mines might think he had the advantage here. But he had no idea what he was facing, no matter what stories he'd heard about the Queen of Secrets and her Brutal Prince.

"You will forgive me, Palomides," I drawled, tilting my chin so the braid across my forehead fell back, and my ears were fully visible. He was not the only one dripping in amorite. "In Baylaur, it is customary for vassals to bow before the High Queen."

He did not move.

Arran did—so slightly, that I was certain I was the only one who had noted it. Palomides had chosen to fixate on me. Under other circumstances, I would have been pleased to be perceived as the bigger threat. Now it made me wonder—what rumors were spreading across Annwyn about Arran? Surely no one knew the details of his injury, but that he'd been parted from his queen and mate... those would be impossible to quell.

The ramifications difficult to predict.

Just like my mate.

He did not reach for the battle axe at his belt. There was no need.

The growl filled the hall, so deep at first that I felt it before I heard it. A slight reverberation, building with each second, until it thrummed in my eardrums. Not just for me, this time, but for everyone. The guards lining the walls shifted on their feet.

It filled the space around us until it felt like the force of Arran's power had sucked all of the air from the room.

I did not need air, not when I had the essence of *him* to feast upon.

"You will not disappoint my queen, Palomides." The Brutal Prince did not ask. He commanded.

I wanted to reach for his hand, to speak into his mind and tell him what those words meant. No memory at all, and yet still he understood. Maybe it was the mating bond. Maybe his beast. I did not fucking care. The possessiveness and threat in those words touched the broken part of me that had been ripped asunder.

Feet scraped against the ground—Palomides rising. I imagined I could hear his bones creak as he knelt on the floor, and I fantasized about what it would feel like to snap a few of them.

The two younger terrestrials remained stock still on either side of the throne.

I clicked my tongue, and they sprang into motion. They lacked the elder's grace of movement, sinking into awkward bows that revealed their inexperience. They might stand on either side of Palomides' makeshift throne, but neither of these terrestrials had been coached in courtly manners.

When all three sets of knees pressed firmly to the floor, I exhaled a slow, appreciative sound.

"Very good," I purred, so softly that it almost could have been a hum, an exhale, not a word at all.

But Palomides heard it. His mouth tightened as he pulled himself back to his feet.

I was drunk on the power of it, tempted to remind him that he should stay on his knees until I invited him to stand. But that would be counterproductive. He'd knelt before all of his guards, his wards, and witnesses from the elemental and terrestrial kingdoms. That would do.

For now.

I flicked my hand, and the others rose. Arran did not move from my side.

Palomides elected to stand before his throne, rather than seat himself in our presence. Wise choice.

"We did not receive word of your visit," our host said, tenting his fingers in front of his body.

"And yet, you were well prepared for us," Arran said. There was no inflection in his voice, but he did not need it. He was terrifying on his own. Maybe that was the best course of action—pretend that there was nothing amiss. If he acted as if he had something to prove, it would only spur rumors.

Arran Earthborn did not explain himself or cater to the whims of a would-be lord. He was the most powerful fae in millennia. His power spoke for itself.

Palomides merely shrugged. "Castle Chariot is unfortunately situated. We have had to take unconventional measures to defend ourselves."

I wondered how many shifters had hidden in the woods, reporting upon our approach. The serpent, who now stood at his side, could not be the only one.

"Did your predecessor employ similar defenses?" I cut in. As I spoke, I fingered the hilt of my dagger in its jeweled scabbard. Shifted my shoulders to accentuate the twin rapiers sheathed there.

Palomides recognized the threat, but his dark eyes were amused, rather than wary. "He did not."

This time, I beat him to the shrug. "More the pity, him."

He smiled, a poisonous thing that reckoned mine for wickedness. "Indeed."

In the elemental kingdom, it would have been a crime punishable by death and torture to eliminate an ancient, noble house. But on this side of the Split Sea, where strength ruled, anything worth having was open to challenge.

I desperately wished to speak to Arran. We should have spoken before this, but we were so damned skittish of each other. We should have come into this hall with a plan—more of a plan. I'd been sorting through possibilities from the moment the black castle had appeared on the horizon.. But he'd asked me to stay out of his mind—ordered me, actually.

And I would not force myself upon him.

Not yet.

I lifted my chin, affecting an air of boredom with the proceedings. Time to cut through the bullshit. "We require access to your mines," I said plainly.

Nothing in Palomides' face shifted. He knew why we'd come, then.

But still, he said, "Which ones? I possess many mines."

Ancestors-damned hell. I knew it. There was more to this terrestrial usurper styling himself as a lord. What other mines did he possess and would they be important to the war effort against the succubus?

I did not know what he wanted yet, but I doubted it would align with what was best for Annwyn. In which case, if we could not find sufficient leverage, we might have to take what we needed and ask questions later.

Palomides' life for the rest of my subjects was an easy trade.

The thin female on his left twitched, unused to standing still for such long periods. Three lives, then, for the safety of my kingdom.

I could certainly live with that. I'd survived worse.

But I'd play the game a few minutes longer.

I touched a hand to the shell of my ear as I spoke: "Amorite."

That serpentine smile deepened. "Amorite is very valuable. Is it possible the elemental kingdom is not as prosperous as we terrestrials are taught to believe, that you must loot our kingdom to enrich your own?"

"It is all *her* kingdom," Arran said sharply. "And mine."

My heart surged with emotions I did not dare examine in the middle of the fraught negotiation.

Palomides bowed his chin, but his eyes were clear. "And yet you came here, to speak with me, rather than seizing the mines with your... considerable force."

Did he know about Barkke, ensconced in the woods?

Was he really arrogant enough to think that Arran and I could not slaughter him, his kin, and every guard here before they could make it to the outer bailey?

My fingers itched for my dagger.

"We have no wish for strife. You will be compensated for every stone we take from the mines," Arran countered.

He must have negotiated like this before; hundreds of times, maybe, over hundreds of years leading the terrestrial armies. Though if the legends were true, he'd mostly accepted surrenders.

"But to what purpose?" Palomides pushed.

Arran's face hardened.

My stomach turned.

Arran.

He did not respond. His gaze did not flicker.

I wasn't even sure what I would have said to him if he answered, what I would have asked. But to feel the caress of his beast, brushing against my consciousness, might have given me a measure of confidence that I was making the right choice.

Nothing came.

Bravado it is.

I shrugged off my cloak, tossing it toward the line of guards along the wall with total disregard. Nevermind that I would soon be shivering without it. This was about performance and cunning.

"Annwyn is beset by an ancient enemy." As I spoke, I walked to the young female. I dragged my eyes over her, like a predator about to eat. I reached for her throat. The male on the other side of the throne inhaled sharply. But the female did not flinch, even when my sharp fingernails grazed her throat as I lifted the heavy amorite necklace.

"The succubus comes at night, while men and males sleep in their beds, to feast upon their minds and turn their bodies into weapons." I recounted each detail as if I was reporting the weather. Detached. Bored.

"If you have not yet seen this horror, then consider yourself lucky and your time counted. The succubus will come for you eventually," I said. But I did not look at Palomides as I spoke. I gave him my back, knowing that Lyrena and Arran would die to protect it.

I looked into the female's dark eyes.

She did not flinch. But I knew the look of fear.

A wicked twist of my wrist, and the heavy necklace came apart in my hand. I slid it into my pocket and walked back to join Arran as if it—and she—were nothing.

Palomides was angry, though he tried to cover it. His hands were not tented anymore, but at his side in fists that were only half-buried by the floor-length robes he wore. They actually reminded me of the attire the priestesses in Avalon favored. But they were black, like everything else in this cursed castle.

I licked my lips, ready to finish my accounting. But Arran spoke.

"The amorite is one in an arsenal of weapons we will use to defeat the succubus." Arran may not be an elemental, and he certainly did not lie. But he had a way with words, a force that he put behind them, that was difficult to counter. It was power given sound. Death as a promise.

Palomides' mind and mouth recovered faster than his body. "The female you are so interested in is my niece, Synora. The one you stabbed, my nephew, Syros."

I bared my teeth at the latter.

Palomides was unmoved. "But I think now is the time to introduce you the last member of my court."

Court.

I wanted to cut the word from his lips. He might imagine himself a king, but I would not leave this cursed castle without disabusing him of that notion.

But first, the amorite.

Before we could speak, a door to the left of the throne opened.

It was a window into the void. A portal. A rift. *This isn't possible.* I grabbed for Arran's hand, waiting for the tingling sensation in my fingers. What was this? Would I be able to control it? I'd never encountered such magic—

Then the swirling stopped.

It was not swirling at all.

It was a body—a figure, moving out of the darkness. A figure that *was* the darkness.

He stepped into the hall, and the breath emptied from my body. As big as Arran. Just as broad, too. But that was not what was striking. It was the armor. Head to toe, not a single fraction of skin or clothing was visible. Just armor.

Black.

But not like the castle itself.

This black *moved*. It swirled and twinkled and sharpened. Like the night sky. Darker.

Like the void itself, given shape.

I felt sick.

Arran's fingers tightened around mine.

I was still holding Arran's hand.

"This is the Black Knight," Palomides said, his smile no longer worthy of the word. As he spoke, Palomides pounded his fist against the Black Knight's breastplate.

The metal did not move. Neither did the Black Knight.

But he was solid. Touching him was not a trick to free-fall into the void.

Inside me, something solidified as well. Or maybe that was because Arran was still holding my hand.

"I am not interested in payment, not of the sort you offer, in any case. In the terrestrial kingdom, we value strength. Prove that you are strong enough to take the amorite."

"I could prove that by killing you now."

"You could. But then you'd have to instill someone else in my place." Palomides said it because he knew it was a costly option. If I was as powerful as I'd intimated, even a hulking black knight in eerie armor should be no match for me. Maybe I should have played this differently—been a retiring female rather than a brazen one. But it was too late for that.

"Duel with the Black Knight. If you defeat him, you will have access to the mines," Palomides said simply.

It was anything but simple. A duel could encompass a thousand different scenarios. Would magic be in play? What magic did the Black Knight possess? Did that mysterious armor shift with him, or was he flora-gifted?

None of that mattered.

We needed the amorite. Annwyn needed it.

"If we defeat the Black Knight, we will have full and unconditional access to the amorite mines until such time as the High King and Queen concurrently decide to return them to you," I said slowly. I paused, waiting for Arran to interject.

His black eyes darted down to our joined hands, but he did not speak.

This was not just about proving my strength or worth. Palomides was up to something. I could feel the lies he spoke as they burrowed their way under my skin. But I could play his game. For now.

Palomides did let the opportunity for an amendment hang open. "Very well. But I shall set the terms of the duel."

"I accept."

Arran's eyes slammed into me with all the force of one of the black stones that built the castle around us. He dropped my hand, his eyes turning murderous.

Get in line, I wanted to say to him, *or Lyrena will beat you to it.*

But I did not.

"Synora and Syros will see to your accommodations. The duel shall take place after midday tomorrow." Palomides sank back onto his throne once again. Relaxed.

This had been his intent all along.

There was only one reason for us to come to this desolate castle. He had something we wanted, and he had known the price before we'd ever walked through the portcullis. Why he wanted us to duel... I'd use the time between now and the duel to figure that out.

I slowed my steps, falling in beside Kay as we followed Synora and Syros out of the great hall. Every step, I kept one eye fixed upon the Black Knight. That feeling in my stomach had not entirely quelled. I doubted it would. "What was Castle Chariot called before Palomides arrived?"

Kay followed my gaze, his grimace saying everything I could not. "Basdove."

The black death.

56
VEYKA

The image of the Black Knight followed me up the stairs to the richly appointed bedroom that Palomides had prepared. It was a royal suite, obvious from the jewel-studded border along the vanity mirror and the gold-flake in the paint adorning the wooden headboard. Palomides had known we would come eventually. Maybe not me and Arran, specifically. But this room had been waiting for the High Queen and King's arrival.

Palomides knew the value of the amorite in his mines. He must have known it when he killed the previous occupants of the castle. Which meant he'd encountered the succubus and figured out that the amorite was key to defeating them. There was no other plausible reason for his posturing.

But what did he hope to achieve through a duel? If either Arran or I was killed, entirely new heirs would have to be appointed. It would throw Annwyn into disarray, and then there would be no one to buy his amorite or whatever else he mined, because everyone would eventually be turned or devoured by the succubus.

There was a piece missing to this puzzle.

But Palomides would not offer answers of his own free will. Every scrap of information would have to be bartered for.

The willowy young female led us into the suite as she'd been bid. But instead of waiting with downcast eyes, she watched our reactions. No doubt, she would be reporting back to Palomides at the first chance.

Lyrena tossed down our travel packs, snapped her fingers to light a fire in the hearth, and surveyed the rest of the room. Whether it was her years in Baylaur or her excellent elemental skills, she looked thoroughly unimpressed.

Synora looked past Lyrena to me. "His lordship has gifted me to you for the duration of your stay, Your Majesty." As she spoke, she swayed her hips and dragged a hand down the centerline of her bodice.

I did not want to know everything that offer entailed.

"We will manage fine on our own," I said, walking to peer out the window. Parting the drapes gave me the opportunity to scan for any obscured entrances. I knew that Lyrena was surreptitiously doing the same. We'd both lost too much to the hidden passageways in Baylaur to take such things for granted.

When I glanced back over my shoulder, Synora had not moved. I rolled my eyes. "You are relieved," I said emphatically, layering my voice with the command I'd seen Arran use—the one that had elementals and terrestrials shaking.

The young female's dark eyes flared with anger, but she could not gainsay me. She may be used to having her way as the lady of the castle, but when I was in residence, she was nothing and no one. But she was not afraid of me, either. I let myself enjoy the chagrin on her face.

Lyrena only waited until the door was closed before tipping a painting forward to check the stone wall behind it. "Glad you said it, so I didn't have to. That one is a snake."

I sighed, my eyes drifting to the sweet oblivion of the bed. "They are all snakes." I paused, rethinking. "Vipers."

That earned a smirking chuckle from Lyrena. How she still managed it, after everything we'd seen and endured, I'd never know.

She must have deemed the bedroom secure, because she crossed to the travel packs she'd shucked on the floor and began unlacing the top of mine. "Cyara gave me annoyingly thorough directions on how I should tend to you—"

"Lyrena." She only stopped because I used the same tone with her as I had on Palomides' niece. Unlike Synora, Lyrena did not retreat. She lifted her golden brows and gave me a look that dared me to push her. Of course, I did. "You are my Goldstone Guard, my Knight, my friend. You do not have to unpack for me or dress me," I said firmly.

She dismissed that argument and went back to work. "Cyara does it."

"As if I could ever get her to stop." I did enjoy being pampered. But I did not require it. I'd spent twenty years locked away in the water gardens with only my nursemaid and my torturers for company. I was perfectly capable of dressing myself.

I closed the space between us and kicked the pack hard, sending it sprawling across the floor and out of Lyrena's reach. She flashed a menacing smile, all gold teeth, letting the warrior show. I crossed my arms.

"I know you will not consent to sleep anytime soon. But talk to Vera and set the watch outside my door. I can manage for myself in here."

Her desire to argue was so deep, so visceral, that I thought she might not be able to control it. I hardly expected blind subservience from my Knights. But she recognized it for what it was—an order. And despite her preference, one she did not have a good reason to fight.

Lyrena stepped back, her orange-gold cape billowing behind her. How she kept her goldstone armor gleaming even when we traveled in snow and muck, I'd never know. She was every inch my glorious golden knight as she nodded. "Stay out of trouble, Veyka." She softened it with a wink.

After days of close contact, with Arran in proximity and my nerves near fraying, I exhaled a sigh of relief as the door closed behind her.

As I expected, the travel pack I'd carried with me for the last several days was a treasure trove. I'd only needed to breach the top several inches over the course of our journey to the coast. It was too damn cold to change clothing or bathe. But now that there was a fire roaring in the hearth—I'd have to remind myself to feed it, since neither of my fire-wielding friends were here to tend it for me—I was warm enough to strip out of my layers of travel-worn clothing.

I almost regretted sending Synora away, if only because she might have drawn me a bath. But I made do with a soft cloth and water heated in a kettle by the fire. By the time I changed into a soft nightgown of translucent dove gray silk and reached for the silver gilt hairbrush, my mind had quieted.

The last hurdle was my hair. At least it did not reach all the way down to my waist these days. I untangled the plait and began to work the brush through the layers. It took an inordinate amount of time. I allowed myself to get lost in the repetitive strokes. It was not quite as soothing as Cyara brushing my hair, but it helped. One stroke, another and another. My eyes drifted closed. Maybe, just maybe, tonight I would actually be able to sleep.

Then the door opened.

The scent of spice and earth accosted my senses before I'd even managed to get my eyes open. But after I'd grabbed the dagger off the vanity.

My first instinct was to scream into his mind, to snarl right back at the beast. But he'd asked me to stay away. So it was my voice that demanded for the second time in only a few days, "What are you doing here?"

His own travel pack was slung over his broad shoulder. He'd taken the time to brush his own dark locks, tying the back in a neat knot at the base of his skull. I wanted to drive my fingers into it and muss that perfection. And then perhaps I would wrap my fingers around his throat and strangle him.

Arran dropped his pack and kicked the door shut behind him. I imagined whoever guarded our door cringing in the corridor. *Not our door. My door.* Whoever it was, they had not barred his access.

I should have expected this. It was exactly the sort of thing that the Arran who had arrived in Baylaur all those months ago would have done. Except that neither of us was that person any longer.

He crossed his arms and planted his feet, ready for a fight. "You have made a point of reminding me that I am the High King of Annwyn."

"And?" I leaned down to pick up the brush I'd dropped to the floor, still clutching the dagger in its place, though I loosened my hold. Any stabbing would be premeditated at this point.

When I straightened, Arran's eyes were burning with black fire. I hadn't meant to do it, but I realized immediately. The nightgown had long sleeves, but its only closure was a single clasp situated at the midpoint between my navel and breasts. And when I'd leaned down to retrieve the brush...

It was almost laughable. How many times had I used my curves against him, to try and manipulate him into doing what I wanted?

I wanted was him desperately.

And I knew that if I had him, my heart might never recover.

Physical joining would not restore what we had lost. Arran had seen the darkness within me, the scars left by the water gardens, and loved me through it. Because of it. Now it felt like darkness and scars were all I had left.

That brutal scowl was back in place on his face. I knew what that meant. He did not want me to know how he was feeling. How much he wanted me. "The High King sleeps with the High Queen," he growled.

My heart stopped entirely. "Like hell."

He advanced a step, his beast's growl rolling through me. My head tilted back like it was a fucking caress. He might as well have licked my throat. I clamped my thighs together, but knew it was useless. I was soft and weak when it came to Arran Earthborn.

"You expect me to believe that my beast allows you to sleep in your own chambers?" As he spoke, his elongated canines flashed. I wanted them sinking into my veins, nipping at my clit.

"We don't share a bedroom," I choked out. Which was almost the truth. In Baylaur, he'd joined me in mine without any formal discussion. But he'd never added any personal belongings or tried to change the arrangement of my things. Other than the time he'd burned my bedsheets after finding Parys in them. A spurt of wet heat slid between my legs at the memory.

Arran's hand rose, his fingers curling toward my chin. "We do now."

He was going to touch me. His fingers would skate along the soft column of my throat, then he would take my chin in his powerful grip. He'd hold me steady as he brought his lips down to mine with punishing force that I would meet thrust for thrust. Then there would be nothing but *us*. Hot limbs and soft curves and perfect rightness—

Arran stepped back.

I wished for cold air to rush in between us. But the room was hot from the fire Lyrena had lit. And the space between us would surely have ignited into an inferno if exposed to even the barest hint of a spark.

I thought I might die, but somehow I managed to get the words out. "Sleep on the floor."

"No."

I closed my eyes. If I had to look at him for a second longer, I would lose control. Maybe if I deprived one of my senses of him, I might be able to claw my way back to rationality.

"What are you so afraid of, Princess?"

I sank my teeth into my lower lip so hard it drew blood. I heard Arran shift on his feet. The scent of it must be doing things to him, to his beast. I could not care about that. I had to preserve myself. Cyara had urged me to let him in, but it hurt so much. And if he saw me now, if he saw who and what I was and did not want me... I crushed the thoughts into oblivion. There was no place for them here and now.

"Do not call me that," I said softly. "Just shut up and let me go to sleep."

That brutal mask was back in place, so I could not tell if Arran was hurt or disappointed or just as frustrated as me. With half a thought, I could have followed the bond that connected our hearts, that precious golden thread, and bathed in his feelings and emotions. But he'd asked me to stay away. So I would.

I walked to the opposite side of the bed. Arran groaned as I retreated. Yes, the translucent nightgown and the swish of my hips was torture. I buried myself under a mountain of blankets and knew it would not be enough.

Arran moved around the room. I'd spent enough nights with him to recognize the movements. But I did not let myself roll to my back and admire the broad outline of him as he completed his evening ablutions. He always slept without a shirt. The sight of a bare-chested Arran might very well kill me.

Eventually he sat, the mattress bowing under his weight. When he didn't lie down, I knew we weren't finished.

"We should talk about the Black Knight," he said, voice carefully devoid of the heat that had almost incinerated us minutes before.

I kept my back to him. "What is there to talk about? Tomorrow, I will face him in the ring, defeat him, and we will have our amorite."

Another pressure on the mattress. He'd leaned back on his fist, was digging it into the soft fabric. If I looked, would I see wolf's claws digging into the thick quilts and blankets?

"Palomides gets to set the terms. They will not be favorable. They may even be impossible."

He wanted to say more. I could feel it, the words he did not say, in the charged space between us. But just like Arran was fighting his physical attraction to me, I was fighting opening up my heart.

The words burned out of my throat. "We could kill Palomides, his family, and all of his guards. Summon terrestrials to man the mines, establish supply lines. We could waste weeks arranging all of it." I had thought through the possibility again and again. But after what had happened with the terrestrials and Isolde, I was not even less sure. Even the terrestrials at Eilean Gayl could not be counted upon for loyalty. "Do you think that a better plan?"

He sucked in a breath, exhaled it slowly. Anger wouldn't have been so easy to diffuse. So, this was something else. I could not decipher it in the simple syllable he gave in answer. "No."

I did not respond.

Arran shifted, stretching his legs onto the bed.

Despite the weight of what was between us, and the worry over the battles the next day would bring, my eyes were heavy. As my thoughts became cloudy, I vaguely wondered if it was Arran's presence in my bed. Wearing his tunic had been a comfort. But the weight of his body mere inches away... it inflamed me, but it also spoke to something else deep within my soul. With Arran here, I was safe.

Just as sleep took me, Arran spoke again. This time, it came out as a low growl, so deep I could have sworn he said it into my mind rather than the fraught air between us. "I do not want to see you hurt."

But that was impossible, of course, because he had asked me to stay away.

57
ARRAN

I'd known from the moment I walked into the bedchamber that I'd made a colossal mistake.

We could not show Palomides any sign of weakness or conflict. He had no doubt seen the desire burning in both of our eyes. If we did anything other than share a bedroom, he would see it as an opening to try to drive a wedge between us. Worse, he might find out that he did not even need to. It was already there, firmly lodged.

But no sense of duty or strategic thought could have prepared me for the sight of Veyka in that fucking nightgown. What business did she have being so beautiful? It was as if the Ancestors had crafted a female perfectly designed to test my control. Her moon white hair was unique, a shade I'd never seen before on this continent or any other. And those eyes... Ancestors, those eyes of hers were dangerous. Too keen by half, and too damn good at looking past the wall I erected around myself.

And that fucking nightgown. How had she managed to bring such a thing along? My travel pack was full of thick woolen clothing and emergency rations. Hers clearly had been packed with less rational thoughts in mind. Though I doubted it was Veyka's doing.

She had not even wanted me in the room. There was no chance she'd packed that scintillating garment with the intent of me seeing it.

But she had not tried to cover herself, either.

She may not want me here with her, but she wanted me. And the more time I spent in her presence, the more I did as well. Not just her luscious body, but her dangerously sharp mind. She was manipulating Palomides, I had no doubt. Agreeing to the duel, letting him set the terms and keep us in the castle overnight were calculated choices, they had to be. That bravado, while inherent to who she was, was also a strategic weapon—being used in the service of Annwyn.

I wanted her to let me in.

I wanted her to agree with me about the amorite not because I was the stronger willed of the two of us, but because I'd convinced that cunning mind that it was the best course of action.

Yet my rational mind would not allow me to give myself to her. Not entirely. Not even if my body and soul demanded it. I wanted Veyka with every beat of my heart, but that did not mean I could trust her. She was an elemental. She knew more about the succubus and about what had happened to me than she was letting on.

There were holes in the recounting she'd given me. I'd prodded at them while we traveled to the coast, trying anything to keep my mind off of the female herself. Veyka was keeping secrets. She did not trust me any more than I did her.

That was going to be a problem sooner than either of us was comfortable with.

I laid awake for a long while, staring up at the bed hangings. Only when Veyka's even breaths turned to soft snores did I finally feel my muscles beginning to relax. Kay was stationed at the door. Lyrena at the end of the hall. Vera would relieve Kay at midnight. We were secure enough that I did eventually drift off.

I dreamt of a barren, orange-gold plain with swirling dust and dunes of sand, ringed by tall mountain peaks. The image had come to me again and again in the days since my awakening in Avalon.

But I still did not recognize it, and I had not yet consulted a map. It was nowhere I'd been in my memory... at least, no memory that still resided safe within my mind.

That confusing tableau gave way to something much more pleasant.

A long, languorous caress across my shoulder and down my pectoral muscle. A sharper prickling sensation followed. Methodical, steady. My Talisman. The sprawling tree tattooed across my chest was burning with pleasant but persistent sensation.

Then it was past my Talisman. Lower.

My eyes snapped open, but there was nothing to see in the dark. The fire was nearly out, reduced to embers and tiny licks of flame. But I did not need light to realize what was happening as Veyka slid down my body, her fingernails and tongue working in tandem to draw the startled groan from my throat.

Somehow, I managed to shape it into words. "What are you doing?"

"What I should have done the moment you woke up," she purred, and I felt it against my skin. Her scorching breath, her soft lips, her complete possession of me.

Her hand closed around my cock and I did not need to question her intent again. Not when she flicked her tongue over the head and a moan ripped from her chest as well. Her head dipped down again, licking the first beads of cum from the tip with such greed I found myself thrusting up into her mouth.

Veyka took it in stride. She began to work my length with her hand in a rhythmic twirling motion while her mouth sucked me down, deeper and deeper. At some point she pulled her hand away, and a growl so visceral and demanding ripped from me that she chuckled maniacally. In the haze of my pleasure, I realized she was not in full control of herself. Nor was I.

But I did not stop it.

When her hand returned, slick and wet, and the scent of her own arousal hit my nostrils, I nearly spilled my load of cum down her throat on the spot.

But Veyka knew me, that much was obvious. I did not care to interrogate that realization, not when it felt so fucking good. She took me right to the edge, again and again, until I felt my control flagging. Veyka knew it too. She dragged her tongue in one last long, languid stroke over the head of my cock before sliding up my body, her soft curves caressing everywhere her tongue had paid homage on the way down.

She paused, rising up on one elbow above me. I could just see the outline of her face in the failing light from the hearth. For the space of several heartbeats, she balanced herself above me. The muscles of her arm did not quaver under her weight, used to bearing that and more. Every inch of Veyka was strong, right down to the soul that I was quickly learning was indominable.

It was too dark to see anything in her eyes other than the burning ring of blue around the pupils. But I knew the question they must hold. An opportunity to pull away. From her, from this. Because we both knew that this would change things. I had no idea what it meant to her, but for me...

I waited too long, and she decided she did not care about my answer. When her mouth closed over mine, I realized I didn't either.

She sank her hips down over mine, the weight of her substantial and powerful. Veyka was no slender waif, breakable and weak. She was strength and power and every sexual fantasy I'd ever had. Maybe they had not been fantasies at all. Maybe they had been visions of my future. A future with this female, my mate.

Veyka's hand curled around my cock one more time, guiding me to her slick center. Then she shoved her hips down, seating me to the hilt in one brutal stroke. There was no memory or thought of past, present, future. There was only this moment, this female, this excruciating perfection and pleasure.

I reached for her for the first time. Ancestors, how had that happened? How had I not taken every second to explore her glorious body? But she swatted my hand away, pinning a hand to my shoulder.

I could have fought her. But then I felt her other hand between us, her nimble fingers tangling in the thick curls, stroking her clit as she rode me. She could not see my face, I could not see hers. And yet, there was no doubt of who and what we were as we drove each other toward climax.

Mates.

The word sang through my veins, embedded itself in the sinew of my muscles. For the first time since awakening, the bond in my chest did not ache. It glowed. If I blinked, I might see that golden thread between us come to life. Conjured by this—by us.

The walls of her pussy clung to my cock tighter with every thrust. I wanted to reach for her hips, to slam her down harder, or to warn her. But some instinct told me that if I touched her, the magical suspension between us would be broken and we'd come crashing back to reality.

It was too late anyway. I exploded inside of her, spurt after spurt of my hot seed coating the insides of her cunt. Veyka did not slow at all, the thrust of her hips milking every last drop of seed from my length. I realized why a second later as she gripped around me again, her climax so intense I felt my cock hardening in response. It should not have been possible, not so fast, so soon.

But I was spilling again, and she was crying out, screaming as she rode me through wave after wave of pleasure. I clung to it, to her. Nothing had ever felt so perfect, so right.

She was shaking as she lowered herself back down, her breasts pillowing out against the hard planes of my chest. I caught her, unafraid to touch her now. Unable to stop myself. I eased her onto the bed until she was in my arm, her face buried in my shoulder and her body still half-draped over mine. I did not dare try to kiss her, not even to press one to the top of her silky hair.

Only when she finally stopped shaking did I close my eyes.

The sleep that came for me was dreamless.

58

ARRAN

I woke again in the liminal hour just before dawn, when light begins to seep back into the world and creatures of the night retreat back to their dark refuges. My arm reached across the bed, seeking without conscious thought or intent, only to find the space cold. Empty.

But the scent of primrose and plum lingered.

The room was dark, the fire gone to nothing. But I could hear faint movements near the foot of the bed. Another second, and I knew from the slide and cadence that it was Veyka.

She was dressing.

"You are leaving."

The sounds ceased, but silence did not come. Was that Veyka's heart beating wildly in her chest, or my own?

"I will be back by sunrise, Brutal Prince," Veyka finally said. She resumed her careful movements, the soft scrape of leather and fur giving way to the harsher sounds of metal as she strapped on the harness she wore over her chest—the one that as coincidentally showcased her magnificent breasts.

As if anything Veyka did was coincidental.

"No harm shall come to me," she said into the darkness between us. An offering, after those last words of concern I'd given. My own weakness, exposed.

A sharp pain stabbed into my gut, as real as if someone had shoved in a blade. Where was she going—to who? Barkke was beyond, waiting in the forest, but with her void power Veyka could be at his side in a matter of moments.

My mind may not remember her, but my beast and my body did.

"Hush," Veyka whispered. I could imagine her lips pursing together, the soft hiss of her breath between those luscious lips. But I felt it in my chest—the thread that was wrapped so tightly around my heart, surging, shining. She was not speaking to me, but to my beast. "You know that I am yours."

I was gripped with need—not just to be inside her again, though I could feel my cock tightening—but to have her. *Possess* her. Every part, not just her body.

The sex had been... less than I expected.

It had eased the primal ache in my chest, the climaxes real and more visceral than any I'd ever experiences.

But I knew there was more, something we had not touched.

Maybe we were both too afraid. Maybe I was a coward, after all. The Brutal Prince, High King of Annwyn, too terrified to be honest with himself or his mate.

That did not stop me from wanting her.

From needing her.

My feet hit the floor. "I will come with you."

Silence.

It was too dark to search her eyes. But a few steps on the cold stone floor, and I was close enough to see the shape of her face, even with only slivers of starlight from the window to illuminate her.

Veyka was a master of masking her emotions. I'd watched her do it with Palomides, showing just what was useful, holding back what was dangerous. But here, between us in the dark, it was different. She was different.

The pout of her lips betrayed her—lips still swollen from where they'd scraped across mine. She was trying to harden herself, to create a protective shell around her heart. Her bottom lip trembled. She was failing.

For a moment, I thought she would refuse. Simply disappear into the darkness, into the void, where I could not follow.

Then into the space between us, she held out her hand.

59
VEYKA

The castle was certainly warded to protect from intruders, but that had not stopped me from moving through the void and landing on the battlements. I hoped that reasoning would hold within the castle itself. I had not yet encountered any ward or room that could hold me. Only Arran.

He could pull me back if he tried hard enough—had done, and saved my life, when I'd first fallen through the realms uncontrollably after our Joining.

But I doubted he could do it now. I had not even explained the tether of my power to our mating bond.

Arran had loved me at our Joining. I'd loved him, even if I'd been unable to admit it.

Now...

I did not want to test it.

After what happened... No. I would not allow myself to regret it.

I had been unable to stop myself. Together in that bed, even if he'd asked me to stop, I would not have. Could not have. The mating bond demanded. And I did not try to argue.

But afterward I felt... hollow.

Anytime our bodies came together, it was wild and eviscerating and earth-shaking. It had been all of that.

But it had also been empty.

A mockery of what should have been between us, of the way we had consummated our bond in the faerie pools. Even in those earliest days in Baylaur, the anger and hate between us... that had felt like *more*. Something so solid I could almost wrap my hands around and hold it.

But this ephemeral echo of love... it was going to tear me apart.

So, naturally, I needed to tear something else apart.

I pulled us from the void and into a darkness that felt oppressive, rather than freeing.

Arran immediately released my hand, drawing the battle axe from his belt. I could not blame him; the black stones around us reeked of blood and decay. But I still wondered if the Arran before the Battle of Avalon would have kept hold.

We stood just inside a thick wooden door studded with metal reinforcements. One torch was pinned to the wall beside the door, casting the ground in front of us in flickering light. My stomach tightened at the sight. These might have once been the same black stones that built the rest of the Castle Chariot, but they were so crusted with dirt and gore that they were unrecognizable.

"I aimed for where the dungeons ought to be," I said, nearly choking on the scent of the place. Clearly, I'd found them.

Arran moved on silent feet toward the corner where the wall turned and the light ran out. "Aimed?"

I did not know how else to describe it. Moving through the void was not exact. At least, not for me. *Not yet*—a voice whispered in my mind. I ignored it.

We moved in silent tandem around the corner, finding a row of empty cells. Empty, because whoever had been held here was dead. A rotting corpse huddled in one corner, covered in its own refuse. In another, there was nothing left but bones. Scattered bones. As if the body been ripped apart before being left to bleed out.

Impressive, in terms of torture techniques.

Concerning, for a king and queen in need of an ally.

Another door, a set of stairs downward. Not a single guard to be seen.

Palomides must consider this place secure enough without them, at least inside the dungeons themselves. Later, we'd see how many guards waited beyond the door where Arran and I had first arrived.

We were halfway down the stairs when the scent hit me.

No. It couldn't be, not here. They can't—we are too late—

"Arran, take one of my rapiers." I kept my voice low. Did they hear? There was still so much we did not know. I shoved the blade into Arran's hand. "You cannot bleed with the scabbard, but they can still injure you—"

"The scabbard?"

Arran's eyes blew wide as the scent accosted him as well. Decay and death, but worse. The smell of darkness. Not the darkness within me, or even within Arran. This was a darkness that took and took until there was nothing left; a darkness from which there was no return.

What is that?

My soul sang in response to his voice inside of me, stroking me through the bond despite the lurking danger.

Answering him was as easy as breathing. *You cannot bleed while you wear the scabbard. It protects you.* And then, *the succubus can kill without drawing blood.*

Understanding flashed through the bond, companion to confusion and questions. But I did not have time to answer them. Not now.

I grabbed Arran's arm, letting the warmth of him run through me even as the cold, calm of killing overtook my senses. "I love you."

Maybe it was unfair, to drop those words on him in a moment like this when he could not hope to process them. But I knew what awaited us but a few steps ahead, and I would not go to my death or let him to go to his without the truth between us. No matter what had happened, who Arran was, I loved him.

For a thousand years and a thousand more.

The scent was overwhelming. I could hardly breathe. But killing was natural to me, it was my sustenance. When nothing else in my life made sense, the feel of blood and blade was clear.

I would stand between my mate and death. I would not put him in danger again.

I charged down the stairs, rapier in one hand and dagger in the other.

There were no torches, no light at all. Maybe the succubus did not need it to hunt. My eyes sharpened, pupils widening to let in every bit of life-saving light. But my blade was already swinging outward in a defensive sweep. Arran was behind me. Not Arran—his beast. He'd shifted, and the brush of his thick fur against my midsection as he pushed past bolstered me. We'd face this together. We would survive.

Arran snarled, muscles tensing to leap.

But no attack came.

My hands dropped to my sides, weapons with them, as my eyes fully adjusted and realization took over.

I felt Arran shift beside me, the soft fur replaced by leather and wool.

"Ancestors save us," he breathed.

If I had any faith left in the Ancestors, I might have said the same.

They were behind bars. Caged, like animals.

But so much worse.

Arran gave me a look—*do not do anything stupid*—before disappearing briefly back up the stairs. He reappeared a minute later with a torch.

I expected to see the face of the hardened battle commander, taking stock of his enemy, studying them for weaknesses. I was wrong.

I should have been flattered. He did not bother to hide his horror from me.

Instead, I felt deflated.

He had believed me, but he hadn't trusted my account. He had not fully understood until this moment, when faced with the reality of it. Another part of my heart fractured at that—a part that could not be healed by any amount of fucking.

The cells stretched beyond the reach of the torchlight in both directions. They did not seem to be purpose-made for the succubus, but the thick metal bars contained them just the same. And the cells were packed. I counted ten in the one directly in front of us.

"Mostly humans," Arran said, stepping closer despite the smell. The noxious black bile of the succubus coated the ground, the bars, the bodies. And yet, some of them were not actively spewing the stuff anymore.

Their souls.

The black bile was their souls, being ejected forcibly from their bodies, until nothing remained but a shell for the succubus to exploit.

My own soul recoiled at the thought, the golden thread of Arran and I's mating bond tightening in my chest, protecting itself.

I had a soul worth protecting. And a kingdom as well.

I had changed. My first instinct was to kill them all—and we would. There was no way I would leave this kind of threat waiting in the dungeons for Palomides to unleash on us or on unsuspecting innocents. But this was also an opportunity.

"I knew that Palomides was hiding something. The duel is a distraction, to keep us from finding this. Or maybe to spring them upon us somehow." The possibilities I'd been sorting through it my mind had narrowed, but had yet to fully solidify.

"A distraction," Arran repeated quietly. "Just like everything you did in the throne room."

Despite what stood in front of us, my gaze was drawn to him. I dipped my chin.

He did not move, and it was hard to read his expression in the faint light. But his voice was raw. "You do not have to hide from me."

An offer. To share myself—my plans, my worries. To let him see me, again.

I did not know if I could do it.

I stepped closer to the cells, refusing to flinch away from the desiccated black hand that reached out for me, fingers rubbed away to bony points. Scratch marks covered the floor. The succubus had sharpened its nails.

"They do not need the light to know we are here," I said.

Arran moved to stand beside me. I wanted to lean into him. But he did not reach for me.

He had done me the courtesy of ignoring my declaration of love. The least I could do was keep my hands to myself.

"And they have no interest in ripping each other apart. Only us," Arran said, raising the torch above his head. The succubus strained toward us, pressing up against the bars. They could have easily taken a bite of each other, but their focus was singular.

Arran took a few steps down the corridor, cold, fetid air taking his place. "Are they sentient?"

I wished I could say no. But the more I looked at them, the more I sorted through my memories...

"A pack of them, dozens, attacked us in the jungle above the faerie caves. It could not have been an accident, not as isolated as we were," I said. Arran did not remember, but I did. "I've never heard one speak, if that is what you're asking."

I felt Arran's grumble of annoyance. A few steps further down the corridor, while I held my place. But the succubus were wholly focused. Even the ones in the cells further down, nearest to Arran, surged all together in one direction.

Mine.

"They want you," Arran breathed.

I swallowed past something in my throat that felt a lot like fear. "So it would seem."

He was back at my side. "Why?"

I did not dare press my eyes closed, not even with the succubus behind thick metal bars. I'd known this moment would come. Arran was much too smart not to work it out. But I hadn't expected it here, now, when I my pussy still ached from the feeling of his cock inside of me and with my words of love hanging heavy in the air around us.

"I am the reason they came to Annwyn again, after all these millennia. My void power opened the pathways that had been closed."

Silence.

The horrible, unearthly sounds of the succubus continued. The gurgling of black bile, the scraping of bones and hiss of death. But I did not hear any of it—not even the pounding of my own heart in my chest. I waited for Arran to speak.

Instead, he took my hand.

I heard my heart now. It was about to explode.

"Wouldn't killing you close those rifts?" he said quietly.

"Or keep them open forever," I whispered.

Arran's hand tightened. "They cannot have you." *You are mine.*

Fae or beast, male or mate, I *felt* those words.

I inhaled sharply, regretted it instantly, and was pulled back to the cruel reality around us. "If they are human, he must have brought them here through a rift. There are the official ones, but we discovered months ago that there are others, secret or forgotten. There must be one nearby. Human minds are easier for the succubus to overtake. He may very well have brought them here as human men, and then bided his time. Eventually, without any amorite, the succubus invaded their bodies and turned them into this." I shook my head at all that implied. "Palomides knows what is at stake, and yet still he plays games."

Arran held my gaze for several more seconds. His eyes blazed with black fire that I would gladly have let burn me to nothing.

Then his jaw ticked, his dark brows drew together, and he forced his eyes back to the cells.

"Yes. But to a purpose. He is keeping them here…" Arran paused as if weighing his words. "He knows the amorite protects him and his guards. He is building his own army."

I shivered, unable to repress the chill that slithered down my spine. The betrayals would never cease. First Gawayn, who believed he knew what was best for Annwyn. Roksana, thinking I would be the easier Pendragon sibling to control. My mother and Gorlois, whose plot had been decades in the making so that they might command the kingdom of Annwyn for themselves. And now, another ambitious lord who sought to overthrow my throne.

It should not have been possible.

"How do you know?" I hated how melancholy my voice sounded in that dungeon of death, where strength was required above all else.

"Because it is what I would do, if I wanted what he wants." Arran dragged a hand up through his hair. "Power."

Arran had never wanted power. It had been seeded in him from birth. Thrust upon him by Arthur's death.

I had longed for it. The power to defend myself. To free myself. I claimed those things eventually, and they had nothing to do with magic. The power that flowed through my veins now, ignited by the male at my side, was nothing without the ability to claim it. To master it.

Arran had taught me that.

In the time we'd been apart, when I'd been forced to stand on my own, I had started to learn what that power could truly do.

Before I had been terrified of my power.

But now I had bigger things to fear. And the power to protect those I loved.

Arran was not holding my hand any longer. His fingers stroked over the head of his battle axe, tucked back into his belt. "War is coming."

"I will not let it get to that," I said fiercely.

My fault.

I was the reason the succubus had returned to Annwyn. I had to find a way to defeat them, to push them back before their death and darkness spilled over from the human realm. I would not let it come to all-out war. I couldn't.

I could not send my subjects to die knowing that it was my fault.

That my happiness—my mating bond with Arran—was the cause.

I missed the cold, scowling mask of the Brutal Prince. The pity in his eyes was so much worse. How many legions had Arran led into battle? Even in victory, there had surely been losses on the field.. Once, I would have scoffed at the notion of guilt. Arran was a tool made for death and destruction. I understood because I was his counterpart.

But it was one thing to stab and kill and maim. It was something else entirely to contemplate sending the ones I loved into danger on my behalf.

Stab. Kill. Maim.

Maybe that would dull the edge of my agonizing guilt.

I drew my weapons once more.

Arran's eyes flicked up at the movement, tracking it. I blinked, and his battle axe was in his hand.

"Can you get us into those cells?" he said, tucking the torch into a notch high above the reach of the succubus in their cells.

"Of course." I flashed a wicked smile sharp as the blades in my hands. "It would be my pleasure."

60

ARRAN

We arrived back in the bedchamber just as the bottom arc of the sun crested over the hill. My heart throbbed in my chest, my beast howling and clawing to be freed. Slaughtering the succubus had only whetted his appetite.

Veyka released my hand instantly, stalking to the window.

I could not even pretend to not watch her.

She dropped the weapons first.

Then the cinched linen shirt that highlighted the too-generous curve of her hips. I sucked in a breath and turned away when her fingers went to the laces of her bustier.

More fabric hit the floor as she reached for a wet cloth and began scrubbing away the remnants of our encounter with the succubus.

This was punishment for that bloody, feral possessiveness I'd shown in the dungeons. I told myself not to look. What had happened before... not a mistake. But rash. Driven by need rather than rational thought.

But rationality and strategy had failed me where Veyka was concerned. I had no memories to use as their basis. All I had was feeling and need.

And I needed her more than I needed my next breath.

A long, languorous groan filled the room, surging straight for my cock. My eyes were on her before I could stop myself, devouring every detail—every luscious curve silhouetted by the morning sun, every dip and dimple of her magnificent backside visible as she stretched her arms overhead.

Fuck it.

The duel would not take place until midday.

"Wake me in time for lunch," Veyka said, shattering my delusion.

She threw herself into the bed without a backward glance in my direction. Wrapped bedsheets that still smelled of our sex tight around her. And did not even open an eye to taunt me with a wink.

Ancestors.

I was so truly fucked.

61

VEYKA

I woke with my fingers in my cunt and Arran's name on my lips.

It hadn't been enough. I'd hoped that giving in to the physical desire between us would ease the clawing need in my chest. But it had only reminded my body of what I'd gone without for all these weeks. Months, now.

Not anymore.

Hours. It had been mere hours since Arran's cock was buried inside of me, and already it was too long.

My fingers were already wet with my desire. I stroked lower, toying with my entrance—

And froze.

I was not alone.

I should have known by the feeling in my chest, burning with need, but not aching. Arran was near.

A slow, repetitive sound filled the bedchamber. Metallic. He was sharpening a blade. I listened for a few strokes more—his battle axe. Again and again, I listed to the long lashes of the file over the blade. He did not realize I was awake.

My fingers began to move again.

Arran swiped the file over the head of his axe. I drew a fingertip along the length of my slit. Again, again. I forced myself to follow his cadence, to imagine it was his touch on me.

My hips started to arch, desperate to increase the pressure. But I forced myself to lie still, to not alert Arran.

His pace increased. He'd found the right angle, his body falling into rhythm. I'd seen him sharpen his axe dozens of times. I could imagine the intense focus on his face, the way his tongue would dart out from between his lips.

I wanted his tongue on me. But all I had were my own fingers, stroking deeper with each swipe of the file against the blade. I could not help myself. I slid a one finger into my pussy. Then two. It still wasn't enough. I ached with longing, for Arran's thick fingers stroking inside of me—

The sounds stopped.

I'm caught.

My cheeks burned. So did my breasts. Not from embarrassment, but anticipation. If I threw off the sheets, if I presented my body, needy and trembling, there was no way Arran or his beast would be able to resist.

But then it began again.

Quieter, more precise.

File traded for whetstone.

I sank my teeth into my bottom lip to hold in the moan as my fingers echoed the movement. No more long, repetitive strokes, but continuous, precise circles. I dragged my fingertips around and around my clit as Arran honed his blade.

Oh, Arran. My entire body filled with heat. The sheets burned my skin, but I didn't pull them off. The scent of Arran's spice and earth still clung to them. I breathed it in and my pussy began to tremble. I was so close—

A pause.

The almost imperceptible sound of Arran turning over the axe to work on the other side of the blade.

Bastard. He knew. He was torturing me.

But that would not stop me now.

Arran was moving faster. So was I.

I was going to come, to fill the bedchamber with the scent of my satisfaction. My body begged for release. I arched into my own hand, and this time I did not stop myself.

I heard Arran stand, honing the axe against the leather strop. The final step. I shoved two fingers inside of myself, my other hand desperately working my clit.

My eyes clenched shut, but I swore I could *feel* the strength of Arran's fingers where they curled around the handle of his axe, as if they were curling inside of me. The pressure was too intense. My chest tightened. So did my pussy. A growl, low and deep, rolled through me.

I plunged over the edge, the walls of my cunt squeezing my hand as waves of wetness soaked the bedsheets.

But I could not stop. My flesh was raw. So was I. But I drove my fingers into myself, harder, deeper, until I came again. I didn't care what sounds I made. Maybe my growl matched Arran's beast, primal and harsh.

I had no idea how much time passed as my body stilled, the last tremors of my climax finally settling around me. There were no more sounds of blades and weapons. Only ragged breaths. Mine— and Arran's.

I should open my eyes.

"Veyka," Arran growled, his voice raw with need. Nearly shaking. "Veyka," he said again. Insistent. A demand.

Knock. Knock.

I thought he might ignore it. Damn strategy and duty and everything except *us*.

But I was disappointed.

He threw open the door so hard the hinges cracked.

"Good morning!" Lyrena said brightly. "I found some..."

My cheeks were burning again.

"I can come back later," Lyrena said firmly.

But the scent hit me before Arran could slam the door in her face. I scrambled out of the bed, nakedness entirely forgotten. "Are those—"

"Veyka!"

"—chocolate croissants?!"

⋄⋄⋄

"You need something other than pastries if you want to keep your energy up," Lyrena admonished as I polished off my third chocolate croissant.

"Yes, yes," I said, waving my hand toward the cured meats. "I will get there eventually."

"You do not find it suspiciously coincidental that Palomides happened to prepare your favorite breakfast?" Arran scowled from the window.

The sun had disappeared, eclipsed by thick gray clouds. Arran had been scowling at their progress for an hour.

"My favorite *food*. Period," I corrected, licking a stray bit of chocolate off my fingertip. Arran tried and failed to cover his groan as he turned back to the window.

Lyrena swiped the plate of chocolate croissants away, replacing it with one bearing thick slices of bacon. "Arran has a point. It could be poisoned."

"I do not care," I said. I took a bite of bacon for my own sake, not to appease my hovering skoupuma mothers. Besides, it did not play into the game that Palomides was playing. He was assembling an army of succubus, challenging me to a duel so he could take over my kingdom. If I died quietly from poisoning, he would not get to take credit for the kill. "Death by chocolate croissant would be the best way to go."

Arran covered the ground between us in a blink. His hands pinned mine to the chair, pressing me down into the wooden arms to the point of pain.

"Don't do that," he snarled, an inch from my face. "Do not ever joke about your death."

The stubborn, rebellious core of me wanted to push back, to shove him away and insist he had no right.

But that was wrong.

He was my mate. He had *every* right. The thread within me, the manifestation of our mating bond, which had frayed and stretched, began to glow. Bright, golden, solid.

"I am yours," I said, quiet by strong. Unflinching before the most powerful fae to ever walk this continent.

Arran's black eyes blazed with ebony fire as he took my words inside of him. As he gave them back to me, his voice gravelly and not wholly his own— "And I will never let you go."

62

ARRAN

The day darkened well before nightfall, the morose gray clouds an appropriate match for my mood. Midday had come and gone. It was Lyrena who recalled Palomides' exact words—*the duel will take place after midday*.

After.

Palomides was up to something—more than just keeping succubus in his dungeons, which was damning enough. Whatever it was, I had no doubt it was meant to disadvantage Veyka in the duel. Put her off balance.

More the fool, him. Palomides may have learned Veyka's favorite food, but he did not know her as well as he thought. Veyka was perfectly at ease, spending the day eating pastries and playing cards with Lyrena. Occasionally, they paused for a bit of sparring. But after they shattered a vase, they contented themselves with verbal barbs rather than physical ones.

I was the one on edge.

Maybe fucking Veyka again would have released some of the tension. The Ancestors knew, I was a second away from giving in when Lyrena had interrupted.

The scent of her still lingered in the air. Her usual primrose and plum, yes, but also the tangy sweetness that had exploded from between her legs.

Everything she'd shared in the dungeons, the tenuous connection we'd made, had only intensified the compulsion to be with her. My mind was fighting my beast, and losing.

I pressed my forehead to the chilled window pane. The need for her was going to burn me alive from the inside out. I fixed my eyes on the distant hilltop, tracing the outline of the trees. Nothing of note. Down to the plane, the white snow turned to dirt and muck, and a lone spot of black.

I sucked in a breath just as the knock sounded on the door. When I turned, Veyka and Lyrena were already on their feet, ready. We all knew.

"It is time."

※

Syros, the snake shifter, led us out of the castle. The rain came down in sheets as we cleared the inner bailey. Guards lined the battlements now, but they were as silent and immovable as the day before.

I already knew where we were going.

The Black Knight waited in the center of the lifeless plain.

Behind him, many yards away, Palomides and his niece stood at the base of the hill. They both wore heavy cloaks to shield them from the storm. We did not.

Veyka had left behind her heavy fur mantle. If she was cold, she did not show it. The rain slid in rivulets from her leather armor, but she swaggered along, utterly unbothered.

Begrudging admiration yawned awake in my chest.

"Welcome, Majesties," Palomides' voice boomed, loud despite the distance and pelting rain.

Veyka and I stopped at the same moment, our bodies in sync, even if our minds and hearts were not. In the periphery of my vision, I watched her prop one first on her hip while Palomides yammered on.

"Not even Castle Chariot is grand enough to host a duel of the magnitude you have conferred upon us," Palomides said. "Henceforth, this plain shall be consecrated by the royal blood spilled—"

"No royal blood shall be spilt today," Veyka interrupted. "I grow tired of your proselytizing. Remember that if you are ever summoned to Baylaur."

Palomides' eyes narrowed to slits. A serpent shifter, like his nephew. I could have guessed.

But Veyka was unimpressed by the promise of fangs. "Set your terms," she ordered.

Palomides licked his lips. Even from the distance, I could see— it was forked, even in his fae form. "I am a simple male. Defeat the Black Knight, and you shall have your amorite."

Veyka unsheathed the blades from across her back. "Fine."

"To the death," Palomides added.

Veyka rolled her shoulders. "Yes, yes," she said, sounding thoroughly bored. "Prove I am strong enough to rule the terrestrial kingdom and all that."

Palomides laughed.

"I have no doubt you could, Majesty."

Veyka stilled.

"But you will not be the one dueling."

Palomides turned to me, his eyes black slits. Monstrous. "The Brutal Prince shall be the one to prove himself today."

63

VEYKA

This was a test.

For Arran and I both, and for all of the terrestrial kingdom.

If Arran died, Annwyn would be thrown into chaos. Palomides would use his succubus to take over more than just mines. At least we'd foiled that plan by slaughtering them all. Palomides of the Mines would no doubt send his guards in every direction, to every land holding, to report on the outcome of this duel.

But why take the risk? Arran was the most powerful fae in millennia. There was every reason to believe he would win this duel, unless...

Unless Palomides knew that Arran had been injured.

I did not let any of the emotion ricocheting through my body show on my face or travel through the bond to my mate.

I forced a wide, wicked grin to my face, despite the rain. I was fucking cold, but there was no time for such mundane concerns as personal discomfort.

I turned that lazy smile to Arran. "I shall enjoy watching you cleave him into tiny pieces," I purred to Arran, just loud enough that it would carry through the rain to Palomides' ears.

Are you ready for this? I asked Arran. He could have his feelings about speaking through the bond later.

I received a low growl in response—and not the sensual kind.

Great.

I grabbed Lyrena's arm. A second later, we were on the opposite end of the killing field, far from Palomides and his sycophantic family. Kay and Vera could go where they wanted. I was certain Barkke watched from the shadows of the tree line, in his fae or beast form. I did not dare put my back to the still surface of the Split Sea. Legend said that its surface had not been broken in seven thousand years.

But I was living proof that legends were not always what they seemed.

In the distance, Palomides lifted his arm toward the sky. Even here, with a deluge of rain and all that space separating us, I heard his booming voice. "Begin."

Arran shifted, the motion blurred by the sluicing torrent of water. Even at a distance his wolf was massive. As big as the Black Knight, who stood unmoving in the center of the plain. Like he had not even heard Palomides order.

Arran stalked forward. At an angle—circling his opponent. I'd seen him do the same thing in the sparring ring. A slow approach, choosing the best course of attack. Waiting to see how his opponent would react—turn with him or expose their side. A good way of assessing the Black Knight's arrogance, using it.

The Black Knight stood solid, unmoving. He had not even drawn his broadsword.

A shiver of unease slid down my spine.

Just a raindrop.

Arran is the most powerful fae in millennia. Blessed with both flora and fauna gifts. There is no opponent he cannot defeat.

Except the nearest flora were the trees of the forest, far away even for Arran. That was why he'd shifted into his wolf.

One more snarl, and Arran bounded forward. I did not even have time to drag in a breath. He was that fast.

But the Black Knight still did not draw his sword.

He only lifted a hand to the sky.

Every hair on my body rose.

No. Impossible.

Lightning streaked down the dark gray sky, directly into the Black Knight's outstretched arm. Except his armor was not black anymore. He glowed with light—with deadly energy. Then he swung that arm down and aimed at my mate.

I swallowed my scream, closed an internal fist around the golden thread that connected us. I would not let myself be a distraction, could not let him die because of me.

Not again. It can't be happening again.

Arran twisted in midair, evading the deadly arc of sizzling power. His growl rolled through the water-logged plain, the ground seeming to vibrate as he crashed into the Black Knight, sending them both tumbling to the ground.

A lightning wielder—an elemental. What in the humans' bloody hell was an elemental doing here, serving Palomides?

My skin began to crawl again, that awful sizzling. The Black Knight had gotten his arm up, was trying to channel power from the sky. But Arran knocked him aside.

Who?

"It can't be," Lyrena breathed beside me. But I could not look away, did not dare.

Even as my mind spiraled. Lightning wielders were rare—had I ever even met one? Teo, my traitorous royal councilor, had been able to summon storms. But he was dead. A relative?

Lyrena was shaking her head beside me—she'd arrived at no firm conclusion either.

On the plain, Arran was a storm of death, a dance of fangs and fur.

The Black Knight shoved him off, managed to get the sword into his hand.

Arran pounced, dodging the blade, clamping down on the Black

Knight's arm. Bone snapped—I heard it from the other side of the plain even through the rushing rain.

Blood. Blood flowing out, pooling, coating my hands.

I dug my nails into the flesh of my palms, trying to focus on the pinpricks of pain. That was rainwater wetting my hands. Not Arran's blood.

He'd injured the Black Knight. But the elemental did not cry out, did not show any sign of slowing. He threw up his other arm, drawing down another streak of lightning until his armor glowed brightly once again.

Arran was already running.

He did not make himself an easy target—like dodging arrows, he ran from side the side, changing his direction so rapidly the Black Knight could not predict. He sent down bolt after bolt of lightning.

"He's going to get himself killed," Lyrena muttered.

The scabbard could have protected Arran from the Black Knight's sword. But it would do nothing to stop him from being roasted alive from the inside.

The scabbard could not protect him.

Not from me, not from his soul-bonded mate...

"He's testing the range," Lyrena said. She was clear-headed. She could see what I failed to. Arran moved side to side, yes, but also farther and then closer. Testing the accuracy of that lightning.

But why? Why did that matter? Why not attack, wrestle the Black Knight to the ground, rip off his head?

I realized the answer a minute later.

Arran's movements had changed. No less erratic, but more controlled. Tighter. He was moving in closer, preparing to launch an attack that would be final. That must be final.

Because he was tiring.

Palomides knew it too. His chuckle should have been lost to the elements, but somehow it reached me on the other side of the plain. He had one elemental in his charge; maybe he had another hidden away nearby, a wind-wielder who could amplify and carry the sound. Nausea churned in my gut at the thought. My own kind... betraying me, again.

As I'd betrayed Arran, when it was my sword that pierced his chest.

My fault. My fault. My fault.

Not just the elementals—terrestrials, too. How could we fight the succubus when our own kind were betraying us at every turn?

When my mate was tiring on that blood-soaked plain.

Lyrena must have realized what was happening. "He is not fully recovered," she breathed.

My head was moving. Faster with each breath. Side to side.

"Veyka, you cannot intervene. We need the amorite." She grabbed for my hand. But all she found was air.

64
ARRAN

There was such roaring in my head. The sound of the rain and thunder, the blood rushing through my veins, the wolf's snarling growl. I moved on instinct alone until those too began to fail me.

My beast was slowing.

Not the lack of sleep—I'd fought under worse conditions than this, dozens of times.

The injury.

The wound on my chest appeared healed; not even a scar to mark where Excalibur had cleaved my chest. But I should not have been tiring. Not this quickly. My beast had ripped apart enemies on the battlefield for hours. Days, even.

But the beast was slowing.

I had to make what remained of my strength count. For the amorite we desperately needed, for Annwyn. For my mate, who was trying so hard to keep her emotions locked down. But I could feel her panic through the bond.

The Black Knight was formidable—a lightning wielder. I knew precious little about the intricacies of elemental power, but even I knew it was rare. Who—Veyka must know who I faced. There could not be so many lightning wielders that she would not recognize them once I ripped off that black helm.

And I would rip it off.

I would win. I would survive.

My muscles tensed beneath my rain-soaked fur, readying for that final push. The Black Knight would throw another bolt of lightning. I would dodge it, rally my speed to go wide and launch myself at him from behind. I'd rip off his arm first, the one I had not broken. More strength; more force to get through that black armor. Then he would not be able to pull down the lightning from the storm.

The storm that Palomides had known was coming. He'd waited to summon us for the duel until it coalesced right above the plain, to give the Black Knight as much advantage as possible.

I dug into the dregs of my power, loosening the restraints on my beast as much as I dared, and sprang forward.

The Black Knight lifted his arm again, his armor taking on that unearthly glow.

Deeper, down into my power, calling up everything I had—

The scent of burning fur filled my nostrils, the zing of light and power slicing over my back as I arced into the sky, leaping well above his head. But before I could turn, before I could launch my final attack, she appeared.

Veyka.

She brought her rapier up, fast and fierce. Such power and force behind her blow, she only needed one swipe of the slender blade. One brutal, beautifully accurate swipe in that narrow strip where the armor on the Black Knight's body met the plating on his arms. Not down, where the shoulder was protected. But up from the armpit, through sinew and bone.

The massive arm hit the sodden ground with a sickening *thud*.

"You cannot interfere!" Palomides' voice boomed across the field.

I snarled—my kill. My mate, putting herself in danger, to kill the threat that was *mine*. She was mine.

Veyka ignored me.

She kicked the Black Knight hard, forcing him down to his knees. Crossed her rapiers at the nape of his neck. The helm would not protect him now.

"You have misjudged, Palomides," Veyka yelled across the plain. "Arran's blood flows in my veins."

From the rage contracting on his face, I knew he'd heard every word. "You—"

"The mating bond is deeper than anything you can conceive of in your feeble mind. I am every breath he takes and he is every beat of my heart. We cannot be separated—not by foolish bargains, not by realms, not even by death."

My wolf moved, without my will or intention. To stand beside her, to snarl.

"We are one." Then she sliced off the Black Knight's head.

I lifted my head to the dark sky and howled.

When I shifted back to my fae form, Veyka's blades were already sheathed. She stomped across the sodden ground to where the Black Knight's head had rolled and landed in a puddle. She ripped off the glittering black helm.

"Who is it?" I heard myself ask.

Veyka stared at the face. Male. Unremarkable. She did not answer, stood there in silence until Lyrena reached her side. The knight, her golden hair dark with rain, studied the face for several long moments. Then she shook her head.

"No one," Veyka said hollowly.

She disappeared, leaving the anonymous elemental male to rot in the mud.

But she was not gone for long. Kay and Vera reached my side. We were halfway across the plain when Veyka reappeared in the mud before Palomides. She was not alone.

She dumped the succubus—the only one we'd left alive—on the ground at Palomides' feet.

"We found your pets."

She did not wait to see if or how Palomides would fight it off before disappearing into the void once again.

The rain had stopped.

65

VEYKA

"What the hell was that?"

Arran wrenched his arm away from me. "It was nothing."

I had meant to take us to the privacy of the bedchamber, but we landed on the battlements instead. One look at the Brutal Prince, and the guards scattered into the falling darkness.

I grabbed him back, my fingernails digging into the leather tunic and the steel muscles beneath. He was wet—sweat, rain, all Arran. My core began to pound. But my desire was no match for my anger.

He tried to shake me off, using what remained of his brutally superior strength. But I would not give him the satisfaction of watching me fall on my ass. I caught myself easily, planting one hand on each hip.

"It is not *nothing*," I seethed, my voice silky in its threat. Made for battlefields and bedrooms. "You said you were healed. I let you walk into that duel under the belief that you were at full strength."

"You do not *let* me do anything," he bit back, canines flashing. Even after nearly being defeated, the exhaustion lining his eyes, he was so ruggedly beautiful. I was so completely gone for him, that brutal slash of a mouth as he snarled— "I am fine."

My hands curled into fists. "None of this is fucking *fine*."

I spun away from him—had to get away. If I stared at him for too long, I'd start tracing the lines of his face. Cataloguing the curved lines of his muscles to reassure myself that he was alive and safe. The little indent in his chin where I liked to catch my teeth—

Fuck!

I started running along the battlements, desperate to get away. Night was falling quickly. So were Palomides' guards, jumping out of my way. At least something had come from the disaster on the plain.

Arran did not follow.

Only when I was clear of his scent did I let myself stop. I still hated running. But the feeling of air knifing in and out of my chest was enough to obscure the pain and worry.

Seconds turned to minutes as the moon rose, the first rays of white light hitting the top of the Split Sea and splitting across the smooth surface. I toyed with the ends of my hair, still damp, but bright white against the darkness. Just like the moonlight on the sea.

"You are angry with me."

I pressed my eyes closed. At some point, my legs had melted from under me. Now they hung over the edge of the Castle Chariot, reaching down to the endless darkness beneath.

Arran's voice was even. Conciliatory, even.

But I did not have it in me. I was so tired. "Go to bed, Arran."

He didn't, because that would have been too fucking easy. And nothing about this had ever been easy.

A low growl slid through my consciousness, languid heat unspooling inside my core in response. *Except that.*

He closed the physical distance between us, coming to stand at the edge of the turret. But he did not swing his legs over to sit beside me. He did not reach for me.

My heart fractured a little bit more.

I could feel the heat of him, mere inches away. I knew that if I turned my head, just a fraction, I'd see the outline of his familiar profile against the shining moon.

So instead I kept my gaze steadfastly fixed on the horizon. Perfectly still. Crystalline. What tempest raged beneath the unbroken surface of the Split Sea? How did it compare to the torrent inside of me?

I felt Arran's power before I saw it. He must have been mustering it for... I was not sure how long. But there was no life on this barren plane, one of the reasons that Palomides had insisted on Arran dueling instead of me. To pull the flora from the forest, all the way here to the castle itself... his way of insisting that he *was fine*.

Vines crawled up over the stone ledge. Dark, snarling briars meant to hold enemies, to cause pain. A window into the state of his soul.

Guilt whipped through me, killing the vestiges of desire and leaving darkness in its wake.

"Who was the Black Knight?"

"No one." I'd said it on the plain, and meant it. "I did not recognize him. Neither did Lyrena."

"That means—"

"We cannot trust anyone. Why was Palomides' voice booming like that? Because he has a wind wielder somewhere around here. Elementals—*my* subjects—serving a terrestrial. And they are not even elementals I know to be traitors. They could be *anyone*. This is another new threat. Elementals, terrestrials, succubus. They are all coming for us. And you aren't even at full strength!"

"I did not ask for this," Arran said.

"You would not remember if you had," I snapped back.

I hated myself immediately. None of this was Arran's fault.

He recoiled, his warmth too far for even my senses. But those black vines twisted higher, higher, threatening to block out the moon entirely.

My fingernails dug into the flesh of my palms. "That was cruel." *And I am sorry.*

I am sorry for all of it.

And yet, I would do it again. Lose my mate again, if that was the cost of his life.

I waited for his retort. I expected and deserved every harsh word. He'd lobbed plenty of them in my direction during those first months in Baylaur, before...

Before.

Another step backward, too loud against quiet of the night. The vines stopped. I knew Arran was gone without turning to look.

66

VEYKA

I was silent.

Behind the heavy curtains and thick-paned windows, the winds of a winter storm howled.

My feet did not make a sound. Neither did my dagger.

A fire roared in the hearth. Crackling, popping. A hiss, almost serpentine.

But no lithe, scaled body appeared.

A pity.

"Awaken, Palomides."

He bolted awake—the reaction of a male who knew his days were haunted. I almost regretted dropping the succubus at his feet, revealing that we'd discovered his secret. It made this just a little less fun. The amorite he wore did not protect him from attack, only from possession. But he'd managed to get away, and I'd dispatched Lyrena with one of my amorite blades to kill the succubus.

Palomides hands dug into the bedsheets, one slithering beneath the pillow.

"You shouldn't bother with weapons," I said, stroking my fingertips lovingly over the hilt of my own dagger. Other than that, I did not move, remaining near the warmth of the fire.

Palomides moved quickly for his age.

But no one was faster than me.

He whipped the knife from under his pillow, flinging it forward with considerable strength and decent aim.

I stepped into the void, reappeared behind him, and caught his wrist as it swung backward.

The knife hit the black stone carved mantle and clattered to the floor.

"How—" his cry of rage died against the swirled steel and amorite of my blade, pressed to his throat.

I chuckled, low and harsh. "What was that, *Lord* Palomides?"

He grunted, testing my hold on his wrist. Fool. Stupid, arrogant fool.

I drew blood. Not with my dagger—with my nails. I punctured the vein at the base of his wrist. He hissed, but did not move. If he did, my nail would dislodge and his blood would begin spurting.

"You cannot use your cursed power here. I have warded this room against you," he ground out.

I threw back my head and laughed. Fully, deeply. Slightly unhinged.

"How did you know about the King's injury?"

When he did not answer, I thrust my thumb nail deep into his wound, savoring his below of pain, tasting it on my tongue.

"Informants," Palomides grunted. "In Eilean Gayl."

"Names?"

"I do not know their names."

His answer remained unchanged after several thrusts of my thumb into his wound. I did it once more for good measure before hurling myself into the void. When I reappeared, his wasted dagger was in my hand. I turned it over in the firelight.

The blade was swirled. An amorite weapon. I tucked it into my belt and turned back to the bed, where Palomides was busy writhing around in a puddle of his own blood.

I rolled my eyes. "Embarrassing."

"You—"

"Your Majesty," I purred before he made a fatal mistake. "I do not want to kill you, Palomides. Not yet."

He held his silence now. Except for the whimpering.

"You will honor our bargain," I said, examining my fingernail. Even the scent of his blood was irritating. "If you do not, I will return to Castle Chariot. Alone."

I disappeared. Materialized by the window. "You must know by now that the High King is the level-headed one."

Disappear. Reappear. Now at the foot of his bed.

"But I am faster on my own," I whispered in his ear.

Before he could flinch away, I'd moved to the fire once again. "I will not need anyone's help to punish you for your disobedience. Tomorrow, you will take us to the amorite mines. We will take as much as we can carry with us now, and make all the arrangements to set up the supply lines."

His bleeding had slowed. That wouldn't do.

I threw myself through the void one last time.

When I landed at his bedside, my dagger was already in my hand. I swiped it up across his face, flaying the skin from his jawline to his graying eyebrow.

Palomides collapsed back on the bed, screaming and clutching his face. I stalked back to the warmth of the fire on my own two feet. Warm once again, I sheathed my knife and rested a hand on each hip.

"Palomides."

He silenced at the command. His whole body shook, but for a moment he managed to drag himself back up to face me.

"Remember, when you think of betraying Annwyn... there are no wards that can hold me."

My feet were too loud on the stone floor, but Arran was already awake. The fire raged in the hearth here as well, illuminating his bare chest, the brutal black lines of his Talisman a sharp contrast to his glowing golden skin.

"Is it done?" he asked evenly.

I jerked my head as I unbuckled my weapons, letting my belt fall to the floor. "Palomides will do as he's told."

Arran's chin dropped. The barest suggestion of a nod.

It may have been a trick of the light, or his chin might have shifted to the side a fraction of an inch. Question or invitation.

It did not matter. I threw myself into the chair before the fire and pretended to sleep for the rest of the night.

67

ARRAN

I love you.

In that moment of true fear, when Veyka thought one or both of us might not survive, those were the words she had given me.

That was how serious she considered the threat of the succubus. And she was right. Palomides may have been the first to see the utility of those mindless monsters, but he would not be the last. The ambitious lords and ladies of Annwyn, or even kings and queens on continents beyond, could take the amorite for themselves and set the succubus upon their enemies. The less powerful, the poor, the fae citizens of Annwyn, would be sacrificed to the succubus on the altar of power. If our enemies learned that the succubus wanted Veyka... it would be too easy.

But those concerns, the safety my kingdom, those were not what echoed in my head.

I love you. I love you. I love you.

Before those three words, nothing else mattered.

My beast had tried to snarl them back. They'd been on my tongue in the moments when my bones cracked beneath the strain of the Black Knight's attack.

It should not have been possible. I had never said those words to anyone—not even my family. And yet Veyka—this Queen of Secrets, as she'd proclaimed herself at our first meeting—her soul spoke to mine in languages that my mind could not comprehend.

Why can't I fucking remember?

I wanted to.

I wanted to know what words had passed between us. What touches. Promises.

If I had loved her... did love her... as much as everyone around us seemed to believe, as my beast insisted with every snarl, how had it happened? Why had I been given such a thing, only to have it taken away?

For killing.

Three hundred years spent being the worst version of myself. A male who killed with impudence. When I planned a battle, I did not think about how to ensure the least deaths. I thought about winning. Glory for Annwyn, and ultimately, glory for myself. Power, to protect my mother. A reputation for violence that protected my family even when I could not be at Eilean Gayl myself.

Selfish.

I had not done my duty because I cared about the citizens of Annwyn. It was all for me. I was not worthy of love. That was the part of myself that I never let anyone else see.

But had I shown it to Veyka?

She turned, as if she could hear the intensity of her name flashing through my consciousness.

Lyrena sat at her side, their heads tipped together as they spoke quietly. The golden knight said something to make herself laugh. Veyka's full, pink lips quirked slightly. Then she rolled her eyes.

They snagged on me.

The smile dropped away.

Barkke shoved a cold sausage roll and a flask of mulled wine into my hands. I wanted to let the hot liquid slosh all over him, the ass. But I'd been scouting ahead in my wolf form and had missed breakfast.

If I took the food, maybe he would leave me alone.

Instead, he took a bite of his own luncheon, flakes of pastry sticking in his beard. "Trouble in paradise?" he said around a mouthful.

"You are an ass."

"And your friend."

Friend. Had I ever really had those? Barkke and I had grown up with one another. His father had brought him to Eilean Gayl as an offering. An agemate, to train alongside the monster of the north. I had not seen him in decades, though he appeared unchanged.

Guinevere was the closest to a friend I'd had in maturity. A competent lieutenant, proving her prowess and power on and off the battlefield. When Uther Pendragon died and Arthur assumed the throne, she'd left the war camps and went to Wolf Bay to compete for the title of Terrestrial Heir.

How would I have described Veyka, if I'd had my memories?

Mate, my beast growled.

A word whose implications I might never sort out.

I was still watching her, even as I ate. Even as Barkke blathered on.

"...all I am saying is that if I had a female like that waiting in my bedroll, I would not be sleeping outside," Barkke said.

Stupidly.

The beast inside of me surged up, ready to kill. *Mine.*

Barkke met the death in my eyes with an irreverent grin, wiping droplets of mulled wine from his beard. He looked past me to Veyka.

His eyes glowed.

I drew the axe from my belt, food forgotten. Nothing else mattered but punishment. How dare he—

But Barkke had trained at my side. His mace was in his hand just as fast, meeting my axe, holding steady. I could kill him—he was strong, but I was stronger. The strongest fae in millennia. The High King of fucking Annwyn. How fucking dare he desire my mate—

"You better get used to it, Majesty," Barkke said. He pressed his mace hard into my axe. Every member of our party watched us, but they could hear nothing over my growl. Barkke gnashed his teeth, his own growl meeting mine. His beast form may not be a wolf, but he could be just as vicious. "Veyka deserves to be worshipped by every male who sets eyes upon her. You cannot slaughter every male in Annwyn."

"I could slaughter you."

He threw back his head and laughed, exposing his throat. An act of submission. My wolf recognized it on a primal level. I stepped back.

"Maybe someday," Barkke said, lowering his mace.

"Consider it a promise."

His eyes were undimmed. "Done." He nodded over my shoulder. "Now go talk to your wife."

Veyka did not even pretend to not be watching.

Her white hair, loose around her shoulders except for the part in front that she braided away from her face, blended with the wall of snow behind her as the northern edge of the Spine rose toward the bleak winter sky.

We'd traded the thin layers of snow at the coast for thick drifts several feet deep. It was the most precarious part of our journey. We had paused on the edge of the forest to eat, but when we rose we would begin the treacherous trek across the ice field. The snow provided a barrier to give our feet purchase on the slick ice, but it also disguised any number of dangers. Solabear dens. Crevices so deep that even a fae could not survive. Another month, when the spring thaw began, and this area would be impassible for any but aerial shifters.

Veyka could have moved across it easily, avoiding the thick drifts of snow and precarious ice. But she had not offered. Maybe she was exhausted after the duel with the Black Knight. All magic had a cost.

I'd long ago accepted that the cost of mine was being alone, apart.

But there sat my mate, licking her lips as she ate her own sausage roll. I walked to her, not bothering with a pretense of anything else. There was no room for pretense and posturing between us.

Veyka stared straight into my eyes as she wrapped her entire mouth around the girth of the sausage roll. Ancestors fucking kill me.

Lyrena laughed at us brazenly as she left.

"Not quite chocolate croissants," I choked out.

Veyka licked her lips again. "Not even close."

She did not move over to make more room for me on the rock beside her. While everyone else stood to avoid wet backsides, Lyrena had melted the snow off of this rock so the queen had somewhere to sit.

Veyka tilted her head to the bare bit of black rock in silent invitation.

It was not big enough for me to sit without touching her. Veyka knew that.

An offering, after the harsh words we'd exchanged on the battlements of Castle Chariot.

I took it.

We sat in silence. Veyka offered me the remaining half of her sausage roll—she'd watched me drop mine in the snow in favor of trying to kill Barkke. I accepted it and ate.

The others moved around the edge of the forest, speaking quietly. Barkke was pointing out toward the horizon as he spoke with Lyrena, likely explaining our route. Vera and Kay had remained at Castle Chariot, to ensure Palomides' compliance and oversee the shipments of amorite.

We'd spent a day touring the mines, during which Veyka had deferred to me entirely. I told myself it was because of my history. I'd been fighting wars for hundreds of years; I knew the importance of weapons and necessary steps for establishing supply lines to support an army. But that was not the only reason she kept her distance.

The tenuous offerings of trust we'd made in Palomides' dungeons had been fractured by the duel. But maybe now, on the reprieve of the journey back to Eilean Gayl, with mostly each other for company, we could try again.

I forced myself to ignore the soft feel of Veyka's hip where it pressed into my thigh. Such soft skin, soft folds, that concealed a body and a will of iron.

It was so easy to give in to the physical needs of our bodies. The desire to take her, to bury my cock inside of her and forget the rest of the world... a thousand times simpler than sorting out the disaster that was our mating, our Joining.

"I did not know," I finally said. Veyka made a questioning sound, her lips forming a painfully kissable moue. I cleared my throat to keep from doing just that. "I did not know I was not at full strength. Not until it happened."

Her lips parted, a heavy sigh. "I should have sparred with you. I would have known."

I turned to look at her. Mistake. We were too close. My face was inches from hers. My mouth... "How?" I choked out.

She shrugged. "I cannot always explain it. The bond... it is like breathing. It is a part of me that I do not have to think about it because it is always just *there*."

"Always demanding." Like right then—demanding that I claim what was mine.

She smiled. "Yes, always." Very tentatively, she reached out and laid her hand on my knee. Heat surged through me, marking the spot, cataloging the pinpricks of contact between us. "It helps, the touching. To take the edge off."

"Speak for yourself."

Her smile turned absolutely wicked. She kept her hand on me, her fingers drumming casually across the fleece-lined leather stretched taught over my skin. With her other, she reached for a wooden cup nestled into the snow at her feet and took a long, savoring draw.

It was unusual, as tall as a wine glass by cylindrical. "What is that?"

Veyka held it up for me to see. "Osheen made it for me. I am always cold, even in Baylaur. But since we left, it has been worse. I don't know how it works, if he's infused it with flora magic... if that is even possible. But it keeps the tea warm."

"Osheen."

"You remember who he is," Veyka said carefully.

"Of course." That was not the problem.

The surge of anger I'd felt when I saw the glow in Barkke's eyes was nothing to what I felt when Veyka said another male's name with such affection.

Veyka's hand on my leg had stopped moving. She set down the special made cup on the other side of the rock—outside of my view. She knew *exactly* what was happening.

"He traveled with you to Baylaur for the Offering. He accompanied us to Avalon," Veyka said, her voice even.

"Where is he now?" I ground out.

She slid her hand up my leg, her fingernails leaving a burning trail of possessiveness to match my own. She pressed harder into my side, working her cloak up over her shoulder so that the curves of her body pressed into the hard planes of mine.

Every nerve in my body stood alert, ready. The need to possess her, to make her mine in every fucking way, was almost impossible to bear. Veyka was trying to soothe me, to connect with my beast, to bring me back to where I could wrestle control around my power again.

"He remained with the Faeries of the Fen," she continued, voice so carefully even. "Maisri—" her voice broke off, sharp as a knife. "Arran."

Something was coming.

The world around me sharpened—brighter, clearer than before. Every sense was at work, fae and beast.

Veyka's hand tightened around my leg. "Arran," she said again, breathing in sharply. Her hand already moving for a weapon. "What is it?"

I did not have time to answer as my beast wrested control and leapt for the the solabear as it lunged for my mate.

68

VEYKA

At first, all I felt was the sharp contrast of cold and warmth. I fell backward into the snow, my cloak bunching up behind me and leaving my shoulder exposed. Even the wool of Arran's green tunic —the one I was still wearing daily—was no match for the penetrating cold. Above me, pinning me to the ground, was warmth. Thick fur as white as the snow beneath me. *Arran.*

He was vibrating. *I* was vibrating.

That was not in either of our powers...

I tried to move him off of me—

The entire world spun. I pressed my eyes closed, and could have sworn I saw the void there. But my fingers did not tingle, and the ember of power inside of me did not brighten.

The wolf above me bunched his muscles, pressing down tighter against me. Bracing against an attack. Why wasn't he the one attacking?

What was happening?

My head flooded with a growl, blocking out all other thoughts. My chest vibrated with it. That was the vibration I felt.

Arran's wolf stood over me, protecting me. I did not need to be protected. I reached for my knife—

Fuuccckkkkk.

Pain roared through my skull. My hand fell away into the snow, useless.

Breathe, I ordered myself. *Arran will keep you safe.*

I had not survived decades of torture by being unable to function while in pain. Pain made the world sharper, enemies clearer.

Slowly, I lifted my hand again. The pain was still there, but not as sharp. I lifted my fingers to the base of my skull and began to feel around, finding the culprit almost immediately.

I'd struck my head on a rock.

I tried to reach farther back, to see if there was any blood. *No, no blood, there couldn't be.* I wore the scabbard. But it still fucking hurt.

Arran must know. He must have been able to feel it through the bond. If not the precise injury, at least that I was incapacitated.

My mind was clearing, bit by agonizing bit.

Arran stood above me, defending me. From what?

The snow and his thick white fur muffled the sound, but I could hear Lyrena yelling. Why was she yelling so fucking loud? My head throbbed.

A sharp bark joined Lyrena's cries. Not Arran's howl—another shifter?

Barkke, I realized. I laughed. I started convulsing with laughter in the snow, while my mate and companions fought off... something deadly.

I must have hit my head harder than I'd initially thought.

I took another long breath.

In, out. In, out.

I reached for my dagger with my hand while my mind speared for my mate. *I am fine. Let me fight.*

My answer was a growl and an unshifting white body.

I shoved him aside. He moved begrudgingly.

He planted himself in front of me as I sat up, rather than over my prone body. Only then did I see what he'd been snarling at.

A solabear.

It made the skoupuma seem meek. Easily ten feet tall, with claws that matched Arran's fangs for ferocity. I understood Lyrena's yelling—she'd been drawing it away from me and Arran. Now, she swung for the beast with her mighty sword, deftly using her goldstone armor to deflect when the bear swiped for her. At her side, a massive dark brown hound snarled, exposing an already bloody maw. Barrke's animal form. I'd make fun of him for it later, when my head was not spinning dangerously.

The solabear shook its arm, dislodging Barrke's jaws and sending him sprawling across the snow. Lyrena screamed and charged, but she slid in the snow and the solabear deflected easily. It was not interested in her—it turned back towards me and Arran.

Arran was not fully recovered from his enchanted sleep in Avalon, he'd just pushed himself to the limit dueling the Black Knight. It was up to me—

I fell back on my ass in the snow.

Stay down! Arran snarled into my swirling consciousness.

I wanted to argue with him, but I couldn't get the words out, through my lips or my mind. I could not even get the solabear into focus. It blurred with the landscape, at once white and then brownish gray as it melded into the tree line behind it.

No, that wasn't my mind playing tricks. Its fur reflected the area around it.

That's how it had gotten so close. It had blended right into the snowy mountainside.

It did not matter how it had gotten here. It was close, too close. Arran was bracing himself, muscles tensing. I forced my legs underneath me, forced my body to obey.

Arran leapt for the solabear, going straight for its throat. But the huge ursine was not afraid of Arran's wolf. One massive swipe of its paw and—

"Arran!" The scream tore from my throat.

My mate hit the snow hard, his huge form nearly disappearing into the drift. I was on my feet now, dagger in hand. I'd kill the thing myself.

It was too fast. I was unsteady on my feet. I tried to duck out of the way of that massive paw, but I couldn't make my body move fast enough. I hit the snow a few feet from Arran. He was on his feet, struggling to get out of deep drift.

But the solabear was made for this terrain. Its massive paws did not sink into the drifts like we did. I braced myself, dagger ready. Arran and I were all that stood between the succubus and Annwyn. I would not leave my subjects to suffer. I would not die without a fight.

The pain in my head was nothing as its jaw closed around my leg.

I heard Arran's scream—felt it through the bond, reverberating through my body. He was not in his beast form anymore. Those were his hands, grabbing for me. But I was slipping away through the snow and ice... not slipping... dragging...

The solabear wasn't ripping me limb from limb. It was dragging me away.

I tried to rise up. I could drive my dagger into its face, that would make it release me. Then I could go into the void. The world spun around me... not the void... I would not be able to control it...

My arms flailed around me, trying to find purchase. But there was nothing—just barren snow that slipped through my frozen fingers. I clenched the muscles in my abdomen, determined to pull myself up.

I screamed as I did it—the pain in my leg, in my head, the will to live—

Something heavy hit my side, knocking me back down. The edge of the forest, we were nearly there. Where was it taking me... what was that... animals. Eyes. Creatures... monsters... something was waiting, lurking.

Suddenly all the air was knocked from my lungs. Arran was on top of me. The solabear roared, the air filled with the scent of blood.

Not mine.

Not Arran's.

I tried to suck in a breath of relief, but then the world fell away. No more snow at my back, no more blue sky overhead. A whisper of spice and earth, and then nothing at all.

69

ARRAN

I held her tight against my body, shielding her as we fell. Shards of ice scraped over my skin, but none of them touched her. I refused. Not mine. Not Veyka.

We landed hard, the impact reverberating through us. Veyka did not moan or show any sign of life.

She had to be alive. *She had to.* If she was mortally wounded, if she was dying, I would know. I would feel it. I would have to. She was fae. She could not die. She was wearing the scabbard.

I expected the ground to shift beneath us, the snow to give way. But everything stilled. The only movement was the irregular up and down of my chest as I dragged in ragged breath after ragged breath. Veyka was still—too still.

Very slowly, I eased my hand up her back. She'd hit her head when I threw her out of the way of the solabear. That was before the solabear had dragged her a dozen yards and we'd tumbled down into the ice cave. But there was no blood on her. Thank the Ancestors.

I reached her throat. Her hair was matted with sweat and grime and cold snow. I slid my fingers beneath it, searching along her throat. Her skin was so impossibly smooth and soft. So fragile. A flick of my fingernail, and I could have punctured the delicate layer of skin that protected her lifeblood.

There.

Something inside of me released as my fingertips found the steady, resolute thump of her pulse. My eyes were burning. I must have gotten a shard of ice in them as we fell.

I eased myself up to sit, keeping Veyka in my arms. I tried to move her as little as possible, afraid of hurting her more. But then I saw her leg. Her calf hung from the knee socket at an unnatural angle, her shin exposed where the solabear had ripped through her leather leggings with its fangs.

Still, no blood.

Ancestors be praised.

I had been in situations like this before. Pinned down with injured soldiers. Injured myself. There was no place for panic. I summoned up the battle commander, and shoved down the roaring beast.

I forced myself to take stock of the situation. Veyka was not bleeding. Her pulse was strong. Her fae blood would keep her alive. But I needed to know where in the Ancestors-damned hell we were.

The realization took only a few painful seconds. An ice cave turned solabear den. Above our heads was the tunnel we'd fallen through. The angle was steep, but not so sharp we couldn't have climbed out. But with her leg like that, Veyka was not climbing anywhere. At least until the next morning.

The solabear was dead. I'd ripped out its throat with my bare hands, my beast's sharp claws poking right through my skin. I had never done that before—a strange, partial-shift. But I had not been thinking. When the solabear began to drag my mate away, thought and strategy had ceased to exist.

At least we would not have to contend with the solabear returning to its den.

The cave was about the size of a large bed. One way in and one way out, typical of a solabear. At our feet, there was a pile of freshly shredded snow and claw marks in the wall. No bones or half-eaten animals; the solabear had not been awake long before it attacked.

The ice around us glowed faintly blue, reflecting the light from overhead. But it would not last long. Veyka was still unconscious; that might be better for what I had to do.

I cut away her legging from mid-thigh down. She'd be cold later, but I needed to see what I was working with. It was worse than I'd thought, the bone below her knee was snapped in at least two places.

She did not make a sound when I set the bones back into place, securing them with a leather strip cut from the tatters of her legging. I checked her pulse again.

Da dum. Da dum. Da dum.

I listened to it for far longer than I needed to determine it was regular and strong.

I covered her with my own cloak—hers was providing a barrier between her body and the ice. Then I shifted into my beast form and curled against her side to share my warmth and to wait.

One hour turned to two.

Neither of our companions appeared. They might not realize what had happened. Even if they did, reaching us would be treacherous. Night came early north of the Spine in the winter. Already, the blue glow of the ice was receding.

Another hour passed. It was fully dark.

In the third hour, I began appealing to the Ancestors. It had been too long. She was still not awake.

She'd taken an injury to the head. Her body was healing itself.

But I needed to hear her voice.

Veyka. Veyka, please, I pleaded through that shared space in our minds that I'd ordered her not to touch.

The irony of it... I had been in an enchanted sleep for weeks. I did not remember what had passed between us before I awoke in

Avalon, but Veyka did. Her feelings for me were strong, fully developed. She loved me.

This was the worst thing I had ever experienced.

Worse than my own torture, or hearing about my mother's. Worse than the bloody battlefields, the innocents I had killed when I was new to my power and could not control it. The beating of my heart synced with Veyka's. If hers stopped, I would know it because so would mine. There was no world that I wanted to live in, no realm human or fae, without Veyka Pendragon in it.

Is this what it means to love?

A low, pained groan slid into my consciousness.

Veyka.

I shifted in an instant, on my knees before her. It was fully dark. Even with the sharpness of fae eyes, I could not see anything. My wolf form was slightly better. But then I could not talk to her. But I could, through the bond.

Veyka hissed through her teeth. "I think it is broken."

"We are trapped in a solabear den. It is night," I said quickly, trying to assuage any worry or fear.

Veyka grunted, apparently unbothered by darkness. "How bad is my leg?"

"Worse than your head, I hope?"

She laughed softly into the darkness. I hated that I could not see her. But I *felt* that sound, softening the jagged edges of my soul.

"It all hurts," she admitted. "But it is nothing to what I've endured before."

I heard the soft sound of her laying her head back against the wall of ice. It was the last sound I heard as my blood rushed in my own ears.

"Who?"

Something deeper than anger clawed at my insides. Parents told their children stories of my beast to keep them in their beds at night. Nothing that anyone had seen, on any battlefield, would compare to what I would do to the ones who had hurt my mate.

"Hmm?"

"Who hurt you?"

Veyka swallowed, the sound too loud in the small space. I was sitting very close to her. She could surely hear the sound of my blood pounding through my veins. Could she scent the rage as well?

"I killed Gorlois the day I injured you, in the cursed clearing across the lake from Avalon," Veyka said. Her voice was so tired. The tension inside of me loosened a notch. "The other... my mother. Igraine."

"The Dowager Queen." All the possibilities flashing through my mind, none of them made sense.

Veyka sighed. "I do not want to talk about it. Not now."

I wanted to demand—I was her mate. It was my duty to avenge the wrongs done to her. Whatever the state of things between us—love, almost love, maybe love, definite duty—I owed her that much at least.

"Arran." Her voice broke. "Please."

I would not be the one to break her. That pain in her voice... I recognized it. I did not need to know the details to understand the torture of a soul.

I could not see her. Probably would have failed at offering an expression of comfort, anyway. But I touched her leg—the uninjured one. Her fingers settled over mine.

We sat in silence for several heartbeats.

"The scabbards really do keep you from bleeding," I finally said. Me, as well. Exactly as she'd explained.

Her voice sounded distant, distracted, as she said, "They were a gift from my brother." There was more to that than she was saying. But I didn't push that either. She exhaled, half laugh, half sigh. "If only they prevented injury of any kind."

If only.

"Can you use your power?" I asked, though I already knew the answer. Few things could hinder fae power. There were the natural limits of each individual. The cost—manifested as pain, exhaustion, sleep, and so on. And then there was illness and injury. We healed so quickly, that the latter were rarely an issue. But Veyka had dislocated her knee, broken her leg in two places, and hit her head.

I knew her answer would be—

"No."

I could just imagine her pouting out her lips. But I could not see them.

She was leaning back against the cave edge, legs out straight before her. I'd knelt at her side when I first shifted, but I settled myself next to her now. As soon as I stilled, Veyka's head dropped down onto my shoulder.

"I feel... naked," she said quietly.

Fuck.

My cock thickened instantly, my beast snarling awake. Veyka was still holding my hand. I tried to pull it away, on instinct, to stop myself from feasting on my injured mate. But she held tight. I did not fight her.

"I did not have power, in the beginning," she said into the darkness. "I was born without it. It was only after our Joining that the void power within me awakened."

The darkness changed something between us. There were no nuances to interpret, no expressions to guard. Even as my body yearned for hers, I forced myself to remain still. I wanted every bit of herself that Veyka was willing to offer me.

She sighed, her breath warm against my cheek. She'd tilted her head up as she spoke, as if she could see me even in the dark. "I did not realize how much I'd come to appreciate it, to rely on it."

To love it.

I caught the delicate sound of her tracing her lips with her tongue before she asked. "Do you love your beast?"

It was not that simple. "Do you?" I parroted back; he certainly was fond of her.

Veyka graced me with a low, sultry chuckle. "How could I not love that tongue?"

Oh, Ancestors. Was she implying that at some point, we'd actually... while I was in my beast form... *Oh fucking Ancestors.*

I felt like I was speaking through water, but I got coherent words out. "The beast is a part of me. Like my arm. I do not love my arm. It is another tool for survival."

"I do not believe that," Veyka said confidently.

Whether she meant that I loved my beast, or I loathed it, I was not certain. I was not certain I even wanted to know, either way.

But she did not press it, settling deeper into my arm. She nudged my shoulder with her nose. What—oh. She wanted me to put my arm around her.

I lifted my arm and she tried to maneuver herself into place. She tried to mask the soft hiss as she shifted her weight, but I was too attuned to every sound and scent. I squeezed her hand hard, and she stopped fidgeting, allowing me to be the one to arrange us.

She fit perfectly against my side.

Ancestors be damned.

This felt too fucking good. Too right.

There had to be a catch—a cost. I had done nothing to deserve this, to deserve her.

"We'll bed down for the night," Veyka was saying. "By morning, I should be healed enough to use my power to get us out of here."

"I am not going to sleep while you are injured." I doubted I could. My beast would never allow it. Neither would I.

She vibrated softly against me. "Then let's do something else."

I groaned. Loud, unrestrained. She laughed harder, groaned in pain, let out a very unqueenly snort as she tried to repress her mirth. Her hand started burrowing around between us, lower and lower—

"Veyka," I groaned again. This female was going to be the death of me.

She withdrew her hand and pressed it back down into mine. But now, there was something long, hard and smooth between our palms.

"Communication crystal," she said, her smirk evident in every syllable.

She'd mentioned them before—but I had never seen or used

one. They were rare in Annwyn. A few of the continents I'd traveled to over the centuries had them in greater numbers. But it was only as good as the person who was on the other end. "Does Lyrena have one?"

"No. But Cyara does."

70

VEYKA

It should have been impossible to be as aroused as I was while also in mind-numbing pain. My leg ached terribly, to say nothing of the pokers of hot fire that shot through my shin if I shifted at all. At least my head had stopped hurting. I'd never missed Isolde and her bright, beautiful healing magic more. And still, the heat of Arran's body pressed up against mine was slowly devouring me from the inside out.

His throaty groans were certainly not helping things.

I forced myself to focus on the communication crystal in my hand.

I muttered the incantation quickly, sighed with relief when the crystal began to glow bright white.

I felt Arran's sharp intake of breath, then the slower release as he caught himself, trying hard not to move me even a fraction of an inch for fear of causing me pain. Brutal Prince, and overprotective skoupuma mother. High King of Annwyn... and my love. My mate.

Cyara's tentative voice spared me that line of thought.

"Veyka?" she said into the darkness of the cave, the crystal quivering with light. It didn't do much, illuminating our thighs pressed together. The light did not reach past my knee—thank the... whoever. I did not want to see the mess Arran had had to sort out.

Nor did I allow myself to look up at his face.

"Yes, I am here," I said, fingers closing tight around the crystal. "As is Arran."

Several beats of silence. "And everyone else?"

Arran made a sound low in his throat. He wasn't the sort to shift about under the weight of other's judgment or expectations. But I could tell from the way his muscles tensed that he was uncomfortable.

And I could not resist needling him. It was almost as good as kissing him.

"We are alone," I told Cyara.

"And you are contacting me?"

Arran's chest contracted as he stifled another groan.

"We are trapped in a solabear cave," he said.

Several months of silence passed. I heard the soft sound of Arran opening his mouth, but the words came directly into my mind, rather than my ears. *Will she hear everything we say?*

Are you worried? I shot back.

Before he could respond, I spoke aloud. "We will be out by the time you can send help from Eilean Gayl."

There was no pause in Cyara's response this time. "Why can't you get yourself out using the void?"

Shit.

Now I was the one leaving long, heavy pauses.

"She is injured. But she will be fine." Arran spoke with such certainty—as if he had not been begging me to wake mere minutes before. I had barely let myself believe it, the yearning in that plea that had echoed in my heart in the half-conscious moments before opening my eyes. It almost sounded as if he...

Nope. No way. I could not allow myself to go there.

Maybe there was something resembling trust beginning to grow between us again. Mutual respect, perhaps. But not love. Not yet.

I fought back the sob that rose in my chest. "See," I ground out. "If Arran says I will fine, you know it is true."

Arran tensed—recognizing the strain in my voice.

If Cyara did as well, I could not tell over the chastising. "In all the time you've been in my care, you have never once been injured. As soon as you leave me behind, you are trapped in a cave and hurt."

I did not remind her about the Joining, where I'd fallen through the void, crashed onto the floor of my bedroom, and broken nearly every bone in my body.

"You asked to stay behind to monitor Percival and Diana," I said. "And a handmaiden is not the same thing as a nursemaid. Though we could have used your harpy to fight off the solabear."

"She is a harpy?" Arran asked sharply. Reprove, disappointment.

I had not meant to keep it from him. But there were so many things that we'd shared, it was impossible to remember them all, to apprise him of them all. I did not want to remind him. I wanted him to remember. I wanted my mate back. Suddenly, I wanted to jerk away, to sit by myself, even if it meant shivering all night. But my blasted leg held me in place.

"Shall I leave you two alone?" Cyara hummed through the crystal.

I focused all of my attention on the glowing white crystal, refusing to note Arran's movements in the periphery of my vision. "Tell us what you have found out from the priestess."

Cyara reported like the observant, competent sentinel she was quickly becoming. "Percival is the most useful he's ever been. He knows a lot of human history and can match up events with the histories of Annwyn here in Eilean Gayl. They have several legends about the Nightwalkers, but we are still trying to figure out how those fit with Annwyn. If they do at all.

"The priestess and her acolyte have taken to Diana. Most of the time I only understand half of what they are saying. There are several mentions of a book called *The Travelers*, but it is not in the collection here at Eilean Gayl."

Percival being helpful. I almost snorted again. But if there was one thing to motivate him, it was his sister. And Diana was moldable; Cyara had proved as much. Maybe it made me ruthless to use the two human prisoners like this. Or maybe it just made me a queen.

"So... not much progress," I said after I'd finished digesting.

"Nothing that changes our course of action," Cyara agreed. She did not sigh—she was much too practice for that. She did add, "Diana has an idea, but..." Another long pause, "We can discuss it when you return."

If I had looked up, I would have seen Arran's jaw ticking. I felt certain. Not being able to see was sharpening all of my other senses. I could hear the subtle inhales and exhales he tried to modulate. He had not missed Cyara's implication.

Cyara, ever faithful, spared me from having to defend myself either way.

"Did you get the amorite?" she asked.

I nodded, even though she could not see it. "Yes."

Vera and Kay were already preparing the first shipment. When we arrived back in Eilean Gayl, we would send back more terrestrials to help with the transport. In the meantime, we each carried bags full of as much amorite as we could carry without impeding our movements.

"Thank the Ancestors," Cyara said through the crystal.

"We should be able to outfit all of the males at Eilean Gayl with amorite amulets or earrings. But beyond that, we shall have to decide who and what. There will not be enough."

The weight of that thought had settled upon my shoulders with each step away from Castle Chariot. How would we allocate the amorite? Who would be most important? Guards and warriors would be the most dangerous if vulnerable to the succubus, but fathers and brothers living across Annwyn could decimate their entire families in the span of a few minutes. The memory of the burning human village seared through my mind. It might have already begun in Annwyn. If word had been sent to Baylaur, or if citizens had petitioned there, I would have no way of knowing, sequestered as I was in Eilean Gayl above the Spine.

The guilt turned my stomach.

Arran cleared his throat. "Especially once we start making weapons."

Now the guilt threatened to choke me.

"I did not agree to that," I said sharply.

Hell—it was hell to be pressed together like this and unable to move. Unable to glare at him or bare my teeth.

"War is coming, whether you can acknowledge it or not. There is not enough amorite to protect all the males in Annwyn. We must be able to kill the succubus who do come," Arran said. He was not even being cruel, no disdain or superiority in his voice. Just a battle commander stating the facts of the enemy at hand.

It made me want to vomit.

"It will not get to war," I said. I would not let it. That was the reason Cyara was searching with Diana and Percival. We had to find a way to stop the succubus before it came to war—a war we could not possibly win. A war that would mean the death of thousands of fae to the succubus, both in possession and murder.

Seven thousand years later, we still called it The Great War. I would not allow history to repeat itself.

"This argument is immaterial at the moment. You are trapped in a cave," Cyara said through the crystal, her voice flaring around us. Chastising us like children.

It *was* about to become an argument. I could feel the tightness of Arran's arm where it curved around me. The fingers, which had held my arm with soft possession, were now stiff.

"We will be back at Eilean Gayl in a few days," I said. Cyara had given me an out—I would take it.

"Good," she said, voice already fading. "Contact me again if you need help."

The crystal went dark.

I wondered how long we would sit in silent darkness, both of us too stubborn or afraid to breach the chasm that had opened between us. We'd made no progress on this argument—defensive or offensive. Protect or prepare. We had no round table to sit around and hash it out. That should not have mattered, we should have been able to discuss it anywhere.

Except that we were not the High Queen and King who had left Baylaur months ago. Neither of us.

"She is quite formidable," Arran finally said when I moved to tuck the communication crystal back into my pocket.

I chuckled, careful this time not to jar my leg. "The former captain of my Goldstones was afraid of her."

I heard the sound of Arran's teeth clenching together before he wrenched them open to say, "The one who tried to kill you."

"One and the same," I nodded.

Neither of us expanded on that. Arran's reaction to my joking while eating croissants at Castle Chariot was burned into my mind. Part of me savored it, his protectiveness. But the other part... it was empty. An instinct borne of the mating bond, not of any real love for me.

With the crystal put away and darkness all around us, there was nothing left to do but sleep. Yet I knew that neither of us would be able to anytime soon. I knew Arran like I knew myself; better, probably. I understood the tension he tried to coax out of his fingertips where they were curled around my shoulder. I caught the soft, surprised exhale when I leaned my head onto his shoulder.

He wanted to give in, to let himself trust me. Maybe love me. But he was afraid. As I had been, before. It was torture, to have the roles reversed. Arran had been the steady one. *I would have waited a thousand years for you to realize what was right in front of you,* he'd said in the faerie caves. Yet, here we were, scant months later, and I was the one bursting with love while he struggled to parse need and the mating bond from real emotions.

I understood. I really did.

He had none of the last months together for context. He'd been dropped into a life wholly different from the one he remembered.

But understanding did not make it hurt any less.

I felt his throat working a second before he spoke.

"The solabear hibernates all winter," he said, quietly even though it was just the two of us. Something about the darkness hushed our voice.

"And I thought I was grumpy in the morning," I scoffed. But I understood the thrust of his thoughts. "Is it possible we got too close to its den? Woke it up?"

"Or someone else did." The cool veneer fractured with those words. Battling the succubus was one thing; threatening his mate was another. His beast responded on a primal level.

Those words promised death.

"I saw... something. An animal, or several, retreating into the woods. Right before I lost consciousness," I admitted. The images were vague, addled by my head wound. But my instinct told me they were real, not a delusion conjured by my mind.

Arran's arm tightened around me. Shockingly—thankfully—the slight movement did not cause a lash of pain. My leg was healing.

"Maybe you were not as effective at threatening Palomides as you thought," he said.

"Or maybe one of the terrestrials in Eilean Gayl saw an opportunity to be clear of the conniving elementals," I sassed back.

Arran went rigid. "What do you mean by that?"

I should tell him.

The vines that had tried to pull me down on the bridge when we'd first arrived. The threat carved into the stairwell, bathed in blood. The looks that the terrestrials gave me. How I'd figured out that the guards Elayne stationed at our doors, the secluded tower suite she'd given us, were not to trap us but to protect me. The attack on Isolde. And finally, Palomides admission that someone within Eilean Gayl had reported about Arran's injury.

But it was so much to explain. And I was so tired. And if I did tell him... how could I know he would not take the side of the terrestrials, his own people, over me? The female who had been forced upon him?

So instead of the truth, I said, "Terrestrials hate elementals."

And I pretended like I was not part of the reason for the chasm between us.

71

ARRAN

My entire life, the terrestrial court had sneered at my mother. *She'd allowed herself to be debased. She was not powerful enough to fight back against the males who'd raped her for the heir she would one day bear.*

I had systematically slaughtered everyone who dared to utter those words.

I knew they had not stopped, that those evil words still lived in the minds and on the tongues of the powerful at Wolf Bay.

Now I was their king. Now, I could truly punish them. Kill anyone—

Except we needed able-bodied warriors. A war was coming, whether Veyka accepted it or not. The succubus would not wait for her and her companions to research. Even if they did find a solution, a way to stop the succubus from entering Annwyn, it could come too late. We had to prepare. We needed warriors, elementals and terrestrials—

Terrestrials, who sneered at their queen. My wife. My mate.

"You are the High Queen of Annwyn." *And I will punish anyone who treats you as anything less.*

I knew she heard my unspoken words. I listened to her teeth

scrape across her lower lip before she responded— "I am an elemental."

I pulled her tighter against me without thinking, without regard for her injury. But she did not wince this time. She even pulled away —just a bit. Just enough that I knew she'd turned her face to mine, even though I could not see anything in the blackness of the cave.

"Arran, *you* used to hate me," Veyka said softly.

The heat of her breath caressed my skin. For a heartbeat, I let myself savor it. This stolen moment, this sacred space between us where we shared breath and no one else existed.

"Why?" I had to know. I wanted to know every detail that had been stolen from me. "Why did I hate you?"

She laughed softly. Not at me, I thought. But at the memory. "You told me that I was selfish. That I only cared about myself and not my kingdom."

I could not see her face, but I had to know. I reached out, so slowly, until my fingertips grazed her silk-smooth skin. The curve of her lips. The soft smile that melted away under my touch.

"And you were right," she breathed against my fingertips.

No.

I did not remember anything that had happened between us. Not even an echo. All I had was the tug of the mating bond in my chest, the low growl of my beast pushing me ever-closer to her. But I did not need the memories to know that I'd been wrong.

Veyka loved her golden knight and her handmaiden. I'd seen it with my own eyes.

She loved her kingdom—why else would she be so insistent on protecting as many as possible with the amorite? She was not selfish, even if she was wrong about the best way to go about it.

She had fallen in love with me.

And only I could understand the depth of selflessness that would have taken.

And it must have been the darkness, the depth of desperation, the threat of her injury that made me say softly, inches from her lips, "I can see how I fell in love with you."

She tried to pull away. I caught her chin between my forefinger and thumb.

"You are more clever than you let anyone see."

Was that her lip trembling? Or was she fighting to pull away. I eased my hold on her. She stayed. I pressed my thumb into the center of her lower lip.

"Part of being an elemental," Veyka said. Her chest was moving too, in time with her trembling mouth.

I wanted to ease that pain, the same way I had set her wounded leg. It would hurt. I knew it would. But I wanted to heal it, to heal her. *Us.*

"You use the expectations people have of you against them, subvert them. All while flashing that wicked smile and luscious body." It had worked on me, too well. She had to know that it would—she'd used it against me before, I was certain, even if I could not remember. I did not resent her for it, not in that moment.

Veyka attempted a muted laugh. "Use what you have."

"And all of it for Annwyn."

I waited for her to deny it—to explain away the best parts of herself. To tell me I had misjudged her. But she did not, because she could not.

"That isn't the female you fell in love with," she said softly. "I'm not the female you fell in love with... not anymore."

If it had not been so dark, I might not have noticed. But every nerve, fae and beast, was attuned to her. I could feel her in my soul. So, I had no doubt that the tiny droplet of water that hit my hand was not a melted bit of ice, but a singular tear.

Veyka spoke again—faster, desperate. "I was angry and selfish and depressed bloodthirsty—"

"You're still plenty bloodthirsty," I interrupted. My cock was already hard, had been since she'd first tucked herself in against my side. But the mention of blood, of her unbridled vengeance and glorious brutality, had me near ready to explode.

Still, Veyka tried to deny who and what she was. "The queen I was... I ..."

She lost her words.

I had them.

"Why can't it be both? Why can't both versions of you be worthy?"

Another tear. I could smell them now, the faint saltiness merging with the ever-present primrose and plum that was so perfectly Veyka. There was no hint of blood; the scabbards did not allow it. But I imagined I could smell the coppery tang of her through the delicate skin of her throat. A throat I wanted to taste. To claim, because she was mine.

And whether I was ready to accept it or not, I was hers.

Slowly, guided only by instinct in the dark and that golden thread that connected our souls, I replaced my fingers with my lips.

"Arran, I..." Veyka trembled against my mouth.

I pulled back, just enough to let her speak. She was injured, more fragile than perhaps even she realized. I would sit here at her side for the entire night, cock aching to be sheathed inside of her, soul yearning to touch hers.

"Tell me to stop," I breathed.

Her words were as tortured as my own— "I can't."

Thank the Ancestors.

"I won't hurt you."

Yes, you will.

72

VEYKA

If Arran heard the words I let slip through the bond, he did not respond to them. Desperate, wanton thing that I was, I was grateful that he didn't. His mouth was on mine, gentle but insistent. His hand dropped between us, already questing beneath the heavy fur of my cloak. I did not want it to stop. The darkness and isolation of the ice cave was giving us something beautiful amidst a desert of despair, and I was too weak to turn away from it.

I leaned further into him, one hand reaching to unfasten my cloak while the other slid up his leg. But Arran's fingers hovered in the air between us.

"You can touch me," I moaned against him. "I will not break."

Not physically, at least.

The pain in my head was gone. My leg ached, but it was not sharp anymore. The throb of healing. We would have to be careful, but I was strong. My need for him more powerful than any wound.

Softly, so gently I almost thought it was a wish, his fingertips touched my stomach. There were layers and layers of clothing between us, and I would happily shed them all, despite the oppressive cold. But when Arran touched me, through the thick wool of the tunic I wore—his tunic—the linen shirt and boned bustier beneath, it was reverent. His fingers stroked again and again, massaging the layers of fabric, the soft skin a curve of my stomach beneath. It was the sweetest sort of torture as his lips mirrored the slow, persistent exploration against mine.

He was discovering, as if for the first time, all over again.

The weight of it could have suffocated me. This would not be the half-conscious fucking of a few nights ago, driven by unbridled need.

That need was still there, to be sure.

But this was deeper. This was a choice.

Finally—*oh, yes, finally*—Arran slipped his hand beneath the layers of fabric to touch my fevered skin. He caressed the inch of exposed skin between the bottom of the bustier and the waistband of my leather leggings. I pressed my hips into his hand, urging him to slide lower. But Brutal Prince that he was, he chuckled against my mouth.

"Needy thing, aren't you?" he murmured.

The darkness was so intense, every other sense was heightened. Every breath felt like fire as it skittered across my skin.

"Only for you," I said, shivering at the intensity. "Always for you."

Arran's beast rewarded me with a low growl that filled up my being nearly as full as if Arran's cock was buried inside of me.

The hand that was not teasing my waistband cupped my chin, thick fingers splayed out across my throat. "You truly are at my mercy," he said, so low it was nearly a growl.

Desire, liquid and hot, pooled between my legs. The cave was steadily filling with the scent of desire. I whimpered—every bit as needy as he'd said—as he slid his fingers back into my hair and lowered his mouth to replace where his palm had been.

Such long, languorous swipes of his tongue—along the line of my jaw, over the pulse hammering in my throat. He paused, sucking hard enough that I knew there would be a mark. I thrust into his hand again, using my uninjured leg to press myself up, to do something to ease that painful, building ache.

I could not get myself close enough, and he knew it. I wanted control, to at least drive the direction of this. But I was stuck there, back against the wall of the ice cave, legs straight out in front of me. I could turn, I could reach for him, but Arran was in charge.

Fuck that.

"Put my cloak down on the ground. Lay with me," I moaned as his lips reached the bottom of my ear, teeth closing around the earlobe.

Arran caught his canine against the amorite stud, dragging it over the tender skin with such precision while his hand drew infernal circles on that tiny sliver of exposed skin.

"Not yet," he said into my ear, before sliding his tongue rapidly up the shell to the pointed tip.

I whimpered again. I was a mess. A needy mess, emotional and physically injured and—

"I can practically hear the tempest in your mind," Arran said against the nape of my neck this time. "Am I not doing a good enough job distracting you?"

"Arran," I said, not bothering to hide the desperation in my voice. "I need you, naked against me. I need your mouth everywhere. I need your cock buried inside of me until I am so full, I think I will burst, and then I need you to fuck me until we are both screaming loud enough to bring this ice cave down around us."

He froze.

Tongue on precise point of the curve where my neck became my shoulder, tunic shoved out of the way to make room for his mouth, fingers curled under the rigid lower edge of my bustier.

"Veyka," he said hoarsely. "Are you trying to kill me?"

I laughed, which scraped my nipples against the tight constraints of my bustier, and the laugh turned to a moan. "Maybe," I admitted through my teeth.

Arran sucked in a breath, his mouth so close to my skin it felt as if he was trying to sustain himself on *me*, rather than the thick air around us.

"Hold still," he ordered.

I revolted against that command immediately when he drew his hands away from me. I tried to grab them back, but he caught my wrists deftly, even in the dark. Our bodies in sync, as always, even when nothing else about us was.

"I said *hold still*," he growled. It was not the male that spoke, but the beast. I could tell by the way the command reverberated through my body, my soul bowing instinctively while heat raced through me, unrestrained.

No. I cannot. I need to touch you—the growl rose up again, fierce and menacing.

I stilled, my struggles against his grip halting instantly.

Good girl, his beast growled. My pussy was drenched. But I did not move as Arran carefully released my wrists, waiting several heartbeats to see what I would do. I lowered them to my lap and kept them there.

His hands went to my throat again, fingertips skating over the hollow of my throat. But then they went to the knot that held my cloak in place. Released it with deft, practiced ease. It took all of my restraint to keep myself still as Arran's hands skimmed my breasts through the wool tunic, down to the hem, catching the linen undershirt as well and drawing them up over my head.

I had to shift my head to the side, shimmy my body to help him get them off. A low warning growl.

I paused with my hands over head. Let him see my breasts curving, straining against the bustier. Even Arran's legendary control would falter. He adored my breasts.

But it was dark. So fucking dark, he could not see them.

I let out a growl of my own and arched my back so that when his fingers came back down, he could not help but touch me.

This time, we growled in unison.

"You are terrible at taking orders," Arran said, his voice strained. I took sadistic pleasure in knowing he was just as tortured as me.

"Give better ones." I rolled my shoulders back, pressing my breasts into his palms. He hissed through his teeth. "Take it off."

"Are you the one giving commands now?"

Ancestors spare me, but he sounded like he might actually enjoy it if I did.

Another time, I promised myself.

I needed his hands on me—here, now.

"Take it off. And do not rip the ribbons. I do not have another set with me."

Arran's mouth was on mine as the last syllable left my tongue. Gone was the gentle exploration of mere minutes before, replaced by the feral need that coated every interaction between us. I would not let him rip apart my bustier, so he nipped at my tongue and lips instead. Not sharp enough to draw blood, but enough to have me moaning for more—more pain, more intensity, more Arran.

I was so caught up in the savage battle of our mouths, I did not realize he'd unlaced my bustier until it fell away. My breasts sprang free, heavy and full and tingling at the cold air. If he did not touch them soon, circle his tongue around a nipple and suck it tight and hard, I was going to die just to spite him.

Instead, bastard that he was, he skimmed my burning skin with only his fingertips.

Arran was an absolute fucking liar.

He was the one trying to kill *me*.

Because instead of sucking a nipple into his mouth, or taking the weight of my breasts into his hands, he leaned forward oh-so-carefully and kissed my throat again. He braced one hand on the ground, the other against the wall of ice just above my shoulder, as he branded me with his tongue but did not touch another inch of my body.

And Ancestors be damned, but I loved it. I savored the sweet torture—that Arran even wanted to torture me like this. That on some instinctual level, he knew what this would do to me, how sweet it would make that final joining. It felt like a step closer, to who and what we'd been. Whether he could hear it or not, that tentative hope colored every beat of my heart, every moan that he coaxed from my lips.

Arran's mouth finally, finally moved lower. Past where the skin of my neck was pulled taut by the weight of my breasts, to the spot right above my heart.

"I need to taste you," he breathed, so low I almost did not hear it between my gasps and moans.

"You've already destroyed my leggings." I did not clarify whether I referred to the pieces he'd cut away to tend my leg, or the mess of sticky desire between my legs.

"Not that—yes, always that," he amended. But he paused where he was, elongated canines snagging on my breast. Pressing into the skin, just where the curve began. "This."

Oh. *Oh.*

There was no hesitation. He'd asked—sort of—but he did not need to. Not of me.

Maybe another female would have been cowed before him, this powerful male, the most powerful in millennia. But even before I'd inherited a power to match his, I'd given myself to him without restraint, showed him the darkest parts of myself.

Giving him my body was nothing, everything—because it already belonged to him.

"Yes," I breathed. "Always, yes."

Arran's breath shook as he exhaled. He slid his hand between us. "That Ancestors-damned scabbard—"

"It cannot stop you." I pressed my eyes closed, even in the dark. I would not let those memories, that terror, into this moment. This stolen, sacred place between us. I had walled off parts of myself for years, I could do it now, even as I was forced to explain. "You are the other half of my soul. The scabbard cannot protect me from you."

If Arran realized the implications, it was impossible for me to see. All I had was the flaring ring of desire in his eyes, a black circle of fire visible even in the interminable darkness of the ice cave.

I felt his nod, because I could not see it. And then a second later, I felt him sink his elongated canines—the mark of a terrestrial, of the beast within, of the differences between us—into my vein.

Neither of us moved. It was too excruciating and exquisite.

Every sensation was heightened.

I could feel the curve of his teeth embedded in my skin. The contrast of his lips, soft against my breast. Then the scrape of stubble on his chin, pleasant but dull compared to the sharpness of his bite. He sucked, drawing my blood into his mouth.

"Arran," I moaned, every vein in my body sizzling in awareness. "Arran, yesss."

He pulled his mouth away from my skin, pressing his lips to mine. Our tongues tangled, the taste of my blood coppery and sweet but mixed with the essence of him. *Oh yes*, it was intoxicating to taste the way we joined together.

But that was not all. The twin wounds where his canines had broken my skin bled.

My senses screamed in awareness, tracking the thin line of blood as it slid down my breast, circling around my nipple. Another second, and it would slide downward. Further, over the hills of my stomach, toward my pussy.

Arran did not let it get that far. He kneeled over me and caught that rivulet of blood against with his tongue just before it reached my navel. Traced it upward, over my stomach, turning his head so he did not miss a single drop as his mouth curved up my breast.

He reached my nipple, twirling his tongue around it, biting. Not hard enough to draw blood this time—no, there was no need. That wetness that around the taut bud was part Arran, part me.

He had tasted my blood before, but never like this. While his mouth worshipped my breasts, his fingers slid higher.

He pressed at the wound, coating his fingertips in my blood. The pain was sharp, intense, but not too much. Especially when he slid his hand inside my leggings and found my clit.

Arran did not tease, now. He massaged my clit in hard, tight circles that drew cries of pleasure from deep in my chest. It did something to me, that massaging, knowing that it was *me* that provided the lubrication. Not just my desire, but the very blood from my veins.

At the edge of my awareness, I felt his other hand in my hair. Stroking, slowly rubbing at the roots. Then moving around to my face, pressing against my mouth.

An offering.

I wanted to do it—to sink my teeth into the mound of flesh of flesh at the base of his thumb. I wanted to smell both of us, taste the way we mingled together.

But I couldn't. Something inside of me recoiled with fear. I could not hurt him—not again. Not after Avalon.

"Arran," I whimpered again. Even in his lust, he heard the plea in my voice. His hands were on my face, holding me steady, his forehead pressed against mine.

"Stay with me."

It was a command I desperately wanted to obey. I answered by pressing my mouth to his and tasting myself on his lips.

Without pulling away, somehow still avoiding my healing leg, Arran lowered me to lie on my fur cloak, now spread beneath us. I recognized the motions of his hands, urgent now—pulling down my leggings, then his own.

Then his cock was nudging at my entrance. For the first time, I wanted to curse the darkness of the cave that had, until that moment, made everything about this even more erotic. I longed to push myself up onto my elbows and watch the moment he slid his cock into my cunt, to see him pull himself in and out, his shaft shiny and wet with *me*.

I lifted my uninjured leg, opening myself for him, trying to get him deeper, closer. Arran caught it, lifting it to his shoulder.

He held tight as he slid inside of me, deeper and deeper. No easing in, no testing some of his length and pulling out. He knew I could take it, and the arch of my hips said what I needed—every inch of him. *Now*.

There were no more words between us. Only the rough gasps as he pumped into me again and again. Maybe the wound on my breast had healed. I was too far gone to care. All I knew was that Arran was inside of me. *My* Arran. My mate.

He pressed a kiss to the inside of my ankle. Then more—snagged his teeth on the bone, and grazed just deep enough to draw a well of blood. Too dark to see, but I knew it was there by the way his mouth fitted around it and sucked hard. I felt myself filling his mouth, filling him. A second later, his cock began to pulse inside of me, spurt after spurt of his come coating the insides of my pussy. The heat of it, the way we filled each other in time—I lost myself entirely.

Who and what I was did not matter as I cascaded over the edge, climax ripping through me. My pussy clenched, milking every last bit of come from Arran's cock until my legs were shaking with the force of my orgasm.

Arran pulled his mouth away from my ankle, and I whimpered as loudly as if he'd pulled his cock from me. The feeling of loss was just as profound. But then his tongue was back, smoothing over the cut that had already begun to heal. His hands stroked down my leg, constant and smooth until I finally stopped shaking.

"Arran," I whispered into the darkness. Half plea, half prayer. All love.

"Veyka." He lowered himself down to the fur cloak, not nearly big enough for two, especially of our sizes.

Good thing we were one.

Avoiding my injured leg, he settling himself, tugging me flush against him. I did not resist. How could I—in this moment, just for a moment, everything was perfect.

73
ARRAN

The morning sun turned the cave shades of crystalline blue whose beauty was rivaled only by the eyes of the female curled against my side. We woke slowly. Veyka's stomach grumbled, mine answered, we both laughed softly. The ring of bright blue in Veyka's eyes glowed brightly. I was loath to give it up, this refuge. The closeness it had brought, if not clarity.

I had known Veyka was powerful, clever. But I had not expected the depth at which she cared. She'd made herself into an enigma, even to me. Yet, in the darkness, I felt like I had truly seen her for the first time since waking in Avalon.

The ease the darkness had created between us lingered, if slightly altered by the light of day. We could see each other now. The wound on her breast had healed. More importantly, she pulled herself up to stand easily when I offered her my hand.

"Are you ready?" I asked, wishing I did not have to.

Veyka caught her lower lip between her teeth. She stared at my chest, rather than my face. Maybe she regretted the night between us. My beast snarled his answer to that—*impossible*.

When she did lift her eyes to mine, the answer was there, plain. The love.

I love you. She had not said those words last night; but her voice echoed in my head just the same. Except now, perhaps, even louder than before.

Veyka held out her hand and I took it, knowing she would deliver us back to our companions. Her power, at least, I could trust her to judge for herself.

A second later, and my feet were still on compacted snow, but there was the sun shining overhead and the startled, relieved cries of Lyrena and Barkke.

I dropped Veyka's hand by reflex. She blinked repeatedly. I waited for her to say something, aloud or through the bond between us. But after a few seconds, she walked away, into Lyrena's unrestrained embrace.

Part of me—the beast—roared to go after her. To reestablish the connection between us. Here, back with our companions, it might be impossible to recreate. Lyrena would keep Veyka close. Barkke would report to me out of responsibility and routine. Veyka and I would be on opposing sides once again.

But my feet did not move.

Barkke approached, a grin on his face, ready to make a lewd joke about how we'd passed the night. And still, I did not move.

Because we were not protected by the darkness anymore. As much as I respected her, I did not agree with her about the amorite or the coming conflict. And I knew there was more about the succubus that she was not telling me.

There was more between us, and I could not be the only one responsible for tearing that wall down.

74
ARRAN

The distance between us was nearly unbearable. Not physical—we were never more than a few yards apart, except for when I scouted ahead in my beast form. Even then, I tracked Veyka through the pull in my chest. Harder, I was farther away. When it eased, I knew I was getting close to her. Something that had been a myth to me but a few weeks ago exercised a huge amount of power in my life, and I was not sure how I felt about it. Nor how I felt about her.

I wanted her. But ruling a kingdom would require more than a physical bond between us. Veyka loved me. If everyone around me was to believed, I had loved her as well.

I did not know how to love. I was the Brutal Prince.

Had never wanted it; did not deserve it.

I stayed in my wolf form for the remainder of the journey. No one talked to me, not even Veyka. I told myself it was for the better.

Yet as we neared the end of our journey, I found myself shifting. I needed to speak with her. These last few moments were not the same as the ice cave, but it was a hell of a lot more privacy than we'd have once we arrived at the castle.

A few more steps, and Eilean Gayl would be in view. My legs

moved faster, the need to speak to Veyka, to say *something*, compulsory. Overwhelming. Even if I did not know what to say.

Barkke muttered something under his breath as I shoved past him that he was lucky I ignored. Lyrena lifted her brows but did not bar my way.

Veyka had to hear my approach. The pull of the bond. I was almost alongside her as Eilean Gayl appeared—

"Something has happened."

The bridge was crowded, gates thrown open. Veyka already had a blade from her back. My battle axe was in hand.

"I'm sorry," she said over her shoulder to Lyrena.

I understood a second before she took my hand and we disappeared.

☙❧

Veyka pulled us from the void a quarter of the way across the bridge. Lyrena and Barkke were running, the latter in his beast form, but they were on the other side of the lake. Veyka was at my side, formidable and fierce, ready to defend Eilean Gayl.

Until she lowered her weapon.

A broad smile spread across her face, fuller and more unrestrained than she'd ever given me. Jealousy bloomed as a dark blur shot across the bridge in her direction.

Veyka cried out, weapon sheathed, arms wide, scooping the blur into her arms.

A child.

The crowd turned to face us. Frenzied—but with excitement. Erratic movements—terrestrials clapping a tall male on the back. Beside me, Veyka was making nonsensical joyous sounds that seemed to be reciprocated by the child in her arms. Dark hair, pointed ears, and judging from the massive bouquet of flowers she held out to Veyka, a terrestrial.

The tall male broke off from the group. Several others trailed him—my mother and father, Veyka's handmaiden, and the white-skinned faerie who'd hassled me all the way to Eilean Gayl. But the male, I recognized.

"Osheen," I said, right arm across my chest, fist clenched—a typical warrior's greeting. Osheen was among the finest I'd ever commanded. A powerful flora-gifted terrestrial, yes, but that was not what made him so useful. There was not a hint of pride or artifice in the male's body. He was confident, steady, and loyal.

Then my mate threw her arm around his shoulder and I decided I could live without him.

"Your Majesty," he said to Veyka, rolling his eyes as she turned to speak with the white faerie, the child still on her hip. "Arran. You look healed."

Not well.

Not happy.

Not healed, either. Not fully.

Only when Veyka was several feet away from Osheen was I able to speak without growling. "What has brought you to Eilean Gayl?"

Osheen's brows drew together. "Isolde came for us," he said.

Not a lie, obviously. But not an explanation.

"Osheen! I thought we might never get you to leave those caves!" Lyrena greeted the warrior warmly. Despite the run to reach us, she was barely winded.

The throng was growing. Our traveling party, Osheen and the child, the residents of Eilean Gayl. Veyka got further away from me by the moment. I needed to speak with her. I needed a report from Osheen. Veyka knew him; surely he could fill in the gaps in my memory that she still shied away from.

"I have called for food, to provide succor to our weary travelers and celebrate their return," my mother said, voice rising above the rabble.

My jaw clenched.

There was no privacy to a communal meal. Food and wine would devolve to music and fucking. My eyes went straight to Veyka. They had never left her, not really. Could not possibly.

She heard my call. Turned, because she'd never lost sight of me either. But her blazing blue eyes did not meet mine as she opened that too-luscious mouth.

"The meal will have to wait," she said, offering no apologetic smiles. Giving no quarter. "Every male in Eilean Gayl is to report to the great hall. Immediately."

75
VEYKA

I knew it was going to piss him off.

I did it anyway. It was why I'd avoided him for the remainder of our journey. Even if I was beginning to trust him again... I had to do this.

I did not allow myself to look back over my shoulder as Elayne escorted me into the castle. I could feel Arran's presence, knew he followed with all the others. Elayne dispatched servants without breaking step, so that by the time we reached the head table, now bare, the great hall behind us was already filling.

Arran walked at Osheen's side.

The tension in my chest eased a little.

Cyara had held my hands on the bridge and told me that after Arran followed me to the mines, she'd asked Isolde to go back to the faerie caves to retrieve Osheen and Maisri. Ever loyal, Isolde had not hesitated.

I should have thought of it sooner. Osheen had been one of Arran's lieutenants for centuries. Arran trusted him implicitly. He was also the only one who knew us both, who Arran still remembered, other than Gwen.

Gwen. Had word come from Baylaur while we were away?

Cyara would have told me, surely.

But there were so many terrestrials around. I needed to speak with her first, then—

No.

This had to be done, now.

I nodded to Elayne.

She hesitated, probably wondering if she'd misinterpreted the gesture. I nodded again, toward the wall where Pant stood, waiting. I was not addressing the congregation as her guest, but as their queen.

My Knights moved through the hall, falling in at my side. I wished Guinevere was with me. Cyara and Lyrena, both formidable in their own ways, were elementals. Which meant that now was finally the moment for Arran to be a king.

What are you planning?

I betrayed nothing as he came to stand at my side. His jaw ticked. He knew I'd heard his question and chosen not to answer.

Please, trust me. But I kept that plea safe inside my own head.

I pulled my dagger, its blade swirled with amorite. I lifted it high above my head. Slowly, the voices died away. Their eyes found me at the apex of the grand, ancient hall. I held the blade aloft. My arm began to ache, but I did not allow it to tremble. I waited. Until every single set of eyes was on me.

"Citizens of Annwyn." I took a breath long enough to hear my own heartbeat. A second longer, and I might lose my nerve. "We face a grave threat. An enemy so old, we have forgotten its name. But they have not forgotten us. I am the queen of the Void Prophecy. The darkness is coming for Annwyn."

76
ARRAN

It could have been worse. Most of those assembled merely blinked up at Veyka in confusion. Terrestrials were warriors. They all knew the Void Prophecy existed. But I doubted any of them could recite it. It was a legend—like mates.

But there Veyka stood. Real. My mate, not a legend.

And not done talking.

"The humans call them nightwalkers, because they come while we sleep. They creep into the minds of our males and turn them into monsters. Mindless, vicious monsters who will kill a wife, a child, a friend." She paused. "We know them by their true name. The succubus."

Silence.

Shifting of feet, but not shifting to beasts. A small miracle. The silence would not hold. Veyka knew it, by the expectant tilt of her chin. But what else did she have to say?

What are you doing?

My mind was silent. Not even a growl.

She did not trust me, even after the ice cave.

"Amorite is our only defense, the only thing that will repel them." She dropped her travel pack, tugging loose the plump pouch strapped to the side. She held it aloft where her blade had been. "By royal decree—every male in Eilean Gayl will step forward to have his flesh pierced by amorite."

The great hall erupted.

I grabbed her wrist. "You should have told me," I growled.

Veyka did not waver. "You would have tried to stop me."

"Because you are wrong."

She cut her eyes to me, spearing me with those shards of blue ice.

I did not flinch, my grip on her wrist tightening. "We rule together."

Her eyes flashed again. "You cannot decide to play king when it suits you. You are either my mate and king, or you are not."

She ripped her hand away—too easily. Like I'd never really had her at all.

"Osheen, step forward and receive the amorite," Veyka yelled.

The hall quieted again. Waiting.

Osheen stepped forward, ever the dutiful soldier. Cyara was there, handing Veyka a needle heated with the handmaiden's flame. Another few seconds and it was over, a small amorite stud winking in Osheen's earlobe.

Barkke stepped forward next.

I wanted to strangle her.

So fucking clever. She'd seen Osheen, seen the warm welcome he received, and seized her opportunity. But it did not change the fact that she was wrong. Or that she had not trusted me enough to share her plans, however quickly they'd come together.

She could speak into my fucking mind. But she'd chosen not to.

More terrestrials came forward. Veyka did each piercing herself. A queen, serving her subjects. My father. Male after male. Until the crowed parted and revealed a line of unmoving males.

I stepped closer to Veyka.

"Come," Veyka purred, licking her lower lip. "I promise to be gentle."

None of the males' eyes flared with desire. None of them moved. Lyrena shifted closer.

The eight males held a solid, unmoving line. I recognized none of them, but that meant little. I had not been to Eilean Gayl in decades. The one at the center looked oldest, though they were all young. It was he who spoke.

"We have seen no evidence of this supposed darkness."

Lyrena dropped a not-so-casual hand to her sword. Veyka merely cocked her head to the side.

"Nor have any of you graced the halls of the Goldstone Palace. And yet, the Gremog waits to taste your flesh, just the same," she said.

A velvet wrapped threat. Veyka did love violence.

Still, the males did not move.

"Come," Veyka said again. Her voice made the promise—she would not ask a third time.

No movement.

Lyrena drew her sword. "Your Queen gave you a command."

The leader smiled.

This was what Veyka had meant. A queen, but to many terrestrials, in name only. She needed me at her side. Not only as her mate, but to make good on an agreement made seven thousand years ago by the Ancestors.

Veyka handed the needle back to Cyara and pulled the drawstring on the pouch of amorite.

"Any male who refuses the amorite is a danger to Annwyn. A traitor." She smiled as she gave Lyrena the order. "Kill them."

The hall erupted once more.

Veyka.

Some terrestrials applauded. Bloodshed was entertainment. Many stepped back, forming a circle for the fight. Executions. Lyrena would not lose.

Veyka. We need every fighting, able-bodied soldier.

Her back was to me. She was re-stowing the amorite.

Listen to me.

She straightened. *We do not need traitors.*

Just because someone disagrees with you does not make them a traitor.

She turned, slowly. But her eyes did not go to the males, some shifting, some brandishing weapons. Lyrena laughed in their faces and encircled the makeshift arena with a ring of fire.

Veyka ignored them all, her eyes fixed on me. Beautiful, raging storm clouds gone to shards of ice.

"Who are you?" she hissed.

I did not flinch. "I am the High King of Annwyn." I turned back to the spectacle. "No one shall die today."

Lyrena's flames banked. She looked past me. I did not turn to see the betrayal in Veyka's eyes. I could feel it in my soul.

77
ARRAN

Osheen followed me upstairs to the study I'd commandeered. The halls were crowded with males returning to their tasks, recounting what had occurred in the great hall to the females who hadn't made it down to witness the spectacle themselves.

The door closed. I turned. I expected to see Osheen standing at attention, hands folded behind his back, waiting to report.

But he crossed his arms over his chest, and he did not wait for me to speak before demanding, "What the hell was that?"

I had never seen Osheen angry. But there it was, in the stubborn set of his jaw and the narrow line of his mouth.

"Care to soften those words?" I said carefully. I did not sit, nor cross my arms. This study was a mistake. I was not made to be contained by four walls.

"No, I do not," Osheen said sharply. "Why would you undermine Veyka like that, in front of all those courtiers?"

Few would have dared to challenge me like this; Osheen never had. Maybe that was why he could do it, and I did not instantly shift into my wolf and rip his head off.

I shook my head. "They are not courtiers. This is Eilean Gayl, not Baylaur or Cayltay."

Osheen did not take my dismissal. He took a step forward. Outside, I heard the telltale creep of vines on the wall. His power was boiling very close to the surface. "Terrestrials gossip just as much as elementals. You have weakened her position, and for what? A few extra soldiers?"

My hands turned to fists, but my voice was even. "We may need those soldiers."

"Eight males are nothing in the coming conflict, we both know it." Osheen did not give an inch of quarter. He stood in the middle of the study, refusing to be cowed. "Why?"

Because she does not trust me. "The amorite is better used for weapons. There is not enough to protect every male in Annwyn."

"You may be right," Osheen allowed. "But the male I knew would have slaughtered anyone who dared to gainsay his queen. He would have been proud that she was so devoted to duty, to her kingdom."

Because I am not worthy of her.

I walked to the window and threw it open. Let his vines come. My own were more than a match. "You have changed, Osheen."

He laughed ruefully. Another sound that I'd heard so rarely. "No. I am merely saying something you dislike."

And I was reacting exactly as I'd accused Veyka of doing —selfishly.

Fuck.

I forced myself back to the desk and down into the chair. I stared over Osheen's shoulder at the door. "Report."

"On what?" Osheen's tone was wary.

My voice scratched out of my throat. "Everything."

He began with the news that Arthur Pendragon was dead, beheaded by humans on the same night that he'd been poised to announce his betrothal to Guinevere. We'd been in the war camps on the northeastern edge of Wolf Bay, Osheen said.

I remembered none of it.

I did not let my gaze shift an inch while he spoke. I did not want to see the pity in his eyes.

He spoke of our arrival in Baylaur, waiting hours in the desert for admittance. The Offering, and the desire that burned in my eyes from the first time they found Veyka. Desire that every elemental and terrestrial in Baylaur had seen. He elaborated on Veyka's description of the assassin who came for her in the night, how I had asked him to shore up the defenses around the goldstone palace. How he had seen the fondness growing between Veyka and I from a distance. He spoke of the Joining. Of Veyka being ripped away from me and the rage I'd felt, the twenty courtiers I'd killed when I lost control of my beast.

Finally, he recounted the journey from Baylaur to the caves of the mysterious Faeries of the Fen. The burned human village and Veyka's dismay. Finding Percival. He described the joy in Veyka's eyes when she'd finally begun to master her power, and the pride in mine.

He ended with our departure from the Faeries of the Fen. Before I had been injured—not just injured. Stabbed, by the legendary Excalibur. By Veyka.

It cannot stop you. That was what Veyka had said when I tried to remove her scabbard in the ice cave. *You are the other half of my soul.*

Realization barreled through me, cold and harsh. I had been wearing the scabbard. That was how Veyka knew that I could draw her blood even while wearing it. She had thought I was safe, because I wore the scabbard. And instead, I'd nearly died.

I stared into the wood grain of the door. My eyes traced the ancient knots, as old as the castle itself. If I looked away, I did not know what would happen.

"The Battle of Avalon. Tell me how it happened," I said.

"I was not there."

My eyes tried to move away, to search Osheen's face. But I held resolute. "Why?"

"The vision the faerie priestess gave to Veyka promised bloodshed on the shores of Avalon. We all agreed not to take Maisri into known danger," he explained.

"Maisri..." I searched my mind.

"My niece. My ward." From the periphery of my vision, still fixed on that blasted door, I saw him shaking his head side to side. "You remember nothing? Truly?"

A low growl rolled up inside of me, through my chest. I knew Osheen could not hear it. Would Veyka? "My beast remembers her," I said. "But I do not."

Osheen did not speak for several moments. Once he did, I realized he'd been weighing his words—and should have kept them to himself.

"Maybe there is less of a difference between you and your beast than you imagine," he said.

"You are flora-gifted. You cannot understand," I snapped back.

An insult.

Not a jest. I rarely made those. I had just insulted my most faithful lieutenant. More—my friend. There were some terrestrials—many terrestrials—who believed the fauna-gifted shifters among us more powerful than our flora-gifted counterparts. It was nonsense. I'd seen Osheen put his trees and vines to better use than nearly every other shifter I'd encountered.

Of all the terrestrials, I was the only one who'd ever been born with both gifts. I, above all others, had the ability to understand that one was not intrinsically more powerful than the other, that it all depended upon the individual who wielded them.

Osheen had never complained. Never shown a hint of resentment toward the power he'd been given or the gift he had not.

I forced myself to look at him. To see what I had done.

There it was.

Hurt.

Fuck.

Osheen did not try to hide it. He let me see the damage. After a few moments, he dropped his folded arms back down to his sides.

"You and Veyka are mates. But you loved her before that," he said plainly. Answering the question I had not dared to ask. "When your memories return, you will regret every wound you've left. Every barb. They will haunt you for the next thousand years."

"And what if my memories never return?" I breathed.

There was no looking away from the pity in his eyes as he said, "Then I hope you're not stupid enough to squander a gift you waited three hundred years to find."

He bowed slightly at the waist. "If you wish to find me, I will be with Maisri. I am certain she is currently eating her weight in sweets in your queen's chambers." Then he left.

I sat alone for a long time.

I'd betrayed Veyka. Osheen was correct, even if I hated it. From every angle, I'd been wrong. I disagreed with her about the amorite; she was living in denial about the true threat the succubus posed. This conflict would be settled on a battlefield, not through ear piercings. But she was young. I was a battle commander with three hundred years of experience. If she trusted me, maybe I could convince her.

But none of that changed what had happened in the great hall. Even if I disagreed, I should not have done so publicly. Those soldiers were nothing. Veyka's stature was worth more than my pride. Veyka was worth everything.

And I had still been stupid and selfish.

Everything I'd supposedly accused her of being when we first met.

To make matters worse, I'd insulted Osheen, a male who had been nothing but loyal to me and to my queen.

I was back to staring at the door. There were three knots in the wood. Elegant swirls that spun around and around before they found their way and straightened out.

I did not much like the male I was allowing myself to become.

I could not force Veyka to tell me her schemes. But maybe I could earn back her trust. Maybe I could be the male she had fallen in love with.

Maybe I could be worthy of her.

78

VEYKA

The door opened, and I did not need the mating bond in my chest to know who it was. Cyara's silence said enough.

"Go away," I said without looking up.

I was writing letters—*fucking letters*—about the amorite. I'd portioned out what we'd taken from Castle Chariot and would send it with the aerial shifters on to Cayltay and Baylaur. Word still had not come from either city in response to the missives Elayne and I had sent weeks ago.

I should take it myself, through the void. And when I got back, Lyrena would tie me to a chair—little good it would do her. And Arran... was standing right behind me.

"We must speak."

"You've said enough," I snapped. "High fucking King of Annwyn."

He did not move. Cyara didn't either, bless her.

"I should not have countermanded you."

I dropped the quill.

"Who are you?" I asked for the second time, turning in the chair. The first time, because I'd been unable to recognize my mate, the male I loved, in the one who had openly undermined me before our subjects. Now, because he was apologizing. Sort of.

This was not the male I had fallen in love with. Maybe neither of us was that person anymore. Maybe we could never be again. Not in the face of all that had happened.

But maybe we could be something else.

I swallowed down that traitorous shred of hope.

"You have been High Queen of months," Arran said. "I have only had a matter of weeks."

Still not quite an apology.

I wanted to hate him for what had happened in the great hall. But I couldn't, because I understood it. I knew what it felt like to be broken and lost and alone. That is what Arran was—alone. Just like I had been in the water gardens for all those years. When I emerged, only to have Arthur taken from me, I'd recoiled in on myself. Arran had been the one to rescue me, to pull me out of that darkness.

He was my mate. My love. And instead of being gentle and kind, I was sharp. Hard. The queen I needed to be for Annwyn, but not the wife I needed to be for Arran.

I should have told him about my plan. Argued with him about it. Persuaded him to see things my way.

Trusted him.

I had not trusted him, and he had repaid me in kind. We were both behaving like children, not High King and Queen.

For Arran, I could swallow my pride and my hurt. For my kingdom, I could try and make peace. "I should have shared my plan with you."

Arran worked his jaw slowly. "You closed off your mind."

"It's horrible, isn't it?" I sighed heavily. "But even before then... before we arrived back at Eilean Gayl. I knew what I wanted to do, and I was afraid you would refuse."

He took a step closer. "I betrayed both you and Annwyn. It will never happen again."

I bit hard into my lip to keep from closing my eyes as the

weight of that vow hit me square in the chest. I knew—just like I had known when we made our vows to one another in the faerie pools—that this was forever.

And that both comforted and scared the shit out of me.

Does that mean you will always let me have my way? I hoped I sounded more flippant than I felt.

A soft, rumbling growl. *It means I won't argue with you in front of our courtiers.*

I suppose you want me to promise the same.

The next growl sounded more like a chuckle. *That would be ideal.*

I pressed my palm to my forehead. "You are the one who is good at this. Not me."

Arran rewarded me with a rueful laugh. "Perhaps we can learn together."

My heart thumped painfully in my chest. "Perhaps we can," I echoed.

"Ahem," Cyara cleared her throat from the corner. "Shall I call the Round Table to order?"

I grimaced, thinking of the dismally small rectangular table in the sitting room. "I suppose you should."

79
ARRAN

It took less than ten minutes to assemble everyone Veyka wanted in the sitting room connected to the bedchamber. The sun had long disappeared behind the tall leaded-glass windows, but Veyka was the only one in her nightclothes. Another flowing, sensuous garment that skimmed over her figure and begged for my touch.

She saw the glow in my eyes, made a sound in her throat that might have been reprimand or repressed whimper, and pulled on a thick velvet wrapper over the top. Which did approximately nothing, other than add warmth and give me another layer to imagine peeling off of her alabaster skin.

Control.

This meeting was my chance to demonstrate to her that I could control myself and be a supportive partner rather than a total ass.

Veyka breezed into the room, going straight to the sideboard in the corner and its waiting bottle of wine. She was lifting the rim to her lush lips for her first sip when the exterior door opened to admit Osheen, Lyrena at his heels.

"Where is Maisri?" Veyka asked by way of greeting—and holding out the bottle of wine. Lyrena grinned and took a swig directly from the narrow neck.

"Running wild with the other children, telling tales about the faeries. She's very popular at the moment." Osheen shook his head at Lyrena's antics before fixing me with a long look.

He would not let me avoid the words traded between us. I'd have expected nothing less. I inclined my head. When Lyrena stopped chugging wine, I took the bottle, poured a glass, and handed it to my friend.

Lyrena's eyes danced with mischief, jumping between me and Osheen. Veyka elbowed her before she could say something indecorous.

A second later, and the door opened again. Cyara, with the two human prisoners in tow. I had not taken a good look at either of them before this moment. Matching deep ochre skin and black hair, the sibling bond between them was apparent. The woman kept her eyes downcast, hurrying past. The man—Percival, I recalled—fixed me with a look halfway between disgust and disbelief.

My beast snarled back.

I jerked at the impulse—only to find Veyka grinning at me from the other side of the room, where she'd arranged herself in a chair at a small rectangular table. She crossed her legs, exposing a long, fully-healed, and deliciously muscled calf. *You may growl at Percival any time you like.*

My beast made a sound I'd never heard before. A growl so low, it was almost like a purr. And it was all for Veyka.

This female did things to me on levels I could not even begin to comprehend.

Veyka's smile was absolutely feline. She knew it, too.

A final, timid knock sounded at the door and drew my queen's glowing blue eyes away from me. Thank the Ancestors. I used the moments as we all turned to gather myself. Veyka knew I wanted her. What she did not know is if I could be the king she needed to stand at her side.

In truth, I did not know either.

Cyara opened the door to the tiny white faerie. She gave me a small smile as she moved to stand beside Lyrena. "You tended to the Queen's leg quiet well, Your Majesty."

Your Majesty. She meant me. I cleared my throat awkwardly. "Thank you."

I turned back just in time to see Veyka rolling her eyes. Minx.

She waved a hand at the chairs—a mix of styles that had clearly been drawn from wherever Cyara or Lyrena could muster.

"Cyara and Lyrena are Knights of the Round Table," she began. "As are Parys and Gwen." Parys—an elemental courtier and Veyka's closest friend, Osheen had told me. Guinevere I did not need explained.

Veyka continued around the room. "Osheen and Isolde have earned my trust."

She was doing this for me. We could not regain the months of memory that had been lost between us, but if we were to move into the future, I needed to know the shape of things. Cyara had known without a word of explanation from Veyka who she wanted in this room.

Still, I had questions. How had she, or we, decided the Knights of the Round Table? How had she ended up with the Round Table at all? It was an heirloom of Gwen's family. A thousand more sprang to mind. I said none of them.

"So they will have mine, as well," I said, nodding to Osheen and then Isolde, who vibrated with something like embarrassment. *Could a white faerie blush?* Which left the humans clinging to the stone wall. "What about these two?"

"Diana is not so bad," Veyka said slowly.

Percival was the one who had betrayed her—us. Shoved a knife into Lyrena's back. Yet, Veyka kept them with her. A thousand more questions rose to compete with the first thousand.

Veyka stood with slow, methodical grace. A warrior in command of every muscle, even in the guise of rest and respite. A flick of her hand, and a blade graced her palm. Where she'd hidden it in those flowing layers...

Swift as an adder, she pressed the blade to Percival's throat.

Diana flinched, but did not back away, holding her ground directly beside her brother. The man's throat bobbed, but he gave nothing else.

"You are at my mercy," Veyka purred.

Percival's eyes were thick with hate. That would be a problem soon, if it was not already. *And this male was sleeping a door away from my mate. That was a question I would not wait to have answered.*

"As always," Percival ground out.

Veyka swiped her tongue over her lower lip, as if she could taste his fear. Enjoying it. But her words were cold when she spoke again. "Why were Arran's memories taken?"

Percival's face did not shift an inch. "I cannot answer that."

"How can we get them back?"

"I don't know."

To all the rest of the room, she must have appeared calm.

Veyka did not have any tells. She chose what and when to show her feelings. But she could not hide from the bond between us. I felt her agony and frustration as if it were my own. *Because it is*, I realized. One soul, two bodies.

My hand closed around the back of the chair so hard the wood groaned.

Cyara stepped forward, white wings flaring behind her. "He cannot be lying," she said with quiet force.

Veyka did not care. She wanted answers, and she was ready to slaughter Percival for them. In a breath, the mood had shifted from casual to deadly. Because of me—because of what Veyka needed and wanted. I had underestimated her, and the depth of what she felt. Her love.

My other hand joined the first. The chair would not survive the night.

"We are only half-witch," Diana said softly, her voice trembling. But she continued. "The witch curse in our blood compels us to answer your questions truthfully. But we only have knowledge about what we have personally experienced or witnessed."

"That is not how it happened in the Tower of Myda," Veyka bit back. Even with Cyara at her side now, she had not eased her blade from Percival's throat.

"You encountered a true witch," Diana breathed.

"Yes."

Witches had been hunted down by the Ancestors after the Great War, at the same time the priestesses had been stripped of their power. Avalon only remained because it was in the human realm, rather than Annwyn. And even so, I'd thought it little more than a legend until I'd woke up on the sacred isle.

But according to legend, two witches survived. Hidden by the Ancestors, in case some future generation needed to call upon their power. One, in the Tower of Myda. According to the sketchy details Osheen had been able to give me, Veyka had killed that one. The other was said to dwell somewhere in the icy caves of the Spine.

"A witch—a full witch—is not tethered to her body," Diana explained, still trembling. "Their minds can unfurl, travel to the past and the future, to other realms. Just their minds. But it is how they can answer any question, no matter the topic." She was a second away from bursting into tears, but she managed to get the last few words out. "Can you take that away from his throat?"

Veyka narrowed her eyes at the woman, but gave no other hint of what calculations she made behind those swirling blue orbs. Whatever it was, she was not feeling strongly enough for my beast to sense it.

As suddenly as she'd advanced, Veyka stepped back. "Fine."

She dropped into her chair, set the knife on the table—a reminder for Percival and Diana, and turned to her handmaiden. "What have you found out about the Sacred Trinity?"

Lyrena stole the question from mouth. "You had them looking into the Sacred Trinity? I thought we were trying to find a way to banish the succubus back to their own realm for good."

Veyka very pointedly did not look at her golden knight. "Arthur thought it was important."

Lyrena gnashed her teeth, gold flashing. "Arthur lied."

The dynamic was strange. Not like the council at the terrestrial court, nor any war council I'd ever led. Those she'd assembled in this room—aside from the prisoners—spoke with no reservation.

Veyka pursed her lips, eyes still averted. Lyrena was having none of that. She planted herself directly in the Veyka's line of sight.

The queen did not look away. "Why?" No response. "Why would Arthur have lied if it was not tied to this, to the succubus? Why would he give me amorite weapons, the one thing that can defeat them? Why set you, Lyrena, a Goldstone Guard sworn to protect the king, with your fire that can hold the succubus at bay, as my protector when such a thing had never been done before?"

Lyrena did not back down. "Because he loved you."

"I do not accept that." Veyka's throat bobbed before she added, "That it's a coincidence."

She'd loved her brother fiercely. That much was easy to read. And the feeling had been returned. Loved him, only to see him murdered before her eyes. Taken from her. As I had nearly been. Sorrow filled my gut—but it was not my mate's. It was my own.

Veyka.

Cyara stepped around Lyrena, hands folded before her and wings now steady. "We have found nothing to indicate otherwise. No mention of the Sacred Trinity at all. From what Percival says, it is a human legend. Not a fae one."

Behind her, Percival straightened. "Yes, but—"

Cyara ignored him. "In Baylaur, there may be clues to what Arthur was thinking. Blacksmiths who made your blades, servants who waited on Arthur. But we are not in Baylaur."

Lyrena and Cyara stood shoulder to shoulder—Veyka's Knights of the Round Table. Her most trusted friends and advisors.

"You have to let it go," Lyrena said, more gently.

"I will not."

The room fell silent. Veyka's stubbornness was unmatched.

"I think she is right," Percival said.

Lyrena and Cyara parted like a set of twin doors, both fixing the man with their own incredulous looks. Behind me, Osheen swallowed a laugh.

Veyka threw her hands up in the air. "Someone save me. Percival is the one who agrees with me."

But Percival continued, much steadier than his sister, even if every word dripped with distaste for those he spoke them to. "The sacred trinity was made in Avalon. Avalon is where the priestess who made the Void Prophecy dwelt for thousands of years. Our legend says that the bearer of the Sacred Trinity will be the master of death. She commands the depths of the voids of darkness. Sounds pretty similar to death."

It was a fair point.

But a distraction.

I felt the shift in the too-small room. And Veyka, caressing my wolf through the bond. *Will you challenge me too?*

It was no different from any war council I'd ever commanded, with egos and opinions competing and conflicting. Except I was not in command—*we* were.

What if I do?

Veyka had no inner beast, but I could have sworn I felt her low growl in response. *Then I will punish you.*

There was enough heat in that promise that I let myself say, "We focus on what is before us. What we can do here, concrete actions we can take to push back the succubus. For now."

For a second, Veyka's eyes glowed with desire. I knew mine burned with black fire.

But then she shrugged her shoulders and turned back to her handmaiden, who'd positioned herself slightly in front of the two humans.

"What *have* you found?"

Cyara's wing twitched. "There are no direct mentions of the succubus. But there are many records of the Great War. Even some information which does not align with our own history."

Veyka sighed. "History or legends?"

"It seems that the former has become the latter," Cyara said slowly.

"Tell us."

"In the absence of information about the succubus, we have spent many hours looking into the Great War itself," Cyara continued. "The elemental histories tell us that Accolon and Nimue's joining ended the Great War between our two territories and created the united fae kingdom of Annwyn."

Veyka nodded; so did Lyrena.

"That is the story I am familiar with as well," I said, finally able to loosen my grip on the back of the chair. Legends and histories seemed safer territory.

From over my shoulder, Osheen inclined his head in agreement. He hadn't contributed anything thus far, but I knew from centuries of having him under my command that he'd internalized every minute detail.

Cyara glanced over her shoulder, toward Diana. A subtle warning, but to who?

"It matches the official record as well, in the histories kept by the priestesses. But in addition to the official record, the priestess here at Eilean Gayl maintains a collection of journals."

Veyka cocked her head to the side. "Journals?"

"A passion project of her predecessor that she has continued." Cyara paused, drawing in a long and careful breath. I did not reach for the chair again, but I knew in a few moments, I'd wish I had something to crush beneath my fingers. "There is one recollection—not of the story itself. But an entry written by a terrestrial soldier who was stationed at the entrance to Wolf Bay."

"There is a rift at the entrance to Wolf Bay." Veyka was sitting straight up now.

Cyara's turquoise eyes drifted to mine. "It is also the location of Accolon's ancestral home."

I held her gaze. "And what does this entry say?"

"It mentions another story, an alternative to the widely known version of Accolon and Nimue. In which, they were mated on the eve of the Great War, rather than at its conclusion."

"What else?"

"We do not know."

Veyka sighed heavily, throwing herself back hard enough the chair creaked beneath her. "So it is a dead end."

But Cyara stepped forward, eyes back on Veyka and bright. "No. The writer mentions carvings, which told the story in full. Carvings which may still exist."

"So, we visit our Ancestor's old homeland," Veyka said slowly.

Cyara's wings twitched, catching Veyka's attention. Her eyes clouded with confusion. She did not understand—but I did.

"What is the problem?" Veyka asked.

"It is lost. Hidden, destroyed. No one has been there in thousands of years," I said. Osheen made a low noise of agreement. That was one of our legends.

Veyka swiped the half-full glass of wine off the table and drained it. "Great."

Behind me, Isolde murmured something to Osheen. Lyrena paced to the window, one hand on the pommel of her broadsword. Veyka was halfway across the room, aiming for the next bottle of wine, when Diana spoke.

"There is a spell."

"Diana," Percival warned. He was at his sister's side, grabbing her hand tightly, imploring her not to speak. But her dark eyes darted between me and Veyka.

"There is an old witch spell. He..." Her voice broke. She pressed her eyes closed, fighting internal demons none of us could see. At the table, Veyka had gone deadly still. Diana mastered herself enough to open her eyes, then her mouth. "G... Gorlois forced me to use it, to help him travel between realms."

Veyka was silent.

So I asked—"What does the spell do?"

Cyara answered, one eye on Diana and the other on Veyka. Dangerous. This conversation walked a tenuous line that I did not understand. Gorlois—the one who had attacked in the Battle of Avalon. But Veyka's stillness... Gorlois had hurt her, before. Gorlois and the Dowager.

"The spell untethers her mind, like a true witch. It allows her mind to travel through space, through realms. Even through time," Cyara explained. "To the past."

"To find out where Accolon's home is," I finished.

It was not a guarantee, but it was a real plan, at least. A tangible action we could take toward finding out about the Great War, and how they had defeated the succubus seven thousand years ago.

"It is dangerous," Percival growled, his voice an impressive match for my own beast. "She could become permanently untethered, her mind lost while her body remains."

"Like being lost in the void without the tether of a mate," Veyka said softly.

What in the Ancestors' living hell did that mean?

"Which is why she is not going to do it," Percival said sharply.

Diana tugged her hand from his. "You are not my master. No one is."

Wrong. She was held at the mercy of Veyka, me, and an entire castle of terrestrials. An untrained human, she had no defense here. My beast would snap her neck in a second.

But I was not thinking about Diana.

Lost in the void without the tether of a mate.

Veyka's power... was it tied to me?

I stared at my mate, but she did not look back. She was watching Diana struggle to draw in breath after ragged breath. The wine was forgotten. So was the dagger. Veyka's hand was flat against the tabletop, and I could hardly tell if she was breathing.

"He," Diana breathed, looking straight at her brother. "Gorlois forced me. Before that, I was bound to the Lady of the Lake. Even you, shouting at me through the communication crystals whenever Gorlois was not speaking to Baylaur, were always telling me what to do. I can choose for myself. I can choose this."

Cyara's wings fluttered. Her hand was pale against Diana's bare arm as she offered comfort.

But Veyka's voice sliced through the room. A cold, frozen thing sharper than any blade. "There is a communication crystal in Baylaur?"

80

VEYKA

My soul was a void of roaring darkness. I was the void. There was no slipping into it, no traveling through it. It was part of me. Had always been there in the darkest corners of myself, waiting to be awakened.

"Who?" I asked, in a voice that I hardly recognized as my own.

Diana was trembling again. "I do not know. He never told me."

Percival jerked his head to the side, gnashing his teeth in threat. As if he, feeble human, was any match to the darkness inside of me.

I stood, but I did not feel the ground. "The Dowager. It has to be."

"Veyka," Lyrena said slowly. "We knew she was involved with Gorlois. You said as much in the letter you sent to Gwen."

Veyka.

Arran's beast, brushing against my consciousness, trying to steady me. He did not know, not this Arran. He could sense my distress, but he did not *know*.

I did not bother to walk. Why, when I was the void?

A heartbeat, and I was back in the bedroom, pulling the crystal from the travel pack that Cyara had not finished unpacking. Another, and I was back.

I must have said the incantation, for the communication crystal began to glow. But I did not hear it, even as the words passed my own lips.

"Answer me," I commanded. Yelled. Not begged. I was not begging. "Answer me, you heartless bitch!" I screamed at the crystal. "Answer me!"

My cheeks were not wet. I was not crying.

The crystal did not glow again.

"Gwen may have received your letter by now. Igraine could very well be under arrest, in the dungeons or her quarters. Gwen may even be in possession of the crystal," Lyrena said gently. So gently. Because I was broken, breaking. And those were tears.

I swallowed down the lump in my throat. "Guinevere. Gwen, your queen commands that you answer."

No response came from Baylaur or anywhere else.

Veyka.

It was too hard to answer. But I felt his hand a second before it landed on my shoulder. The other carefully took the crystal from my hand, lifting it into his own.

I closed my eyes, listening to Arran's voice. Letting its warmth sink into me. "Gwen?"

Nothing.

Either Gwen was not receptive to any of our messages, she did not have the crystal, or she did not know how to use it. So close to having that connection. To knowing those I cared for were safe. And yet, nothing came of it.

Who knew what havoc Igraine was wreaking in the goldstone palace?

My eyes were still closed, Arran's hand still on my shoulder, but there was movement. The scuffing of boots. Light, slippered steps. Then stillness.

When I opened my eyes, they were arrayed in a half circle around me and Arran. Lyrena and Cyara, of course. But also Osheen and Isolde. Diana and Percival stood, backs to the wall. Still prisoners, but not quite. Helpful, but dangerous. Complicated. Like everything in my life.

Everything except the allegiance of the four warriors before me.

It was Osheen who spoke. Even, steady Osheen. "What would you have us do, Majesty?"

Slowly, so slowly, I exhaled through my nose, forcing myself to look at each of them in turn before I spoke. "We must find Accolon's stronghold, and whatever records are there. It is the best lead we have regarding the succubus. We move forward with the spell." When I looked at Diana, she was no longer trembling. Small mercies. "How long do you need?"

"I can be ready tomorrow."

"Thank you."

I could have kissed Arran when he spoke next, saving me from having to form any more coherent words. "How long has it been since you first sent word to Baylaur and Cayltay?"

Cyara answered for me. "Nearly four weeks."

He released my shoulder, taking a few steps toward the window. It was too dark to see across the lake, but his eyes were far off anyway, doing the calculations. "It is still feasible that word is coming from Baylaur within the next week. But the council at Cayltay should have responded."

This was the Arran I needed. The experienced battle commander, cool and calculated.

"There is a forge at Cayltay. We go assure their allegiance, and solidify the supply lines for the amorite so we can begin making weapons. We will need to muster the terrestrial forces from the army camps."

No.

Not that.

I was thankful he was no longer touching me. I did not know what I would have done. "That sounds like we are preparing for war."

That could not happen.

I needed Arran to help us avoid a war, not start one.

He did not sigh—no, he'd never be as demonstrative as that. He turned from the window without a hint of emotion. "This will be a war, Veyka."

Mere minutes ago, he'd been hesitant to disagree with me. Then this. He did not understand. He did not understand me. This was not Arran—not my Arran.

I stepped forward, hands at my sides. No need to put them on my hips, not for this challenge. I was not posturing. "What, then, is the point of the spell, of searching out Accolon and Nimue's secrets?"

Arran squared his shoulders, facing me fully. "Even if the spell is successful, that does not mean it will lead to a way to banish the succubus."

"They did it before, to end the Great War. There must be a way to do it again."

"What if it is too late?"

"Too late for what? Too late for who?" My voice was rising. The void howled in my veins. There were no tears this time—only rage. "What about the males that will be taken by the succubus, who will murder their friends and families, while we use the amorite for weapons, instead? Too late for them?"

Our companions said nothing. Did nothing. What could they, how could they, when this was Arran and I, against each other.

"There are no easy choices in war."

The nerve. Choices. There had never been an easy choice in my Ancestors-damned life.

"This is no choice at all," I spat. "I will protect Annwyn. Not sentence its subjects to death."

Arran's eyes were burning now, but not with desire. With challenge.

Trust me.

Two words, so soft, so secret, I could pretend I had not heard them at all. *No.*

My mate hardened before my eyes. Inside of me, there was no warmth, no brush of his beast. Only the howling void as he stared me down with those fathomless black eyes and said, "You do not understand."

Something broke inside of me. It felt a whole lot like my heart.

"*I* do not understand?"

81
VEYKA

We were alone. Suddenly. Finally.

A few measly feet separated us, and yet I could have sworn we stood on opposite sides of the void. Arran had played nice. So had I. But it was always going to come to this.

"You are afraid," he said. No accusation. A truth given, by the male who could see into my soul as easily as his own.

Given and received.

"Of course, I am." My voice did not shake. The last hour had been a tempest, and now I stood in the eye of the storm. "Every day, every minute in your presence is a reminder of what I stand to lose."

Tell me I have not lost you. Tell me that you love me.

But my mind was silent. A howling void.

Arran, my Arran, looked at me as if he were trying to figure me out. As if he did not know or understand me at all.

He shook his head slowly, dark locks nearly freed from the que at the back of his head. "You are queen. You cannot be selfish—"

"Do not dare. Not you. Not after all of this." My restraint was slipping. My sanity. The void was calling and soon I would go.

"Everything I have done has been for Annwyn. Even at the cost of you."

A low growl. "I do not understand."

My heart was already broken. What did it matter if I smashed it into a few more pieces?

"What if I had not left?" I whispered. "What if the first thing you'd seen upon waking in Avalon had been my face?" I had asked myself those questions again and again. Sleeping, waking, with every inhale and exhale, I asked the Ancestors and the void, "Would you have remembered?"

He stared at me, assessing. A battle to be fought, a foe to be unraveled. Not his mate or his love.

"I don't know," he finally said.

Neither did I. But I supposed it did not matter. I reached for the dagger on the table, angled my leg so the scabbard strapped to my leg was visible and slid it home. My fingers grazed over the jeweled scabbard, so intricate. One of the sacred trinity. Important. But useless to this moment, and to my true fate.

I could not bring myself to meet Arran's eyes as I said, "It is my fault."

"You could not have known. Not with the scabbards."

It was an easy mistake to make. I was touching one, after all. "Not that. Yes, that, actually."

Arran stepped closer. The scent of him—earth and spice and warmth, such heady warmth... it made me want to throw aside everything. To throw him down and forget reality.

"I do not blame you," he said quietly.

I almost gave in then. I almost let myself be the coward he'd once accused me of being. I was so, so afraid. Because at least now, I had some shred of him.

"But you should," I said softly.

I forced myself to look into his eyes as I finally told him the truth, the one I'd held back in every conversation since he'd awoken. "My void power is the reason the succubus has returned."

He did not move. Did not understand. I had already told him

this, in the dungeons of Castle Chariot. But it was more than fact that motivated me. It was the gaping hole those facts had left in my soul.

"I planned to leave after I avenged Arthur. I was going to leave Baylaur, leave Annwyn, travel to some distant continent where I could live out my powerless days in peace, without bringing ruin down upon my kingdom. But I fell in love with you."

I turned over my palm, as if I could see the place where Merlin had slashed my flesh.

"I stayed. I joined my blood with yours and awakened the void power, and doomed my kingdom. I gave the succubus a way back in. That is why they hunt me, Arran. Why even the mindless, soulless shells of bodies are drawn to me. Because it is *my fault*. All of it is my fault."

My fault.

I thought it with every breath.

My fault.

Knew it with every beat of my heart.

Arran dropped a hand to the head of his battle axe. The Brutal Prince—a place of safety for him. I should have expected what he said next.

"Then go to war. Go to war to protect them."

Nothing for me. Nothing about me. No words of comfort—because I did not deserve them. All of it was my fault. "So that more of my subjects can die for me and my mistakes?"

"The succubus is coming," Arran said. "You may not have a choice."

I laughed at that, a sound as cold and broken and empty as the void that I was quickly becoming. "I have never had many choices. And when I have, I've always seemed to choose wrong."

Arran did not reach for me. He did not offer anything. I understood, I really did. We had lost months that felt like lifetimes. Memories and trials that we may never regain. It had been a blessing, if a fleeting one. Borrowed time.

But if I kept reaching out for him, if I kept waiting, I would chip away until there was nothing left. And if it were just for me, that would have been enough. But Annwyn depended on me. I would not fail them again.

"I won't beg you to love me, Arran," I said. And even though I hated the Ancestors, I sent up a genuine prayer of thanks that my voice did not break. "But I do love you. Even this fucked up version. And if I have to spend the next thousand years without seeing love in your eyes, I will pay that price. Because I made a vow. A thousand years and a thousand more."

Not the vow we'd made before Annwyn. The one whispered in the secret waters of the faerie pools the night we'd consummated the mating bond between us.

Arran stared at me like the world was ending. In some ways, it was. This world, our world, the one we'd made between us, was shrinking away to nothing with every second. What emerged on the other side would never be the same.

I walked to the corner. Waited. Filled a glass of wine. Waited. Drank it. Waited.

I turned back to my mate.

"Perhaps it would be better if we went our separate ways."

No reaction.

"I can return to Baylaur. Deal with my mother, dispatch the elemental forces."

No movement.

"You can tend to Cayltay. The war camps, the forge. Maybe it would be better than this."

Only those endless black depths, where I could have lost myself forever.

"Anything would be better than this," I whispered.

My fingers began to tingle. My arms. The golden thread was there, would always be there, to keep me from fully letting go. But when the void pulled, when the ember of power inside of me blazed to life, I did not fight it.

I did not let myself imagine that there was a low growl there, at the edge of my consciousness, before I disappeared.

And if that was my name on his lips, I did not want to hear it. Not as I gave myself to the yawning emptiness inside of me and slipped away. As the voids of darkness welcomed me home.

82

ARRAN

The walls of Eilean Gayl pressed in around me. Tighter, tighter. So close, I could not shift. I could not breathe.

On two legs, I stumbled down the stairs. No one to see me. Too late, too dark. Too alone. These walls had once shielded me, but long ago, so long ago, had failed. Then caged.

I had to get out. My beast tore at my control, shredding the ties that bound him.

I wanted to feel the cold winter air on my skin. Needed it. But the beast was in control. I shifted before I burst through the doors. Over the bridge in four massive bounds.

Then it was just me and the forest. There was no moonlight to glint off of the lake, to remind me of Veyka's hair. A ceiling of ominous shadows blocked out every star. Soon, it would rain. Maybe snow. Snow as white as my mate's skin.

Veyka, who was the other half of me. Who needed me, loved me.

But I could not give her what she needed.

She had vowed to love me forever.

I could be the High King of Annwyn, if that was what the

Ancestors demanded of me. It was my duty. But to give myself to Veyka, to love her—

My beast flooded my mind with a snarl. The line between the two of us was blurring with every bound, deeper into the snowy mountains. The wolf inside of me loved her, needed her. No conditions. No questions.

But I was not the beast.

I controlled the beast.

Controlling the beast was the only way I survived. Without that control, I would turn into a monster.

But without Veyka, would I become something worse?

83
CYARA

She dispatched Percival and Diana to the kitchens to help prepare the evening meal. The kitchen servants and the priestess were the only terrestrials in Eilean Gayl who did not look at the two humans as if they were calculating how they would taste. But at that moment, anywhere was safer than near Veyka. The queen might finally decide to rip out Percival's throat, just to calm the roaring pain inside of her.

She even sent away Osheen and Lyrena, encouraging them to join Maisri for the communal meal. But Cyara herself lingered in the corridor, ears alert, wings tucked in tight in the narrow space. The guard at the stairs ignored her. She returned the favor. Most of her attention was focused inside the sitting room. Even her sharp ears could not make out the words; she would not have wanted to. That would be an intrusion.

But as soon as the voices died, she moved.

Cyara was through the door into the queen's bedchamber, door closed, before Arran opened the one into the corridor and disappeared, his gait even heavier than usual. The bedroom was empty.

Veyka had taken to the void. Either to find some other place of solace, or to lose herself in that endless in between. She had done that more and more, used the void not as a means of transportation, but as an escape.

How long would it be before that was her true home, and Annwyn the mere stopover?

Cyara picked the first garment from the never-ending pile of clothing in need of mending and settled in to wait.

※

Dinner came and went. Veyka had lost weight from missing meals. Had anyone else noticed? Cyara set aside a loaf of crusty bread and kept the rich stew warm with her flames. Damn the cost. Her wrists could ache every minute from now until she was five hundred years old, and she would consider the price justly paid.

The sun was peeking over the horizon when Veyka appeared. Right in the center of the room, white hair a tangle around her shoulders, blue eyes turned sapphire dark. Cyara ached to reach for her, to hold her close the way she had done for her younger sisters. Simple days, those had been, when she could soothe a slight or scrape with a bit of chocolate and gentle caresses of their copper hair.

There was nothing simple about the tempest that had encircled Veyka.

Cyara set aside her long-forgotten sewing and stood, palms out. "What can I do?" she asked quietly.

Veyka sighed and dragged a hand through her hair, fingers catching on the tangles. She pulled on the snarls mercilessly, her face hardly showing any reaction other than exhaustion. "Pack."

Cyara nodded. "Where are we going?"

Veyka's hand dropped.

But it was her eyes that gave her away. Those miraculous blue eyes that could soften with kindness or darken with ire. Sharp as ice when she was angry, bright as the sky when they sparkled with mischievousness. Now, they were the blue of a sea that Cyara had only seen in her mind, in her father's stories. Unmoored and shifting.

Veyka did not know where they were going—not yet.

It did not matter, Cyara told herself. They would take all of their possessions, regardless. "I see." She nodded, matter-of-factly. "Are we bringing Percival and Diana?"

For a second, the queen's eyes flashed with gratitude. Then she walked to the bed, back to Cyara, unstrapping her weapons as she went.

"Yes. Lyrena, Isolde, everyone. Ask Osheen." Veyka pulled her weapons from her belt, arranging them on the bed. Her two curved rapiers, her daggers, and then she opened the drawer beside the bed and added a few small but wicked knives. She did not plan on sleeping anytime soon, then.

Her brother's mighty sword was conspicuously absent.

Cyara still had not found where Veyka had stashed it, despite combing over their chambers multiple times over the past month and a half.

But that was a question for another day. Now, there was only one that mattered. "What about Arran?"

This time, Veyka gave the answer in words. "I don't know."

She kept her back to Cyara.

But that sort of pain could not be contained. Cyara could feel it in the air they shared, the current of a kingdom. A friendship forged in pain and the light at the end of a long darkness.

Yet in that moment, Cyara knew the light in her friend had dimmed.

"I see," she said softly.

Veyka's voice cracked. "Do you?"

Cyara closed the steps between them. So slowly, gentle as if she were reaching for a scared animal, she took hold of Veyka's shoulder and eased her around. She expected tears, but they were none. Veyka had left them in the void, along with the last shreds of her hope.

"I see a female who is stronger than she knows," Cyara said

softly. Her grip on Veyka's shoulder was anything but. "A friend who has made me laugh, and cry, and forced me to reconcile the parts of myself that I once feared. I see a queen who has risen from darkness again and again. A queen who will keep rising, every day, no matter how her enemies try to keep her down. My queen."

Veyka closed her eyes. Cyara did not speak again, tracking the bob of Veyka's throat, and the slight sway of her shoulders as she tried to get command of herself. When she did open her eyes, they were clearer than before, if only by a tiny fraction.

"I must ask you one last thing, and you are going to hate it."

Cyara's wings twitched. "Go on, then."

"There is something I must do before we leave Eilean Gayl."

Cyara stepped back enough that she could cross her arms. "Something dangerous," she guessed. "That you do not plan on telling Arran about."

Veyka laughed softly, and the sound was only slightly hollow. "How do you always know what is on my mind?"

"If I told you, I would be giving up my advantage."

"An elemental to your core." Veyka's small smile faded. She turned back to assessing her weapons. "I will be back in a few days."

Cyara watched as she unsheathed the rapiers, examining the blades. "I can manage Percival and Diana without Lyrena. Though if it will make you feel better, I shall ask Osheen to look in periodically."

"I am not taking Lyrena with me."

Despite what her queen thought, Cyara was not actually able to predict her every move. "Veyka—"

"If I have not returned in three days, you can send Arran and Lyrena and the rest of them to retrieve me from the Spine. But until then, tell no one where I have gone." Veyka began repacking her blades. She would not linger long, then.

Cyara knew it was a useless appeal, but she made it anyway. "Please, do not do this."

"Cyara," Veyka paused, offering a grim smile over her shoulder.

"You know better than most that sometimes, the darkness must be faced alone."

The harpy.

Yes, Cyara had been alone when that dark monster inside of her awakened for the first time. She had carried the secret of what she was—what Gawayn had made her by slaughtering her sisters—as a lone burden for as long as she could. Until Maisri was in danger, when the harpy had clawed her way out.

"Be careful, Veyka," Cyara finally said.

Veyka's smile was nowhere in sight as she nodded sharply. "Be ready to leave when I return."

84
VEYKA

"Lady Elayne to see you, Your Majesty."

I had almost made it. Another five minutes, and I'd have been gone. I'd paused long enough to eat the stew that Cyara had kept warm and waiting all night long. It just seemed rude to let her effort be for nothing. There was so little she could do to help; that anyone could. So, I'd forced down the stew even though my stomach was in knots. And delayed my departure long enough that I had to lay aside the satchel—a smaller version of the travel pack—and meet my mother-in-law.

Elayne swept into the room, graceful as ever. Cyara's eyes traced over me from head to foot, as if she were trying to memorize me. As if part of her thought I might not come back.

I'd kept my plans to myself, but running was not part of them. I'd given up on that foolish hope back in Baylaur, after the Tower of Myda.

There was nowhere I could run to escape my heartbreak.

"Thank you, Cyara," I said. "I will speak to you soon. I am certain you have preparations well under way."

My handmaiden narrowed her eyes, but did not ask me to stay or try to change my mind before she withdrew to the sitting room.

I did not do Elayne the dishonor of dissembling. I faced her directly. The time for anything less had passed. "What is it?"

"You are leaving," Elayne said with equal candor.

She'd come through the sitting room, where Cyara was already gathering their things. "Not for a few days."

Elayne shook her head slowly. "*You* are leaving."

She had either spoken to Arran, or made a good guess. It had to be that—the sorry state of my soul could not be that painfully visible. "I did not realize I was so transparent."

I waited for the arguments. Instead, Elayne came to stand beside me. I was wrapping traveling cakes. Each in a layer of thin linen, then stacked five high, then wrapped again in a thicker swatch before stowing them in a pouch. I doubted I'd need them all before I returned, but it was better than being hungry. I doubted there would be much hunting where I was headed.

Elayne watched me wrap one, then nudged my hands aside and took over the mundane task herself. I checked over my weapons one last time.

"I do not know much about the mating bond. Only the legends that we have all heard." Elayne said as she worked. "Once, I fancied that Pant and I enjoyed such a connection." She let out a soft, breathy laugh.

The image of Pant, the Lord of Eilean Gayl, with Lady Sylestria spread across his lap at Yule came back to me, sharp as if I'd seen it yesterday. Not my heartbreak. But real.

"How do you manage?"

Elayne did not pause her work as her slim shoulders moved up and down her back in a graceful shrug. "I love him. And he loves me. For the things we can give each other, and the things we cannot. I was hurt badly, before my marriage."

So casual a reference to such a monumental wrong.

Elayne had been raped, again and again, by terrestrial males hoping they would be the one to sire upon her the child of immeasurable power that she would one day bear.

"Arran told me."

Only after the birth of her first son, Arran's elder brother, had the attacks stopped. When her first child was born ordinary—with power, but nothing remarkable—she'd been discarded. She eventually fell in love with Pant and bore Arran, the most powerful fae born in millennia.

"Their births were treacherous, especially Arran," Elayne continued. "I found that after my sons were born, I could not bear to be touched, not in that way, never again. Pant was kind and loving. As the decades passed, I gave him the freedom to find those comforts elsewhere. I have his heart, and that is enough."

I tried to process that. Hundreds of years together. That was what it an immortal lifetime promised. She and Pant had looked into that future, decades stretching into centuries, and decided to find their way forward together.

Because they loved each other.

A thousand years, and a thousand more.

"But what if you did not have even that?" I asked softly.

Elayne finished wrapping the last of the travel cakes, closed the drawstring pouch, and met my eyes with her dark, steady gaze. "What you and Arran share is nothing like my own marriage."

No, it was not.

I loved Arran. Every beat of my broken heart belonged to him. But even if his beast knew me and loved me, the male did not.

I took the parcel from her hands. "Thank you, for providing safe harbor here. It is more than I could have asked or hoped for."

Elayne exhaled. "But you are still leaving."

I held her gaze long enough to nod, then turned to stow the pouch. The last item to be added to my satchel. "This time has been but an interlude. We have secured the amorite and more is coming. We have sent warnings to Cayltay and Baylaur, but that will not be enough. The succubus can prey on villages and castles alike. I need to be with my people, need to send warnings and amorite in every direction. Prepare soldiers. Prepare for battle." I could taste the bitterness of those last two sentences on my tongue.

"Those are Arran's words."

They were. But just because I hated them, did not mean they were wrong. Maybe neither of us was right. But the argument was only a symptom of the much deeper divide between us.

Later. When I return. Then, I would start making decisions.

"There is too much to do. It may be better for Arran and I to manage separately, to each play to our own strengths." I wasn't sure what mine were, but I knew his. "He will be needed in the war camps. My place is in Baylaur." By some miracle, my voice did not crack.

I heard her sharp intake of breath, but I kept moving. Adjusted the buckle on the harness that held my rapiers. Fitted the satchel over my shoulder and around on my hip. Reached for my thick fur cloak.

"Arran will never allow that. He will not be parted from his mate. He will not let you go."

I wished she were right.

I turned to face her. Ready.

"Are you certain?"

If she said yes, that would be something. Something to hold on to, threw the next grueling hours of my journey. A ray of hope, when I was drowning in a well of darkness. But that was not what she said.

Her answer shone in her eyes, and it was not the one I wanted.

I bowed my head. "Thank you for your help, Elayne. I will not leave without saying goodbye."

Then I was gone.

85
ARRAN

The beast curled up before a fire long gone cold. No one brought food. No one disturbed the monster. I forgot who I was, what I was. Brutal Prince. High King. Mate.

The beast wanted control, so I gave it to him.

I knew Veyka would not come, but still my beastly senses pricked at every sound. A rustle of skirts, a whipping wind. None of it came to anything.

There I remained for hours, locked behind a door that would not do much if my beast decided to tear it down.

A door to which only one person had a key.

The beast scented her cool lavender before the pin slid into the lock. By the time the door swung open, the male stood before her.

My mother did not pause until she'd locked the door behind her. Only then did she stop to regard me. Starting with the filthy boots, past the trousers with torn-out knees, up to the ragged tunic and vest. Her gaze lingered on my face—unshaven, gaunt. I did not need a mirror to know how awful I must look.

My mother merely cleared her throat and folded her hands. "Veyka prepares to leave Eilean Gayl."

My chest began to burn. When I spoke, my voice was hoarse.

"Cayltay must be brought to heel. The war camps will need to be readied; who knows how many months they have been loitering without action."

Two gracefully arched eyebrows lifted. "Your queen has agreed to go to Wolf Bay?"

Ancestors spare me.

"You ask questions you already know the answers to. Why, Mother?"

A slow exhale through her nose. Control—this was the female who had taught me control. The only one in the entire terrestrial kingdom who had dared to approach me, spend time with me, when I was still learning to master my power. "I hope if I ask enough, eventually I will receive a different answer."

My wolf had torn across the countryside, ripping apart any creature that crossed his path. But still, the power simmered in my veins. I curled my fingers in toward my palms, and two thick vines curled through the open window.

I let them grow. Let my power out in a slow, steady stream. "I know that you have grown fond of Veyka. But we must do what is best for Annwyn."

My mother watched the advance of the vines with one eye. "Duty above all else."

They curled around the bookshelves that lined the wall, thick thorns the size of my beast's fang forming, blocking out the gilded spines. "Yes."

She said nothing. "Even above yourself."

Up and up and up the vines climbed toward the flat wooden ceiling. "When necessary."

My mother walked to the window, nudging it open fully. To prevent it from shattering, probably. Small, controlled actions, always.

She stroked one hand over the vine lovingly. As if it was a child's cheek she caressed instead of a thorn-covered tendril of death.

. . .

"Will you ever stop punishing yourself?" she asked softly.

It was a question she'd asked me before. The answer was on the tip of my tongue. "It is either punish myself or punish them."

Punish myself for what I had done, the hundreds of terrestrials I had slaughtered in the years it took me to get control of my powers. Force myself to serve a country that had done my own family such harm as penance for the monster that lived inside of me.

It was either that, or tear the world apart for what they had done to my mother.

What it had done to Veyka.

The vines stilled.

What had been done to Veyka? She was a warrior, but a survivor... it would make sense... but I had no memory... *No. That is a memory. That feeling of vengeance, a promise not yet fulfilled. To avenge those that had hurt my mate.* That was a memory.

My mother turned to face me again, the wall of vines thick behind her, no fear in her eyes even as those thorns swelled in size.

"I am safe, Arran. Whole. Protected. I should be the least of your worries."

I said nothing.

She would never be safe enough. *Neither would Veyka.*

"Is this about your brother?"

That was a door I kept firmly closed, always. Only my mother would have dared to try and wrench it open. "No."

But my mother was not assuaged. "Have you told Veyka, about what happened?"

"If I did, I don't remember," I bit back. The vines were creeping across the floor now, circling around the legs of the chair and the desk. Soon, there would be no stone left uncovered.

My mother huffed a sigh. "You two are quite the pair. When she told me about your injury, about how it was her hand that drove Excalibur into your chest, I told her I forgave her. She refused me. I imagine you would do the same if I told you, for the thousandth time, that I do not blame you for your brother's death."

It did not matter what she said, how many thousands of times she said it. Because none of that mattered in face of the truth.

"My beast killed him."

I had killed many, in those days. I could hardly recall them. They were a blur of pain and blood. The beast would wrest control at the smallest slight. The vines would shoot through windows, shattering ancient stained glass and wrapping around the offender's throat before I could blink.

None of those faces lived in my memory. Except one.

"Is there a difference between?" my mother asked carefully. So carefully.

That was the true question, the one I had never fully faced. What was the beast, and what was me? Where was the line? For three centuries, I had kept them separate. I had maintained control by forcing the beast into restraints and never fully releasing them. Never.

But when I awoke in Avalon, the line between myself and the wolf was blurred. The mating bond in my chest compelled both male and beast.

If I admitted that they were one and the same—*we* were one and the same, then I was responsible for my brother's death.

Then I was in love with Veyka.

The burning in my chest was an inferno. It filled my head, my eyes, my heart. I was going to burn up, burn out. Right there, in a lonely tower study that I hated.

Until a cool hand touched my cheek.

I closed my eyes, and exhaled the words that burned my throat. "I killed him." And a second later— "I love her."

In an instant, the vines withered to nothing. A soft swish, and they fell away from the wall. Nothing but tiny fragments on the stone floor, soon to be lost underfoot.

When I opened my eyes, my mother was smiling up at me. "Of course you do."

"But that does not solve anything, Mother." It did not banish the succubus. It did not restore my memories. It did not take back any of the pain.

Her smile just deepened as she dropped her hand, refolding it in front of her. Regal and composed, as always. "Don't you understand, my son? Every trial, every ordeal, every death—it has all been to bring you here. To bring you to her."

My head shook of its own accord. "And what if after all of that, we still are not enough?"

Her head snapped up sharply. "Are you saying that Veyka is not enough?"

"Veyka is everything," my beast growled—I growled—at the mere insinuation.

"Yes, she is," my mother nodded, turning for the door. "And all she wants is you."

86
VEYKA

Three days. One to go, one to return. An extra for all the time I spent bumbling about, trying to find the right spot. The accounts were vague and the mountains of the Spine towering. But I did not appreciate just how massive they were until I stood at the base of one. The jagged peaks made the mountains ringing Baylaur and the Effren Valley appear pitiful by comparison.

Their presence made Eilean Gayl, the amorite mines, everything north of them even more remarkable. For millennia, the terrestrials had traversed these mountains. Thankfully, they'd also written down hundreds of accounts of their excursions.

Those accounts had been my nighttime reading since our arrival in Eilean Gayl.

It was not enough to give me a precise location. But I knew where to start.

I murmured a prayer of thanks to whoever was listening, Ancestors or human gods or some other benevolent being, and entered the void. Hopefully there would be solid ground awaiting me when I stepped out on the other side.

Closer. Every jump through the void brought me closer to that final destination. I was damn prideful, but even I could admit to myself that without my void power I might not have managed it. In what would have taken days of treacherous climbing, I was able to appear in a mountain pass in the space of one inhale and exhale. Crossing a glacier that would have surely claimed at least one victim, I saw only the view from one and then the other.

But even my void power failed me now.

I stared up... and up, and up, and up.

A solid wall of ice towered hundreds of feet above my head.

Maybe if I'd had these as my model, I would have been more successful at guarding my heart.

I squinted, testing the limits of my sharp fae eyesight. There were narrow protrusions that might serves as ledges, but even if I was able to aim and land myself directly on one of them, the force of impact might have the ice crumbling beneath my feet.

There was no use—I'd have to do this the slow way.

I choked down a few travel cakes, their wrappings still faintly laced with Elayne's soothing lavender scent. Took a swig from the canteen tied to my belt. Then started to truly prepare.

Leather thongs served to affix the small knives I'd brought to the soles of my boots. I doubted they would hold my weight entirely, but they'd steady me and allow me to ease the strain on my arms. I left my cloak behind. It pained me to do it. I'd thought Eilean Gayl cold—that was a fucking joke. But the leather and fur cloak was heavy, and I had my own weight of contend with. A single pound might be the different between life and death. I doubted that even my innate healing abilities would matter if I smashed into the stone and ice from five hundred feet up.

Soon I'd be coated in sweat, anyway.

One last glance upward. That was all I allowed myself.

Then I bent my knees and leapt. Slammed one dagger into the wall of ice, and began to climb.

I did not allow myself to look down. I counted the seconds and minutes to keep myself from noticing how ragged my breaths had become. Twenty minutes. Thirty.

If I looked down, I might see that I'd only made it a few dozen yards. The exhaustion would start to win, and I would never make it. Or I would realize how far the fall was, lose my nerve, become sloppy, and fall to my death. I told myself that I would be able to plunge myself into the void before I splattered across the icy ground.

Better not to look down at all.

Hand over hand, I slammed one dagger into the wall, hoisted myself up, then slammed in the other. Up and up and up. I had to remind myself to keep kicking in the small knives affixed to my boots. They would not hold me if I slipped; but they might slow me down enough to save myself.

Maybe coming alone had been a bad idea. Cyara could have flown, picked out where the entrance was and then I could have used my void power... it wasn't too far for her wings... I flicked my gaze downward to check—

Oh shit. No. No. No. No. No.

I could not even see the ground below. It had disappeared entirely behind a veil of swirling mist.

I swung upward, harder. The ice shifted beneath the force, sending a showing of snow and shards of ice cascading down over my face. There was nothing I could do. I clamped my eyes shut. I may not be able to bleed, but I did not know if that protection extended to my eyeballs.

I dug both boot-daggers deep into the wall. My other dagger, too. Just a minute. I could rest for a minute.

I counted the seconds as my heart raced.

Fifty-seven, fifty-eight, fifty-nine, sixty.

I summoned every ounce of strength in my aching muscles and hoisted myself up. Inch by agonizing inch. Somewhere in this wall of ice, I would find the entrance. Every few yards, I paused long enough to look from one side, then to the other, to make sure I had not inadvertently climbed right past it. But yard after yard, I saw nothing but barren white-blue ice.

My body screamed for rest, but I refused to listen. The air around me fogged with each breath. I was getting higher. The air was thinning. Soon, I whispered to myself. Soon, I'd have the answers I sought.

Above my head, a few feet away, I spied a ledge. I hauled myself up with renewed resolve. Three more feet. Two. I aimed my daggers wide, wary of any impact that might damage the integrity of the icy ledge. Then I was there. Daggers still buried in the wall, I did not dare release them. But I eased my grip, let my exhausted arms have a few seconds.

My head fell forward, resting against the ice. I could not leave it there for long. My sweat may very well freeze to the sheet of ice. But just for a second...

CRACK.

No. No. I will not die here.

But the fissure raced up the ice, splintering the wall beneath me. I tightened my grip on the daggers, holding tight. But the crack was spreading, a second and they wouldn't be safe. I pulled one away, swinging wide, trying to find a stable patch of ice that would hold. But I missed.

The ledge crumbled beneath me. Another loud crack. A sickening lurch.

And I was falling.

In some ways, it was just like that first time I'd plunged into the void. My entire body ached. I had no control. The world was rushing by me faster than I could process it.

Time seemed to slow.

It would have been so easy to just let it happen. Once, I would have.

But I was not that lost, sad princess anymore.

I will not die here.

The ember of power inside of me exploded. I threw myself into the void. A second later, I was on the other side, crashing into the wall of ice. I got my arm up, just in time, with just enough force. Embedded my dagger to the hilt.

I hung there, by one arm, as the world took shape around me once more. Every muscle in my body was trembling, but not from exertion. I forced my breathing to steady, my heartbeat to slow. I checked my body for wounds; found none. The golden thread of the mating bond was tight around my heart. My ember of magic glowing happily deep inside of me.

I lifted the other dagger and swung upward, lodging it deep into the ice. Only then did I look upward, ready to haul myself the rest of the distance. It took several pulls to dislodge the first dagger where I'd embedded it as I fell out of the void.

I swung upward again, but my dagger met air.

One final pull, and I was heaving myself over the edge, onto a floor of solid ice. I did not turn around to watch the sun setting over the mountains behind me. I did not allow myself the wave of relief or the glow of triumph. I pulled myself up to stand, knowing that what lay ahead would be infinitely worse than the treacherous climb.

The witch unfolded from her icy throne.

"Welcome, Veyka Pendragon. I have been waiting for you."

87
ARRAN

Veyka wasn't anywhere in the castle. The taut pull of the bond in my chest told me as much; but I still took the time to verify it with my own eyes before seeking out Osheen. The latent energy, the thoughts burning through me—they needed an outlet. Sparring would have to do. I hoped that pairing with Osheen would make some small step toward healing what I'd so thoughtlessly broken. But by the time I hit the training courtyard, Osheen still nowhere to be seen, I was starting to talk myself round to accepting Barkke as an opponent instead. Even if that meant enduring his endless yammering.

But the training courtyard was deserted.

And festooned in flowers.

And not empty.

The small, dark-haired child who had thrown herself so emphatically into Veyka's arms stood at the end of the line of arched alcoves, gently twirling her finger. Even from a distance, I was struck by the beauty as she coaxed a tiny bud into a wide, yawning gardenia bloom. She was a daisy fae.

Maisri. Osheen's niece.

It looked like she'd been at work on the training courtyard for hours. Of course, with that sort of power, it might have only been a matter of minutes.

It explained why there was no one around. No one would have dared to disturb this kind of masterpiece; not even the prideful shifters who scorned the flora-gifted.

I would find no sparring partner today. I'd have to satisfy myself with shifting into my wolf and running through the mountains to take off the burning edge of—

"Stop! You're crushing them!" the child cried. She was across the courtyard in a flash, shoving me backward.

Not a hint of hesitation. She did not even look at me as she fell to her knees, then her elbows, wriggling her fingers at what I'd thought was a patch of moss. But before my eyes, they sprang back to life. Tiny star-shaped blue flowers. The color of Veyka's eyes.

Maisri rocked back on her heels, staring at the blooms for a few moments before lifting her accusatory glare to me.

I started to step backward, stilled the motion, and put my hands up in outright submission. "I'm sorry."

Her dark eyes widened—*impossibly, how could anyone's eyes get that big?* —and then just as quickly as she'd moved before, she danced back across the courtyard to a little leather satchel I had not noticed before, resting near the gardenias she'd been attending to.

She tugged out a small book and what appeared to be a tiny bit of charcoal.

"What are you doing?"

Her eyes darted my way. This time, they were lined with mischievousness. "Writing down the date. Veyka will want to know."

I caught the barked laugh halfway out of my throat, so that it came out a strange, strangled thing. Maisri seemed utterly unbothered. She finished her scribbling and tucked her book back into its pouch.

"Saucy little thing, aren't you?" I said, looking more carefully around me as I assessed an exit route.

She cocked her head the side, dark hair bouncing. "No."

I'd never understood children, even when I had been one. At least this one wasn't afraid of me. That was... something. I rubbed a hand over my still unshaven jaw. "Where is Osheen?"

She shrugged, moving away from the pillar of gardenias to examine what I thought was an already sufficiently festooned pillar of draping lilacs. Clearly, Maisri disagreed. Another flick of her hand, and more flowers burst into existence.

"He went out with the others on a hunting party for Imbolc," she said over her shoulder.

The festival of females. A week away. I'd forgotten it entirely.

But if my mother was to be believed, Veyka would be gone by then.

I needed to speak to my mate.

I turned, only to have Maisri skip past me, deftly avoiding the patch of flowers I'd squashed and she'd so promptly repaired.

"Where are you going now?"

She paused, huffing with the annoyance that only children could get away with around a male called the Brutal Prince. "To find Veyka. I want to show her the lilacs. They are her favorite color."

This child knew my mate better than I did.

Fuck me.

Even if I did love her, even if we were able to repair things, somehow... we had so far to go.

Maisri pursed her little lips, staring at me hard enough that I got the impression she was trying to see straight into my mind. "You truly do not remember anything?"

I swallowed. "I wish I did."

She chewed her bottom lip as she considered. "I can answer your questions."

I choked. "That... I do not think that would be entirely appropriate."

She lifted her chin, staring down her nose at me with an impertinence that screamed of Veyka Pendragon. "I am a very good listener. Cyara said so."

I couldn't help rolling my eyes. "Well, if Cyara says so."

She was blocking my way. I did not dare take another step into the training courtyard. I'd have to go back the way I'd come, up the staircase. Where Maisri stood poised on the bottom step.

Fine.

"Did we always argue this much?"

Maisri burst out laughing. "Of course," she managed to gasp between giggles. "Ask me something harder."

Ancestors save me.

"Who fell in love first?" I hardly believed I asked it. There was no one else I would have voiced that query too. Only a child, a daisy fae, who worshiped my mate with a ferocity I aspired to.

"I never heard either of you say it," Maisri admitted, toying with the ends of her hair. "But the way you looked at the queen... someday, I hope I have a mate who looks at me like that."

Her eyes went a little dreamy. My throat closed. But I managed to get out a few gruff words. "I hope you do."

She shrugged, eyes drifting over my shoulder. Already bored with the little game she'd devised. "I suppose I ought to go start packing. Osheen said we are leaving again soon."

My beast snarled, sharp and demanding.

Osheen had agreed to accompany Veyka—without knowing whether I would be coming as well.

Good—I wanted the best watching her back.

I should be the one watching her back.

Maisri could not hear the snarl or the growl that was building inside of me. She was halfway up the stairs before she called back one last question. "Are you coming with us?"

My beast growled in answer. I did not fight him. "Yes. Yes, I am."

88

VEYKA

I chucked the amorite amulet at the witch's feet. "Put that on before you take another step."

She lowered her eyes to examine it, exposing the column of her neck to me. One bound, and I could remove her head from her body. Stupid, arrogant, or lethal. Probably some combination of the latter two.

In some ways, she was identical to the sister I'd slain in the Tower of Myda. Her long nails curved downward, but instead of razor-sharp points, hers had grown into graceful curls that brushed the icy floor of the cave. Those eyes were the same as well—all-seeing and damn eerie.

"I have not seen a gemstone like that in an age," the witch cooed, adoration flickering in her eyes. "What a gift you have brought, Veyka Pendragon."

"I am not sympathetic to your circumstances," I said. The daggers were still in my hands; ready if she were to make any move of aggression. "But I would rather not have to kill you before I get my answers. Put it on," I ordered again.

The witch swiped the amulet up without bending her waist at all, courtesy of those grotesquely long nails.

"You have discovered the one weakness of the succubus." As she spoke, she turned over the amulet in her hands. It was simple. A stone the size of my thumbnail in a rough gold setting, affixed to a narrow leather strap. She did not lift her gaze back to me as she considered it. "I am a female. What need have I of your trinket?"

Already, she was asking me questions. The witch in the Tower of Myda had tried to do the same, to distract me so that she could gain the upper hand.

I gritted my teeth. "A test? You shall have to answer my questions regardless once I have my blade pressed to your throat."

Maybe her throat was not the best bet. Too close to those vicious nails. My rapiers crossed behind her neck, forcing her down to her knees before me... yes, that was a better idea.

The witch's nails clicked together in an unnerving symphony. "Humor an old female."

So many times, I'd thrown myself into the void over the last month and a half. A sweet escape, yes. But most of those times, I had appeared in Eilean Gayl's library. In the priestess's reading room. In Pant's private studies, dotted throughout the castle. Each time, inching a bit closer to this—to the witch. The last remaining one in Annwyn, if the history was to be believed.

I almost laughed aloud at the absurdity of that.

But I stifled the impulse, my face cool. Giving the witch nothing. "You are not like the other," I observed.

"Are you like every other elemental?"

Point taken.

"Your counterpart in the Tower of Myda, her mind was taken by the succubus. Her body turned to a weapon, used against her will. Even though she was female."

She was not staring at the amulet anymore. No, she'd lifted those eyes to me. I'd thought the nails were bad? Her eyes were worse. It felt as if she could see directly into my soul, past every barrier real and internal.

A second—that was all it would take for the succubus to invade her body and for me to lose this chance.

"Put it on," I commanded. I left the other half of the sentence unsaid—*and then I will tell you the rest.*

Her eyes did not twitch from mine as she lifted the amulet overhead and lowered it to her shoulders. Only when she pulled her hands away, and the amorite remained, did I feel my stomach begin to unclench.

"A witch's mind is not tethered to her body. It is a powerful magic. But a dangerous one, particularly when it leaves your mind open and accessible to the succubus, regardless of gender."

The witch smiled. Horrible. Every instinct inside of me screamed. "You always were so very clever. Even as a child. But I have watched you for years, Queen of Death and Darkness. You and many others. Why should I fear the succubus now?"

"Because they want me." And proximity to me might very well draw the succubus directly to the witch. One of the many reasons I'd needed to make this journey alone. I would not put my friends in this kind of danger.

Parys had nearly died in the Tower of Myda. The feat required to reach the witch here in the Spine was different, but no less harrowing. I would not sacrifice another friend on the altar of my own agony.

The witch sank down on a stone, not unlike the one where Excalibur had been lodged, waiting for me to claim all those months ago. She'd called me queen, but she was the one seated upon a throne, grinning as she said, "Indeed, they do."

I did not linger on that thought. I already knew the succubus was drawn to me; Arran and I had discovered that truth in Palomides' dungeons.

"My terms are simple," I said as I stalked around the perimeter of the cave, angling my body so that my strong arm was always angled toward the witch. "Allow me to hold you at my mercy, answer my questions, and you shall live."

"And then you shall leave me in this frozen hell for another seven thousand years."

Well, that was my first question, answered. This witch *was* the one of legend, the one deposited by the Ancestors in the terrestrial kingdom after the witches were stripped of their power following the Great War.

"I do take after my Ancestor in more ways than one," I said, with a casual shrug. Entirely faked. I was aware of every breath the witch took, every twitch of her mouth or cheek or disgusting nails.

"She was a self-righteous, arrogant thing as well," the witch muttered.

And there was my second. Nimue had been the one to entomb the witches—Nimue and Accolon. For this moment, they'd done it.

They'd known about the Void Prophecy. They'd known the succubus would return. And they had trapped the two witches, one in each of the fae kingdoms, so that when the time came, a prophesized queen would be able to come here to demand answers.

But unlike the witch in the Tower of Myda, I did not taunt this one with the knowledge that I'd extracted answers from her for free. This witch needed to survive, so that if some future descendant—or me, myself—needed her, she would be right here, waiting.

I sighed heavily, the perfect mask of impertinence. "You have watched me for years. You are aware of my skill with a blade. Agree to my terms, or I shall start slicing off limbs. Then, once I have you at my mercy, you will answer my questions as you bleed out."

I expected her to take longer to consider, but the witch's eyes only flickered once.

"Very well." She folded her hands in her lap, the curled tips of her fingernails scratching across the cave floor. "Come, Queen of blood and vengeance. Ask your questions."

I approached her from the back, with both blades drawn, just as I'd planned.

When I reached her stone pedestal, I pressed the blades to the back of her neck—not hard, but enough that she could feel the kiss of the amorite-swirled blades. She flicked her colorless eyes over her shoulder for just a second.

She would still try to kill me.

But I would be ready. And in the meantime, I would get the

answers to my three questions. I recited the words carefully, just as I had in the tower in Baylaur.

"I have conquered the terrors of the Spine. I come bearing blades and power. You are at my mercy. You will answer my questions."

Inside of me, the ember of my power danced awake at its mention.

"How do I banish the succubus for good?" One question for Annwyn.

Her voice was otherworldly now—a strange, forced quality to the tones. I recognized the power of compulsion from interrogating Percival and Diana. "Fulfill the prophecy. All of it."

Outside of the cave, the wind was picking up, beginning to howl. A winter storm, descending upon the Spine. An hour, maybe half, and the snow would begin to accumulate, sealing the witch in. And me, with her.

No, my bright core reminded me. I had the power to leave, at any time.

"You are not nearly as poetic as your sister was," I observed, even as I repeated the witch's words to myself. I'd write them down as soon as I returned to Eilean Gayl. The wording might be important.

She hissed through her teeth. Pointed teeth—ones she had not revealed until just then. Just like Arran's canines, but every single tooth. Made for shredding flesh.

Oh, yes. She planned on killing me. Whatever had motivated her more mild approach, it was quickly losing to her baser nature. I could not tarry.

"What must be done to restore Arran's memories?" One question for my mate.

This time, she wanted to answer. There was no sense of her fighting the compulsion in her blood. She even laughed, a wicked, horrible sound that I did not allow to send a shiver down my spine.

"You begged for his life. Powerful magic was required to save him from a wound like that—a soul wound. This is the price, foolish queen. You could never have become what you needed to be with him at your side."

Not an answer.

I pressed my blades hard into her neck, the desire to keep her alive for future generations suddenly forgotten—

"I cannot see if or when his memories will be returned."

I fought hard to keep my hands from trembling. To keep them still and hard against that knob at the top of her spine.

One more, and then I would be gone. I could go back to Eilean Gayl. To warmth.

Twenty-five years of elemental influence kept my voice steady. "What is the cost of my power?" One question for me.

I thought it had been the loss of his memories. I'd fooled myself into thinking that maybe his loss of memories was not because of what I'd done at Avalon, but because of my void power. That, at least, had been beyond my control.

But I received no such respite.

Which meant the cost of my power... my ever-growing power, the lack of fatigue even as it grew... the cost was still hanging over my head.

The witch must have sensed the thoughts in my mind. The witch in the Tower of Myda had been able to, had mocked me for the unruly tangle of emotions.

"The cost has already been paid," she crooned. A heartbeat later —"Arthur."

I did not hear the howling of the wind. Nor the clicking of the witch's nails. Not even the beating of my own heart.

I should have known.

A duality in the world that was never meant to exist. It was only a matter of time.

The witch in the Tower of Myda had told me as much. But that was before the Joining, before my power awoke, before the succubus... *oh, Arthur.*

I stepped backward, letting my blades go slack.

The witch fell right into the trap.

She whipped her nails around, wicked fast and hard. They thrashed into my body, the curled ends going around my legs, holding me in place.

Clever trick.

I even gave the witch a heartbeat to savor her victory before I flashed a wicked grin that would have made my mate proud.

"Nice try," I said.

As I disappeared into the void, leaving nothing but gaping air for her talons to slash at, I imagined I heard her raging roar even amid the swirling dark.

89
ARRAN

I had not been to the temple in Eilean Gayl since before my powers had manifested. My devotion to the Ancestors had always been nominal at best. After my beast took over, and I began that killing rampage, coming here seemed like a slap in the face. Though I wasn't sure to whom.

Most of the castle had been rebuilt after the Great War, including the temple. It was small, in keeping with the power allotted to the priestesses after the Great War. The history I'd been taught was that the priestesses had sided with the elementals in that nasty, protracted period of hate and bloodshed. The dismantling of their power had been a terrestrial condition of the hard-won peace.

But now, after everything we'd found out about the succubus and the true causes of the Great War, I could not help but wonder... what role had the priestesses truly played? What crime had they committed to see them so denigrated?

Before the Great War, entire palaces had been erected in their honor, for their work and study. Places like Avalon had existed throughout Annwyn and the human realm. Now, no more than two were allowed to dwell in a place at any one time. Priestess and acolyte, and not a soul more.

Just then, the temple was empty.

Priestess, acolyte, perhaps even the half-human prisoners, all tucked away elsewhere. I'd never seen the priestess' quarters; never had a need.

For now, I was alone.

Me and the Ancestors.

Even three hundred years later, I remembered the ritual.

The room was dark, without a single window. In the temple, it could be any time of day, and day of the year. It was meant to deprive the senses so that one could more easily hone their focus on the Ancestors. Only one candle danced with light, just beside the arched doorway I'd entered through. More than enough light for sharp fae eyes.

There were six altars—four elemental and two terrestrial. One for each of the elemental powers—wind, water, fire, and ice; as well as the two terrestrial gifts—flora and fauna. Here in Eilean Gayl, the four elemental altars were bare. I did not even know what praying or offering to those Ancestors would look like. Did not know the names of the Ancestors who stood for each of the powers.

I knew mine.

First, to the flora altar. The pedestal was carved with various plant matter, so worn away by the centuries that it was hard to distinguish. In the center of the shallow bowl, a single shriveled leaf waited.

A flick of my hand, and it uncurled, emerald life spreading through it until the leaf looked like it might have been plucked from its tree just a moment ago.

But I did not linger at the flora altar. I'd never felt drawn there, though I always performed the ritual. I stepped up to the fauna.

The bowl was dark, stained with the blood of all those that had come before. I quickly drew my knife across my palm, spilling several drops into the bowl. A few seconds, and my hand was already healing, the blood I'd spilled absorbed by the dark stone.

I was the only terrestrial who had ever worshipped at more than one altar.

But perhaps not the only fae.

My eyes traveled slowly over the four elemental altars. Nimue had been an elemental. I tried to recall what her power had been, other than the legendary power of void. Had she had any other magic? Or had all power slumbered within her until her mating, like Veyka?

I almost asked myself where Veyka would choose to worship, were she with me. I knew the answer immediately—she'd probably kick over the altars for spite. For the lies that had been told to us about Accolon and Nimue, about the succubus and the Great War, lies that we just now were beginning to unravel.

But that was not why I had come.

I waited another few moments, the only sound in the dark temple the beating of my own heart. No one came. I sank to my knees.

"Sacred Ancestors. Accolon. Warrior King." The words were hollow on my tongue; words that did not belong to me, but to the ancient priestess who had first taught me these rituals. Long dead.

This was probably a waste of time.

I had never prayed to the Ancestors, not truly. What good could beings dead seven thousand years possibly do for me?

But something kept me on my knees. Not quite a compulsion the way the mating bond was, though this also felt internal. Like the echo of a memory.

Accolon.

I sucked in a breath of dank, dark air and tried again. "I suppose we are the only two males to have ever loved a female with the power of the void." I sighed, only because there was no one around to hear it. "Not exactly an easy path."

No answer. No response. Not even a memory. But I did not get up.

"I love her," I breathed, so quietly. I was not afraid of the words. But I was afraid. And once the words started, I could not keep them in.

"I love her. But... I am hurting her. Every moment I cannot remember is a knife in her heart. Even if I tell her, I am afraid... that it will not be enough. That it is not what we had before, and that even what I can offer... it will carve her out until there is nothing of the female she is. The one she deserves to be."

Veyka was trying. So was I. But maybe it was not enough. Maybe...

"Maybe it would be better to let her live with the memory of what was, rather than to have that memory constantly mocked by comparison."

There it was. The thought that had haunted every breath since I acknowledged to myself that I loved her, and had lingered unseen even before, a dark, ever-present specter.

"Maybe she would be happier with the memory than with the male."

My beast growled. *I* growled. There was no delineation. We were one, male and beast. And we loved Veyka. But loving her... it might mean letting her go.

There was nothing more to say. No answer came from the ancient Ancestors. I had not expected one.

But I lingered on in the darkness and wondered when, or if, I would find the strength for what needed to be done.

90

CYARA

Cyara summoned every skill at her disposal. The curious young child, hiding behind a cracked door while her father recounted his days in the goldstone palace library to her mother. The watchful older sister, nearby but silent, ready if needed to jump in and defray an argument between her siblings. The royal handmaiden, seen but not noticed, unheard and unbothersome.

Not a feather moved. No twitch of her white wings to give her away. She had pulled them in tight to her body, shrinking into the pocket of shadow as much as she could. It still was not far enough for her to help overhearing Arran's prayers.

When he finally stood, she said a prayer of her own, beseeching the Ancestors to hide her from view long enough—

"Cyara." Arran's voice was a mix of surprise and resignation.

She eased her wings down her back. "Your Majesty," she said, bowing her head.

She kept it there, giving him the chance to pass her by without having to meet her eyes. His thoughts were private and deserved to remain so. She had only come to the temple because on the opposite end of it was the door that led to the priestess's sanctum, where Percival and Diana awaited her.

But the king did not move.

"Does a harpy pray to the shifters?"

Slowly, she lifted her eyes to his, finding the black orbs unreadable. Her wings relaxed another inch. "I am a fire-wielder. An elemental," she said. "But before all of that, I am a Knight of the Round Table."

Arran inclined his head, the corner of his mouth twitching. Not quite a smile. Maybe a grimace. Even after months of observing him, Cyara struggled to understand his small tells. Veyka was easy. But the Brutal Prince... High King...

"She is lucky to have you at her side."

Her throat threatened to close with emotion. "I would say the same about you, Majesty."

"Arran," he corrected.

Cyara dipped her head again. "As you wish. It is time."

His dark eyes asked the question.

"Diana is going to cast her spell. Very soon, we may finally have answers."

"Or more questions."

"Come with me." "You are a terrestrial. You may notice or understand something that is beyond my knowledge."

<hr />

Cyara led Arran through the temple and into the quarters kept by the priestess and her acolyte. There was a reading room lined with bookshelves, a small bedroom the two females shared, and a bathing room. She had spent countless hours in the reading room with Diana and Percival over the last several weeks. As she did each time, she bid the priestess and her acolyte welcome and offered a small bow.

Behind her, Arran did the same.

If the priestess or acolyte were surprised by the Brutal Prince's sudden appearance, they did not show it. They merely bowed their own heads in response, as always, and continued at the work table where the priestess was providing instruction to her student in calm, steady tones. Mostly, was content to let them conduct their own research.

"It is time," Cyara said again, this time directing her words to Diana.

Diana nodded, closing the book that had been spread in front of her. Cyara noted all the minute details—the bob of the woman's chin, the slight sway of her hips, as if the ground was unsteady beneath her feet.

But her voice was firm as she pulled her lavender robes tighter around herself. "Not here."

Percival was on his feet as well. "You do not have to do this."

Diana's voice remained even but firm as she circled the table. "We have spoken about this at length, brother."

Cyara could not help the pride that rose in her chest at Diana's tone. Strength. New and hard won, directed mostly toward her brother, but noteworthy all the same.

Percival's bushy dark brows formed a single dark line across his forehead. Cyara steeled herself, ready to intervene, to offer silent or vociferous support as needed. But Arran beat her to it.

"Where?" the king asked. A question laced with command. To Diana, the query. To Percival, the promise of painful death if he did not shut his mouth.

Cyara swallowed her small smile. She did not quite want Percival dead—not anymore. She could understand his allegiance to his sister. But she had not forgotten or forgiven the dagger he had shoved into Lyrena's back.

Diana chewed her lower lip. "Will we bring down the wrath of your Ancestors if we use the temple?"

Arran cut his gaze to Cyara—as if he had not just been praying himself. But it was the priestess who answered.

"I should think our Ancestors would be honored, as it is their world you seek to save," she said softly from her worktable.

She made no bones about watching them. Her acolyte was less sure, eyes darting between the humans, the King, and the floor.

Arran thanked the priestess, and the acolyte actually began to quiver.

With permission obtained, it was the work of mere minutes to assemble what they needed. Diana quietly but firmly directed them to sit in a circle—Cyara, Arran, Percival, and herself. At their center, she placed a small pile of stones.

She turned to Cyara, seated at her right. "I shall need your fire."

A gentle, steady nod. Every movement smooth and careful. She did not want to spook Diana now that they were on the precipice. "Tell me what to do."

"After I say the spell, light the flame there, in the center." Diana pointed to the pile of stones. "I will not be able to hear you. I have prepared my mind as best I can, and thought on what answers we seek. We will have to trust the spell to take my mind where it needs to go."

They were all silent as she dragged in a breath and exhaled audibly.

Cyara's sisterly core, the female she had been before her sisters were murdered before her eyes, wanted to put her arm around Diana. Assure her that she did not need to take this risk. But the Knight held her silence and hoped that all the work she had done these last weeks would be enough.

Diana's next breath was steadier. "Percival, hold my hand." He gave it to her, reluctantly. "He is my tether," she explained. "If my mind becomes lost, he will pull me back to this realm, this place and time."

"Hopefully." Percival opened his mouth to say more, to argue more, but he was too late.

His sister was already chanting.

"Grant me wisdom, grant me sight, as I wander realms beyond my might. By ancient magics, this spell is cast. Guide me home, when the journey's past."

A strange pall came over Diana's face. She was still upright, still rigid. But her features softened into complete relaxation. Her eyes glazed, then darkened. Cyara swore she saw starlight flickering in those dark orbs.

Arran inhaled sharply. "What is happening?"

"She is traveling," Cyara breathed.

She was so entranced, she almost forgot to light the fire. A wave of her hand, and a flame danced to life above the pile of stones. Her eyes were fixed on Diana, lips moving constantly. Repeated the spell, again and again, in a breathy whisper that Cyara could hardly make out.

A wave of heat pressed at her cheek. She could not have lost control of the flame—

"What is that?" Arran said, shifting forward to get a better look at the flames… at the image that appeared there, wreathed in undulating red and gold.

Cyara recognized the goldstone palace immediately, even if it was not the version she was familiar with. This one was stunted, still built into the orange-red mountain itself, rather than rising above it. But that was not what drew her eye. It was the sea of black. Where Baylaur should have been, and the sand of the Effren Valley, there was only black. The succubus. A throbbing darkness that stretched all the way to, and around, another familiar monument. The Tower of Myda. Then the undulating black wave retreated. Contracted. Until there was nothing but red sand.

Diana's voice was getting louder.

The flames devoured the image as quickly as it had appeared.

Two figures stood on the edge of a vast ocean. Waves lapped at their feet, around their ankles. Higher, until they were wet to the knees. But they were both smiling; staring at each other, completely lost to the rest of the world. Accolon and Nimue. It had to be. This was the mating, the one that had truly happened before the Great War, not to end it. Even as Cyara realized, a third figure rose out of the water. Everything about him was foreign—the tilt of his eyes, the knot that held the cerulean loincloth in place around his hips… he drew a dagger, its hilt made of embedded bit of sea glass, and slashed it across their hands. First Accolon, then Nimue—

The image dissolved.

Diana's voice filled the temple. Cyara spared her only a glance, only long enough to see that her face and eyes were unchanged before turning her eyes back to the ball of fire. Her heart raced, trying to fit in every detail against what she already knew, to find the incongruities.

Another vision—another place.

Towering white cliffs rose, up and up and up to the very tip of the flame. Waves crashed against them, battering the stone with unforgiving, endless swells.

The Ancestors had battled the succubus in the Effren Valley seven thousand years ago, caught them between the goldstone palace and the Tower of Myda, and emerged triumphant.

Accolon and Nimue had been Joined—mated—before the Great War. Because that was the Split Sea they had stood in, and it had not been breached in seven thousand years. Not since the end of the Great War.

But even as Cyara stared and stared at the white cliffs, she could not make sense of it.

There was too much noise. She could not think at all. Everyone needed to stop yelling...

Diana.

Diana was yelling—the words of the enchantment, each one a battle cry ripped from her lips.

Arran's sharp voice—a commander's voice—cut through everything else. "How do we get her back?"

"There is no getting her back! Didn't you hear what she said?" Percival screamed over Diana. "Is it worth it to you, if she dies here?"

"No one is dying today." Cyara said. Yelled. She had to yell to be heard. She grabbed Percival's other hand, while he clung to his sister with the other. "You are her tether. Pull her back."

"I do not even know what that means!" he cried.

But someone did.

Cyara spun. "Arran. You are Veyka's tether when she goes into the void."

"What?"

"The mating bond—that is how she finds her way back. How she does not get lost..." Panic bubbled to life in her gut. "She did not tell you."

She had to stay calm. Everyone else could panic, she would stay calm.

"Later," Cyara said sharply. "What does the bond between you feel like?"

Diana's cries were not getting louder, but they were more tortured by the moment. Percival was crying, his entire body shaking with the force of it.

"A thread," Arran said. "Through my entire body, through every layer of consciousness. But mostly around my heart, concentrated in my chest. A golden string that connects us, at any distance."

"Percival?"

"We are not mates," he cried through the sobs. "She is my sister."

Cyara gripped his hand fiercely. For Diana. For Charis and Carly. "And before my sisters died, there was no being in the world who I cared for more. Find it—find something."

He could not stop crying. But the sobs ebbed to quieter tears. He closed his eyes. It felt like minutes passed, but Cyara knew that was the Ancestors playing tricks on her.

"I... I can feel her."

"Bring her back."

"How?"

Arran knelt before them. The fire was out. Whether he had smothered it or she had let it die away to nothing... Cyara did not care. Not as Arran grabbed the man's knee and spoke, his voice dark as the space between stars and the corners of souls. "You love her more than anything in the world. You demand that she comes back to you, that she stays with you. Because there is no other option. There is no world without her. No air worth breathing, no kingdom to save. There is you, and her, and everything else is a distraction from that truth."

Percival's eyes were still closed. Tears leaked down them, but he was silent. Then, suddenly, Diana was too.

Arran retreated; Cyara moved forward instantly into his space. But Percival beat them both. Faster than a human should have been able to move—even a half-witch human—he had Diana's face between his hands.

"Are you here?" he demanded.

Diana blinked. "Yes." Her voice was horribly hoarse, but she got the words out. "I am here. I am fine."

Cyara pulled herself to her feet, retreated several steps. Percival and Diana were both talking quickly, embracing, muttering reassurances that she did not need to hear. She was too keenly aware of the male at her side to notice their words.

She did not flinch, did not still her impulse to study him. After what they had just seen, what Diana had endured... Cyara let herself study every inch of her king's face, looking for any clue. She only found one.

Arran's golden skin was eerily pale, his mouth wan as he spoke. "The white cliffs. I've seen cliffs like that before, at the entrance to Wolf Bay. They stretch for less than a mile, to the east. That must be where Accolon's fortress is hidden."

He did not mention the first two visions. Little bits of the past, from seven thousand years ago. Miraculous.

Cyara closed her eyes, let her back rest against the damp stone wall as she started the monumental task of sorting through the memories and their meanings.

But Arran did not linger.

Cyara jerked to attention. "Veyka."

All of those words, the way he described the bond to Percival, the power of it... all of it was about Veyka.

Arran froze, his hulking body blocking the entire doorway. "Yes."

"Tell her, Arran." Cyara's voice broke as she sank to her knees before her king. "I beg you. Tell her."

91
VEYKA

The satisfaction of escaping the witch had dwindled away to nearly nothing by the time I arrived back Eilean Gayl. I did not go into the castle itself; was not quite ready to face my friends. Or Elayne. Or Arran.

Alone, then.

I walked alone through the woods, night falling fast and thick around me. Over the rugged hills. The lake appeared below me just in time to greet the moon and stars. Despite the storm that had raged outside the witch's cave, the night here was silent and still. Cold. So fucking cold.

But the exertion of climbing and walking warmed me. I even jogged for a while, despite my visceral hate for running. A benefit of the leggings the cold weather necessitated—no chafed thighs.

Every step was a chance to turn over what the witch had revealed.

There was no telling when Arran's memories would return. More—the witch could not see whether they would ever return. Witches knew all. That was the entire fucking point of one still existing, seven thousand years after the Ancestors had decimated them.

If the witch could not see... what did that mean? That had to be significant. It had to mean... maybe that future was not set? That my choices, Arran's choices, the succubus... those things might determine if and when his memories returned?

Fuck all of that.

Fuck. Fuck. Fuck. Fuck.

I could not take it a second longer. I planted my feet, throwing my arms up at the sky. At the Ancestors, in whatever afterlife, in whatever realm—I screamed loud enough for all of them to hear. "Fuck you!"

"Fuck you for taking his memories as punishment. That's what this is, right? Punishment for needing him? For begging for his life? For daring to be happy for a single fucking moment?"

I couldn't breathe. The cold air was heavy as stone in my chest. But I was strong. I shoved the stones aside and dragged in another ragged breath, because I was not done yet. Not nearly.

"I need him. Do you understand? He was the wise one, the careful the one, the one who knows how to protect Annwyn. Without him, all they have is me!" My voice caught painfully in my throat.

My legs could not hold me.

I collapsed down into the snow and grass. First to my knees, then forward onto my palms, and then onto my back. So that I was staring back up at the stars again.

"All they have is me," I whispered. "What sort of sick fucking joke is that?"

I laid there for so long, the stars overhead shifted their positions. The change was minute, but I'd spent hours marking them out.

All the while, the witch's words echoed in my head.

Again and again, one sentence. Not about the succubus, or about Arthur. But selfishly—fittingly, perhaps—about me.

You could never have become what you needed to be with him at your side.

I wished I did not know exactly what she meant. Everything else was subject to interpretation, but that line echoed through me because of the stark, painful truth of it.

When I'd made the decision to stay in Baylaur after the Tower of Myda, it had not been for the good of Annwyn. It had been for Arran. The same was true of my pleas to the Lady of the Lake, my superior, imperious, *neutral* half-sister. I'd spoken of Annwyn, but I'd begged for myself.

I had been every bit as selfish as Arran had accused me of being.

Until I could not be.

Until Arran was taken from me, and I was the only thing standing between a kingdom and utter ruination.

When I finally pushed myself back up, sliding my feet underneath me, my muscles groaned in protest. Cold and tight from laying prone for so long. But I commanded them to function, to take me down the mountainside one step after another, toward Eilean Gayl.

And I understood the witch's half answer.

It did not matter when or if Arran ever regained his memories. I had to be the High Queen of Annwyn either way. I would go on, with or without my mate at my side.

92

VEYKA

No torches lit the bridge. I found my way all the same. Eilean Gayl had called to me since the very first time I'd glimpsed it, falling through the void in the moments after the Joining. And even though I'd been threatened, and glared at, and cried more tears here than I ever had in Baylaur, it still felt like coming home as I passed into the keep, cutting across the training courtyard.

If the moonlight had not given it away, the thick floral scent would have. The courtyard had been transformed. Flowers bloomed on every pillar and archway, so thick it was hard to see the greenery that supported them. I recognized Maisri's sweet magic instantly.

The courtyard felt like joy.

I let myself linger—there was no one to see me close my eyes and inhale the lilac and gardenia.

But another scent twined with the fresh floral notes. Darker, spicier. A thrum in my chest. I opened my eyes in time to watch him shift from his wolf to fae form.

I took another deep breath, willing the fragrances of Maisri's garden oasis to soothe the jagged edges of my soul. "It is the middle of the night."

Arran lingered in the shadow of the archway—this one blooming with the primrose. My heart clenched.

"I knew you were getting closer," he said. "I could feel it—here." He touched his chest—his heart.

I knew. I felt it too. "Are you going to ask where I went?"

"Would you tell me if I did?"

"I don't know." I could be honest about that, at least.

But everything else... I was so fucking tired. Screaming at the Ancestors hadn't helped. Neither had refusing my impulse to invoke their name. Maybe sleep would. I started for the spiral staircase at the opposite corner, the one that would lead me past that awful carving, then up to the relative safety of my bedroom.

"Veyka, it cannot go on like this between us." Ancestors, his voice... it was tortured. Is that what I sounded like?

"Like what?" No. I sounded worse.

Arran pushed out of the archway. Closer—dangerously close. I could hear his heart hammering in his chest. Or was that mine?

"This—dancing around one another. Pulling closer, then apart again. It is... I can see it tearing you apart." He stared at my chest as if he could see the heart and soul within, see the damage.

But I was not the only one who was damaged. "And what about you?"

His answer was immediate. "I want you to be happy."

I shook my head. "What about you?"

"What I want does not matter."

"You are afraid." I'd already admitted I was. For some reason, I needed to hear him say it too. No matter what happened, how this conversation or the next one or the next one, I would go on, because Annwyn needed me. But I wanted to know how he felt. Needed it, or I might suffocate.

I grabbed his shoulder, the contact sizzling up my arm. *Tell me.*

His eyes started to burn. "Yes, Veyka," he growled. "I love you, and I am afraid of what that means. I am afraid that it will not be enough for you because it is not what we had before, and that it will break you, and I just…" He broke off, looking at my face, my eyes, the sky. Searching for words.

Words that I had. "Annwyn needs me."

Arran's eyes jerked back to me. This time, he grabbed my shoulders, shaking me hard. "I need *you*. I need you whole and flashing that wicked smile and meaning it. I love you, Veyka. Annwyn can die in darkness, if that is what it costs for you to be safe and happy."

Oh, Ancestors. Fucking Ancestors.

My insides were melting.

"Some of us aren't meant to be happy," I rasped. Arran did not let me go. So I eased myself out of his grip. Closer to the stairs.

I love you.

He was right to be afraid. I was afraid too—afraid to give in to those words again, to risk losing him again… knowing that I would have to pull myself up again for the good of my fucking kingdom.

I had not stopped loving him for a single second. I never would. Somehow, I would have to figure out how to save my kingdom, help Arran through this torment, and keep myself standing. Tomorrow, I would tell him and the others about the witch. Tomorrow, I would start building back my life, brick by brick. But tonight, I was just tired.

I waited until there was plenty of cold air between us before speaking again. "I am leaving in the morning."

Arran's eyes darkened. "Wherever you are going, I am going too." His muscles were so tense, the outline of his body rigid. But he held his ground and did not advance. Not physically, anyway. "I love you."

I could not have stopped the words, not in a thousand years. "I love you more."

I turned to go up the staircase before he could see the tears burning in my eyes.

"Why do you always have to argue?"

My heart stopped.

It can't be.

Not a single beat. How was I still alive and breathing?

I thought I had known fear before. But not like this, never like this.

It can't be.

The witch... she'd implied it might never happen—

Arran stumbled forward. "Veyka."

The world ceased to exist. I could not see anything beyond the male in front of me. His brutal, beautiful face, twisted with such emotion. Such longing. And pain. Pain I knew, because it had arched through me with every single breath. Then fear—fear that it was a dream. That this was not real. That in a second, a minute, he would forget me again.

I did not recall crossing the courtyard again, only knew that I needed to touch him and then suddenly I was. Maybe I'd slipped through the void.

But I stopped short of touching him. Scared, that the mirage would fall away.

Arran was the braver of the two of us. He was the one who reached out, his hand cupping my face.

"Ancestors, Veyka," he breathed, skating his thumb over my cheekbone and down over my lips. "I am so sorry."

I melted.

Collapsed.

My muscles ceased to function. So did my mind.

Arran's arms were around me as my knees hit the ground. His mouth was on mine, silencing the strangled sobs that shook my chest. I was still afraid to touch him—but then his hands were on mine, shoving them into his hair, over his shoulder. The contact awakened me. I could not get close enough, hold him tight enough. That golden thread of our mating bond, it did not just connect our hearts through our chests. I swore that I could feel it threaded and shining through every inch of my body, one long string that did not just connect us—it was us. And we were one.

"Veyka," Arran said my name, again and again as he rained down kisses on my face, my neck, my ears. "I'm sorry. I am so sorry."

"You do not get to be sorry."

"I said awful things—"

"I stabbed you in the heart."

He paused, hands splayed on either side of my face, pressing my forehead to his. "Even that was not enough to drive us apart. Not for long."

Breathing was not necessary, not when Arran's mouth was on mine. His tongue was in my mouth, reclaiming every corner. Twirling around mine in that exquisite, teasing dance. He caught my lower lip between his teeth, sucking hard as he pulled away.

"You taste," he shuttered. "You taste so fucking perfect."

I tried to tell him that I tasted the same as I had the last time we'd kissed, but words were impossible. Not when his mouth dropped to my throat, scalding hot kisses and scraping canines and — "Arran. Arran, please. You are going to kill me."

He growled at the mere suggestion. Male and beast, in unison. Wet, hot desire slid between my thighs, soaking my leggings. I needed these clothes off—his, mine. I needed him naked against me.

Nothing between us. Never again.

Arran must have heard my thoughts—I might have been screaming them through the mating bond. I was too out of my mind to notice or care. He tugged the thick wool tunic over my head. His tunic.

The growl in his throat turned possessive. His hands were too as they cupped my breasts, held in place with only a tightly wound piece of linen. Hardly sufficient for climbing mountains, but I hadn't wanted to risk my single bustier.

Arran glared down at the wrapping.

I pulled the dagger from my belt.

He slid it through in one precise slice, the very tip of the blade skimming my skin. I inhaled sharply, eyes flying up, only to find Arran's eyes glowing. "I shall make you pay for that."

"And every harsh word I have said." Guilt flashed in his eyes. No, I would not allow that.

I began undressing him, tugging loose the buttons across his chest, shoving the leather vest over his shoulders. I raked my fingernails along the tawny skin as it emerged.

"How?" he murmured. "Why now?"

It took me a moment to realize what he was asking.

When I did, I rocked back onto my heels. Not releasing him entirely. I doubted I would stop touching him anytime in the next month, at least.

"I—" I scraped my teeth across my lower lip. "I hunted down the witch in the Spine. I asked her what I had to do—how to get your memories back." There was my heart—wild and frantic in my chest. "But she said—she said it might never happen, there was no way..."

Realization spread through me like ice over the lake.

Arran was in my space immediately, stroking my cheek, gripping my waist. Unwilling to let me retreat back into myself. "What is it?"

I closed my eyes, too afraid to look at his perfect face as I confessed. "It is because I decided I would go on without you."

"Oh, Ancestors. You are going to hate me." His hands were going to withdraw any second. A betrayal—that is what it was. Elayne had told me once, that I could love them both, my kingdom and my mate. But it was a lie—a foolish fallacy. "I decided that no matter what happened between us, whether you chose me or not... I would go on. I would keep fighting—for Annwyn, I would—"

Arran grabbed my hands. He lifted them to his mouth, pressing his lips to each knuckle. "I could never hate you, Veyka." Then my palm, the inside of my wrist. "You are the other half of my soul. I... I do not think I could have survived, if our fates had been reversed."

He dragged his tongue over the thrumming pulse just above my wrist. "I am proud of you, Veyka." Scraped his canines over the vein. "I love you. I will love you for a thousand years."

"And a thousand more."

I had no more words. They were too hard, there had been too many. I needed my mate. All of my mate—the male who'd fallen in

463

love with me in Baylaur, who'd taught me to love him as we crossed a continent, who'd declared his allegiance and chosen me again here at Eilean Gayl, even in the face of pain and loss.

I realized then—this bond between us was something else. A mating bond, yes. The primal connection of our souls. But it was a bond we'd chosen, both of us, again and again. It was not destiny that made our love strong. It was the fact that we were willing to give ourselves to one another, to choose each other day after brutal day.

I stood only long enough to shimmy out of my leggings. Arran, bless him, did the same. Slower—because his eyes were fixed upon me. His gaze traced the lines of my body as I exposed them to the cold, layer by layer. Gooseflesh spread across my skin, my nipples pebbling into tight buds.

I knew that when I spread my legs, the wetness on the insides of my thighs would be gilded with moonlight.

"Veyka." Arran's voice was hoarse. Desperate. A prayer, but not to the Ancestors. No, this male belonged entirely to me.

I cupped one breast, letting its weight fill my palm before pinching my nipple. The other dipped to my pussy. I was so wet, so ready for him. Beyond ready. Needy. But I savored the feral longing on his face as I dipped my fingertips between my folds. When I drew them out, they glistened with *me*.

For a second, I contemplated licking them clean myself. But I was much too impatient. I needed Arran inside me.

His hands were ready, digging into the soft folds of flesh at my waist and lowering me down. Ancestors, his cock was magnificent. Had it only been a week since it was buried inside of me? It felt like a lifetime. As I angled myself above him, the moonlight caught the bead of come on his tip. I longed to lick it off. Later, I promised myself.

When Arrran nudged at my entrance, all thoughts of later disappeared from my mind. There was only now—us, this, together. Forever. I shoved my wet fingers into his mouth at the same moment that he thrust up into me. I did not know which of us moaned louder, but we moaned in unison.

The entire castle would be awake by the time we were through. But a thousand eyes could not have stopped me. Not with Arran sucking on my fingers, licking away my wetness as if it was the sweetest nectar. Not with his cock buried inside of me, stroking up and up and deeper and...

"Arran," I pleaded. "Arran, oh fucking... Arran."

He grabbed my hips, trying to control the pace. To slow me down. But it was impossible. I was certain that if I slowed even a fraction, I would die. I rode him, driving my hips forward, my knees into the stones of the training ring, the scent of lilac all around us. I felt all of it, all at once, a glorious cacophony of sensations. Rising. Higher and higher.

My pussy began to clench. I was so close. The stars began to swim before my eyes. Arran grabbed my wrist, pulling my hand from his mouth. He laced his fingers with mine, pulling me back. My eyes met his and stayed, the demand in those blazing black orbs impossible to escape.

Mine.

The word was a growl through the bond.

Forever.

I was coming. No drawing it out, no stopping it. I was too close to the edge, the friction against my clit combined with his rigid, demanding cock inside of me—

Never again, Veyka.

I whimpered. Tried to cling to him. But Arran held my hand fast.

We will never be parted again.

"Never," I promised. Then I flung myself over that edge. Pleasure ricocheted through my body, from my clenching cunt to the hard points of my nipples to every follicle of hair in my scalp where Arran's other hand was buried.

And then Arran was coming inside of me. Hot spurts, in time with the rocking of my hips. I kept going, taking every bit of him that he would give. All of it. All of him. My lover. My king. My mate.

Finally, after all this torturous time—mine.

※

When the pleasure ebbed and the cold of the night air finally began to sink in, I took us through the void. To the bed where I'd dreamed of him. Where I'd cried and ached for him to be returned to me.

Arran pulled me against him, twining our hands and legs and fitting us together in every possible way. When we'd both settled, our heartbeats evening out, the darkness pressing in, Arran's breath kissed the shell of my ear. "Tell me everything. Every secret, every insecurity you were trying to protect me from."

"Everything?" I swallowed audibly.

"Everything." He squeezed me tighter. "I want it all, Veyka. I want you." And those words—maybe I'd needed them even more than all the others.

When we'd both come again, the air of the bedroom thick with the scent of our arousal and pleasure and every muscle in our bodies gloriously sated, I did.

I told him every worry that I'd held in my burdened heart.

And then, finally—finally, I fell asleep in my mate's arms.

93
CYARA

They crossed a continent in a moment. This time, they did not have to work out an order so that no one got killed. Veyka merely held out her hand, an invitation to whomever was bravest to join her for her longest journey through the void yet.

Cyara stepped forward.

No matter how many times she went through, the void always terrified her. It clawed at her being, tried to separate her soul from her body. She knew Veyka was with her, could sense her lifeforce, but she could not see or hear or feel her friend.

Then just as suddenly as it started, it was over.

They landed on a bluff high above the entrance to Wolf Bay.

It took every bit of internal fortitude to keep from going to her knees. Cyara drew in breath after breath. The first—that was air around her. Real, life-giving air. The second—the air was salted, cold. The third gave her back enough of herself that she was able to take in her surroundings.

"Is this close enough? Can you tell?" Veyka asked, utterly unbothered by the void. She edged closer to the drop, peering down.

The way Veyka sucked in her breath between her teeth told

Cyara enough. But still, she flapped her wings, catching a gust of ocean air that carried her out over the ledge, to where there was nothing but brine and mist.

A wall of white cliffs spread out before her.

Cyara knew they would glow with the rising sun. But something was not quite right.

She lingered in the air, her wings beating on the wind. She arced in a graceful curve before coming up to land beside Veyka once more.

"There."

From the corner of her vision, Cyara was aware of her queen turning, tracing her arm, her extended finger, beyond.

Beyond.

To an island cast in shades of blue and gray by the setting sun.

Veyka's swallow was audible, even over the rushing wind and incoming waves of an evening tide crashing against the white walls, as pale as her hair. "So be it."

※

Veyka brought them one after the other to the rocky beach of the island. Lyrena, Percival, Diana. Arran waited at Eilean Gayl for her return. Anxiously, Cyara was certain.

Cyara waited, unspeaking, eyes fixed on the rising white cliffs in the distance. It was only nominally warmer in the southern reaches of Annwyn than it had been north of the Spine. Cyara knew that the temperatures did not begin to rise until the other side of the Spit, in the elemental kingdom. Still, she found herself surprised. She rubbed up and down the arms of her thick gray tunic and wished she had brought her cloak.

It did not matter. Soon, they would be hiking up into the forested hills that made up this island on the edge of the world. She would be warm enough.

The crunch of gravel gave Veyka away.

"Are you ready?" the queen asked.

Veyka was not even winded. Four trips from Eilean Gayl, all the way south, to the entrance of Wolf Bay. Each carrying another person. Each in rapid succession. But her blue eyes glittered.

Her power was growing.

What would she be able to do in a month? A year? A hundred years?

Cyara swallowed down the thought. If they lived that long, she would worry then.

"Are you?" she countered, giving her queen a long look.

Veyka flashed that wicked grin—real, true. It eased something inside of Cyara to see it, finally. "Imbolc is the festival of females. I think I'll manage."

She lifted her hand and waved to the trio waiting further up the beach. Then, with a smile and wink, Veyka was gone.

The communication crystal weighed heavy in her pocket. She would use it to contact Veyka and Arran once they'd found Accolon's fortress.

Cyara prayed to the Ancestors, the human gods, whoever might hear her pleas for her kingdom, her queen, and herself. She prayed that when she reached for the crystal, she would have answers to give her queen.

When none of those mighty beings answered her prayers, Cyara turned from the water and began to climb.

94
ARRAN

"What should I expect?" Veyka asked from the dressing table.

With Cyara and the others gone, she'd dressed herself and styled her own hair. She had managed a simple but elegant plait that started at the center of her forehead and continued straight down her spine. Instead of weaving jewels into the braid, she'd created a circlet that crossed over her forehead and then disappeared into the braid at the back. The tail of her plait swayed over the center of her back, teasing me. Begging me to press my mouth to the beauty mark that stood out sharply against her pale, bare skin.

Veyka turned in her seat, depriving me of the view I'd been enjoying, and catching her lower lip between her teeth at the same moment that she caught my eye.

She was torturing me.

Two could play that game.

I paused buttoning my tunic, lifting my arms high above my head to stretch. Exposing the sharp-cut planes of my chest and abdomen. "Imbolc is the festival of females." Veyka's eyes glassed over. "The regeneration. A promise of the coming spring."

Promises. We'd made even more of them between each other. But instead of a weight, they were a comfort. Etched into my soul as permanently as the sprawling tree Talisman tattooed onto my skin.

Her hands flexed on the table.

"I am already used to being waited upon," she purred.

I held her gaze as I buttoned the tunic sideways across my chest, up to the shoulder. Hiding myself from view. "That is indeed part of it,"

"And what is the other part?"

"Worship."

The shift was slight, but she could not hide it from. Not the growing scent of her arousal, nor the way she pressed her thighs tighter together. "I very much like the sound of that."

"Unfortunately, you will not be participating fully."

She pouted out a lip. Ancestors, I had missed her without even knowing it. I'd missed the familiarity, the ease. I'd longed for it, for that piece that was missing between us...

Now it was sharper. More urgent. We had to touch each other, talk to each other, to reassure ourselves that it was real.

And Veyka... I would do anything to erase that haunted look that lingered in her eyes.

"It is our custom for females to choose their partners—as many partners as they like." Her brows rose as I added, "Anything less than three is an insult to the Ancestors."

Veyka tilted her head to the side. *Are you so eager to share me?*

Any male—or female—foolish enough to approach you will deserve their fate.

She chose that moment to stand, to show off the gown she'd chosen for the evening. "Perhaps I should change. It almost seems cruel."

The dark blue bodice curved over her breasts, but did not rise to cover her shoulders. It cut outward, to her arms, which were fully enclosed in tight-fitting blue. Leaving the expanse of creamy skin of her breasts, shoulders, and throat exposed. Her skirts were fuller than the terrestrial style, more modest than I'd expected. But as she walked to me, I saw the slits cut up the sides, nearly to her waist. Revealing the long, muscular line of her thigh and calf.

The low growl of appreciation filled my body, my consciousness. Veyka tilted her head back, moaning softly as if the sound were a physical caress.

Ancestors. We were never going to make it down to the great hall.

Veyka grinned wickedly, the ring of blue in her eyes vibrant. I knew my own burned with black fire in return—my cock was hard, demanding in my tight-fitted trousers. Ready for her again, even when we'd risen from the bed mere minutes before.

"I shall pass your compliments along to Cyara."

"Cyara might be the most powerful elemental I have ever encountered."

Veyka pinched my bicep. "*I* am the most powerful elemental you have ever encountered."

So easy, to get lost in the moment. To forget the reality—the death that lingered at the doorstep of our kingdom.

Imbolc was an interlude. A brief escape. Even as we did our duty here, Cyara, Lyrena, and the humans were searching for Accolon's ancient keep. It felt selfish, to be basking in Veyka's glory while the rest of them toiled in search of answers.

The logical voice in my head reminded me that this was part of being High King—ceremony and spectacle were important. So was demonstrating our unity and strength, after the events of the last two months.

The selfish one did not give a damn that others were suffering. Me, my beast—we wanted to savor every second with her. Worshipping her. Every second of the next thousand years, and a thousand more beyond that.

"If you look at me like that, we will never leave this room." Veyka's voice was more than a little breathless.

I slid my hand into hers. "I am yours, Princess."

95
CYARA

Percival complained. Loudly.

Even after Lyrena shoved into him—accidentally, of course—on her way to take the lead.

It as a steeper climb than she had realized from the rocky beach to the center of the island. Every few minutes, Cyara would pause and flutter up into the sky, peering back the way they had come. Every time, there was the wall of white cliffs, precisely as it had appeared in the flames of Diana's spell. They had to be getting close. But when she looked ahead, she did not see any sign of a castle or fortress.

She almost flew ahead, away from the others. Scouting, like Arran had often done in his wolf form while they traveled across the human realm. But the queen and king's orders had been clear—stay together. *Do not let anyone out of your sight.*

Cyara swallowed the impulse and landed again at the rear of their party. It would be a while before Veyka was willing to let anyone she cared for go far.

Diana's breaths came in loud huffs, her heavy purple robes catching on roots and debris as they climbed up and up and up. At the front, Lyrena cut away the worst of the branches and understory with her sword. But it was still slow going.

Cyara was about to suggest a stop—she did not need Diana fainting dead away and injuring herself, especially with Isolde all the way back at Eilean Gayl.

Lyrena beat her to it.

Diana was already looking for a log or stump to sit on. Percival urged her ahead, pointing to what appeared to be a clearing just beyond where Lyrena had paused. Cyara shifted the pack she carried, mentally mapping out which provisions she would take out and where they were stored.

But Lyrena was still not moving.

Neither were Diana and Percival.

Cyara's stomach flipped as she closed the last few yards between them, all the sounds of the forest melting away.

Even Percival fell silent.

"It is not a castle at all," Diana murmured.

Accolon's ancestral home. They had expected a fortress of some kind, an old round tower, perhaps—or at least the crumbling remnants of one.

The clearing was certainly wide enough. The journal had mentioned Accolon's home; Diana's vision had shown the white cliffs. But it had never occurred to Cyara that they were not actually seeking Accolon's residence. Until she stepped into the clearing.

Because instead of the ruins of a seven-thousand-year-old keep, the clearing was ringed with massive monoliths. Standing stones.

Every single one of them was carved.

96
VEYKA

It was a wonder that Elayne and Pant even bothered with torches, when every single set of eyes in the great hall glowed with desire and barely contained lust.

It began like every other communal meal I'd attended at Eilean Gayl—without any ceremony at all. The priestess and her acolyte were present, standing between Elayne and Pant and offering benedictions to anyone who approached. But that was where the formality ended.

The only difference I could detect was that the revelry had moved towards fucking more quickly. Usually, the terrestrials did not start openly straddling or mounting each other until at least the third course.

But by the time the first round of meat hit the table—curried lamb with a tangy cream sauce—the scent of arousal was already thick in the air.

Most of the terrestrials ignored the platters. I, however, was hungry.

Arran's breath warmed my ear, making me drop the portion of lamb I'd been aiming for my plate. I should have been able to sense him coming. But since I'd returned from the Spine, the mating bond had been humming so loud, it was nearly impossible to tell whether it was to indicate his nearness or an aftereffect of our most recent round of bed play.

Not that we'd confined ourselves to the bed.

We'd fucked on nearly every surface in my suite of rooms. And the study Arran had commandeered. Twice.

Arran leaned around me, cutting a new slice of lamb and placing it on my plate. "Eat up, Princess. I do not want you to lose another pound of that lovely round ass of yours."

How the fuck was I supposed to eat when he said things like that?

Arran's eyes glowed, dark brows lifting in challenge.

I forced myself to cut the meat, to lift a bite to my mouth. My stomach betrayed me as the mouthwatering scent filled my lungs. Clearly, my stomach and my cunt were not in communication with one another.

I decided not to look at him. Seeing those burning black eyes, imagining the stubble on his chin as it scraped over my skin... Nope. I definitely could not look at him.

I trained my gaze on the crowd in front of us as I forced down bite after bite, appeasing both my mate and my stomach. There was a growing group of terrestrials in the center of the great hall, dancing. Or fucking while dancing. As I watched, a male lowered himself to the ground right in the center of the pack, bringing a female down with him. She shoved aside his pants, her otherwise demure skirt, and mounted him, rocking her hips in time with the music. A few seconds later, two more males had joined her—one tugging down her bodice to pay homage to her breasts, the other coming behind and toying with her rear entrance.

I put down my fork.

Arran's mouth was back at my ear.

Ancestors, have you paused to eat anything tonight?

A low growl caressed me from the inside. *I'd much rather feast on you.*

"Shall I take you here, before our subjects?"

Yes.

But before he could make good on that promise, we both turned.

The exultant fervor had shifted. Panic—those were cries of panic and fear.

Arran stood with me, a solid wall at my side. I rose to my toes, trying to see into the crowd. It was hard to make out anything in the frenzy of movement.

But then the scent hit me. Stronger than the thick clouds of arousal and aromas of sizzling meat. Putrid, decaying, death.

They're here.

97

CYARA

She counted, and then counted again. Eight monoliths, arranged in a near perfect circle around the clearing, each towering several feet above the top of their heads. Even Arran would have to lean back to see to the top of them. And seeing the top would be essential, because every inch of the inner face of the standing stones was engraved.

"What now?" Lyrena asked, walking the perimeter for at least the third time in as many minutes. "They are similar to the one outside the faerie caves," she observed.

"Yes," Cyara agreed.

On the other side of the clearing, Diana sat cross-legged in front of one of the stones, sipping water from a canteen and peering at the inscriptions. Percival was sour faced but silent beside her.

Cyara moved slowly in their direction, steps steady and unthreatening. Diana had made great strides in her self-confidence, but the monoliths were enough to set anyone on edge. Only her decades of training in the elemental court were keeping Cyara's pulse steady.

"Have you ever seen anything like this, in Avalon, or elsewhere in the human realm?"

Diana tilted her head to the side, then the other way, but finally, she shook her head.

For a moment, Cyara considered pulling the small knife from her belt. Something about Diana's answer felt... insufficient. But only with her blade pressed to some vital organ would she truly know if the human spoke the truth.

"There are carvings in Avalon," Percival said. He pushed to his feet, stepping slightly in front of Diana. "But they are not like this. The carvings there tell the legend of the sacred trinity."

"You did not tell Veyka."

"You piece of shit," Lyrena seethed, sword already in her hand.

"I agreed with her that it was worth investigating more," he bit back. "But you all told her it was not."

Lyrena gnashed her teeth, golden tooth glinting with menace. "She will flay you while your sister—"

"I think these carvings tell the story of your Accolon and Nimue," Diana said softly. Even just above a whisper, her words cut through everything else. "And I do not think it is the one you are accustomed to hearing."

Lyrena's sword dropped a fraction.

"The Queen commanded that we all return in one piece," Cyara reminded them. She ignored the sound in Lyrena's throat at the reminder. "Spread out. This is going to take us a while."

98
VEYKA

Chaos erupted.

The terrestrial fae of Annwyn were a warrior race. But they had never met this enemy before. The shifters took to their beast forms, claws and fangs and wings joining the melee. Weapons began to swing—Barkke's wicked mace, massive axes and long spears.

But none of it was enough.

The succubus kept on coming. Without the amorite blades to take them down, the terrestrials were at a disadvantage. They kept fighting, defending the weaker among them. But the succubus did not tire.

That black bile poured from their mouths and eyes and nostrils, coating the terrestrials who fought back. Their jaws closed around arms and throats, thick red blood coating the flagstones of the great hall.

In a second, I saw what a battlefield would look like.

This, but worse. An enemy who could go on indefinitely. Who were immune to magic. Who had nothing to lose.

Arran was right.

We needed weapons that could actually bring them down.

The pressure of that realization nearly suffocated me.

I let Arran choose his own angle of attack, pressing one of my swirled amorite daggers into his hand. His battle axe would be useless. I was in and out of the void in less than a second, my own dagger ready. They were the only weapon we had, my rapiers in the bedroom upstairs. I did not waste the time it would take to retrieve them, even as quick as it would be through the void. I would not leave my subjects alone to die, even for a second.

A black blur lunged for me—I ducked, came up beneath it and drove my blade straight into its heart. Or what was left of it. If that black bile that spilled from the succubus' orifices was the soul of the male leaking away, I did not know what remained of his heart.

But the succubus went down, and stayed there.

I muttered a prayer to the Ancestors and kept swinging.

Stab, kick, lunge.

I was made for this. Trained for it. Whenever one of them got too close, I fell back into the void and reappeared on their other side. Still, it was taking too long. I could only fight one at a time, Arran another, which left the rest to feast on the terrestrial revelers.

Eight, I counted as they went down. There were eight of them.

And I knew their faces.

The males that had refused the amorite.

Guilt burned in my throat, as toxic as the black bile coating my wrists. I had failed them. I should have fought Arran harder—fought for my subjects. *My fault.*

No.

This was not my fault.

The succubus were coming for my kingdom. They could not have it.

Then comes a queen in the age of uncertainty, when shadows cast doubt upon the realm. Born under a double moon and marked by a radiant star, a faerie queen shall rise to command the depths of the voids of darkness.

The words of the Void Prophecy echoed in my mind as I brought down one succubus and then another.

The succubus had come, in a time of upheaval for Annwyn,

after the death of Arthur and my mating with Arran. And I had risen to command the void. It was not a coincidence that these things happened together. It was not my fault they had come.

I had been given this power so I could stop them.

So I would use it.

I sheathed my dagger. Too slow, taking them out one at a time. Not when I could grab one with each hand.

I'd been born fast. All fae were blessed with deadly speed. But I had spent twenty-five years of my life without a single flicker of power in my veins. I'd trained myself to be even faster, even deadlier. A weapon to defend myself. Now, I used that weapon to defend those I loved.

My fingers closed around one throat. A second later, I grabbed an arm, slick with black bile. I dug in my nails and took them with me into the void.

But I did not emerge at a different location in Eilean Gayl. Or Annwyn. Or the human realm.

I brought those monsters back to where they belonged—in hell.

99
CYARA

It took a while to determine where the story began. It was a circle, after all.

But eventually they found it. The upper reaches of the stone that faced the white cliffs depicted two kingdoms at war. One elemental—an upright triangle for fire, an inverted one for water, a bisected one for wind. The other kingdom was represented with curving vines and fierce monsters. The terrestrials. This was the Great War as she had been taught.

But it was only the beginning.

The stones depicted many battles. Outlines that looked like Annwyn. Mountains that could have been the Spine or the ones that bordered the Effren Valley.

Cyara wanted to look at each monolith in detail. Maybe there would be time later. She would have to bring Veyka and Arran here to see the sight for themselves. But for now, they spread out, each taking a stone, moving between them as needed to make sense of things.

Lyrena spoke first, from across the clearing. "I think this is meant to be the Tower of Myda," she said, tracing her fingers over an engraving. "It stands alone on a flat line, and there are levels inside, just like the ones we fought through."

Percival cleared his throat a few minutes later. "This is the ceremony we saw in the fire. Three figures—one elemental, one terrestrial."

Cyara came to look closer. "What about the third?"

He shook his head. "There is only an inverted triangle."

"The symbol for water," Cyara murmured. So, the third figure was a water wielder? Why was that important?

Too many pieces. Even her clever mind was struggling to fit them together.

She returned to the stone she had been examining. "Keep looking."

100
ARRAN

Veyka vanished.

My heart stopped beating.

The pressure in my chest intensified, so suddenly I staggered forward. Got my dagger up just in time to protect myself, but only dealt the succubus a glancing blow.

She was gone.

Away. Not in the void for a second. She'd gone far—farther than ever before.

I was her tether.

I wrapped ever bit of my iron will, my love for my mate, around that golden thread that connected us and *yanked*.

Veyka crashed into me, hard enough to send us both sprawling.

"What the fuck was that?" I demanded.

She was already rolling to her feet. "If the succubus can come to our realm, there is nothing to stop me from going to theirs and dumping their kind back where they belong."

She'd gone to the succubus realm.

She'd been there once before, when she fell through the realms after our Joining. Then, we had not known what it was. But now, I could fully envision the cold, dank dark of that place. The vile smell and clawing to get inside, to reach her soul and claim it. To kill her.

And she had gone there—willingly, purposefully, taking the succubus with her. Her power had grown. She'd claimed it, just as I'd always known she could.

Pride burned hot in my chest, along with worry and a dozen other terrible, debilitating feelings—all cut off as a scream rent the air. A scream I knew. That had haunted my dreams for three hundred years.

Mother.

I was fast, but Veyka was faster. She had the void.

But I was not thinking of that as I shoved other terrestrials out of the way, clawing my way toward the sound of her shrieks. My mother would not—could not pick up a weapon. Even to defend herself. She would not be able to deflect the succubus, even for a second.

I burst through the panicked throng. My father was on the ground, not moving. My mother shrank down, away, covering her face. I threw my dagger—

Veyka caught it.

Tossed it back in my direction, grabbed the succubus, and disappeared again.

101
CYARA

"The elemental and terrestrial kingdoms were at war, just as we were taught. Accolon and Nimue were Joined, just as we were taught. That ended the conflict between the two kingdoms and created Annwyn. But all of that was before the succubus appeared," Lyrena summarized.

She was just repeated Cyara's words from a few moments before, but Cyara was not annoyed. She understood the need to speak, to process this monumental shift in reality.

Because it was monumental. It confirmed everything they had learned so far about the truth of the Great War, and more.

"These whorls," Diana said, voice still soft. She had not spoken above a whisper since they had entered the clearing. "These whorls seem to be coming from Nimue herself."

Percival peered over her shoulder. "Then they coalesce—into the misshapen things. You have seen these before?" he asked.

"Yes. Both in Baylaur and on the monolith about the faerie caves. Those must be the succubus," Cyara confirmed.

Lyrena's feet crunched it the dirt behind them. "These all show battles between the succubus and the fae," she said, pointing to three of the stones as she passed them by. "But this one... I don't know what in the Ancestors' names is going on here."

Cyara moved to look closer. Percival did as well, only pausing when he realized that Diana had not moved. She was tracing the whorls again and again with her finger. Cyara's heart hurt for him—for the sister he cared so deeply to protect. She could understand it. But she could not offer Diana comfort now.

Lyrena stood before the monolith with her hands on each hip. "There is a sun, and what look like rays of light shining down, but then it is blocked by a cloud. And there is the moon, but actually its two moons with a star in between them." She shook her head. "It looks like a child's drawing."

Understanding clicked into place in Cyara's mind. It was like a child's drawing—symbolic. Simplified. But like a child's drawing, there was more behind it than the carver could convey.

"It is the prophecy," Cyara breathed.

She lifted her fingers and traced over each symbol as she spoke. "*Then comes a queen in the age of uncertainty, when shadows cast doubt upon the realm. Born under a double moon and marked by a radiant star, a faerie queen shall rise to command the depths of the voids of darkness.*"

Lyrena's eyes went wide. She was already moving closer to see the next set of carvings that began at waist-height. "This looks like Annwyn."

Cyara leaned down. Indeed—there were the outlines of the continent, stretched across from one side of the standing stone to the other. The land was marked with mountains, the bodies of water—the Northern Way, the Southern Way, and the Split Sea—with waves.

"The next part of the prophecy says, *Twice blessed, the realm of shift and mist, when comes the awaited queen who shall possess ethereal might. With a touch, she will feel the heartbeat of her subjects and she will unlock the secrets they guard within,*" Cyara recited.

"So this second queen will come from somewhere in Annwyn? How is that possible?"

Cyara shook her head. "I do not know. Maybe it is not Annwyn at all. Maybe it is another realm entirely, and that is where she will hail from."

She knelt down, scraping her thumbnail across the stone. There—a bit of moss gave way. Those whorls again, just like the ones Diana was tracing. But smaller, and dotting what should have been the Split Sea, if the continent truly was Annwyn.

"I do not know," Cyara admitted, shaking her head.

"There is a whorl at the top of your tower. I think it might represent your Nimue," Diana said. She had progressed to the next stone. Slowly considering, slowly tracing.

The one she stood before now was the same one that Lyrena had remarked upon earlier, noting the Tower of Myda. The angle was sharp, but Cyara could make out the dark hordes of the mangled succubus all around the tower.

Cyara pushed to her feet, frowning. The standing stones told the story, but it did not give them any answers. Battling fae kingdoms. A Joining. Fighting the succubus. The tower. Then the prophecy.

"There is more."

Percival had come to see.

Cyara tried to ask him what he meant, but he was already kneeling down in the space she had vacated. Weeds covered the bottom foot of the stone. But Percival brushed them aside.

More carvings.

"There isn't any more to the prophecy," Lyrena said sharply.

Cyara sank down beside Percival. "Yes, there is."

She traced her fingers over the two figures, their arms interconnected. A whorl spreading out around them. Below it, an identical whorl—but without the figures.

And then...

"No," Cyara whispered. "Ancestors, please. No."

102
ARRAN

The attack ended as abruptly as it had started. The succubus were gone—dead by our amorite blades, or returned to their realm by Veyka. I could hardly begin to think about what that meant for the future struggle against the succubus. If she'd encountered any succubus there... what form they took without human or fae vessels.

I held my mother's hand as she sipped fortified wine and tried to regain herself. I'd tried to get her to go to her rooms, but she'd insisted she was the Lady of Eilean Gayl. She would stay to see her people tended, even if she could not do it herself.

The healers worked quickly and efficiently. My father was fine, the wound on his side already knitted back together. But Isolde was the true godsend. No longer a novelty—not with that mystical, pure white healing power that poured from her hands.

Less than a dozen terrestrials had died

It was a small relief, at least. The succubus were a formidable foe, but we were hard to kill.

Osheen moved through the crowded hall. Servants had begun to bring food out again. Chairs were set upright. In the far corner, someone strummed a fiddle.

Against all odds, the feast was resuming.

What better way to defy death than by celebrating the rebirth of the world around us?

Osheen looked me up and down. When he was satisfied I was uninjured, his eyes went to my mother, resting against the stone wall behind me. "Go to Veyka. I will see her safely to her rooms."

To my surprise, my mother nodded her acquiesce.

There were few I would have trusted.

I nodded my thanks and retraced the path he had taken as he guided my mother and father out of the great hall.

Veyka was at the middle of it all. Isolde lingered at her side, eyes lined with exhaustion but bright. Veyka had stayed at her side as she moved from terrestrial to terrestrial, healing each with no regard to kingdom or power. As had Veyka.

She'd earned their respect. And now, the terrestrials showed it. They moved to talk to her. A handsome male bowed, inviting her to dance. Veyka shook her head; she could deduce where that would lead.

The low growl that reverberated between us probably helped.

It took too long for me to arrive at her side. To pull her close against me, reminding myself that she was alive. Well. Mine.

She breathed me in with the same fierce need.

She let me lead her away, back toward the head table where we'd been sitting when the succubus attacked. But instead of resuming our seats, we stood in front of it. I knew there were hundreds of terrestrial eyes upon us, but I did not care. Not as I lifted her chin and held her blue gaze.

Her eyes had dimmed slightly, the adrenaline of battle ebbing away. But there was the faint ring, the glow of desire that ignited just from being in one another's presence.

I had to speak to her here, now. If I waited, held the words inside, they would start to gnaw at my soul. I could not have that. I could not have anything between us, not now, after all we'd been through and somehow survived.

"I am meant to stand at your side, to tear down any who might threaten you." Every muscle in my body ached at what came next. "I failed you. I should have shoved amorite into those males myself. This is my fault."

My fault. Veyka's words slid into my mind. I recognized them immediately for what they were—a chant she'd been saying to herself for months.

There is no time for blame. We can only move forward.

But with her mouth, she said, "Was that an apology?"

I growled.

She laughed in my face. "I shall have to ask Maisri to record it in her book."

I growled again. This time, I buried the sound in her neck. She'd washed away the black bile of the males' souls, defiled by the succubus. All that remained now was her plum and primrose mixed with the scent of the wine she'd sipped as she tended to our subjects.

Veyka inhaled sharply, her body arching into mine.

Around us, the sounds of the festival had begun in full thrust. Females, being worshipped once again by their males. Females worshipping each other. All determined to declare that they had survived—that they would survive this new threat.

"Should I take you now, in front of your subjects?" I breathed into her ear.

"Our subjects," she squeaked as I spun her around. The staccato beat of her pulse against my mouth, in time with the rush of her arousal, was all the answer I needed.

"Tonight, they worship you." Her back pressed to my chest, I was free to explore her breasts. And our subjects watched me. I tugged one breast out of her gown, letting it spill into my palm before I pinched the nipple tight between my fingers. Veyka threw her head back, letting out a delicious moan that drew even more eyes to her.

Good. They should see me worshipping her, this powerful, magnificent female, the way she deserved to be worshipped.

"Their queen," I moaned against her ear as my other hand

parted the folds of her gown, dipping inside to find the folds of her cunt. Dripping, ready for me.

My cock throbbed with demand as I pulled my trousers loose and lifted her skirts, her leg, until my cock nudged at her entrance.

Veyka's whimper of need shredded the last remnants of my control.

I shoved myself inside of her as I growled the words into her ear —"My queen."

Queen of the Void. Queen of Annwyn. Queen of every shred of my broken, twisted soul.

As I took her, again and again, words began to echo in my ears.

Your rest has ended, Brutal Prince. She needs you now.

Familiar, but not quite clear. They hovered at the periphery of my understanding, muddled by the haze of need, the intensity of my feelings for Veyka, the feeling of being inside of her. Of what this claiming meant—me, claiming her as my mate. But also the terrestrials of Eilean Gayl, claiming and worshipping their queen.

The High Queen of Annwyn.

Veyka screamed the pleasure of her climax, the walls of her pussy gripping my cock hard. I was a second away from spilling, right there with her, tumbling over the cliff. I threw my head back and howled, beast and male, as that final ecstasy roared through me and I came inside of her.

As the words solidified. A voice I recognized. That spoke with perfect clarity.

The forgotten line of the prophecy.

Together they must stand, to defeat what once thought dead. Together they must give, if any shall live to the end.

Forgotten, until Accolon had given it to me in a dream.

And cursed me and my mate forever.

103

VEYKA

Lyrena met us on the beach.

Percival and Diana sat up on the bank, wrapped in cloaks, warming themselves around a small fire that Lyrena kept going without a thought.

"Cyara is waiting for you at the top," Lyrena said.

Her voice sent a shiver down my spine. That voice... I had not heard it since those dark days after Arthur's death. It reached inside of me and touched a part of my soul that I had thought gone, healed. But there it was, exposed again.

My golden knight was hurting.

I reached for her arm, but Lyrena shook her head. "Go," she said, lifting her sword—up, toward the center of the island.

For once, I did not use the void.

Arran and I walked every step of the way.

We hadn't slept. There had been no time. We'd barely cleaned up the carnage from Imbolc when the communication crystal began to glow, summoning us here.

Up and up we climbed. I was thankful for the thick leather leggings and heavy fur cloak on my shoulders. Even with the exertion, the temperature dropped with each step we took. By the time we reached the clearing, I was shivering.

Arran tucked me in at his side just as Cyara appeared from behind a monolith that towered over even Arran's head. A ring of them.

She did not wait for us to reach her, coming to where we stood on the edge of the clearing.

"The true story of Accolon and Nimue is etched upon the stones," Cyara said. "And the prophecy. All of it."

Fulfill the prophecy. All of it.

The witch's answer to my question, how to banish the succubus for good.

Inside of me, something began to awaken. Not my power—that was slumbering happily after the way I'd used it to defend Eilean Gay. But an awareness that set my fingertips tingling, nonetheless.

Arran must have sensed it. His hand pressed into my waist hard, keeping me firmly anchored to his side.

Cyara merely bowed her head, her face devoid of all emotion. "I shall wait for you on the beach." She was as good as any elemental at hiding her feelings, but this...

"Cyara—"

"No. It is best you do this alone." Then she was gone.

I flexed my hands at my sides, trying to get the tingling to stop. Maybe it was the cold. So damn cold here in the terrestrial kingdom.

We climbed the last few feet into the clearing until the stones surrounded us. Cyara had indicated where to start. Slowly, still pressed together, Arran and I drifted from stone to stone, examining the engravings.

There it was, exactly as Cyara had said.

It was all as we had suspected until we arrived at the last battle of the succubus and the fae carved into stone. The tower with the whorl at the top. Nimue with her void power, my void power, in the Tower of Myda.

Then, on the next stone, the prophecy.

Long ago, in the goldstone palace, Parys had suggested that Nimue was the original recorder of the Void and Ethereal Prophecies.

Now here they were, laid out in full.

The Void Prophecy, with its depiction of the shadows and moons. The Ethereal Prophecy... more abstract, but there. And then...

I had to pull away from Arran to bend down, to see the carvings at the very base of the stone. Arran remained rigid above me. The tingling was in my wrists now. But the void did not pull at me. I tried to feel Arran through the bond, but he'd shut off his emotions. Much as he had before he'd regained his memories, when he'd wanted to keep me out.

It was probably reflex.

Despite the joy of having one another back fully, we were still healing. It would take time to fully adjust, to share all the secret, damaged corners of ourselves again.

I tucked my hands into my cloak as I leaned closer.

A whorl with the two figures—the two queens, Void and Ethereal. And then they were gone. The prophecy ended—and those two queens did not reappear.

I cocked my head to the side. There was one more stone. It was nearly identical to the one that preceded the prophecy. The tower, the valley. Except that the hordes of succubus were gone. And so was the whorl at the top of the tower.

Arran's hand touched the base of my neck.

Drew me up to stand.

Slipped around my waist.

When I was in Avalon, Accolon came to me in my dreams.

I jerked around to look at him. His eyes nearly broke me.

The wall between us was gone, and in its place... an emptiness as deep and howling as the void. His eyes... my mate's eyes, dark and burning for me, always... they were cold with dread.

He spoke of the sacrifices that he and Nimue made to push back the succubus. But even then, they knew it would not last forever.

I opened my mouth to ask one of the dozens of questions rising to my lips. But Arran shook his head. Pressed his fingers to my lips, then his forehead to mine.

He could not say the words aloud.

Together they must stand, to defeat what once thought dead. Together they must give, if any shall live to the end.

The final line of the prophecy.

All of it.

To banish the succubus forever, to save my kingdom, my friends, my mate, I must fulfill the prophecy. I would have to find the Ethereal Queen. And together, we must die.

104

CYARA

It started at the corner of her right eye. A single elegant swirl. Joined with another as it curved over her cheek, down underneath her bejeweled earlobe to caress the elegant curve of her neck.

Arran murmured something in Veyka's ear, drawing an easy smile from her lips as the artist moved farther down. The ribbon of black ink curled over her shoulder, then around her arm in two graceful swirls before it ended at her wrist, just above the beating pulse of life.

It should have looked wrong. The fierce black ink against her pale skin and moon-white hair. But it was beautiful. Everything about her was beautiful. The stark black made her skin and hair glow even brighter, turned her eyes luminous. Or maybe it was the blazing ring of blue fire around her pupil, the glow that never seemed to fade.

No one in the great hall knew. Not a single one of the terrestrials watching the Queen of the Elemental Fae being inked with a Talisman, a marker of her unique power, a sacred terrestrial tradition... not one of them knew that she was doomed.

That the cost of their safety—their survival—was her.

"I almost cannot stand to watch." Lyrena said, her voice

achingly hollow. "Knowing that this is the beginning of the end." Her golden smile had been nowhere in sight since their return to Eilean Gayl.

The artist finished inking Veyka's Talisman. Arran took her hand, lifting it high above her and slowly spinning her so that all the spectators in the hall could get a good look. An appreciative murmur rolled through the crowd.

"She will survive."

"The stones—"

"Damn the stones. Damn the Ancestors," Cyara said softly. "We are the Knights of the Round Table. We will protect her. We will find a different ending."

Lyrena said nothing.

Maybe she did not believe it. Maybe she was afraid to hope. Cyara did not care. She had lost her sisters. Become a monster to protect those she cared for. She would not lose another friend.

Lady Elayne and Lord Pant stepped up beside them and the murmurs softened. Lady Elayne's voice sounded clear and bright over the assembly as she announced—

"Their Royal Majesties—High Queen Veyka Pendragon. High King Arran Earthborn."

A heartbeat of wondering.

And then, as one, the residents of Eilean Gayl bowed low. Exposing their necks.

The sacred submission.

The traditional, formal acceptance of the High Queen and King's reign.

Cyara watched Veyka's throat bob as she fought down emotion at the sight.

Arthur would have used fire. A dancing flame at his fingertips, enough to heat but not burn, a symbolic show of magical dominance over each subject. But Veyka's magic did not function that way.

As she watched, Arran and Veyka exchanged looks, both of

their faces unreadable. They were speaking to each other without words, Cyara knew.

She inhaled, and Veyka disappeared. Exhaled, and she returned —with a mighty sword gripped in her hand.

Beside her, Lyrena's shoulders started to tremble with silent tears.

Cyara bowed her head with the rest of them. She did not glance up until she felt the cool metal of Excalibur's blade kiss the nape of her neck. And looked up into the eyes of a queen.

105
ARRAN

Somewhere around the third course, Veyka eased herself away from my side. It took her a few minutes to extricate herself. Every few steps, terrestrials stopped to bow. To place a fist over their heart—the greeting of one warrior to another. But eventually, she made it to the two-story tall arched doors of the great hall, eased herself over the threshold, and disappeared into the void.

Letting her walk away was torture. But the strength of the bond in my chest told me she had not gone far. As the feasting reached a pinnacle, I slipped out after her, following the pull of the bond into the night.

It led me past the gates of the keep, onto the darkened bridge that connected the island castle to the land of craggy emerald peaks around it. There were no torches burning along the stone parapets on either side. The original builders had not made a place for them, believing the fortress' strength lay in its isolation. Lighting the way would only serve potential enemies. In the thousands of years since, it looked to all appearances that nothing had changed.

Except that *everything* was different now.

I refused to think of it—to acknowledge it. There had to be

another way. I could not have been reunited with my mate, both of us suffering so much, for it to end with... death.

I was willing to sacrifice myself on the altar of duty. But Veyka? Never.

I would let Annwyn be swallowed by the succubus before I allowed it to happen.

Veyka turned, her hair catching in the moonlight, and all the air was sucked from my body. I could not breathe, for loving her.

Her forearms were braced on the parapet, her hips swaying softly to music that leaked from the castle beyond. The moonlight shone in her hair, on her skin, kissing the lines of her freshly inked Talisman.

Isolde had offered to heal the wounds, leaving behind only the black ink. Veyka had refused her. By tomorrow morning, it would be healed anyway, she said. But I knew her soul; she wanted the reminder, for every second she could, of what it felt like to be alive.

I could help with that.

I slid my arms around her waist, pulling her flush against me. Veyka did not resist, lifting herself from the stones of the parapet and painting her body against mine. One hand drifted up to tug at the club of hair at the back of my head. I knew she would not be satisfied until she'd worked it loose and could grab a fistful of my hair.

What do you want, Princess? my wolf growled softly.

Veyka made a small hum of appreciation as she got my hair loose and buried her fingers in it

"You," she said softly. "To stay here forever with you. Right here —where nothing can touch us. Where we are safe and whole. Our friends. Our family."

She was thinking about it, too. How could she not? It was her life, that the prophecy required.

I held her tighter. "We will come back some day, I promise."

You cannot promise that.

I pressed my lips to the shell of her ear. "I do promise." I paused to inhale the plum and primrose scent of her. "A thousand years, and a thousand more."

She did not answer, did not argue. That worried me more than anything. The silence began to press in on us.

"I am certain if you coached the cooks long enough, they could produce an acceptable chocolate croissant."

Veyka snorted. "We might need a thousand years for them to get it right."

She licked her lips, the sound causing every muscle in my body to tighten. I kept on holding her.

"We have to decide now."

She was right. The time to tarry and argue and debate had run out. The succubus could strike anywhere, at any time. The first shipment of amorite had arrived, half of it sent on to the forge at Cayltay, the rest awaiting further discussion and decision. We had to choose a course of action the best we could, based on scenarios and outcomes. And then we would adjust. Every battle went that way—you planned and adjusted. Planned and adjusted.

But I refused to plan or adjust for the possibility of a world without Veyka in it.

I cleared the emotion from my throat. "Parys and Gwen are waiting in Baylaur. Merlin and Igraine... we would be naïve to leave them alone too long. Even in Gwen's capable hands."

"Or paws?" Veyka squeaked, already laughing at her own joke.

Ancestors—how could she laugh? I could barely breathe.

That had to be why the words came out half-choked. "We need armies."

She exhaled, so slowly. Drawing it out, forestalling her response. But it came, eventually. "I know."

Wolf Bay—Cayltay, the war camps. Or Baylaur—to rule, to harness the full power of the Knights of the Round Table.

Veyka rotated her neck, stretching out the tense muscles before eventually letting her head rest on my shoulder, exposing the burn of her new tattoo to the cool night air. We stared out at the stars in silence, letting the night close around us. It was cold, but I'd take any excuse to hold Veyka close.

After what might have been a minute or an eternity, she spoke again. "What if we did not have to choose?"

Unease unspooled in my stomach. "What do you mean?"

I could feel her maelstrom of emotions through the bond. She did not try to keep them from me. I did not try to block them. But I was still unprepared.

"I could go to Baylaur."

I pulled away—just so I could grip her shoulders and spin her to look at me.

She winced at the pressure—her Talisman.

I released her immediately.

But Veyka reached for my hand, curling it around hers and lifting it to her lips.

"I'd only be gone for a moment."

"No."

Her breath skittered across my knuckles. "It's farther than I've ever gone before, but I can do it. What is the point of my power if not for this?"

"We agreed." I ground out. "Together."

The night around us was suddenly oppressive, threatening. Like the void, determined to steal my mate away from me.

Veyka pressed closer, still gripping my hand. "You cannot leave the terrestrials now. We've only just brought them to heel. There is an army to assemble. We must be ready."

"Veyka—"

She squeezed my hand hard enough to break bones. "I can do this."

I closed my eyes, because I could not bear to look at her beautiful face. To see the desire to help, to push herself, sacrifice herself, without knowing the cost...

"I know you can." *You can do anything.* My forehead fell forward against hers. "But I can't."

We stood there, foreheads pressed together, breathing each

other's air. Reminding one another that the other was alive, and whole, and here.

I worked my jaw as another idea—new, untested and unreasoned—formed in my head. "Open a rift."

Her chin stabbed the air. "I will be back. A few minutes, I promise. Just enough time to explain the communication crystals."

I grabbed her arm, afraid she might disappear into the void right then. "No. That is not what I meant." It felt like a risk, taking a hand away from her. Like she might disappear at any moment. But I forced myself to gesture to the bridge before us. "Open a rift."

Veyka's eyes widened. "Rifts don't work that way. They go between the realms."

"You command the voids of darkness. The rift will do what you command."

Her hand slid to mine. Squeezed tightly, once.

Then she stepped free. Letting her was a physical slice into my chest, but I fought it. Watched as she curled her hands into fists at her side.

For a moment, I thought it a lost cause. That she would throw herself into the void, because it had not worked. Panic flooded through me, hot and stifling and—

The air was glowing.

Moon-white, like her hair. A pinprick of light that grew outward in a spiral. Out, and out, and out. Until the spiral was nearly as wide as the bridge. Big enough for the two of us to walk through, and shining bright with her power.

Veyka flicked her wrist, and the white light solidified. An image appeared in its center—no, not an image.

Not just a rift, but a portal.

Those were the familiar stones of the goldstone palace.

They were drenched with noxious black bile.

Vekya's daggers were in her palms. I felt the weight of my battle axe, not even knowing how it had gotten into my hand.

No one had noticed us yet—no one appeared. But the screams

were agonizing. They ripped through the portal Veyka had created, filling the air around us, echoing off the lake.

Veyka lurched forward. "Gwen—"

I grabbed her arm—just as a massive, dark lioness bounded into view.

Gwen shifted in a second, her golden eyes wide with disbelief. They scanned us, the castle in the background, everything taken in, in mere moments.

Veyka tried to wrench from my grasp, to get through the portal. To the screams—the screams of our subjects being ripped apart by the succubus.

But it was Gwen who spoke, who threw out her arms to either side to block Veyka's way. "No, Majesty—you cannot."

She had to raise her voice to be heard over the screams.

"Baylaur has fallen."

EPILOGUE

For seven thousand years, the Split Sea stood perfectly still. No waves lapped at the shoreline. No being alive—fae, human, or beast—had seen its crystalline surface disturbed. No one knew why the once rich, life-giving sea had died in the days following the Great War.

Fisherman's nets, once filled with fat catches of fish and many-limbed crustaceans, all came back empty. Or worse, filled with death and decay. The mammals that had once built their dens along the shore disappeared. Elemental water-wielders tried to channel their magic into its depths, but found it did not answer. Terrestrials who might have once explored its swirling eddies in their beast forms found lakes to swim instead.

But on that day when the faerie queen who was prophesized opened a rift, when she found her home taken by the darkness, destroyed by the ancient evil that her kind had long forgotten... on that day, something changed.

The surface of the Split Sea broke for the first time in seven thousand years.

And from it arose not one figure, but two.

EPILOGUE

A male of cold wind, of ire and anger, well-suited to dwell in those frigid depths... and to tend to the female at his side.

The heir to the realm of shift and mist.

Hand in hand they rose. And when they took that first step onto land, ready to fulfill their own destiny, the entire continent of Annwyn shook.

It is death to all but the one for which it is made—the best of them all— the one who shall come at the moment of direst need.

Far away, on a distant strip of land at the heart of a mighty kingdom, a king reached out a hand to steady his queen. Found her ready, at last, for what was to come.

The end was near. The wheel of time run out.

The moment of direst need.

The Siege Perilous.

THE END

***Queen of Blood and Vengeance*, Book 4 in the Secrets of the Faerie Crown, is coming in November 2024.**

Can't wait that long? Sign up for my newsletter at https://rlink.st/emberlyash to receive a FREE steamy bonus scene. You'll also be the first to find out all the official release details for upcoming books in the series—including exclusive excerpts, cover reveals, and more.

ACKNOWLEDGMENTS

If you've made it this far, hopefully you've stopped hating me for taking Arran's memories away. If not... well, at least read the acknowledgements.

My life shifted drastically two years ago. I lost my mom. The details do not really matter, other than to say that she is still alive, but after more than thirty years, not a part of my life. I felt unmoored and broken and a lot like Veyka in the beginning of *Crown of Earth and Sky*. So, I started to spill my pain out onto the page. Into the things that had always been there for me—books.

Writing this series has given me space to process my trauma. I get to be in charge of the villains and the monsters. I've gotten to heal my main characters as I also heal myself. Maybe it is weird to say, but this series saved me. These characters saved me. The readers who picked up and loved this story *saved me*.

Just like Veyka had to learn in this book, sometimes you have to endure heart-wrecking loss to become who you are meant to be. And I truly, finally, feel like I'm starting to find my place in the world.

So, thank you to Veyka and Arran. To Arthur, Cyara, Parys, Lyrena, Guinevere, Isolde, Osheen, Maisri, Elayne, and all the others who I've had the privilege of bringing to life.

Thank you to every single reader, from the five stars all the way to the DNFs. You have made this dream real. You played a part in this terrifyingly beautiful journey.

Hold on tight—the rest of the ride is going to be wild.

ABOUT THE AUTHOR

Emberly Ash stole her first romance novel off her mom's bookshelf at the age of ten and never looked back. The author of 12 romance books under her first pen name, Emberly craved something darker and steamier--enter the world of fantasy romance. Her books are dark, twisty, and not for the faint of heart. In the real world, she manages a fire-breathing five-year-old and a grumpy mage of a husband. But you'll most often find her in her hot-pink writing cave, dreaming up your next book boyfriend. Spoiler alert: he's fae.

Find Emberly online at:

https://1link.st/emberlyash

https://www.amazon.com/stores/author/B0C55YXHS8

https://www.instagram.com/emberlyashauthor/

https://www.tiktok.com/@emberlyashauthor

Made in the USA
Columbia, SC
02 June 2025